DUST LANDS

Rebel Heart

BOOK TWO

MOIRA YOUNG

MARGARET K. McELDERRY BOOKS

NEW YORK   LONDON   TORONTO   SYDNEY   NEW DELHI

MARGARET K. McELDERRY BOOKS
An imprint of Simon & Schuster Children's Publishing Division
1230 Avenue of the Americas, New York, New York 10020

For information about special discounts for bulk purchases, please contact Simon & Schuster Special Sales at 1-866-506-1949 or business@simonandschuster.com.
The Simon & Schuster Speakers Bureau can bring authors to your live event. For more information or to book an event, contact the Simon & Schuster Speakers Bureau at 1-866-248-3049 or visit our website at www.simonspeakers.com.
The text for this book is set in Dante.
Manufactured in the United States of America
2   4   6   8   10   9   7   5   3   1
Library of Congress Cataloging-in-Publication Data
Young, Moira.
Rebel heart / Moira Young.
p. cm.—(Dust lands; bk. 2)
Summary: After rescuing her twin brother from the Tonton, Saba experiences disturbing telepathic visions while being hunted by a cunning enemy.
ISBN 978-1-4424-3000-6 (hardcover)
ISBN 978-1-4424-3340-3 (eBook)
[1. Telepathy—Fiction. 2. Brothers and sisters—Fiction. 3. Twins—Fiction. 4. Coming of age—Fiction. 5. Orphans—Fiction. 6. Science fiction.] I. Title.
PZ7.Y874Re 2012
[Fic]—dc23
2012018918

FIRST
EDITION

FOR MY SISTERS

CONTENTS

JACK

IT's LATE AFTERNOON. SINCE MORNING, THE TRAIL's BEEN following a line of light towers. That is, the iron remains of what used to be light towers, way back in Wrecker days, time out of mind. It winds through faded, folded hills, burnt grass and prickle bush.

The flat heat of high summer beats on his head. His hat's damp with sweat. The dust of long days coats his skin, his clothes, his boots. He tastes it when he licks his dry lips. It's been a parched, mean road all the way. He crests a ridge, the trail dips down into a little valley and it's suddenly, freshly green. The air is soft. Sharply sweet with the scent of the scrub pine that scatters the slopes.

Jack pulls up his horse. He breathes in. A long, deep, grateful breath. He drinks in the view. On the cleared valley floor, a small lake glints in the sun. Beside it stands a junkshack with a bark and sod roof, the rest of it cobbled together from Wrecker trash, stones, dried mud and the odd tree trunk. A man, a woman and a girl are working in the well-tended patches of cultivated land.

People. At last. Apart from the white mustang, Atlas, he hasn't spoken to a soul for days. His aloneness was starting to weigh him down.

An there was I, he says aloud, thinkin I was th'only person on the planet.

He whistles a tune as he rides on. He calls a hello as they leave their work and come to meet him. They aren't particularly friendly. They've got weary faces. Wary eyes. They're little used to company, take little interest in the wider world and have little to say. Never mind. Just seeing them and having this awkward, mainly one-sided conversation cheers him no end.

The man's worn out. The woman's sick. Dying, if he's any judge of such things. With yellowish skin, her mouth set tight against pain. The girl's sturdy enough, fourteen or so. She stares at her boots. Silent, even when he speaks to her direct. But her plain, flat face lights with love when her brother comes running from the shack, calling her name, Nessa! Nessa!

He's a cheerful berry of a child. A barefoot, round-eyed four-year-old called Robbie. His family gazes at him with such fond wonderment that it's clear they can't quite believe their good fortune. He leans against his sister's legs, sucks his thumb energetically and sizes up Jack.

The battered, wide-brimmed hat. The silver eyes. The lean, tanned face that hasn't seen a razor for weeks. The long, dusty coat and worn boots. The crossbow on his back, his well-stocked weapons belt—bolt shooters, longknife, bolas, slingshot.

Boo, says Jack. Robbie's mouth drops open. His thumb falls out.

Jack growls. The boy shrieks with delight and tears off towards the lake. Nessa gives chase. The valley sings with their shouts and laughter.

They aren't sociable people but they aren't mean. They see to it that he and his horse are watered, washed and fed. They offer him a roof for the night, but he's anxious to keep moving. Dusk is falling as he sets off again. They're hard workers, early risers. They'll be in bed as soon as he's gone.

By his reckoning, the storm belt should be no more than three days' travel from here. And that's where he's headed. The storm belt, a tavern called The Lost Cause and an old friend named Molly. He's the bearer of bad news. The worst. The sooner he delivers it, the sooner he can turn around, retrace his steps and keep on heading west.

West. To the Big Water. Because that's where she is. It's where he promised to meet her.

He pulls out the stone that he wears around his neck, threaded on a leather string. It's smooth and cool to the touch. Pale rosy pink. Shaped like a bird's egg, a thumb's length in size.

It's a heartstone. It'll lead you to your heart's desire, so they say.

She gave it to him. He'll head west and he'll find her.

Saba.

He's only just left the valley when Atlas falters. Tosses his head and whickers. There's something up ahead. Jack doesn't stop to think. In a moment, he's off the trail, into the scrub pine and out of sight. From the cover of the trees, his hand over the mustang's muzzle, he watches them pass.

It's the Tonton. Nine black-robed men and horses. They're escorting a couple in a buffalo-cart. The commander leads the way. Four men behind him, then the cart, followed by three men on horseback. The last man, the ninth, is driving a wagon with an empty prison cage.

He studies them carefully. He knows the Tonton well. They're rough and dirty and casually violent. A loose collection of amoral thugs who swill around the power. Only loyal to each other, only answering to a master if and when it suits them. To a man, they're ruled by self-interest. But these ones seem different. Everything about them is clean and shiny and polished and ordered. They're well armed. They look disciplined. Purposeful.

And that makes him uneasy. It means that the enemy have changed their game.

He checks out the couple in the cart. They're young, strong, healthy looking. A boy and a girl, no more than sixteen or seventeen. They sit close together on the bench seat. The boy's driving. He holds the reins in one hand. His other arm circles the girl's waist. But there's a gap between their bodies. They sit stiffly upright. They aren't comfortable, that's for sure. It's as if they hardly know each other.

They stare straight ahead, their chins held high. They look determined. Proud, even. Obviously not prisoners of the Tonton.

The cart's neatly packed with furniture, bedding and tools. All you'd need to set up house.

As they rattle by, the girl turns her head sharply. She stares into the trees. Almost like she senses that somebody's there. It's dusk and he knows he's well hidden, but he shrinks back anyway. She keeps on looking until they've gone past the woods. No one—not the Tonton, not the boy sitting beside her—seems to notice.

Jack gets a clear view of her forehead. The boy's too. They've been branded. And not long ago. The circle, quartered, in the middle of their foreheads looks raw and sore.

They're headed into the valley. Towards the homestead. With an empty prison wagon.

Now he's more than uneasy. He's worried.

Keeping to the trees, leading his horse, he turns around and follows them.

† † †

From the wood at the top of the valley, as darkness begins to fall, he has a clear view of the homestead he's just left. The Tonton are already entering the shack.

He has to stop his feet from moving towards them. Halt his hand as it reaches for his bow. Because the survivor in him knows that this is a done deal. Whatever's about to happen, he can't stop it.

But he can bear witness. He will bear witness. With clenched fists and a rising rage, he watches what happens below.

By now they've roused the family from their beds. The weary man and woman, their children, Nessa and Robbie. Flushed them out at the point of a firestick. They huddle together in the fading light while the Tonton commander makes a short speech. Probably telling them what's going to happen and why. Words to frighten and confuse people already too frightened and confused to properly listen.

Jack wonders why he bothers. It must be procedure.

The young branded couple wait in the cart, ready to move into their new home. A land grab. A resettlement party. That's what this is about.

Everybody looks small from up here. Doll-sized. He can't hear what's said, not the words. But he can hear the alarm in the raised voices of the family. The girl, Nessa, falls to her knees. Pleading with them, holding her brother tight. One of them takes Robbie while two others grab her by the arms.

They move towards the prison cart. She struggles, yelling, looking back at her parents.

They shoot them at the same time. Husband and wife. A bolt through the forehead and their bodies crumple to the ground.

Nessa screams. And this time, Jack does hear. Run, Robbie! she screams. Run!

The little boy kicks and wriggles in the Tonton's arms. He bites his hand. The man cries out and drops him. Robbie's free. He runs through the fields, as fast as he can, while his sister yells to go faster. But it's summer and the crops are high and he's only four years old.

The commander shouts orders. One man starts after the little boy. Too late. The eager new settler is out of the wagon. Aiming his firestick. He shoots. Robbie drops in his tracks. The wheatgrass folds around him.

The commander's lost control of the situation. It should have gone smoothly. But it's chaos. As he and the settler yell blame at each other, Nessa begins to scream. Her high-pitched wail of grief and rage shivers Jack's skin.

Her shirt has been torn. The men laugh as she tries to cover herself, weeping, screaming, lashing out. They pin her hands behind her. One of them touches her roughly.

The commander sees it. He moves fast. He shoots his man through the head.

Somehow, in all the confusion, Nessa gets hold of a bolt

shooter. She shoves it in her mouth and pulls the trigger.

Jack turns away. He leans his head against the white horse's neck, drawing in deep breaths. Atlas shifts uneasily.

What a mess. A botched job. They were obviously supposed to take Nessa and Robbie, young and healthy, and kill the sickly parents. Instead, all dead.

The Tonton have changed their game all right. He'd heard rumors of land grabs and resettlement months ago. But not this far west, never this far west. They're rolling over the land like the plague.

If this is Tonton territory, then so is the storm belt. And that means Molly's in danger.

Now he's more than worried. He's afraid.

† † †

Jack leaves the trail. It isn't safe.

He and Atlas travel east along unknown roads. The going's hard and unfriendly. Dark, stony ways, never warmed by the sun and seldom used. He spots the odd traveler in the distance—a moving dot in the landscape—but they must be as keen-eyed and eager as he to pass without notice because that's as close as anybody ever gets. He hurries, resting for an hour here, two hours there. He has plenty of time to think about what he saw.

The Tonton. Most recently, the private army of Vicar Pinch: madman, drug lord and self-styled King of the World. Now dead.

They defeated the Tonton at Pine Top Hill. He and Saba and Ike, with the help of Maev, her Free Hawk girl warriors and their road raider allies. And Saba killed Vicar Pinch. But they didn't wipe out the Tonton. They didn't kill every last one. Even if they had, he's lived long enough, he's seen enough to know that you can't kill all the badness in the world. You cut it down in front of you only to find that it's standing right behind you.

The Tonton are most definitely still standing. But different now. They've always been scruffy, grubby even, with long hair and full beards. These were clean-shaven, with short, cropped hair. Their robes were clean. Their boots, too, and all their gear. Their horses were groomed, with shining coats. A new clean-look Tonton.

Not quite clean enough. The operation back at the valley went badly wrong. The commander didn't have control of his men. They were slow to obey him. And the way that one roughed up Nessa showed that some of them still want to play by the old rules. But the commander shot him. Fast. Without hesitation. Message delivered loud and clear to anybody else who might be thinking that way. New game. New rules. No second chances.

So.

The little green valley. A good patch of land. Shelter. Clean water. The Tonton kill the sick wife and the worn-out husband. And if it had gone according to plan, they would have taken Robbie and his sister. Both young and healthy. But where would they have taken them to? Where did the boy and girl in the cart, the resettlers, come from? Maybe they'd been snatched from their families too. But they certainly seemed willing enough. More than willing. The boy joined in with the clearance, took matters into his own hands.

The quartered circle brand on their foreheads means something. In Hopetown, the Tonton branded the whores with a W, but he's never heard of anything else like that. Branding marks you out permanently. Shows what group you belong to.

Healthy young people, branded. Territory expansion. Grabbing the good land and the clean water. Control of resources. A new, more disciplined Tonton carrying out orders. But whose orders? Somebody higher up. Somebody working to a larger plan. A man with a plan.

Such a man would have to be powerful. He'd have to be determined, disciplined, persuasive and very, very smart.

Jack knows of only one such man. A Tonton. He was Vicar Pinch's second in command. The power behind the throne. He rode away from Pine Top Hill before the battle even started. He abandoned his mad master, leaving him to his fate without a backwards glance. And he took a number of men with him.

DeMalo.

All of this must been rolling out for some time. To get to this point, it has to have been well under way while Vicar Pinch was still alive. Alive but toothless. DeMalo must have been building up his operation on the side. That would explain the rumors Jack started to hear a couple of years ago. From the little he knows of the man, that he's seen for himself, he can tell that DeMalo isn't the type to go for a bloody overthrow.

He's much more subtle. He's the stiletto in the dark. The poison in the drink. He'll have been biding his time, waiting for the right moment. Jack can imagine the tiny inward smile DeMalo must have allowed himself when he realized they were about to do his dirty work for him at Pine Top Hill.

The main thing is, he got his plan rolling out of sight and earshot of Pinch. He couldn't have done that without somehow winning the continued loyalty and silence of his Tonton followers.

Unheard of. Very interesting. Very worrying.

Jack would give a great deal to know exactly what DeMalo's up to. Where. How. And why.

The sooner he gets to The Lost Cause, the better.

The tavern stands at the crossroads ahead. It crouches low, hugging the ground. A shabby heap of a place, alone on the dry, wide plain, ringed in by black, brooding peaks.

The Lost Cause. At last.

Thanks to the route he took to avoid any chance of meeting the Tonton, it's taken him a week of hard travel to get here. Much longer than he'd expected.

It's just before dawn. Dawn and dusk, show time here in the storm belt. He checks the sky above. Right on time, ugly brown clouds are piling up over the plain. They scud in from all directions, tumbling and tripping in their haste. There's a mighty blast brewing. A sulphate storm.

Atlas tosses his head, dances a bit. Jack heels him on. Once they reach the tavern, he jumps down and settles him in the stables. The only other horse there is Prue, Molly's reddish longcoat mare. There's fresh fodder in the bin and water in the trough. That's a relief at least. All this time, he's been worried that he'd find the place had been torched by the Tonton. Still, the stable's usually full of customers' mounts: mules, horses, and the odd camel.

As he walks towards the door, the tavern sign creaks in the rising wind. The paint's flaking and faded, but he can just make out the tiny boat foundering on an angry sea, about to be swamped by a huge wave. Every time he's been here, he's half-expected to find that boat gone. Sunk to the bottom of the sea.

The Lost Cause. Never was a name more suited to a place. A pile of Wrecker junk a rat wouldn't sniff at. Tattered shreds of who-knows-what. Battered bits of this and that. It looks like a heavy sigh would do for it. But it's been here forever. Long years. Way before the weather changed and the storms moved in. When this was a grassy, green plain with life in plenty.

Even then, it was a well-known hooch and whores joint. But once Molly's family became landlords, it became notorious. Four generations of Pratts made it the only stop in this part of the world. Famous brawls, rogues plotting mischief in corners, the hectic jangle of music, drink rough enough to numb your hair, and bad girls of all persuasions. He wonders if Lilith's still working the room. She must be knocking on a bit.

He's never known The Lost Cause to be closed, day or night. Molly's likely to be awake, even at this hour. She's an early riser. Gets by on four hours of sleep with a catnap in the afternoon. She might even be working the bar.

Jack pauses outside the door. His stomach's jittery with nerves. He's pondered, over and over again, what he's going to say to her. How he's going to tell her about Ike. And he still doesn't know. He's never had to do this before. He'll just have to hope the right words come to him.

To buy himself a moment or two, he knocks the dust from his hat. Flicks the pigeon feather stuck in the band. A little smile quirks his lips as he remembers the fuss Emmi made, choosing the perfect feather to beautify his battered old hat. He puts it back on. Tilts it to a jaunty angle.

He takes a deep breath. He opens the door. He goes in.

† † †

Molly's behind the bar. She's drying hoochers. The rusty, dented drinking tins and pots look even more harmful than the last time he was here. She's working her way through a stack of them, like she's got a crowd of thirsty drinkers waiting. He's the only punter.

She looks up. She can't hide the little start of surprise. The quick flash of joy that chases over her face. And something else, too. Relief. Then, just as quickly, it's gone. The mask's back in place. The heard-it-all smile. The seen-it-all eyes.

They've got history together, he and Molly. And it goes deep. But that joy wasn't for him. Never for him the wild, hot joy he caught a glimpse of just now. No. She thinks Ike's with him. He swallows around the sudden tightness in his throat.

Well, well, she drawls, look what the wind blew in.

She goes back to her work. Her long tangle of blonde curly hair's tied back in a tail. She's got distracting lips. Dangerous curves. Direct eyes. Traveling men make wide detours just to be in the same room as her. That's the most that even the best of them can hope for.

Molly Pratt, he says. Remind me, what's a heavenly creature like you doin in a dump like this?

Servin rotgut to scoundrels like you, she says. An if you call my place a dump agin, I'll bar you.

You barred me the last time, he says, an the time before that, an the time before the time before that. Remember?

Oh, I remember, she says. Well, step in, don't be shy. Yer hangin back like a virgin on her weddin night. Siddown, have a drink, pull up a stool fer Ike. Where is he? Settlin the horses?

He doesn't answer. He'll work his way up to what he's got to say. Have a drink or three first. Wait for the right moment. He goes to the bar, grabbing a couple of stick stools on the way. He settles himself, slinging his bark saddlesack on the floor, dumping his weapons belt on the bar. There's sand everywhere. Piled in the corners. Drifting around his feet in the draughts from the door.

There's bad stuff goin on out there, Molly, he says.

Welcome to New Eden, she says. It's a brand new shiny world.

A bloody world, you mean, he says.

It's always bin a bloody world, she says. Only nowadays, some people's blood is better than others.

What's the news? he says. The Tonton sure ain't what they

was. What about the man in charge? You ever hear the name DeMalo?

She shakes her head. He's called the Pathfinder, she says. The landgrabbers–pardon me, Stewards of the Earth–they breathe his name like he ain't even human. They say he makes miracles. That he's here to heal the earth.

You shouldn't be here, he says. It ain't safe.

Well, it's true, she says, the Tonton don't like hooch an they don't like whores. My, how times've changed. But them bastards got bigger things on their mind than this place. Storm belt land's no good to 'em. I let Lilith an th'other girls go an, as you can see, I ain't ezzackly overrun with customers. No whores, not much hooch, they ain't gonna bother with me.

You don't know that, he says. You need to leave, Molly.

This is my home, Jack, she says. My business. I had it since I was fifteen. My father had it before me an he got it from his father. I bin dealin with hard-nosed sonsabitches my whole life.

I seen 'em, Molly, I seen 'em in action, he says. Are you willin to give yer life fer this place? Fer this?

It'll never come to that, she says. An if it does, I can take care of myself.

Well, you shouldn't be here by yerself, he says. When did the girls go?

A while back, she says. It's fine, me takin chances on my own account, but not them.

Something about the way she says it makes his eyes narrow. What're you up to? he says.

Leave it, she says. This line of conversation is now closed. She shoves an overflowing, rusty tin at him. There's a dead beetle floating on top.

Drink up, she says. No charge fer the bug. I better pour one fer Ike. You boys must be parched.

While she fills another hoocher and he fishes out the beetle, she glances towards the door. What's keepin him? Oh, don't tell me, I know. Hidin behind his horse. Ain't it jest like him, sendin you ahead to scout out the enemy while he waits fer the all clear. I'll be back in three months, he tells me, three months, Molly, I give you my word, an then I ain't never gonna leave yer side agin. Three months, my aunt patootie. Try three years, ten months an six days. I said it to you then, Jack, an I'll say it to you now: do not step through my door agin unless yer bringin Ike back to make a honest woman of me, ferever an ever amen. If you do, I'll shove you in the still an boil you into bad likker. Did I say that to you or did I not?

You did, he says.

An ain't I a woman who keeps her word?

You are.

Well then, she says.

He throws down his drink. Gasps as it hits his throat. That's unspeakable, he says, when he can speak. What is it?

Wormwood whisky, she says. Brewed last Tuesday. It keeps

off bedbugs, lice an flies. Good fer saddle itch too. The last man to try it ran outta here on all fours, howlin like a wolfdog.

Yer gonna kill somebody one of these days, he says.

Who says I didn't already? What the hell's keepin that man? She asks like she couldn't care less. But her eyes say different.

One more drink, then he'll tell her. He shoves the hoocher at her. Keep it comin, he says.

Help yerself, she says.

She's busy checking her reflection in the shard of looking glass she keeps behind the bar. She pinches her cheeks, bites her lips, and fiddles with her hair, all the while shooting little looks towards the door. Twenty nine, but like a nervous girl, waiting for the one who makes her heart beat faster. To see her so makes his own heart squeeze tight.

He drinks. Nerves twist his stomach. Go on, he tells himself, do it. Tell her now. But he finds himself saying, I swear, Molly, every time I see you, yer more beautiful than the last time. How many hearts you broke today?

Shut up, she says, I know I'm a hag. He snorts with disbelief and she smiles at herself in the glass, pleased. Livin in this dump is playin merry hell with my looks, she says. I've grown old, waitin on Ike. The Lost Cause. That's me all right, Jack, the biggest lost cause ever lived. An you know why? Fer thinkin that man might ever mean what he says. Ike Twelvetrees settle down? You might as well ask the sun to stop shinin.

Now. Tell her now. Molly, says Jack, there's somethin I—

Oh, enough about Ike. He'll show his face when he's worked up his nerve. She leans her elbows on the bar. What's this sorry-lookin object? She flicks the brim of his hat. It tumbles to the floor. That's better, she says. Damn you, Jack, yer a handsome devil an no mistake. You an them moonlight eyes of yers.

Listen. Molly. I, uh—

D'you ever think about her? Molly says it abruptly.

He doesn't answer. He stares into his drink.

She'd be six by now, she says. I know it's stupid, but . . . I like to imagine how she'd be. What kind of character, y'know. Who she might take after. She had eyes jest like yers. She was beautiful, wasn't she?

Yeah, he says. She sure was.

He takes her hand in both of his. Holds it tight and kisses it. They look at each other. The air between them lies heavy with what was. With what had never really been, but still would always bind them together.

Jack? She's peering at him closely, searchingly. She draws back to stare at him, like something about him's suddenly struck her. Ohmigawd, Jack. You got somethin to tell me.

He breathes out. Yeah, he says. Yeah, I do. The thing is, Molly . . . I, uh—

Well, I'll be damned! she says. There's a slow smile creeping across her face.

He frowns. Molly?

Ha ha! I don't believe it! She slaps her hand on the bar. Gawdammit an hallelujah, Jack, who is she?

What? What're you talkin about?

Don't gimme the run around, I know you too well. Who is she? Who's the girl? Molly spots the leather string hanging around his neck. An what's this? She gives a tug and pulls out the heartstone, hidden inside his shirt.

Molly gazes at it. A heartstone, she says. She looks at him with wondering eyes. She gave you a heartstone.

Maybe I found it, he says.

Oh no, she says. I can see her in yer face, Jack. I can see her in yer eyes.

I dunno what yer talkin about, he says.

Hey, she says, it's me, remember? You an me don't pretend. We're past that. All the time I've knowed you, Jack, you kept the door to that heart of yers locked up tight an the key hid away. Looks like she found it.

He says nothing. Molly waits. Then:

Keys ain't her style, he says. She kicked the door down.

You love her, says Molly.

Oh, I dunno about that, he says. I, uh . . . huh. That sounds too safe. This don't feel safe.

Oh. Like that, is it?

I don't want this, Molly, he says. I . . . whatever it is, I sure didn't go lookin fer it.

You don't hafta, she says. If it's meant to be, it'll find you. We like to think we're in charge of our own lives, but we ain't. Not really. You should know that by now.

You couldn't find nobody more pig-headed if you tried, he says. An she's always thinkin she knows best, even when she don't, especially when she don't. She's prickly an stubborn an everythin you'd put at the bottom of a list if you was makin a . . . a list of that kind. Which I ain't. I didn't.

But? says Molly.

But ohmigawd Molly, she shines so bright, he says. The fire of life burns so strong in her. I never realized till I met her . . . I bin cold my whole life, Moll.

I know, she says softly.

It's jest that . . . aw, hell. She thinks I'm a better man than I really am.

Well, yer a better man than you think you are, she says.

She's too young, he says. Eighteen.

Scandalous! she says. Cuz yer so old.

Age ain't about years an you know it, he says. Anyways, settin so much store in one person . . . it's dangerous.

Don't you dare walk away from this, Jack, don't you dare, Molly says fiercely. Most people don't ever feel what yer feelin. Be with her. An if it lasts one hour, one night, a week, a month, it don't matter. Be with her, burn with her, shine with her . . . fer whatever time's given to you. Now. Tell me her name. Tell me.

He takes a deep breath. Saba, he says. Her name's Saba.

Molly rests a hand on his face. Oh, my darlin Jack, she says. This . . . this is what I wanted fer you. All I ever wanted fer you. How could she resist them eyes?

She tried, says Jack. Man, did she try. But . . . listen, Molly, that ain't why I—

A celebration! she cries. This calls fer some serious drinkin! An I mean serious!

She laughs as she slams hoochers down, setting them out in a long line across the bar. Where the hell is Ike? Ike! she hollers. Gawdammit, man, git yer hairy hide in here this minute! We're drinkin to Jack an Saba! She starts to pour, splashing and spilling everywhere. I tell you, Jack, yer a inspiration. I'm gonna rename this place. No more Lost Cause, oh no. Not this place an sure as hell not me. From this moment on, it's gonna be called The Hope Springs Eternal! An when Ike walks through that door—after I finish kissin him to death— I'm gonna tie him to that chair an never let him go, cuz life's too gawdamn short an it's about time I started takin my own advice. I might need yer help, of course, but I'm sure you won't mind, seein how—

Molly! Jack grabs her hand. Stop, Molly, please. Dammit, Moll. Ike ain't gonna walk through the door.

She goes still. Very still. Her smile fades. Please don't say it, she whispers.

He can't bear to. But he has to.

Ike's dead, he says. He's dead, Molly. I'm sorry.

Tears flood her eyes. Spill silently down her face. She looks at him straight.

It was a month ago, he says. No . . . a bit more. There was a . . . it was a big fight. A real one this time, not jest some tavern brawl. The Tonton.

The Tonton, she says.

We went back to Freedom Fields, he says. We burned the chaal fields. They came after us an . . . not jest me an Ike, but Saba too, an some others. We fought 'em, Molly. We beat 'em. An fer a time, fer . . . a little while, the good guys was on top. Me an Ike, the good guys. Who'd of thought it?

Me, she says. I would. I know.

He was with friends, Moll, says Jack. I was with him. I was right there an . . . he died in my arms. He died well. He went out big. The way he would of wanted to. The last thing I said to him, I . . . whispered in his ear. Molly loves you, Ike. That was the last thing he heard.

She stands there a moment. She nods once. Slides her hand free of his. I'm glad it was you told me, she says. Don't waste no more time, Jack. Go to her. Be with her. Burn bright. Promise me.

Leave here, he says. Come with me. Please.

Promise me, she says.

I promise, he says.

G'bye, Jack. She kisses him on the cheek. Then she slips through the door into the back room and closes it behind her.

Silence. She must be holding something over her mouth so's not to make any noise. She might as well let go and have a good howl. He's the only one here. He goes around the bar and knocks on the door.

Molly? No answer. He was comin back to you, Molly, he says. He loved you.

Go away, she says.

I cain't leave you like this, he says. Let me in.

Fergawdsake, jest do what I say! she cries.

He goes back to his stool. He looks at the full hoochers lined up along the bar and starts on the first one. He knows how Molly grieves. Once he's gone, she'll lock the place up. Then she'll cry some and drink some. And she'll do that, over and over again, until the skin over this latest wound has grown tough enough for her to carry on.

He'll wait till the storm passes. Then he'll go. He pulls the heartstone out again. Rubs it between his fingers. It's cool, even though it's been next to his skin. That's the way of a heartstone. Cool until you get close to your heart's desire. The closer you get, the hotter it burns. The last time he saw Saba, she put it around his neck. It was hot.

It'll help you to find me, she'd said.

I don't need no stone to find you, he'd said. I'd find you anywhere.

Then she'd kissed him. Till he couldn't think. Till he was dizzy with wanting her.

He slips the stone back into his shirt.

The storm hits. He hears the sudden, dull thunder of sulphate raining down on The Lost Cause. Soon enough, the rain will follow and wash it away.

The door slams open. The wind wails inside, rattling the rafters, stirring the sand on the floor, plucking at his coat. He gets up to close it.

Two men walk in. They're spattered with sulphate. Leather body armor. Crossbows. Bolt shooters. Long black robes. Long hair. Beards.

Tonton. Old-style. Danger.

Every nerve, every muscle in Jack's body snaps tight and starts to fizz. But he keeps his voice casual as he says, The place is empty, fellas. Looks like everybody cleared off.

I come to see that Lilith, says one. Where is she?

Gone, says Jack, like I said. Check fer yerself.

The Tonton stares at him a moment. He crosses to a door in the corner. It leads to a hallway with four small rooms off it, where the girls used to do business. He goes through, yelling, Lilith! Hey, Lilith! Git on out here! There's the sound of doors being slammed open, one after another.

One Tonton out of the way. Jack's eyes flick to the bar. His weapons belt lies there.

A quick move and the other Tonton's got his bolt

shooter out and aimed at Jack. It was the work of a second. He goes to the bar and drains one of the full hoochers. His gaze never leaves Jack. His shooter stays aimed.

The first Tonton comes back out. Where'd she go? he says.

I dunno, friend, says Jack. Like I said, there ain't nobody here.

Just then, Molly lets out a cry. A long, keening, animal wail of pain.

As it dies down, the one with the drink says, So who's that?

He and Jack stare at each other.

Leave her alone, says Jack.

The Tonton points his bolt shooter at Jack's heart. Lazily. He smiles.

Call her, he says. Go on . . . friend. Call her.

THE WASTE,
ONE MONTH LATER

I STAND ON THE RIDGE. I WATCH THE SUN RISE. WHITE-faced an pitiless, it starts to grill the earth. Another dawn in the Waste. Another day in this nowhere. High summer. Heat an dust. Thirst an hunger an blame.

Me an Lugh an Tommo an Emmi. At each other. About who did what. Who said what. Whose fault it is that we're stuck here. That we're caught in this land of death an bones, when we should be livin it rich out west. Makin a new life fer ourselfs.

Over the mountains. Beside the Big Water. Where the air tastes like honey. Where Jack waits fer me.

Oh, Jack. Please. Wait.

I'm countin on you to wait.

We should of bin there long ago. Weeks ago. Emmi says the land's keepin us here. That it's trapped us. I wish she wouldn't say stuff like that. You know it's stupid but she says it an somehow it gits into yer head an then you cain't stop thinkin about it.

The thing is, we made a bad start. We didn't have no plan. We jest turned our heads west an went. It beggars belief that four people could be so foolish, but there you go. We warn't thinkin clear, none of us. Too much had happened. We'd jest beat the Tonton in a hard fight. An only then by the skin of our teeth, an all thanks to Maev an the Hawks. If they hadn't of showed up, we'd of bin finished.

Then Jack. Tellin me, farewell not goodbye, I'll see you out west an—oh, by the way—yer in my blood, Saba.

So my head was full of him an all of the rest of it an . . . I had Lugh back. Since the day the Tonton snatched him from Silverlake, that's all I'd bin set on. To find Lugh an git him back. An I was jest so glad. So glad an so thankful that him an me was together agin.

I don't mean to say that it don't matter that Ike got killed in the fight. A grievous sadness fills me when I think about him. My heart hurts. Not like Tommo's does, not like that. He mourns Ike hard an deep. I guess no deaf boy's ever gonna be a big talker, but he's bin brought so low we hardly hear his strange, rough voice these days. Em's took to speakin on his account. He don't seem to mind.

But when we started off, the main thing was we was alive. Somehow . . . somehow we lived through it all. An I had my Lugh back. My twin, most dearly loved. An it was like we was giddy with relief an joy an . . . so much relief that we fergot about anythin else.

Like how we'd git where we wanted to go.

We ended up askin the first traveler we met. A salt johnny on camelback who'd jest bin harvestin at one of the great salt lakes on the Waste. Our tradebag was on the thin side an the best we could give him was a belt buckle an a pair of cord bootlaces. That bought us a half-campbell of salt an the advice to head straight across the Waste. He said it was the fastest, most direct way west. We figgered he knew what he was talkin about, so that's what we did. We went straight.

A buckle an bootlaces don't buy good advice.

He didn't tell us what kinda place it is. Why it's called the Waste. He didn't tell us about the deathwater. The bad huntin. The Wrecker plague pits that stretch out fer leagues. The sinkholes that suddenly appear as you cross 'em. One moment yer goin along, the next moment the ground opens an yer down among the dead.

I was the first one to fall in. I bin up to my neck in dead men's bones before. You'd think I'd be used to it. That I wouldn't mind. But I do. I mind.

I'm sick to death of death.

Then it was Buck, Lugh's horse. Lucky he didn't break his leg or worse. Lucky Lugh was leadin him at the time, not ridin him. But he twisted his right leg. It happened a week ago an he still ain't right. So we're stuck here till he's better. Stuck in the Waste.

Maybe the land is tryin to keep us here. Maybe Emmi's right. It warn't so long ago that I wouldn't of paid no mind to what a nine year old little sister had to say. But Em's got a way of seein things, a different way of lookin at the world. I don't dismiss her so quick these days.

One thing's true. One thing I know fer sure. This place

ain't right. There's shadows where there shouldn't oughta be none. I'll see somethin, outta the corner of my eye, an I'll think it's Nero or maybe another bird but it never is. An I hear these . . . these noises. It's like . . . I dunno, like somebody's whisperin or somethin.

I don't say nuthin to th'others. Not no more. I did at first. We'd all hunt around to see what it might be, but nobody ever found nuthin an then they started lookin at me funny, so now I jest keep my mouth shut.

I don't sleep good. I ain't slept good fer so long that I'm pretty much used to it, but it's bin even worse ever since Epona died. Anyways, it means I can keep watch over 'em. Lugh an Emmi an Tommo. Make sure they don't come to no harm. If I don't sleep, nobody can come an take 'em.

Mainly, though, I keep watch over Lugh. He sleeps long an deep. But not easy. Never easy. Most nights he talks in his sleep. Nuthin I can make out, mumblin fer the most part, the odd word or two.

Sometimes he cries. Like a little child. That's the worst. I cry with him. I cain't help it. His tears is mine. They always have bin. Th'only time I ever remember him cryin before was when Ma died when we was eight. There was plenty of tears shed then. Me an Lugh an Pa must of cried enough tears to fill Silverlake three times over. But tears don't bring back the dead. I learned that.

Fer now, I got work to do. Back at camp they'll all be wakin with empty bellies an it's my turn to hunt. Lizard, pouch rat, snake, I ain't fussy. Anythin 'ud do, so long as it ain't locusts. I brought back locusts my last three times an all becuz of— well, everybody's cheesed off with crunchin bugs, that's fer sure.

I frown. I cain't think how I got here this mornin. How I got to this ridge so far from our campsite. I must of come on Hermes. There he is, right over there, rough chestnut coat an sturdy legs, rippin up withered clumps of bunchgrass. You'd think I could recall the ride, but I cain't. Strange.

I lift the long-looker to my eyes. Scan the landscape. The Waste rolls out as far as I can see. To the horizon an beyond. Dry, yellow soil. The odd hill of gray rock, striped with red. Worn smooth by the wind.

This place 'ud make a devil weep, I says.

Suddenly I hear a rumble. I feel it the same time I hear it. A low, steady tremor unner my feet. There's a flash of movement to the left. From the north. I train the looker that way.

Holy crap, I says.

It's a line of twisters. They swirl across the plain, in a long row. Small ones, not more'n forty foot high. I ain't never seen such a thing. They snatch the dust as they head this way.

An there's a windspringer. He races along, in front of the line of twisters, as they chase behind. A two-year buck, judgin by his antlers. He goes flat out. If he don't outrun 'em, he'll be swept up.

Nero's ridin the thermals overhead. I whistle. He swoops down an lands on my outstretched hand.

I point to the springer. See that? I says. That's breakfast, lunch an supper fer the next week.

Nero squawks.

You know what to do, I says. Turn him this way. Bring him to me. Bring him here, Nero! I throw him into the air an he streaks away. Nero's a good hunter. Thinks he's a hawk, not a crow. He'll turn the springer from the twisters' path. He'll drive him right into range of my crossbow.

I start to run.

My feet feel heavy. Like they don't belong to the rest of me. They don't wanna move. But I make 'em. I start to go faster. As I run, I slide my bow from my back. Grab a arrow from my quiver. I leap down the dry slope of the ridge. Right near the bottom there's a flat bit of rock that juts out. I can git a clear shot from there an I'll be far enough away to be safe from the twisters.

I reach the rock. Dust whirls about me. The wind shrieks. I take up position. I nock my arrow to the bowstring.

I gotta stay calm. If I stay calm, it'll be okay. This time, it'll be okay. I take a deep breath.

Nero screams with excitement. He's drivin the springer hard. It swerves right, then left, but he dives at it, shriekin. It heads straight this way. There's a white blaze on its breast. Over its heart. The perfect target.

This is gonna be the perfect kill.

I lift my bow. Take aim. Straight fer the heart.

My hands start to shake. There's a flash of white light.

Epona runnin towards me. Throwin her arms wide.An I shoot her. Straight through the heart.

Cold sweat. On my forehead, in my eyes. I blink. Epona's dead. I killed her.

Saabaa. Saaabaaa.

My name whispers around me. I turn, lookin. Nuthin there. Nobody.

Who is it? I says.

Saaabaaa.

It's the wind. The twisters. That's all. Calm down. Take aim. Shoot the springer. It's only a couple hunnerd paces away now.

I grip my bow harder. The shakin gits worse. It's jest like before. Jest like the last time. An the time before that. Any time I try to shoot.

Then.

I notice.

My breath

tight chest

dry throat

cain't breathe

need air

deep breaths

I cain't, I—
cain't
breathe
cain't
breathe
on my knees on the ground tight throat heart fast
too fast, too—
air
air
cain't breathe cain't see cain't—
Nero.
Screamin.
Nero.
Warnin me.
Danger.
Danger.
Danger.

†   †   †

I lift my head. Everythin's . . . blurred.

Then. I see. Somethin movin. Movin fast. I squint. Try to
see what it is, what—

Wolfdogs, I says.

A pack of wolfdogs chase hard at the springer's heels. Six of 'em. No. Eight. Where'd they come from?

The pack splits. Six wolfdogs stay on the springer's tail. They chase it south, across the Waste. The line of twisters churn after 'em.

Two dogs peel off. Two dogs head towards me. Comin this way.

They smell me. They smell my weakness.

Deep inside, in my belly the red hot flickers. But it's feeble. A weak spark when I need a blaze. A fierce fire to save me. The red hot always . . . saves me.

I haul myself up. Hard to breathe. Hands shakin, but I . . . can do it, I can—my bow drops from my hands. Hits the ground. The flicker's gone. The red hot. Gone.

I'm helpless. Hopeless. Alone.

No. Not quite.

Nero screams with rage. He attacks the wolfdogs. Dives at their heads. But on they come. They're forty foot away now. Thirty.

Move, Saba. Do somethin. Anythin! I scrabble fer rocks, pebbles, sticks.

Nero's slowin 'em down. He darts, draws blood, retreats. Agin an agin an agin. They lunge at him. Strike with their claws. A flurry of fur an feathers an dust. Shrieks an snarls. They'll hurt him. Kill him.

Nero! Nero! I scream. I got rocks in my hands. Throw 'em,

throw 'em. No, no, I might hit Nero. Dust an chaos. I cain't see clear.

My breath, my breath's comin easier. Whatever took hold of me starts to let go. But I'm weak. Shaky.

Nero breaks free. I let fly with the rocks. But I miss. The wolfdogs pace towards me. Ten foot away. Eight. Six.

One dog in front of me. One on my left. Cold, flat heat in their yellow eyes.

Nero shrieks an shrieks. He dives. They cower.

I scream an scream. I fling pebbles an dirt. I throw, they flinch, but they ain't put off. Suddenly I remember the knife in my boot. I reach fer it. My hands, my tremblin hands.

They inch towards me. Eyes fixed. Low in their throats, they hum my death.

Then behind me, from nowhere, a noise an a rush. Before I can move, somethin leaps past me.

A gray shape. Big. Shaggy. Another wolfdog. A new one.

This one, this new wolfdog, he flies at the dog on my left. Goes straight fer his throat an bowls him over. Rips his neck open. As blood spills, th'other wolfdog, the one in front of me, attacks the new one. Teeth flash. Dust flies.

I scramble outta the way.

The new wolfdog warn't runnin with the others. He's a loner. He's got blue eyes. Light blue eyes.

That's rare. I only seen one other before. An he's in a

bad way. Rib-thin, matted fur, an now a bleedin wound on his flank. But he's fightin like a demon.

Think, Saba. I need Hermes. If there's a moment . . . if I git a chance I'll take it. I'll take any chance to git away, but I need Hermes here.

No, no, wait, I cain't, the dogs might go fer him. So confused. Cain't think straight. Move, Saba. Jest move! I start to back away, up the ridge. I keep my eyes on the dogs, tearin at each other, fightin to the death.

Nero screams above.

A loose rock. My foot slips. I go over. I'm down.

An I'm slidin. Tumblin. Fallin.

Back down the slope.

Straight towards the wolfdogs.

†　　†　　†

I'm on my back. Lyin on hard, flat rock. Hot rock. The heat sizzles around me. Cooks me. My bones ache. Eyes heavy. Dry. I squint one open. Too bright. A dull pain throbs at the back of my head.

I groan.

Nero croaks. I can feel the weight of him on my stummick.

The smell of doggy, meaty breath, hot an close. A rough tongue licks my face. My eyes fly open. The blue-eyed wolf-dog's standin over me.

Ahhh! I scrabble away an leap to my feet. Nero screeches off in a flurry.

The dog's backin away, whinin. He stops. He sits, about six foot away. His pink tongue lolls outta his mouth, long an drippin. I frown. Is that—is he . . . smilin at me? Fer the first time, I notice he's got one droopy ear. The right one.

Blue eyes. One droopy ear. Jest like Tracker. Mercy's wolfdog, Tracker. But . . . how can that be? Mercy's place at Crosscreek must be weeks from here.

Tracker? I says.

He stands. Barks twice. Takes a couple of steps towards me. Nero caws from his perch on a nearby rock.

Tracker! I says. Ohmigawd, Tracker, it's you! What're you do—

A arrow comes whizzin through the air. I dive. Tracker darts away. It jest misses his left flank. I look behind to see who's shot it.

It's Lugh. Standin on the ridge above. He's about to shoot agin.

No! I yell. Wait! Don't shoot!

Too late. Then Lugh's leapin down the slope, hollerin an wavin his arms. The arrow bounces offa the rock.

An I'm yellin, Lugh, stop! It's okay! Don't shoot!

An Nero's flyin all over the place, screechin an squawkin.

An Tracker's gone. I can see him high-tailin it across the Waste.

Damn, I says. Ow! A sharp twinge in the back of my head. It's a fair-sized lump an hurts like stink when I give it a prod.

I freeze. There's two wolfdogs not more'n ten foot away from me. What's left of 'em, anyways. It's the ones that attacked me. They lie in pools of their own blood. Both got their throats ripped out. Their teeth bared in a last snarl, their yellow eyes glarin rage at death. The air hums with a hungry buzz. Flies. Hunnerds of 'em. Thousands of 'em. The open wounds, the half-dried lakes of sticky blood heave with their shimmerin bodies.

Tracker did this. Tracker killed the wolfdogs. He saved my life.

Tracker. Here. I don't unnerstand.

Saba! Lugh runs up, crossbow in hand. He's breathin hard. Relief an worry an anger, all at the same time, chase over his face. Saba, are y'okay?

Yeah, I says. I'm fine, thanks.

But I'm thinkin. Tracker here. Alone in the Waste. So . . . does that mean Mercy's somewhere near? No, she cain't be, he's in terrible shape, so thin an ragged. She'd never let him git like that. So what's goin on? How'd he git here? An where's Mercy? Tough, wise Mercy. What's happened to her?

Whaddya mean, fine? Saba! Lugh grabs my arm an shakes

it. Saba, what the hell happened here?

That was Tracker, I says. That wolfdog you jest shot at. It's Tracker. Ohmigawd, Lugh, he saved my life.

Who? He looks blank.

Then I remember. Lugh warn't at Mercy's place at Crosscreek with me an Emmi. That was after he got took by the Tonton. So he don't know Tracker.

Tracker, I says. He's Mercy's tame wolfdog. Y'know, Mercy. Ma's friend . . . from Crosscreek.

He stares at me. Crosscreek? You ain't talkin no sense.

Yes, I am, I says. That wolfdog had one droopy ear an blue eyes. Jest like Tracker. It was him, Lugh, it was Tracker, I'm sure of it.

Wolfdogs got yellow eyes, not blue, says Lugh. Yellow, like these here. An there ain't no such thing as a tame wolfdog. They're vicious bastards. Look at you, Saba, yer a mess.

He's right. I got blood all over me. My boots, my tunic, my britches.

Tracker killed 'em, I says. They was comin fer me an then . . . he come flyin outta nowhere, Lugh, an he fought that one an rippped his throat an then he started in on that one an then I tripped an . . . I remember fallin, I must of hit my head. Must of knocked myself out. When I come to, jest now, Tracker was standin right beside me an—

The moment Lugh hears the words "hit my head", he pulls me to him an starts pressin an pokin at my head an talkin over me. Fergawdsake, Saba, why didn't you say?

Ow! I elbow him away. I'm okay, it's jest a bump.

I'll be the judge of that, he says. He starts checkin me out, holdin up his pointer finger an movin it back an forth. I follow it with my eyes.

It was Tracker, I says. I swear it was him, Lugh.

He takes me by the shoulders. Looks at me straight. Listen to me, he says. You hit yer head. You bin lyin in the sun fer who knows how long. You must of imagined it. Dreamed it.

No, I says, no, I never.

C'mon, Saba, think about it, he says. What's the chances of Tracker showin up here, in the middle of nowhere? Crosscreek must be weeks away.

I know that, I says.

So, what's the chances?

I dunno, I says. I . . . not good, I guess.

More like impossible, he says. An what about this?

Lugh holds up the loose end of a piece of nettlecord rope that's tied around his right ankle. I look down. I got the same as him, essept around my left ankle. The tether's bin cut through with a knife, close to my boot, clean an neat. I stare at the cut rope. I fergot all about him an me bein tied together. Lately, when I do sleep, I've took to sleepwalkin. Tyin us together was Lugh's idea to stop me wanderin off an gittin into trouble. Fer my own good, he said. To keep me safe.

I woke up, he says, the rope was cut an you was gone.

45

Nero flaps down an lands on my head. I wince. Move him to my shoulder. I must of bin sleepwalkin agin, I says.

You tryin to tell me you moved so sneaky in yer sleep? he says. That you cut us apart without wakin me up?

What, you think I did it on purpose? I says.

You tell me, he says.

I–I don't remember cuttin the rope, I says. I don't remember how I got here.

Oh gawd, I dunno, maybe you was sleepwalkin. He shakes his head. Jeez, Saba.

Look, I says, all I can remember is, I was huntin an there was this windspringer, runnin in front of a storm—ohmigawd, Lugh, you never seen nuthin like this storm before. There was this . . . long line of twisters, little ones not more'n forty foot high, an they come rollin outta the east, jest sweepin right along there. It was amazin!

I wave my arm at the plain in front of us. Lugh an me look out over the bleak face of the Waste. The mid-mornin sky's so clear you can see all the way to the horizon an into next week. No bushes ripped out. No churned up ground. Not a single sign that a storm might of passed.

There was a storm, I says, it happened, truly it did. Nero seen it!

I look to him, like he might suddenly start talkin an back me up. But he's busy with crow concerns, tearin at the ripped flesh of one of the wolfies, gorgin hisself on fresh kill.

Well, anyways, I nearly had him, I says, this springer, but then this pack of wolfies come outta nowhere an two of 'em—these two here—they come at me an then Tracker shows up an they start to fight an . . . then I . . . I fell an hit my head an when I come to, you was here an . . . that's it.

We stare at each other.

Lugh. Golden as the sun itself. His skin, his long hair that hangs in a plait to his waist. Eyes the blue of a summer sky. So different from me, with my dark hair an eyes. Ma used to say I was the night-time an Lugh was the day. Th'only thing the same is our birthmoon tattoo on our right cheekbones. Pa put 'em there hisself, to mark us out as special. Twins born at the midwinter moon. A rare thing.

Lugh huffs out his breath. Goes to where my bow an quiver lies on the ground, my knife too. While he picks 'em up, he whistles fer the horses an they start pickin their way down the ridge towards us. Hermes an Rip, Tommo's horse that Lugh rode here on. He comes back. Hands my weapons over.

A full quiver, he says. That means you didn't shoot even one arrow. Not at the windspringer, not at the wolfies. How come?

I go to speak. Stop myself. I nearly said. It nearly came out. About the shakes an the breathin an . . . the rest. But I cain't say. I mustn't. I cain't burden Lugh with my troubles. His soul's heavy enough. Whatever it is that ails me, it'll pass.

Saba! Lugh says. How come you didn't shoot?

I . . . I dunno, I says.

You know what I think? he says. There warn't no storm. There warn't no windspringer an there warn't no blue-eyed wolfdog that come outta nowhere to save yer life. You dreamed the whole thing. You was sleepwalkin.

No, I says. No.

You rode here in yer sleep, he says, an somehow you fell an knocked yerself out. While you was dreamin of blue-eyed wolfdogs an twister storms, these two wolfies an that one I chased off, they sniffed you out an got in a fight over the meat.

What meat? I says.

You, you idiot, he says. I came jest in time to save yer hide. If I hadn't of, they'd of ripped you to shreds an vultures 'ud be pickin at yer bones right this second.

I glance at the sky. Sure enough, the big dead eaters is startin to circle above the wolfies. No, I says, no, it warn't like that, Lugh, I swear it was Tracker who—

Shut up! Jest shut up! he explodes. Gawdammit, Saba, give it a rest an stop lyin to me!

His face is hot. Flushed dark red. The little muscle in his jaw—the one Emmi calls his mad muscle—is bunched tight an jumpin. It happens a lot these days. This quick snap of rage.

I ain't lyin, I says.

Well, you ain't tellin me the truth, he says.

What, like you tell me the truth? I says.

We stare at each other a long moment. There's tired

48

lines carved deep in his face. Dark smudges unner his eyes. Suddenly, his shoulders slump. His anger drains away. As quick as it comes, it's gone.

What'm I gonna do with you? he says. He hooks a arm around my neck an pulls me to him. We lean our foreheads aginst each other. I'm sorry, he says. I'm sorry, I . . . I jest want things to be the way they was. I jest want you an me to be us agin.

Me too, I whisper.

You smell bad, he says.

I know, I says.

No, he says, I mean, you smell real bad. I cain't stand it. He shoves me away. Go cut some big muscle meat offa one of them wolfies, he says. We'll stew some tonight an wind dry the rest.

Hermes an Rip stand waitin, well away from the dead wolfdogs. While I stone off the vultures an git on with slicin one of the wolfies into chunks, Lugh goes an starts checkin the horses over, bridles, bits an reins, the cattail mats on their backs.

We jest need to git outta this place, I says. It's doin all our heads in. Is Buck's leg healed enough fer us to move on?

I ain't riskin a good horse jest because you cain't wait to see Jack, says Lugh.

I didn't say that, I says.

You don't hafta, he says. I know what you mean.

You do not, I says. Heat starts to crawl up my neck.

Oh really? Then how come yer turnin red? I swear, this . . . obsession you got with him . . . all of yuz. Lugh puts on a silly little voice. D'you remember the time Jack said this? Did I tell you about the time Jack did that? I'm sick of hearin his name.

Anybody'd think you was jealous, I says.

I jest don't want you to git hurt, says Lugh. I keep tellin you, Saba, he ain't gonna be there. He ain't gonna show at the Big Water. Jack's long gone. A guy like him . . . he gits a whiff of somethin new an he's off. He's only in it fer hisself, you can see it in his eyes. Once he's got what he wants, he moves on.

Jack ain't like that, I says. My cheeks feel flamin hot now.

What's the matter? he says. Too close to the mark? What did Jack want from you? Did you give it to him?

Shut yer mouth, I says.

Lugh stops what he's doin. Gives me a hard stare. Did you lie with him? he says. Is that how you paid him to help find me?

I gasp. Jump to my feet an face him square. You take that back!

I seen the way he looked at you, he says. The way you looked at him.

The way I look at people's my own business, I says. You took aginst Jack the moment you met him, when all you should be is thankful.

An there it is! he says. The hourly reminder of my debt to Jack.

Well, maybe that's because you don't seem to appreciate that you wouldn't be alive if it warn't fer him, I says. None of us would. I don't unnerstand you, Lugh. Why you ain't grateful that—

Do NOT tell me I oughta be grateful! he yells. He storms over, grabbin my arms, shakin me hard. I am not grateful, d'you hear me? I do not! Wanna! Hafta be . . . grateful.

He ends on a whisper. He stares down at his hands holdin my arms. At his fingers diggin into me. Hangin on to me. Then, Why did you let 'em take me? Why didn't you an Pa stop 'em?

His voice is so low I hafta lean close in to hear.

We tried to, I says. You know we did. They killed Pa.

He lifts his head. His eyes so bleak. So . . . old. My heart pinches.

You should of found me sooner, he says.

His voice sends a white slash of fear through me. It's flat. Empty.

Please, Lugh, I whisper, why won't you tell me what happened to you at Freedom Fields?

Nuthin happened, he says. He turns his eyes away. He lets go my arm. We better git back, he says. They'll be wonderin where we are.

We ride back to camp without talkin. Apart.

My head's tight. It throbs an pounds where the bump is. My eyes burn with uncried tears.

If tears could wash away the bleakness in my brother's eyes, the white fear flatness of his voice, I'd weep till the end of time. But they cain't. An I fear there won't ever be enough tears. Not fer him. Not fer none of us.

All the while I was lookin fer him, all them months, I kept tellin myself the same thing. Over an over. Once I find him, once me an Lugh's back together agin, we're gonna be the same as we was before. The way we've always bin.

Now I know that was jest the story I told myself. To keep goin. To spur me on to find him. To keep me fightin. To keep me alive.

It's a good story. I wish it was true. But it ain't. Because this is the truth.

What happens to you changes you. Fer good or ill, yer changed ferever. There ain't no goin back. No matter how many tears you cry. It sounds simple, but it ain't.

It's a truth that Hopetown nailed through my heart. The first time they put me in the Cage to fight.

My whole life, Lugh's bin my better self. The light to my dark. We shared a heartbeat in the womb. The blood an breath of our mother. We're two halfs of one whole.

Now he cain't help me. I cain't help him. An we sure as hell

52

cain't help ourselfs. No, fer the first time ever, Lugh ain't the one I need.

I need Jack.

Jack.

My longin fer him aches in my bones. His silver eyes, his crooked smile, the smell of his warm skin, sage an sun. But mostly I long fer, mostly I ache fer, his stillness. The stillness at the heart of him. Like calm water.

Lugh's wrong about him. Couldn't be more wrong. If Jack says he'll meet me at the Big Water, he will. He keeps his promises. All I need is to see him agin. To be with him, to talk with him. We'll talk about it, we'll talk about everythin, an he'll listen an he'll help me figger out how to fix things, how to make it all better. How to make me an Lugh better.

He'll banish the shadows. He'll silence the whispers. An the wounds of my soul will heal.

I jest need Jack.

He'll make everythin all right.

✝ ✝ ✝

We're nearly back at camp. Suddenly, somethin catches Lugh's eye. He squints east, into the distance. I do too. There's a trail of dust slowly snakin this way.

Throw me the looker, he says. The first words since we left the ridge. He lifts it to his eyes. Another wagon train, he says. How many's that since we bin stopped here?

Four—no, five, I says.

A lotta people on the move these days, even in this hellhole. He watches fer a bit. Same as always, he says. Sick lookin. Old. Useless.

Let's talk to these ones, Lugh, I says. Maybe they could help us. We could travel with 'em.

I bin takin care of this family since I was eight, he says. I think I know what's best. You sayin I don't?

No, I says, no, I didn't mean to—

We don't need nobody's help, he says. Well, they better not come lookin fer water. We ain't got none to spare.

I'll watch till they pass, I says.

He nods. Tosses me the looker. Sing out if they head this way, he says.

Hey, Lugh?

Yeah?

You an me, we're . . . okay, ain't we?

His smile don't reach his eyes. Of course we are, he says. He clicks at Rip an they disappear around the hill.

Our camp's set up in the lee of the best windbreak fer leagues around—a great carhill, made back in Wrecker times. We had one near us at Silverlake. Pa figgered that carhills must of bin some kinda tech worship thing the Wreckers did.

The land took hold of this one a long time ago. Covered it with earth an grass all over, hid it away from view. But on the windward side, you can see bits of crushed, rusted car. A nose here, a tail end there. Around th'other side, there's a grove of spindly scrub pine an a waterhole an that's where we are. So close to the carhill, you'd esspeck the water to be rustwater, but this one ain't. Still, it's only a puddle, jest enough fer us an the horses.

I git down from Hermes an scramble up the hill. I fix the looker on the dust trail. It ain't long before the travelers come into plain view. There's three wagons in this train. First comes a old woman on boarback, wild haired an bent. Next, a man an woman in a mule cart. She fans flies away from the limp child in her lap. Bringin up the rear, a girl about my age pedals a three-tire trolley.

I wait. They pass, too far away to see me an I'm well hid besides. Still, the driver of the mule cart lifts his head. Turns it this way. Maybe the sun caught on the glass of my looker. A brief glance, then he sets his face forwards once agin.

He's bitter-faced, sick yellow skin. With the look of a man who's left any hope by the side of the road a long way back. A sorry crew, altogether. They look like they're carryin sickness. Maybe the blood lung, maybe worse. Fer definite we don't want 'em stoppin to ask fer no water.

Old folk. Weak men an women. Sickly young. Jest like

th'other wagon trains we seen crossin the Waste. Not one person lookin fit enough to travel good roads, let alone this one. Lugh's right. People's on the move west.

I wonder why.

Not jest wagons, lone travelers too. We found the leftover bits of one fella. Well, Nero did. Dead eaters had bin at him, jackals an vultures, so you couldn't tell much. Jest his hair color an boot size. The boots was good an they fit Tommo. You never feel right, takin from the dead. But he wouldn't be doin no more walkin an Tommo would. We piled rocks over what was left of him an Lugh said a few respeckful words.

I watch till it's clear this train ain't gonna stop. Then I head around the hill to camp.

† † †

There's one good thing in all this. It turns out that Tommo's a genius cook. Ike learned him in the kitchen of The One-Eyed Man, where they had to feed travelers day after day.

He roasts an bastes. He stirs an tastes. He mashes an crushes an boils. Then he'll sprinkle a pinch from his herb bag an whatever limped into the pot comes high-steppin into our mouths. We bin stuck with crickets an small lizard fer some time, which don't even start to kill our hunger. Tommo does champion with the wolfdog an, fer once, our tight bellies ease. Strange to say, but I ain't much bothered by bein hungry. I know I am, my stummick tells me so, I jest don't seem to care. I give half my portion to Tommo.

The day slouches towards night. The pines around us settle in. Their parched needles sigh in the warm breeze. Their tired sweetness gentles the air. After Tommo's finished cookin, we keep the small bitterbrush fire goin, not fer warmth so much as comfort.

I sit unner a tree, apart from everybody. It took three pans of precious water to boil wash the wolfdog blood from my clothes. I huddle in my skivvies, wrapped in a blanket while they drip dry on a branch.

My bones ache with weariness. I long fer sleep. But it won't come. I won't let it. I don't dare.

I can feel the shadows gatherin.

Earlier, Lugh an Tommo made a rack from deadwood an hung thin slices of wolfie meat to air dry. Now they lift an twist in the breeze—rustlin, whisperin wind chimes.

Once we've scoured our eatin tins clean with pine needles, we settle down to eventide tasks. Everybody but me, that is. Tommo starts to fashion two new cleft poles fer his sleep skellie. His old ones snapped in the middle of last night an the whole shebang collapsed on top of him. Lugh's mendin his boot sole with a chunk of goodyear.

Emmi's playin dice with Nero. It's his favorite game, but

ever since Jack learned him to cheat Em's th'only one'll give him a game. She's on a mission to mend his wicked ways. Tonight, she's kept aside a fried locust fer a reward.

No, she says. Cheatin crows do not git bugs. Well, if you want one, play proper. Now, watch me. You see? Okay, now you go. No . . . no, Nero! Oh, I give up.

She leaves him to gobble the bug an comes to crouch beside me. That bird of yers is a lost cause, she says. Jack's a bad inflamence. When I see him, I'm gonna give him a piece of my mind. Fancy teachin innocent crows to cheat.

He tried to pick my pocket th'other day, I says. You can lay that at Jack's door too.

Jack's a rascal, all right, she says. He must be at the Big Water by now. Probly bin there ages. He must think we ain't comin. D'you think he'll . . . he will wait fer us, won't he?

I keep tellin you, Saba, Jack ain't gonna show at the Big Water. He's long gone. A guy like him's only in it fer hisself. Once he's got what he wants, he moves on.

I shut my ears to Lugh's voice in my head.

He'll be there, I says. You know Jack keeps his word.

Yeah, she says. You miss him, I can tell.

Without thinkin, my hand goes to the heartstone around my neck. But of course, it ain't there. Not really, I says.

Yer such a bad liar, she says. Anyways, I seen you an him love kissin that time. You had yer hands on his—

Shut up, Em!

Well, I miss him, she says. I miss him heaps. I wish he was here right this very second. Jack always makes things okay. Even when they're real bad.

Yeah, I says.

Her eyes flick to Lugh. I bet he'd know what to do about Lugh, she says. Seems like he's mad all the time these days. I dunno why. If I ask him what's the matter, it jest makes him worse. I want th'old Lugh back. I miss him most of all.

She's quiet fer a moment, rollin the dice around in her fingers. He told me an Tommo how he found you, she says, with the dead wolfdogs an all. He said you thought you seen Tracker.

Guess I made a mistake, I says. Lugh figgers I was sleepwalkin. Tracker'd never go nowhere without Mercy.

She hesitates, lookin at me sidewise, then says, I'm worried about you, Saba.

Don't be.

Well, I am. You ain't sick, are you? You'd tell me if you was sick.

No, I says. But I ain't.

Jest becuz I'm nine, don't mean I'm a stupid little kid. You should know that by now. She leans in close. Don't tell Lugh, she whispers, but I bin askin the stars how to help you.

Don't git started with all that, Emmi. You know what Lugh thinks about star readin.

Jest then, he calls out, Hey, Em, I nearly fergot! Come meet Fred!

What? Her face lights with surprised delight. She leaps up an scoots over to the boys. I breathe with relief. A dog with a bone ain't got nuthin on my sister.

Em's got this peg doll, Fern, that Pa made when she was two. She's bin buggin Lugh to death an back to whittle a husband fer Fern. The moment she had the idea, she started callin the damn thing Fred.

You made him in secret, I never knew! She takes Fred from Lugh. Gasps an laughs at the same time. No! she cries. Lugh, you made his nose huge! Yer a bad tease . . . Oh, you gotta fix it, Fern wants a handsome husband.

Lugh shakes his head, sayin, Oh no, Fern told me herself, whittle me a distinguished husband, if you please, Lugh. Make sure you give him a fine, big nose.

She did not!

Look what I made! Tommo digs in his pocket an hands her a lump of wood.

Oh! Emmi looks puzzled at it fer a moment, then beams at him. That's good, Tommo. You made a pig! She squishes her nose flat an snorfles like a piggy. She's always actin out so's Tommo knows what she means. She don't need to. He lip-reads easy, so long as you don't talk too fast.

He frowns. No, he says. Their baby.

A wolfdog howl splits the night. Not far away. We tense. Another dog answers. Then another.

Tommo looks a question at Lugh. Wolfdogs, he tells him.

Emmi shivers, her eyes big. They sound near, she says.

Naw, says Lugh, they're a long ways off. But he pulls his bow an quiver a little closer. He shoves more wood on the fire to build up the blaze. Don't worry, Em, yer big bad brother'll keep them big bad wolfies away.

Emmi snugs into his side. He puts his arm around her. Hey, Lugh, she says, what do the stars say about the Big Water?

A mistake. She knows it the moment the words leave her mouth.

Lugh's face darkens. How many times do I gotta tell you, Em? Star readin's a crock. Madmen an simpletons, that's who believes in it. His voice is harsh, lashes at her.

Emmi says, But Pa always—

That's enough! says Lugh.

Tommo breaks the tension. Tell a story, Lugh, he says. Say what it's like at the Big Water.

He moves around to sit at Lugh's feet. Leans in so's he can watch his lips. So's he don't miss a single word. Tommo cain't git enough of Lugh's yarns about what it's like out west. In fact, he cain't git enough of Lugh full stop.

Tommo took Ike's death hard. He's still mournin an no wonder. Ike took him in, starved an half wild, after he found him hidin in the stables of The One-Eyed Man. He kept him, taught him an called him son fer goin on three year. Tommo won't never ferget him.

But the last little while, I noticed how close he watches

Lugh. He's started to copy Lugh's ways. His walk, how he holds his reins an wears his hat. He used to do the same with Ike.

Ike's take on it went like this. Tommo's own pa went off huntin one day an never come back. He told his boy—a young deaf boy, can you believe anybody'd do such a thing? Ike said, shakin his head—he told him not to leave their camp, not to budge from that spot, he'd be back soon. That was the last Tommo ever seen of him. Missin, presumed dead. Killed by the beast he was huntin or injured an couldn't find his way back.

Tommo never got over it, accordin to Ike. He said he'd always be lookin fer his dead pa. I never gave much credence to Ike's notion, but now, seein how Tommo is with Lugh, I wonder if he might not of bin onto somethin.

Our pa was with us. Till the Tonton killed him that day. But he might as well not of bin, fer all the good it did us. Lugh was me an Em's brother, ma an pa all rolled up in one.

Lugh spins his yarn into the night. The Big Water's like somethin from a dream, he says. Think of the best dream you ever had in yer life an it's a thousand times better'n that. A million times more wonderful. It's a land so rich an green an beautiful that when you see it fer the first time, you'll wish you could die right there an then.

Lugh always starts his Big Water tales the same way, with the same words. I yawn. I close my eyes an settle back to listen. This is the Lugh we know. Tellin stories. Makin us smile. Holdin us together.

Say about the rabbits, says Em. They're Tommo's favorite bit.

Agin? All right, says Lugh. Well, there's rabbits everywhere at the Big Water. As far as the eye can see, nuthin but rabbits. You cain't move fer trippin over 'em. An you ain't never seen ones like these fellas. They're big. Fat an juicy an lazy from doin nuthin but nibble on sweet, green grass all day long. An they're so tame an so dumb that when you wanna eat, all you do is set yer pot to boilin, yell out 'Supper time!' an them rabbits march right up to the pot, hop in an pull the lid over. An they whistle while they do it.

Rabbits don't whistle! says Emmi.

Well, you say that, says Lugh, but I heard it from a man, an he heard it from another man who seen it fer hisself an. . .

† † †

A flash of light. Epona stands alone. Darkness all around her.

There's only the sound of my heart. Beat, beat, beat.

She looks over her shoulder. Like there's somethin behind her. She turns back. Sees me. Nods. I look down at my hands. I'm holdin a bow. I ain't seen it before, but I know that it's mine. Pale wood, silvery white.

I bring it up. Fit a arrow to the string. I nock. I aim. She starts to
run towards me. Throws her arms wide open.

I shoot.

There's a flash of light.

An I'm standin over the body. Lookin down on it.

But it ain't Epona.

It's DeMalo.

He opens his eyes.

He smiles.

†   †   †

I jolt awake, sit up, my heart poundin.

He's here. DeMalo's here. I look around, frantic. Lugh an
Tommo an Emmi. They lie in their sleep skellies. Fast to sleep
each one. Nero on his branch. The horses slumberin.

Okay. He ain't here. Calm down. It was jest a dream. I
clutch my blanket to my chest.

DeMalo. Since I seen him last—at Pine Top Hill—I managed to keep him outta my mind. But he's found his way to
my dreams. His powerful body. His long dark hair. Broad
cheekbones. Heavy-lidded eyes. Deep brown, almost black,
glitterin in the torchlight of the cellblock at Hopetown.

Lookin deep inside me. Findin my darkest thoughts, my

64

worst fears. Like he knew me. The strangest thing was this . . . pull that I felt towards him. It was real. Physical. Despite he's th'only person I ever met who gave off warm an cold at the same time. An I still don't unnerstand why he spared my life. Twice, he did it. I'm glad fer it, I'm grateful, but he's Tonton. My enemy. It didn't make sense then an it still don't.

An his last words to me. As he cut the ropes that bound my hands, right there in front of Vicar Pinch. Until next time. Like he knew we'd meet agin.

Until next time.

No. Don't think about it. I take a couple of deep breaths.

I'm still huddled aginst the same tree. I must of dozed off listenin to Lugh talk about the Big Water. It's the flat gray time. Night's on the wane. Maybe two hours till dawn. It ain't cooled down much overnight. The air feels thick an dull.

Sabaaaa. Saabaaaa.

It's Epona's voice.

Epona. Dead by my hand.

Saba.

There she is agin. No, please, I'm . . . so tired . . . I'm still dreamin. That's it, I'm dreamin or . . . maybe it was the wolf-dogs that I heard, howlin agin in the distance.

Then.

A movement in the trees. Straight ahead, on th'other side of the clearin. My heart pitches. Starts to race. I hug the blanket around me.

Epona? I whisper. Epona, is that you?

Even as I speak, even as I ask, I know the answer to be yes.

The merciful thing to do. The right thing. The only thing. That's what they said. That's what they told me. Before I did it an afterwards too. Jack an Ike an Ash. If I hadn't of killed her, one of them would of had to. Jack said he would. He wanted to spare me. But I knew it had to be me. She was only there becuz of me. Helpin me find my brother.

Kill Epona. Kill my friend. One shot from my bow, quick an clean. Or leave her to Vicar Pinch an the Tonton. Men without mercy.

But how do I know I killed her? What if she didn't die outright? What if she was still alive when she fell? What if the Tonton handed her over to them slave workers, crazy from too much chaal? They would of tore her apart. Jest like all the girls I beat in Hopetown. The ones who fell to the gauntlet.

Sabaaaa.

My hands shakin, I reach fer my bow an quiver. I git to my feet. Nero's roostin on a branch above me. He wakes right away. Stretches out his wings an legs.

Another movement. There's somethin there, slippin between the trees, but I cain't quite . . . it seems to change, to shift like . . . smoke or fog. Darker gray than the pre-dawn light, hazy around the edges. I cross the clearin an peer through the gloom.

Saba.

On a sigh, on a murmur, her voice drifts around me. Liftin

my hair, brushin my cheek. It draws me on, into the trees, step by step by step.

Nero flits ahead. A black shape, coastin from branch to branch. A shadow chasin a shadow. He seems to see her. This . . . shade of my friend. We trail her now, twistin an weavin through the trees in a game of follow-the-ghost.

Then we're outta the woods. In the open agin. An she's gone. Epona's gone. But she was here. She was. Here.

Epona, I says. Come back. Please.

The buttes an hills of the Waste wait, crouched dark aginst the skyline. The fadin stars watch. An listen.

Nuthin.

Nuthin.

I hug my arms around me, shiverin. I better git back to camp before I'm missed.

I turn.

An she's here. Right in front of me. Tracker too. He stands by her side.

It's Epona. But not like she was. In life, she gleamed an shone. Her nut-brown skin, her eyes, her hair. So strong an alive you'd swear the earth itself had birthed her.

She's a child of the air now. Fog an mist. She drifts. She gathers. She fades.

Epona, I says.

Sabaaaa, the air whispers.

Tell me what you want, I says.

Tracker whines.

Suddenly I feel it. The weight of my bow. I'm holdin it in my hand.

A bow helps feed you. Helps you defend yerself an yer people. A bow means you got a better chance of stayin alive. But it takes life. Not jest animals. People.

Friends.

Like Epona.

I'm holdin the bow that killed her.

I don't stop to think. With one swift move, I break it over my knee.

It falls to the ground, shattered. The shaft's splintered the whole way along. It cain't be mended.

No more killin. Not by me.

I look up.

Epona's gone.

Tracker's gone.

An Emmi's there.

†　　†　　†

She's standin at the edge of the trees. She comes to me.

Did you see her? I says. It was Epona, she was here. Tracker too, did you see him?

Emmi picks up the pieces of my bow an hides 'em in a split in a nearby rock. Nero perches on top, leanin over to look at what she's doin. Then she takes my hand. Hers is small an warm. Mine's cold.

C'mon, Saba, she says. You need some sleep.

They was right here, I says. You must of seen 'em.

They're gone now, she says.

She starts leadin me back to camp. I look over my shoulder. I don't wanna miss 'em if they come back.

Somewhere out in the nowhere land, a wolfdog howls. Distant an mournful. I stop.

Did you hear that? I says. It's Tracker.

C'mon, says Em.

Our campsite's quiet. Lugh an Tommo's still fast to sleep. Nero settles back to his roost. I lie on the ground an wrap myself in my blanket. Em brings her bedroll an lays down beside me.

I won't tell Lugh, she says. I won't say nuthin. You gotta be okay, Saba. We all need you.

She looks at me. I look at her. At her eyes, jest like Lugh's. Eyes so blue you could sail away on 'em, that's what Ma used to say.

You look different, I says.

I'm taller, she says. I'm growin. That's what kids do. I'm almost ten.

Oh.

Hey, Saba?

Uh huh?

Did you really see Epona? she says.

Yeah, I says.

I wish I could see Pa. I miss him. D'you miss him?

Such a simple question. So like Em. An I'm ambushed by sudden grief. I cain't answer right away.

When I was yer age, I whisper, he was different. You never knew him like that. He was . . . I dunno. He was my pa, that's all. That's who I miss.

It's okay to be sad, she says.

I scrub away the stupid tears.

I wish I could meet Ma, she says. Jest once. D'you think she'd come if I asked her to?

I don't think it works that way, I says.

She's silent fer a moment. Then she says, You ain't gonna die, are you, Saba?

One day, I says. But not today. Go to sleep.

G'night. She snugs down into her bedroll.

I roll onto my back an stare at the sky. I think about Pa an watch the last of the stars fade as dawn creeps in.

Read me the stars, Pa. Tell me what they say.

When Pa was a boy, he met with a traveler. A man who knew many things. He learned Pa how to read the stars. From when we was little, Pa would tell us how our destiny, the story of our lives, is in the night sky. He never would say what he seen there. But it laid heavy on him, you could tell. From the way he looked at Lugh sometimes. The way he looked at me.

Lugh come to disbelieve star readin an all that. I guess he's right. But still, Pa knew somethin. He did. I was there. I heard him say it.

Pa! I yell. They got Lugh! I grab his arm, give him a hard shake. This is real! You gotta fight!

Then it's like he comes to life. He pulls hisself up tall, his eyes spark an the Pa I remember's back. He hauls me to him, holds me so tight I cain't hardly breathe.

My time's nearly up, he says quickly.

No, Pa!

Listen. I dunno what happens after this. I could only see glimpses. But they're gonna need you, Saba. Lugh an Emmi. An there'll be others too. Many others. Don't give in to fear. Be strong, like I know you are. An never give up, d'you unnerstand, never. No matter what happens.

I won't, I says. I ain't no quitter, Pa.

That's my girl.

Then they killed him. The Tonton. They killed my pa an took my Lugh an left the shadows behind.

✝   ✝   ✝

The moment Lugh's awake, he jumps up, checks out Buck's leg an tells us we're on the move agin. Jest like that.

As we break camp an start to pack the horses, nobody says a word. The air's tight. Ready to snap. Lugh's dancin mad about somethin. Tommo keeps his head down, outta the line of fire. Emmi looks at me, wide-eyed. *What's the matter with Lugh?*

So, Saba, he says, where's yer bow? His voice is fake casual. So that's it. He knows. Over Hermes' back, I look at Em. The tiniest shake of her head. She ain't told. I wonder what he knows. I decide to tell as little as I can git away with.

It's broke, I says.

Is that right, he says.

I busy myself adjustin Hermes' bit. I must of bin sleepwalkin agin, I says. Must of fell an broke it.

Emmi? he says. You got anythin to say about this?

She goes bright red. No, she says.

Well, try this, he says. Saba broke her bow on purpose. An you hid the pieces in a rock. An then both of yuz decided to keep it from me. How about that?

All right, I says, you followed us an you seen what happened. Jest leave it, okay?

No, I won't leave it, he says. You broke yer gawdamn bow, Saba. Was you sleepwalkin? An don't lie to me.

I was sleepwalkin, I lie.

Yer lyin, he says. I always know when yer lyin. Why'd you do it? Why would you do that?

I says naught.

Don't jest stand there, he yells, tell me, gawdammit! Why'd you break yer gawdamn bow?

The horses shy an whinny. Lugh looks at me, his face tight with worry an . . . somethin else. Fear. I cain't burden him no more. An if I tell him about Epona, he'll think I'm crazy. I ain't. I ain't crazy. She was there.

I was sleepwalkin, I says.

I'm jest tryin to keep us all together, he says, to give us a better life than Pa did an all you seem to care about is yerself or . . . I dunno, I got no idea what yer thinkin. I feel like I don't know you no more. He shakes his head. Fine. Whatever. What the hell, it ain't like you use the damn thing. It ain't like me an Tommo don't do all the huntin anyways.

We mount up. Nero sails down an lands on my shoulder.

Yer gittin more like Pa every day, says Lugh.

How d'you mean? I says.

You figger it out.

He heels Buck an pushes past. Tommo's right behind him. Em looks at me a moment, her face like a worried old woman, then she hurries after 'em.

I sit there on Hermes. The pines murmur to each other.

More like Pa every day. I favor him in looks—black hair, brown eyes—but that ain't what Lugh meant. No. What he means is I'm goin crazy. Jest like Pa. Our hopeless, helpless father, his reason snatched by death. The death of Ma, who breathed her last as Emmi breathed her first. Pa was left a broke soul with a broke mind. He got worse an worse as time went on.

I ain't like Pa. Nuthin like Pa.

Please.

Don't let me be like Pa.

☩   ☩   ☩

Somethin's followin me. Somethin or . . . somebody. It's bin there most of the day. It's mid-afternoon now.

I could turn around an look. If I did that once, I did it a hunnerd times already. The feelin that somethin's there . . . it's kept me checkin back over my shoulder, agin an agin. Every time I don't see a thing but where we jest come from.

Still. There's this heaviness in the air behind me. Like somethin's settled there. Like somethin's takin up space.

I feel it on the back of my neck. My skin prickles with it. I know it's there. I jest cain't see it.

Not yet, anyways.

☩   ☩   ☩

Now I hear hoofs. The dry thud of hoofs on hard ground. There's a horse behind me. Not in a hurry. Keepin pace. Keepin me company.

A shiver ripples through me. My hands feel so cold. Even though today's the kinda day when the world shimmers white with heat. I huddle inside my sheema.

I gotta take a look.

I hold my breath. I look over my right shoulder.

A little ways behind me, a shape lies jagged along the ground. It's black. Like it's bin cut out of the night sky. It's a horse. An a rider.

My heart starts bangin aginst my ribs. I stare. This ain't the time of day fer shadows. I look away quick. A heavy, sick feelin grips my stummick. Hermes snorts an tosses his head. He's nervous. That ain't like him. I press with my heels an he picks up speed. The hoofbeats behind us quicken. I glance back.

The black shape's keepin pace.

I know the line of that neck. That head. Many times before, when she still drew breath, we'd be ridin an I'd look over my shoulder, jest like now. She'd smile or say somethin to cheer me up.

Epona.

I bring Hermes to a halt. The shadow rider stops too. I stare down at my hands. They tremble on the reins.

Epona, I says. Whaddya want from me?

Silence. Nero flies above. He caw caw caws. Does he see her too?

Breakin my bow warn't enough. I gotta pay proper fer what I did. She'll pace me. Stalk me. Haunt my nights an dog my days till I lay myself down, bare my throat an beg her to finish me off. She must be paid in kind fer her lost life.

Why should I be alive when yer dead? I says. That's it, aint it? I know I got no right to be.

The jangle of her horse's bridle. Hermes sidesteps, his eyes rollin as he tosses his head. I grip the reins harder.

Tell me what to do, I says. Please, Epona. Say somethin.

My whole body's shakin. I'm cold to the bone. Slow, oh so slowly, I turn to look behind me.

She's gone.

† † †

Epona's bin ridin with me fer the past two days. An now it ain't jest her. There's more of 'em.

One by one, they appeared. But these ones ain't on horse-back, like Epona. They're on foot. They hide, jest at the edge of my sight. Or I catch a glimpse of somethin—a flash of light, a rush of dark—as they dart behind a rock or a tree. I hear the sound of runnin feet. Laughter. It's like they're playin a game.

I cain't never git a proper look. They move so quick.

I know who they are. It's Helen. Helen an the rest of 'em from Hopetown. Every girl I ever fought in the Cage. Every girl I beat. An I beat them all.

They call me the Angel of Death. That's cuz I ain't never lost a fight.

If you lost three times, you ran the gauntlet. Nobody survived the gauntlet. The frantic hands of the crowd, tearin at you, pullin you down. I used to turn my back so's I couldn't see. But I could hear. I heard everythin. It all went in. Every touch an smell an taste an sound. Every girl I fought is part of me now. I'm the terror in her eyes, her hunger to live, the scent of death-so-near on her skin.

An here they are. It's a relief to see them. At last, I know who the shades are. Who's bin whisperin on the wind ever since we come to the Waste. They're waitin fer their moment to git me. To take me. I'm so tired. I cain't hold 'em off much longer.

They're bold. Emmi could be ridin beside me, or Lugh or Tommo, an they'll still git up to their tricks. Earlier today, one of 'em even dashed right in front of Hermes. If I hadn't of hauled on his reins, he would of trampled her.

I try not to sleep at night. If I don't sleep, nobody can come an take me. Take me away from Lugh an Emmi an Tommo. Or take them away from me. We'll all be safe as long as I stay awake.

But sometimes, sheer exhaustion snatches me. Not fer long,

but when it does, I dream of Jack. Fevered, shallow dreams or . . . or maybe they're visions, I dunno. They're always the same. He's trapped in the darkness. No, that ain't right—he's trapped by the darkness. Down the corridors I run, up the stairs. I open the door. An I search fer him. I search an I call his name, but I never find him.

I can never find my way to Jack.

Dark dreams by night. Dark shadows by day.

The days an nights melt, one into th'other, till it's hard to tell sleepin from wakin. If the sun didn't rise an set, I might not know at all.

†   †   †

I'm runnin. I gotta find Jack. I know he's here.

Down a long, dark corridor. Torches throw ragged shadows across the stone walls. The only sound is me. My footsteps. My breathin. I got the heartstone in my hand. It's warm. That means Jack's close by.

Saba.

The voice brushes past me on a gust of cold air. The wall torches flicker. I stop. I'm at the bottom of a stone staircase. It's steep, winds sharply upwards.

Saba. Saba.

The voice runs along the walls an up my spine. It settles in the dark places, deep inside of me. Like it belongs there. Jack's voice. Or . . . no, I cain't be certain. All I know is, I heard it before. But I cain't remember where or when.

I clutch the heartstone even tighter.

Jack! I grab a wall torch, shine it up the staircase. Is that you? Stay there, I'm comin!

Hurry, hurry, hurry. The voice sighs down my neck, prickles my arms. I start to climb the stairs. When I git to the top, there's a wooden door. Old, scarred.

I hold up the heartstone. It's burnin hot now. He's on th'other side. The sound of a heartbeat. In my head, all around me, everywhere. So loud.

Jack, I says. Are you there?

I turn the handle. I open the door.

It's ripped from my hand. I cry out. Brace myself. The wind tears the door from its hinges an it flies off into the darkness.

It's a doorway to nowhere.

I'm at the top of a tower. Jagged mountains rise around me. A great chasm yawns below. All is emptiness, vastness, blackness.

I cling to the door frame. The wind sucks at me, plucks at me, shriekin its rage.

Jack! I scream. Jack!

Then I'm fallin. Fallin. Fallin.

79

Lugh pushed us on today. We traveled long an hard. It was dark by the time we set up camp behind the rusted hulk of a great boat, stranded in ancient times when the waters it sailed on dried to dust. It's the best shelter fer miles around, but still the sharpwinds find us. They come whinin, stingin our faces with their fiery bite. Clouds scud across the sky. Break over the face of the moon. There ain't no stars tonight. A wolfdog howls not far away.

I'm crouched on the edge of the campsite. I keep my back to the rest of 'em. If they see, they'll come sniffin around, askin questions. They watch me all the time. I cain't do nuthin without somebody pokin their nose in.

I gotta git it off. This blood on my hands. Soap leaf in boilin water, horsetail . . . it ain't none of it worked. The blood's dried so dark it's almost black. Unner my nails too. I noticed it today, while I was talkin to Epona. They must of got stained when I butchered the wolfdogs. Gotta git 'em clean before Lugh sees. He's ever so particular. He always said Pa might not care but that didn't mean us kids couldn't be decent.

I'm diggin unner my nails with a stick. C'mon, I mutter, c'mon, shift, you bastard. But it won't. I grab a rough stone an start scrubbin at my arms, the palms of my hand. Dammit, why won't it come out? I grit my teeth an scrub harder. I glance over my shoulder. Check to make sure nobody ain't noticed.

They're all starin at me. Tommo, Lugh an Emmi. Sittin there by the fire with their eatin tins.

What? I says.

Tommo's called you three times, says Lugh.

I go to join 'em. They're almost finished. Tommo serves prairie dog stew into my eatin tin. Hey, I says, don't this look good, Tommo. I'm that hungry I could eat my boots.

It's a lie. I ain't hungry. I ain't never hungry these days. I tip most of it to Nero on the sly.

As I go to take my food, Tommo says, Saba! Yer hands!

I shove 'em behind my back. I've gone hot. My face, my neck, my chest. Tommo knows. He seen the stains, he knows what it is. Now they'll all know.

Emmi an Lugh's both jumped up at Tommo's words. Lugh reaches behind me. Grabs my hands an turns 'em over. They all exclaim.

Ohmigawd, Saba! says Lugh. You got blood all over 'em. What've you done?

I tried to clean 'em, I says. I bin scrubbin an scrubbin, but they . . . they won't come out, the bloodstains won't come out. I'm sorry, Lugh.

You poor fool, he says. There ain't no bloodstains. You scrubbed 'em raw.

I stare down at the palms of my hands. He's right. I scraped the skin off. Scraped 'em to a bloody mess. There ain't no dark bloodstains. None at all, not unner my nails, nowhere.

They was there, I says. I swear they was.

Okay, says Lugh. That's it, that's enough. Emmi, git the medicine bag. Tommo, bring some hot water. C'mere, Saba, c'mon. He makes me sit on the ground. He drapes a blanket around my shoulders.

Emmi bustles back with our little skinbag of remedies. Herbs an leafs, tinctures an ointments. Tommo brings a basin of water. Emmi kneels beside me an commences to clean my hands with a soft cloth. I'll try not to hurt you, she says.

Lugh an Tommo crouch in close. Watch me close.

Such serious faces, I says. Am I in trouble?

What's goin on, Saba? says Lugh. An I don't want no snow job. The truth this time.

We wanna help you, says Tommo.

I don't need no help, I says.

You jest tried to scrub away bloodstains that ain't there, says Lugh.

You sleepwalk, says Tommo.

Yer seein things. Emmi don't look at me as she speaks. Her gentle fingers spread sagewort salve on my raw hands, tie strips of cloth around. Like today, she says, when you jumped all of a sudden. You seen somethin. Somethin or somebody. They ran in front of the horses, didn't they? I couldn't see nuthin cuz there warn't nuthin there to see. But you do. You see things all the time.

What is it you see? says Lugh. Who do you see?

My chest's startin to feel tight. Like there's a band around it. Nobody, I says. Nuthin. I dunno what yer on about.

We all seen you, he says. You talk to the air, like somebody's there, beside you. Who is it?

Nobody, I says. Leave me alone.

It's yer dead friend, ain't it? he says. Epona. You see the dead, Saba. You talk to the dead.

I snatch my hands from Emmi. Glare at her. I knew I couldn't trust you! I says.

I warn't gonna say nuthin, she says, truly I warn't, but . . . yer gittin worser an worser all the time. I'm worried about you, Saba. We all are. You need help.

You think I'm crazy, I says. Nobody says naught. Nobody lets their eyes meet mine. Then,

Yeah, says Lugh. We do.

Suddenly, rage takes me. It's nowhere. Then it's everywhere. The red hot. It floods me, blinds me, chokes me. I leap at Lugh. I knock him backwards. We roll on the ground. I punch, I kick, I claw.

From a long ways off, I can hear Emmi screamin. Tommo shoutin. Hands pullin at me. Screamin. Yellin. Lugh kicks an struggles beneath me. I'm sittin on his chest.

Emmi's sobbin. Stop it, Saba! Stop it! You'll kill him!

The red hot starts to fade. I come to. My hands is tight around Lugh's throat. My thumbs pressin on his windpipe.

He's got his hands on mine, tryin to pull 'em away. His eyes wide with panic an fear.

Lugh's afeared of me.

I let go. He gasps. Drags desperate air into his lungs.

My shakin hand reaches out. I touch his throat. The marks of my fingers pressed deep into his flesh. The necklace I made him fer our eighteen year birthday. I touch the little ring of shiny green glass. The memory of our lost selfs. Jest barely do I touch it. In case it disappears.

I climb off. I kneel in the dirt at his side.

I almost killed him. I tried to kill Lugh.

Emmi's weepin. Lugh's chest heaves, his eyes dark with shock. I've blooded his nose.

The red hot's gone. Jest as quick as it come, it went. I'm limp. Exhausted. Numb. I turn my head so's I don't hafta look at him.

He gits slowly to his feet. He reaches down a hand to help me up. We stand there. He swipes his nose with his sleeve.

Tears start to roll down my cheeks. He wipes 'em away, but they keep on comin. Silent. Never endin. They splash in the dust at my feet. But I ain't cryin.

You jest gotta hang on a bit longer, he says. Jest a few more weeks an we'll be at the Big Water an . . . when we git there, when we . . . git out west, it's all gonna be okay. We got such a good life waitin fer us there.

The words halt from him. On a hoarse whisper. Like a story bein told fer the very last time. With nobody there to hear it.

Did I say how the, uh . . . I tell you, Saba, the land out there's so rich . . . all you gotta do is shove a stick in the ground, an the next day there's a full-grown nut tree, right where that stick went in. Wouldn't that be a . . . a wondrous sight? If you seen that, you'd think it was a dream, wouldn't you? I'd sure like to see that. Emmi an Tommo too, we'd . . . we'd all like to see that. An we will. We will.

I watch his lips move. I hear his words. His voice sounds muffled, like he's unner water. He puts his arms around me. He hangs onto me. His whole body's shakin.

Whatever's broke, he says, I can fix it. I'll fix it all. I promise.

† † †

The land's bare of tree. White of rock. No clouds. No shade. No shelter. The sun grills. The earth bakes. Sullen dust dogs our heels.

We plod along, Hermes an me. We lag well behind the rest. I stare at my hands on the reins. Inside my head, I'm more'n halfways to somewhere else. Somewhere blank an white an endless. My brain's flat. I don't care if we ride the Waste ferever.

Somethin dashes in front of us. Cuts across Hermes. He rears an squeals, his forelegs beatin high in the air. I grab the reins to stop from fallin. Sounds crash at me. Slam me. Shock me to life.

It's a blue-eyed wolfdog. With one droopy ear. It's him. It's Tracker. He's here.

He darts at Hermes. In an out. In an out. Hermes shies an dances an squeals. I grip hard with my knees. Hang on the reins. I'm only jest managin to keep my seat.

Up ahead, I can hear Lugh yellin, Wolfdog! The three of 'em wheel around an start gallopin back towards us. Emmi's screamin, Tracker! It's Tracker!

He makes one last dash. Hermes bolts. Then we're racin, flat out, headed due north. I lay low aginst his neck an hang on tight. Tracker chases behind us, a lean gray streak.

He's real. No figment. No dream. The rest of 'em shouted, Emmi called his name, so he ain't jest in my mind.

I glance back over my shoulder. He's still there.

He turned us. No. He turned me. He turned me from the westward trail. On purpose. Like he wants me to go this way. An now he's stickin to my tail, makin sure I stay on course till I git there.

Wherever there is.

We stand on top of a bluff, lookin out over a wide, flat valley. Dry but fer the ribbon of water that loops its way through the middle. Like a thin, silver-skinned snake, it glints in the late afternoon sun. The last, sleepy memory of a once-mighty river.

There's one straight stretch of the river. On the near-side, two rows of ragtag tents, tepees an flotsam skellies straggle along the bank. They're shaded by some good-sized cotton-wood trees. What look to be funeral pyres—three, side by side—burn an smoke some distance from the camp.

Forty shelters at least, Lugh says. He lowers the long-looker. Men an women, kids an dogs. No tellin how many. Horses, camels, carts.

What do we do? says Tommo.

Go down, of course, says Emmi. Why d'you think Tracker brought us here?

Tracker's sittin off to one side. His head moves to who-ever's talkin, like he knows what's bein said. Now he stands. Barks three times. He goes to the edge of the bluff, whinin, then back to us. Barks agin.

You see? says Emmi. He wants us to go.

I'm sorry I didn't believe you before, Lugh says to me. It's jest . . . him bein so far from home didn't seem possible.

I thought I imagined him, I says.

Mercy must be down there, says Emmi. In the camp. I'll jest bet she is!

Nero swoops an soars overhead. He caws at us to git movin.

Scout it first, says Tommo. Make sure it's safe. I'll go.

No, I'll do it, says Lugh. You all wait here.

Sometimes you boys is dumb as stumps, says Emmi. Tracker brought us here to git help fer Saba. He wouldn't of done that if it warn't safe.

Don't gimme that mystical boloney, says Lugh. I swear, Em, you got so much air between yer ears, you wouldn't know common sense if it walked up an slapped you in the face. Tommo's right, we need to check it out.

Is that what you got? says Em. Common sense?

You bet, he says.

Then I'm glad I ain't got none. Emmi takes my reins. C'mon, Saba, I'm gonna git you some help. These two can do what they like. She heels her horse an starts leadin me down the bluff.

In the east, a thunderhead gathers itself. It eyes us up. An heads this way.

THE SNAKE RIVER

WE MAKE OUR WAY TOWARDS THE CAMP. EMMI AN TRACKER lead. Me next, with Nero ridin on my shoulder. Tommo an Lugh bring up the rear. Hermes ain't bothered in the least by Tracker now. You could almost say they're friendly. Which is odd. Considerin.

As we approach, a pack of mangy mutts rushes at us. Tracker snarls a warnin, teeth bared, hackles raised. They yip a swift retreat, tails between their legs.

On the edge of camp, there's a crowd of raggedy kids playin a loud game of bladder ball. The dust flies as they elbow an trip an wrestle. Rough rules. As we git closer, they spot us. They stop. They stare. There's one raggedy scarecrow of a girl around Emmi's age. She gawps at me, open-mouthed. Like she cain't believe her eyes.

Hey, says Emmi. Can you tell me where we could—

It's th'Angel of Death! she yells. Run!

The kids scatter. They race towards the tents, hollerin, Th'Angel of Death! She's here! Ma! It's th'Angel of Death!

They vanish inside. Silence.

Emmi looks back at me. She knew you, she says. She must of bin at Hopetown.

Quite the reputation you got, says Lugh.

Saba's the most famous fighter in the world, says Em. On

her fight days, you couldn't hardly move in Hopetown. People came from all around, jest to—

Can it, Emmi, says Lugh.

I'm only sayin—

Nuthin, he says. I'll say what needs sayin from here on.

He moves up next to me. We ride slowly into camp. There's a wide space between the two lines of shelters, like a road. We make our way along it. All quiet. Not a soul in sight. Nobody watchin the pots that bubble on the cookfires. There's a few stools tipped over, like whoever was sat on 'em left in a hurry.

We edge closer together.

Where is everybody? says Em.

Behind us. Tommo's voice, a cracked whisper.

We look back. A crowd's appeared. Men, women an children. Dried husks of people. With fear in their eyes an weapons in their hands. Sticks an stones, bottles an bones.

Tracker growls. Starts towards 'em.

Tracker, stay! Lugh calls him in. G'day, folks. We don't come to make no trouble. Anybody in charge here?

They don't make no answer. A man at the front starts bangin two sticks together. Others join in. Wood. Stone. Glass. Bone. The steady beat beat beat of bad blood fouls the air.

We turn to face front. My mouth's dry.

Keep movin, says Lugh.

We go on. They follow. They keep a gap between them an us, careful of Tracker.

The wind rises. The sky darkens. The storm from the east is nearly upon us. Thunder grumbles a threat. Lightnin forks in the distance.

Then, in front of us, more people step in our path. They block our way. Armed with wood an stone. Glass an bone. Beat beat beat. A few of 'em hold up odd things. Sticks tied in triangles. A bead an skin dolly.

What're those? says Emmi.

Charms, says Lugh, to pertect 'em from evil. He grabs my reins an pulls Hermes up tight next to Buck.

What evil? Em's squeaky with fright.

They're afeared of Saba, he says. I knew this was a mistake. Let's go.

We cain't, says Tommo.

To the front, at the back, they've blocked our way. There's a wall of shelters on eether side.

The ugly beat closes me in. Traps me. An I'm tremblin. Shakin. I'm back in Hopetown. Back in the Cage.

The ground shakes. The crowd stomps. They chant fer the blood of the defeated fighter.

Gauntlet! Gauntlet! Gauntlet!

I won't let 'em hurt you, Lugh says to me.

Nero screams an dives at their heads.

All this time, the storm's bin movin closer. The wind wails. The red dust whirls. Our horses hate it. The noise of the crowd. The comin storm. They toss their heads. They squeal.

They dance. It's hard to keep 'em in check. Tracker darts an snaps at the crowd in front.

A stone, sharp and quick, flies at Lugh. Hits him in the shoulder. He cries out. Drops my reins. Suddenly, hands reach up. They haul on my leg, tryin to pull me offa Hermes. I kick out.

Lugh! screams Emmi.

He grabs my arm. The horses go crazy. More hands pull at me. I'm kickin wildly. Emmi's yellin. Tommo snatches a stick an starts beatin at their heads. Tracker snarls an slashes. Somebody screams.

Boom! Thunder splits the air. The crowd stops. Falls back. The blood beat stops. They all look to the sky. Like they're only jest noticin the change in the weather.

Mountains of clouds tumble this way. Quickly. Darkly. Their lightnin fingers stab at the earth.

Somebody calls out, The Sky Speaker! She's comin out! Quick!

A woman shouts, Bring her to the Sky Speaker! She'll know what to do!

More hands grab at me. I'm pulled offa Hermes back. I struggle an fight, but four men seize hold of me—two on each arm—an run drag me up the camp. A couple of women run alongside, holdin up charms.

Lugh! I yell. Lugh! As I twist to look behind, I catch sight of 'em bein hauled offa their horses. Emmi, Tommo an Lugh.

The rest of the crowd's dropped their sticks an stones. They're pushin past each other, scoopin up the smallest kids. Everybody rushin in the same direction. Towards the top of the camp.

We come to a piece of open ground along the riverbank, beyond the shelters. There's a small, rough wood platform. It's raised offa the ground about four foot, with steps on the left. A crude slat roof, the sides open to the weather. There's a tattered tent pitched a few paces to the left of the platform. Thunder rumbles. Lightnin forks in the distance. The wind snatches at people's clothes an hair, ripples the tent.

Everybody's startin to kneel, facin the platform. They hush each other. Quiet their fretful kids. They're gonna be caught in the storm, outside when they'd be safer in. But they don't seem worried.

The men drag me to the front. They tie my hands with one of their belts. Kick the back of my legs. I land hard on my knees. I try to turn my head, look fer Lugh, but one of 'em grabs me by the hair. He yanks my head back so's I'm starin up at the platform. I grit my teeth aginst the pain. Lugh! I yell.

Shut up! says the man. We'll see what the Sky Speaker's gotta say about you.

Nero's swoopin an divin, screechin at the men. They hit out at him with their sticks. They'll hurt him. Kill him.

No, Nero, no! I call. Go!

He sails to the tattered tent next to the platform an lands

on top. He opens his wings wide an screams. Unease crackles through the crowd. Crows bring death. That's what a lot of folk think.

The Angel of Death an her crow. At Hopetown, everybody feared Nero. When I fought in the Cage, he used to watch from a nearby light tower. Wouldn't leave till I'd won. People believed I got my powers from him.

Another bunch of men wrestle Lugh, Emmi an Tommo up to the front. Their hands is already tied. A few heavy whacks from a stick an the boys kneel, like me.

Saba! says Lugh. Are y'okay?

Yeah! I says. Em's beside me. Don't be skeered, Em, I says.

I ain't skeered of these cowards, says she.

The wind shrieks. A thump of thunder. A crack of lightnin as the storm draws near.

There she is! cries Emmi.

There's a boy, Emmi's age, comin outta the tattered little tent next to the platform. He's leadin a girl by the hand, helpin her up the steps.

She's got a length of dark cloth tied around her eyes, a blindfold. She's small, fine-boned as a bird, with maybe sixteen year on her. She wears a long white robe. Bare feet, bare arms, bare legs. With skin as white as a white winter moon. Hair of palest fire. It hangs to her waist, loose an alive, threaded with feathers an beads. There's a small skinbox slung around her waist.

The boy ducks to the side, leaves her alone in the middle of the platform. She starts to drum on the skinbox, beatin out a rhythm with her hands. The wind whips her robe around her legs. Flings her hair into a wild dance.

Emmi shouts to be heard. It's the Sky Speaker! She's gonna help you, Saba, I know it! That's why Tracker brought us here.

Jest then, there's the most almighty thunder crash. The boy pulls the blindfold from the Sky Speaker's eyes. She drums ever more frantic, a look of fierce ecstasy on her face. Lightnin slashes at the ground, not thirty paces off. The world lights up. A brilliant flash of blue-white.

The Sky Speaker's shakin, head to foot. Her eyes roll back an she waves her hands wildly. She starts to babble, a endless stream of sounds, no words I can make out, maybe some lingo I ain't never heard before.

Suddenly, her body gives one massive, powerful jerk that slams her upright. She lifts her face to the storm-ripped sky.

The man holdin my hair lets go. She's gonna speak! he yells. He raises his arms, holds 'em high.

The kneelin crowd's all got their arms raised. They look at the Sky Speaker, hope twistin their faces.

Her robe billows. Rain begins to lash. Her head snaps towards me. Her eyes fix on me, here at the front in plain view. She's got eyes like Tracker's. The lightest, palest blue. Wolfdog eyes. Chills runnel my skin.

The boy who helped her to the platform rushes to her side.

He follows her gaze an points at me.

It's her! he cries. The Sky Speaker's choosed her! Bring her up!

There's a boom of thunder. My captor yelps an fumbles to untie my hands, shoutin, Here! Help me! Before I know it, him an two other men's boosted me on to the platform.

Then I'm standin there, three foot away from the Sky Speaker. Starin at her as she's starin at me. Lightnin crackles around us.

She starts to speak, but I cain't hear nuthin over the wild noise of the storm. So I move in, closer an closer till I'm standin right in front of her. She grabs my hands. Grips 'em tight. Her eyes, her strange pale eyes hold me, but I don't think she's seein me. Her pupils is tiny black dots. She speaks quick, in little gasps.

The dead, the dead, they walk in yer footsteps. I see 'em. All around you. I see 'em. So many. Inside you. The shadow. It rises. It's strong in you. It'll take, it'll have you, mind an body an . . . mind an spirit, it'll take you, it'll have you, it'll—

Help me, I whisper. Please.

Jest then, she staggers. I catch her in my arms. Her body starts to shake, uncontrollable. Her eyes roll back.

An she goes limp in my arms.

I'm on my knees, holdin her. She's light as a child. Fer a moment, I fear the savage blast of power through her body might of killed her. I feel fer a neck pulse. She's alive.

The boy's already beside me. Helpin me lay her down.

Turn her on her side, he tells me. He shoves a grubby finger into her mouth an clears her tongue. Then he crams in a filthy cloth. He seems to know what he's doin. Help me lift her, he says. Take her in the tent.

I glance at Lugh an Tommo an Emmi, their hands still bound. They're tense. Wide-eyed. Everybody in the crowd's watchin. This could be my only chance.

Let my friends go, I says.

His foxy face hardens. It'll cost you, he says.

The red hot surges. I grab him. Twist the neck of his shirt. Quick an hard, to cut off his breath. I says, I am the Angel of Death, little man.

As Nero swoops around us, screechin, the boy claws at me, eyes poppin with panic. I let go. He falls back, gaspin in air, then yells to the men holdin Lugh an th'others. Let 'em go! She wants to speak to all of 'em! Now!

They hurry to free them.

The wind wails on, the thunder rolls, but the storm's movin away. You can see the whipcrack of lightnin as it sweeps its way west along the river valley.

I look out on the crowd. At those who so lately would of beat us to death. The Sky Speaker's word holds power over these people. They're startin to go, to disappear into the rainy murk. One or two hold up their charms in my direction. Water drips offa my hair. I'm shiverin.

Lugh an Tommo scramble onto the platform. Tommo hauls up Emmi.

We lift the girl. Lugh an Em take her legs, me an Tommo her arms. Not that we need all of us, she's so light. As we start to move, as the boy leads the way down the stairs, Lugh mutters, Now what?

Now, says Em, we confer with the Sky Speaker.

† † †

Inside the tent it's dim. The boy scurries to light the fat lamps an we lay the girl on a cot by the firepit. He pokes at the banked fire, gits it goin agin.

I stare hard at him. He cain't git away fast enough. As he dives outta the tent, I'm suddenly done. My legs give way an Tommo helps me to a stool. Nero perches on a chest, sets about puttin his damp feathers in order.

Em fusses around the Sky Speaker, gently takin the filthy rag from her mouth. She goes to take the little drum from around her waist.

Don't touch it, the girl says quickly.

Em snatches her hands away like she's bin burnt.

You mustn't ever touch a shaman's drum, the Sky Speaker tells her. Where's Zek?

That little rat? says Lugh. He's gone.

He helps me, she says. Would you give me a hand to sit up?

Her voice is light. Cool. A mountain stream after a long ride. A dawn breeze, before the heat takes hold of the day.

Em helps her sit. The girl unstraps her drum an lays it on a little table beside her. Em drapes a blanket around her thin shoulders. There's a water bucket next to the fire. Lugh fills the dipper an gives her some to drink.

Thank you kindly, she says. My name is Auriel Tai.

She's even more strange lookin, here in the everyday closeness of the shabby little tent. Like nobody on earth, with her wolfdog eyes an moon white skin an hair of palest fire.

Yer beautiful, breathes Emmi, jest like a star.

Auriel hands the dipper back to Lugh. Then she looks at us. One by one. Jest restin her eyes lightly fer a moment. It's a deceptive lightness. I'm last.

She gits up. She comes over to stand in front of me on my stool. Her cool fingers brush my birthmoon tattoo.

I'm glad you found your way to me, she says. An only jest in time, by the look of it.

That was quite the show you put on out there. There's a spiky challenge in Lugh's tone. They was lappin it up, he says. Bunch of simpletons, fallin fer yer flim flam.

Lugh! Emmi gasps. Don't be such a rudesby!

A shaman, huh? he says.

That's right, says Auriel.

She's got a calm, still center, Auriel. So different from all that storm frenzy a moment ago. Lugh's clumsy roughness makes me wince. I know where he's headed with this.

Lugh, I says.

What other tricks do you do? he says. How about . . . star readin? Are you a star reader, Auriel Tai? Lugh's voice is like the sinkholes of the Waste. Smooth earth on top, danger below. A trap fer the unwary.

She falls right in. Yes, she says. Light is my nature guide. Lightnin, the sun, the moon, the stars.

Is that so. He gives her a long, hard, hostile look. Then, Yer pathetic, you know that? he says. You an them loser dirtlanders.

C'mon, Lugh, don't, I says.

Our father thought he was a star reader, he says.

I know, she says. Willem. When he was a boy, he met a traveler who taught him how to read the stars.

Emmi stares at her, big-eyed. How d'you know that? she says.

That traveler was my grandfather, says Auriel. His name was Namid. They called him the Star Dancer. A wise an knowledgeable man.

Wise an knowledgeable, says Lugh. If it warn't so tragic,

I'd laugh. Our feeble-minded father, always lookin to the sky fer answers when he should of bin lookin at us. He kept us in that gawdfersaken place an he starved us. Not jest of food, though that was scarce enough. He starved us of care. Of hope. He read the stars every night an every night he'd say, tomorrow the rain's gonna come. I read it in the stars, son. But the rain never came. It never came. You know what did? Ruination. Our ruination. Me an my sisters'. An all becuz of star readin.

He's kept his voice low. Leashed. Now, in the silence, the air's thick with the roots of our lives. They crowd me. Press me. Choke me.

My sister don't need yer help, he says. C'mon, y'all, we're outta here.

Emmi says, But, Lugh—

Can it, Em, he says. Tommo, bring Saba.

Tommo slips his arm around my waist. Helps me up. Tracker's got to his feet. He's whinin, lookin between us an Auriel. Nero caw caw caws.

We cain't go! cries Emmi. No, Lugh, this is wrong!

Auriel grabs my hand. I can help you, she says. I can heal you. I can banish the dead, put yer bow back in yer hands. I can prepare you fer what lies ahead.

West is what lies ahead, says Lugh. The Big Water.

You won't go west, she says. I'm sorry, that ain't what I see.

What you see, what you see! You big fake! He lunges an

grabs somethin from a table. Suddenly, a spear of light shatters the gloom of the tent. Auriel shrinks away, throwin her hand over her eyes.

Lugh's holdin a piece of lookin glass. He's played it in the light from one of the lamps, right into her face. He tosses it at her feet. Tell yer nature guide to fix yer gawdamn eyes, he says.

As he goes to leave, Auriel starts to speak.

She was a rare beauty, was Allis, in body an soul. Eyes like a spring sky an long golden hair, the same as her firstborn, the child of her heart. She named him Lugh. Lugh, Lugh with yer eyes so blue, I could sail me away on yer eyes.

Lugh's stopped in his tracks. He stands with his back to Auriel, his tense, hunched back. He cain't see what she's doin.

She stands stock still, eyes wide. It's clear she's listenin to somethin. Her voice runs like shallow water over stones. Quickly, lightly. Every now an agin, a shudder racks her body.

My flesh is all goosebumps. It's Ma she's talkin about. The song she made up an sang to Lugh when we was kids. Auriel's goin on.

But Allis couldn't stay. She birthed the baby, then she bled fer two days an died. Don't leave me, sweet Allis, don't leave me, my heartsoul, my life. Poor Willem, her death left him broken, he was never the same. Love makes you weak. Who'd wanna end up like him? I ain't never gonna love nobody, it's better that way.

Auriel stops, a dazed look on her face. She staggers an Emmi catches her. My skin crackles. We stare at her, me, Em an Tommo. She was speakin our lives. How Ma died. How Pa was. What Lugh always says.

Lugh turns slowly back into the tent. He's pale. His eyes dark pools of shock. His voice a bruised whisper as he says, How dare you?

She ain't no fake, Emmi says.

I wanna stay, I says. Please, Lugh.

A long moment. I can see him fight his need to run. Then,

Two days an two nights, he says to Auriel. That's how long you got. Yer time starts now. An I'll be watchin you. I'm gonna pertect my sister. An if you do her wrong, I'll do you wrong tenfold, d'you unnerstand?

Auriel nods.

I need some air, he says. C'mon, Tommo.

With that, Lugh disappears into the rainy night.

An I'm suddenly aware of Tommo. I'm still leanin on his shoulder. He's still got his arm around my waist. He's tall as me. I never noticed till now. A deep flush colors his cheeks.

I'm fine, I says. Go on.

He hesitates a moment. Then he's gone too.

✝   ✝   ✝

The air in the tent, so heavy with tension, lightens with the two of 'em gone.

Auriel sinks onto the cot. Her eyes meet mine. She's got what she wanted. What I need. It's took it outta her, tired her, that last . . . the thing with Lugh, whatever that was.

Em rushes to kneel at her feet. How d'you do that? she says. Can you show me how?

Emmi, let her be, I says.

It's all right. Auriel smiles at her. When I was eight year, she says, I was playin by myself in the woods, when I heard this music. Voices singin, kinda shimmerin in the air. I followed the voices to a little clearin. The sun, the light there was so dazzlin, an that's where the music was comin from, it was the light. It was singin. I stepped outta the trees into it, into the light an the music an . . . I went on a journey of the spirit. I was unconscious fer many days, my family cared fer my body, watched over me, but my spirit was elsewhere. I was brought back by my grandfather, by Namid. He became my teacher. He died last winter. I miss him very much.

Will you teach me? says Emmi.

Auriel shakes her head. First you must hear the call an be brave enough to follow it, she says. Then yer teacher will come.

I'm gonna listen real hard, says Emmi.

Auriel looks at me. Yer exhausted, she says. We'll eat, then you need to git some sleep. You an I, we'll make a start in the mornin.

She serves up tins of thin soup. Emmi, Tracker an Nero

hunker down to fill their bellies. As I take mine, Auriel touches my hand. In a low voice she says, The deaf boy. Take heed, Saba. He's in love with you.

† † †

Lugh an me lie on our backs on the shore at Silverlake. We're eight year old. Pa an Ma lie between us. Ma's got a round belly from the babby that's growin inside of her. It's a soft summer night. We're all lookin at the stars.

Tell us, Pa, says Lugh.

Yeah, Pa, I says. Tell us agin.

Not tonight, he says.

Oh, go on, Willem, says Ma. You know how they love to hear.

He turns his head an they smile at each other. That secret smile they got jest between the two of 'em. It makes my insides go all funny. He takes her hand an kisses it.

Well, he says, everythin's set. It's all fixed. The lives of everybody who's ever bin born.

The lives of everybody still waitin to be born, says Ma, layin her hand on her belly.

It was all set in the stars the moment the world began, says Pa. The time of yer birthin, the time of yer death, even what kinda person yer gonna be, good or bad.

What am I gonna be, Pa? says Lugh.

Oh, yer one of the good ones, says Ma. She strokes Lugh's face, smilin at him. My beautiful golden boy.

An me? I says. What am I gonna be, Pa?

Pa don't answer. He gathers me into his arms, hugs me in tight to his side. His heart beats into me, strong an steady. I breathe his warm, safe skin.

We're flesh an blood an heart an soul. The four of us. Now an always, till the end of time.

Suddenly a star goes streakin across the sky.

Lugh points at it. Look, Saba! A shootin star!

We watch as it slashes through the darkness. So bright. So fast. Gone so quick.

I tug on Pa's shirt. Pa? You never said. What'm I gonna be? Good or bad?

He kisses the top of my head. Whispers in my ear, so's only him an me can hear.

You, my darlin daughter, are gonna be somethin else entirely.

† † †

I open my eyes. I'm lyin curled up on my side on the floor of Auriel's tent. Nero's tucked hisself between my chin an my chest. Lugh sleeps like he always does. With his head hidden in his arms. Pertectin hisself, Ma used to say. They're silent, him an Tommo an Emmi. Deep in the black of slumber.

The rain's stopped. It's night. Stars twinkle through the smokehole.

Auriel's awake. She sits in a small rocker beside the firepit, starin into the low flames. She's wrapped in a dark shawl. Tracker's head rests heavy on her feet. His great paws twitch in his sleep.

Ancient wolfdog dreams, she says.

She didn't look, I didn't make a sound, but she knew I was awake.

He lived with our friend Mercy, I says. Far away from here. It was strange. He jest showed up. Led me right to you.

We speak in low voices, so's not to wake th'others.

He's been hangin around the edges of the camp fer a while now, says Auriel. I wondered about him.

I thought Mercy might be here, I says.

The dog comes an goes, she says. No one claims him. But he's chosen you. He runs with you now. The wolfdog an the crow. Fit companions fer a warrior.

I ain't no warrior, I says. I'm done with all that.

I drape the blanket around my shoulders. I scoop up Nero an go sit on the ground across from Auriel. I hug him to me, buryin my nose in his warm feathers. He grumbles a bit, but don't wake. Auriel reaches down, takes a pinch of somethin from a tin beside her an throws it on the fire. It flares blue fer a second. A strange, sweet smell starts to wind around the tent.

She turns her head an looks at me. You was dreamin jest then, she says.

Not a dream, I says. I was rememberin. Somethin Pa said to me once. A long time ago, when I was a kid. I fergot all about it.

Our eyes meet in the firelight. Hers so pale an wild.

There are some people, she says, not many, who have within them the power to change things. The courage to act in the service of somethin greater than themselves.

To change things, I says.

Through their actions, she says, they can turn the tide of human affairs.

They, I says. You mean me.

The Tonton grow in strength an purpose, she says. They have a new leader, a man of vision. The Pathfinder, they call him.

The Pathfinder, I says.

A new leader fer the Tonton. I git a sudden, clear picture in my mind. Of DeMalo at Pine Top Hill. Turnin his back on Vicar Pinch, ridin away before the battle started, takin a good few Tonton with him. But that don't mean he'd take over. Jest that he warn't willin to put his life on the line fer a madman. He's probly long gone.

Day after day, people arrive here, says Auriel. All with the same story. They've had to flee their homes. Run before they was killed by the Tonton. They're grabbin land. Any earth good enough to work, any clean water. Then they move their own people in to work it—Stewards of the Earth. Any day now, everythin east of the Waste'll be in Tonton hands. New Eden, they call it. An they decide who's allowed to live there. Who's good enough to live in their new world.

I done enough already, I says. Hopetown's gone. Vicar Pinch is dead. All I want is fer you to fix me. Make me myself agin, so I can go west with my family. So I can be with Jack. He's there, waitin fer me.

She throws another pinch on the fire. We all got our parts to play in this, she says. Him, yer sister, yer brother, Tommo. The wolfdog. Me. Nero. Long before you was born, Saba, a train of events was set in motion.

You mean fate, I says. I don't believe in it.

Not fate, she says. Destiny. I'm speakin what my guides tell me, what I see in you. Fer you, Saba, all roads lead to the same place. It's better you act now than later. Many people—not jest now but still to come—many people need you.

The same thing Pa said to me, jest before he died.

They're gonna need you, Saba. Lugh an Emmi. An there'll be others too. Many others. Don't give in to fear. Be strong, like I know you are.

You an I got much to do, says Auriel, an very little time to do it in. But first, you need to sleep. She stirs the flames. The sweet smell grows stronger.

My eyelids start to droop. I lay myself by the fire, me an Nero. I close my eyes. My bones sob. Throb. I'm so weary with tryin to hold myself together. Tryin to hold back the darkness.

The heavy hands of sleep soothe me. Smooth me. Ease me down.

I look down down down to the bottom. To the ancient bed of the lake. Where the dark things crouch. Where the old things wait. Where they crouch an wait . . . fer me.

Don't be afeared. Auriel's voice whispers inside my head. I'll be right here, walkin with you in yer dreams. Fer in our dreams we find ourselves. Who we were. Who we are. Who we can become. Sleep. Dream.

†   †   †

A old man stands by a twisted tree. His skin gleams, a rich nut brown. His white hair coils down his back. We're alone, him an me, on a wide, flat plain. No hills, no grass, no life. There's a darkenin sky. The wind blows hard. The tree shines silver white.

I never seen him before, yet I know him. I know him fer what he is. Warrior. Bowyer. Shaman. He holds a bow in his hands. It's white, like the twisted tree. Pale, silvery white.

An I know why I'm here. What to do.

I go to the tree. I crouch. I wrap my arms round the trunk an pull. It comes easy. No roots. As I lift it free, I can see what lies beneath. A gravepit. A body. Somebody dead, laid out in the pit full length. The head's bin wrapped in a dark red shawl. The body's dressed in armor. Rusted an battered, a warrior, then. Man or woman, who knows?

I look at the man. He nods. I kneel. I draw the shawl away.

There ain't no face. Jest a shape. A blank. Smooth as the smoothest stone. An stone to the touch, too, cold an hard. No eyes, no nose, no lips.

Then the shaman's gone. An I'm alone. The tree bursts green with leaf. Its branches, its trunk, alive an new.

I hold the white bow in my hands. An the wild wide wind mutters my name.

Saba. Saba. Saba.

† † †

More new arrivals, says Auriel.

We stop. I squint aginst the sun, fierce an harsh. Down the far end of camp, a mulecart jolts to a halt. The driver sits there a long moment. Then she climbs out, stiff legged an clumsy. Them that's nearby stir theirselfs to lend a hand. The lone passenger—looks to be a man—don't move.

What're they all doin here? I says.

They're headed west, she says. They cain't go back to New Eden an they cain't stay here fer long. They're on their way to the Big Water, to a better life. They've heard the stories—the good earth, the good air—jest like yer brother. That's what they want too.

Not jest Lugh, I says. Him an me, we want the same.

Lugh dreams of a settled life, she says. He longs to plant hisself in one place, plant the land around him. His hands itch to work good earth, put food on the table that he's grown his-self, raise children. That ain't you. You cain't be tied. You've gotta be free to soar. To fly.

She looks at me. At least, I think she does. She's wearin a dark eyeshield. Any glint of light—the sun hittin water or metal in a certain way—it's liable to set her off in a vision, so she's gotta keep herself pertected. She waits. Like I oughta say somethin. Maybe I should. But I cain't think why or what. I'm slow. Dull. My head's still thick with the dreams of my night.

Auriel's draped her shawl over her head. My eyes keep goin to it. It's dark red. The color of blood. The same as the one in my dream.

Somebody dead, laid out in the pit full length. The head's bin wrapped in a dark red shawl.

I wish she'd take it off. The shades of the dead press on me. I don't see 'em. But I feel 'em, so close around me I cain't hardly breathe.

I dreamed of a old man, I says.

Yes, she says. Namid.

He gave me a bow, I says.

Yes, she says.

We pick our way down the camp, along the road between the shelters. The rain-churned earth's dried into ruts ankle deep.

Her an me's on walkabout. That's what she calls it. She feels responsible fer these people. Lost souls, she calls 'em. She's bin up since before dawn, talkin to the welcome committee an the privy detail an the health an death committee an who knows what else. She's even thinkin she might lead everybody out west herself. She's waitin fer a sign from the light, from her nature guides.

They need a leader, she says. These people ain't like you, Saba. They've spent their lives in the dirt, cowerin at the feet of the strong. They believe it's all they're fit fer.

It's a slow walkabout. Auriel's a mighty wonder. They rush at her, to kiss her hands, to touch her tunic. She speaks to each one, askin about their child, their wife, the old woman they traveled with. Me, they only look at sidewise. Specially with Nero ridin my shoulder an Tracker by my side. But at least people ain't holdin their charms aginst me today.

I look back. Lugh, Tommo an Em dog our footsteps, twenny paces or so behind. Auriel asked that they let her an me alone, but Lugh ain't one to be told. He warned he'd be watchin her an he means it.

Not that there's anythin to watch. The first thing I did today was ask her to git on with it. To gimme a potion or bleed me or read the stars or whatever it is she's gotta do to fix me so's we can git back on the road west. She said it don't work that way. That I'll know when I'm ready. After that, she wouldn't say no more.

The next tent along on the right, two painted ladies sit out front, watchin the world go by. The younger one—plump as a pigeon—sits with her feet up, coaxin a rattly tune from the strings of a banjax. Her friend squats on a stool, her skirt hitched above her knees, smokin a pipe. She's a handsome woman, loaded down with jangly bracelets an necklaces. There's a ring on every toe an finger. Dozens of 'em in her ears too.

In their ragged finery they're a strange sight among these worn-out dusty folk. Like colorful birds blown off course. Nero hops onto the pipe-smoker's shoulder an starts pickin at her flounces.

Would you credit that, Meg? she says. He thinks I'm a crow.

Ferget the bird, Lilith. Unless my eyes deceive me, th' Angel of Death has come to call. Meg lays her banjax aside. She sashays over, lookin me up an down, sayin, You'd be a big hit in our line of business, Angel.

She moves in so close that I can smell her. Sweat an sweetgrass. A big hit, she says. Mean . . . magnificent . . . a bit grubby. I seen you fight once. I still dream about it. She leans in. Her red painted lips brush mine. I always did wanna kiss a girl with a price on her head, she says.

A price, I says.

Lilith takes the pipe outta her mouth. Didn't you know? Oh yeah, the Pathfinder wants you real bad. Anybody harms a hair on th' Angel's head gits theirs chopped off, an it's a parcel of good New Eden land to the person who delivers you alive to Resurrection.

The Pathfinder, I says. What's Resurrection?

His lair, she says. Back in New Eden.

I ain't headed that way, I says.

I'd truss you up an hand you in myself fer a reward like that, she says. But whores ain't allowed in New Eden now. It's all temperance, duty an no fun at all. That's right, ain't it, Meg? No place fer the likes of us.

Saba! Lugh strides towards me. You shouldn't oughta be talkin to . . . to these.

Meg whistles. Fans herself with her hand.

Lilith narrows her eyes. It ain't talkin I wanna do with you, honey boy, she says.

Lugh flushes. He ain't never seen such females in his life before. He's tryin not to look at 'em but he cain't help it.

A taste of ripe fruit, that's what you need, says Lilith. Why doncha let Auntie Lil show you what it's all about? One hour. No charge. Pure pleasure. She's reachin out. She runs a finger up the inside of his thigh.

Don't touch me! Lugh twists away, kickin her hand. So wild an sudden that she goes flyin offa her stool into all their stuff. Pots an tins an a lookin glass crash to the ground. Nero flaps an screeches.

Lugh storms off, tearin hisself free when Tommo grabs at his sleeve. He starts to follow an Lugh shoves him away.

Lemme be, gawdammit! he yells. You ain't my family, Tommo! Back off!

He heads towards the river at a run. Tommo stands there a moment. Shocked. Cracked. Then he turns on his heel an walks fast th'other way. A kinda jagged lurch, huggin his hurt close.

Tommo! Em rushes after him.

Without thinkin, my feet start to go after Lugh. But they're heavy. Slow. Like I'm wadin through sand. Auriel stops me with a hand on my arm. Lugh needs me, I says.

You got nuthin left to spare, she says.

I got nuthin to spare. I repeat her words dully, stupidly.

That's right, she says.

I'm sorry, I says to Lilith. My brother's—

Meg's helpin her to her feet. Lilith shakes her head. Oh, I'm fine, honey, she says. But that brother of yers sure ain't. I'd keep a close eye on him if I was you.

Please, lady, will you come? A man's appeared beside

Auriel, pluckin at her sleeve. Small an wiry, his face carved hollow by hard cares. It's my woman, he says.

If she's sick, says Auriel, it's the health committee you need to—

Not sickness, he says. It's . . . her mind ain't right. Please, lady, she might take notice of you.

He presses his hands together, holds 'em out to Auriel. Beggin fer help.

Take me to her, she says.

We follow as he hurries between the row of tents, talkin all the while. They took our oldest girl, see, our Nell, he says. She's only jest ten. When they run us offa our place an give it to the Stewards, they took Nell away in the prison cart. They took her with 'em.

Ten year old. Emmi's age.

The Tonton, says Auriel.

Ruth blames me, he says. Says I should of fought. But one man got no chance aginst so many, an I ain't no good to nobody dead. After that, she couldn't sleep fer worryin about Nell an she wouldn't let our little one, our Rosie, move from her side.

Jest as we reach his junk shanty, there's a wild scream from inside. The man ducks through the door. Auriel's right behind him. I tell Tracker to stay. As I go in, outta the corner of my eye, I catch a rush of darkness. Hear a shiver of laughter. Cold sweat breaks on my skin.

Go away, I says.

Inside, it's only jest high enough fer me to stand upright. It's dim. No light but what slants through the door. Aginst the far wall, a woman sits in a chair. She cradles the little girl, Rosie, on her lap. Clutches her close to her chest. She rocks back an forth, keenin. It's a raw, animal, unbearable sound. Three other women hover, anxious, around her.

The fever took her two days since, says the man, but Ruth won't give her up to be burnt. The fever, lady. It ain't safe, it ain't right the dead should be among the livin.

Auriel takes off her eyeshield an goes to Ruth. Her cool voice ripples an murmurs, ripples an murmurs. Ruth shakes her head, clutchin her dead child even closer. No, no, no, no, no, she moans. The women an Auriel try to loosen her grip. Another wild scream.

The man looks at me, helpless. Would you try? he says.

Me, I says.

Please, he says.

My feet take me over to Ruth. I kneel beside her as she rocks back an forth. I says nuthin fer a bit, then,

My sister's called Emmi, I says. She's ten, jest like yer Nell. I used to think she was useless. Too young to stand up an be counted. Turns out she's a real fighter. I never thought she would be, but she is. She's a survivor. I bet Nell's jest the same.

She don't look at me, she keeps her face buried in Rosie's hair, but I can tell she's listenin. That's how I know what she's doin right now, I says. Becuz it's what Emmi'd be doin. She'll be watchin an thinkin an . . . plannin how to git away. How to git back to you. An she won't ever give up till she does. So don't you give up neether. You owe it to her. An yer man. It's the livin that need us, not the dead. They're past all that.

Rosie's only wearin a short, thin shift. I take my tunic off, lay it over top of the child.

Here, I says, you want her decent.

My body's heavy. My head's empty. I'm spent.

I'm sorry fer yer loss, I says.

As me an Auriel start to go, the man's face changes. He rushes over to his wife, to Ruth. She's opened her arms. As she begins to weep, as he gathers up his dead child fer the pyre, we leave.

† † †

We step outside. The sun so bright. The colors dazzle my eyes. The trees, the water, the sky. The noise. Too much.

Dogs bark. People chat. Cookfires smoke an crackle. Down at the river they're washin clothes. The pound pound of the washrocks. Children play and chase. The thunder of runnin feet. The bubble of cookpots. The yip of a dog. A sniff. A cough. A sigh.

The shadows of the dead creep out from between the

shelters. They gather at the edges of who I am.

Let us in, they sigh. They crowd me. Press me. They're closin around me. Let us in, let us in, let us in, they chant.

I cain't keep 'em out no more.

Tracker whines.

Saba? says Auriel. Saba, are y'okay?

She's holdin my arm, lookin at me. But all I see is myself. Me. Reflected in the dark of her eyeshield. Another Saba. In the darkness. Lookin out at me.

Jest then, a child shrieks. I turn. Slowly, slowly I turn.

A girl teeters atop a loaded wagon. Her playmates stand below. They egg her on to jump. They shout, they promise to catch her. She shouts back. Showin off. Excited to be with other kids.

It's Emmi, says Auriel. That's way too high. Emmi! she shouts. Stay there! She starts to run towards 'em.

Suddenly Emmi spots me. Hey, Saba! she yells. Look at me!

Suddenly Epona spots me at the edge of the trees. The world slams to a stop. There ain't nuthin an nobody else. Jest Epona an me an the sound of my heart.

Beat, beat, beat.

An it all happens slowly. So slow, I can see the blink of her eyelids. I can see her lips move as she takes in a breath.

Emmi beams. She calls. She waves.

Tears blur my sight. I wipe 'em away. I lift my bow. I take aim. Epona smiles. She nods. She starts to run towards me. She throws her arms wide open an lifts up her face. She leaps offa the roof. She soars through the air. Fer one last moment, she's free.

She flings her arms wide. She leaps.

My hands shake so bad that I cain't shoot. I don't shoot her.

Epona falls. Right into the arms of the Tonton below.

Hands reach out. They grab her. Hit her. Pull her down. Bodies surge, closin over her. She disappears.

Hands reach out. They grab at her. Pull her down. Bodies surge, closin over her. She disappears.

No, I says. Then I scream it, NO! An I start to run.

Then I'm there. Grabbin the Tonton by their arms. Throwin 'em off Epona. Then I got her, I saved her, she's here, she ain't dead, she's okay. An I'm pullin her into my arms.

I got you, I says, I got you, Epona, it's okay, everythin's gonna be okay. Git away! I yell. Don't touch her! I'm sorry, I'm sorry, I'm sorry, I'm sorry, I'm sorry, I'm sorry, I'm sorry.

I hold her to me. Rock us back an forth. Epona's weepin.

Shhh, I says. It's okay. I saved you, I saved you, I didn't kill you.

Saba, she sobs. Saba, what's wrong with you?

Epona. Epona . . . no . . . Emmi. Emmi's voice. Emmi, I . . . I'm holdin Emmi. Her face twisted with fear, streaked with tears.

We was playin Saba an the Tonton, she whispers. I was bein you.

Slowly, my arms loosen around her. She scrambles to

her feet. I raise my head. People all around. Shocked faces. Eyes starin at me. The kids Emmi was playin with. Kids, not Tonton. A couple of 'em cryin. One's nursin his arm, cries out when somebody tries to see what's wrong. Did I do that? Lilith. Meg. Tommo. Lugh, with Emmi clingin to him, her face buried in his side. Auriel. Tracker. Everybody lookin at me.

Nero flutters down to land beside me. Auriel comes over. She holds out her hand. I take it an she helps me to my feet. She takes off her eyeshield an looks at me. The shaman with the wolfdog eyes.

I can banish the dead, she says. Prepare you fer what lies ahead.

I'm ready, I says.

†   †   †

Auriel puts up the vision lodge. It's a special tent that her grandfather used fer many years, set atop a firepit that she gits Lugh an Tommo to dig.

She burns sage leaves an sprinkles herb water to purify the lodge. She lights a fire in the pit. It burns down till the rocks piled in the center glow red-hot. She brews a cactus tea. She puts two water-filled buckets with dippers next to the fire. An one empty basin. She ties seed rattles around her wrists an ankles. Brings her shaman's drum.

Lugh was fixed on bein nearby, in case I need him. He insisted. He argued. But what happens inside the vision lodge ain't fer nobody to know but me an Auriel. They ain't to listen or come in or interrupt, no matter what. So I says farewell to everybody. Him an Tommo an Emmi. Tracker an Nero too.

An it feels strange. Serious, somehow, an sad. Like when a person dies. Or when somebody's startin off on a long journey an you don't know if you'll ever see 'em agin. I hug Lugh last of all.

You don't hafta do this, he says.

Yes I do, I says.

As the sun goes down, we start.

Me an Auriel crawl inside the tent. The air's stuffy. Close. Already too warm. It's only jest big enough fer two to sit cross-legged. She scatters dried clover on the hot stones. Wisps of sweet-smellin smoke fill the air. She lets the thick tent flap down. The world's closed out. We're closed in. Now it's only her an me an the truth of what lies within. I cain't dodge it no more. Cain't hide. Whatever it is, I'm gonna know it. Look it in the eye. Like Pa told me.

Don't give in to fear, Saba. Be strong, like I know you are. An never give up. Never.

It's dark in the tent. Blackness. Eyes open or closed, it's the same. I cain't see a thing. I can only hear.

The dip of the ladle. Water splashin onto hot rock. The angry hiss of steam. Then heat. Fierce waves of heat that tighten around me. Choke me. Right away, I'm sweat wet. Despite I ain't got nuthin on but skivvies.

Auriel starts to chant. To sing. No words I ever heard before. Deep in her throat, then high an keenin, like the wind. She beats the skinbox. Her wrist rattles shimmer the air. The sounds ring in my head, my body.

More steam. My nose, ears, mouth, lungs, filled with steam an heat. Sweat drips offa me. No room to stand. Nowhere to move to. Trapped. In the heat an the sound an the darkness, I'm trapped. My heart flutters like a frightened bird.

But I won't run. I won't.

Auriel holds a dipper of water to my lips. I gasp it down. She spills another over my head. Presses a small cup into my hands. Drink, she says. All of it. Then lie down.

I hesitate. But only fer a moment. I tip my head back an drain it in one. The taste of bark on my tongue. It's like drinkin a tree. Earth. Water. Air. I lay myself on the ground.

Open yerself to the plant, she says. Don't fight it. Let it take you where it will, teach you what it must, give you what you need.

She chants. She beats a rhythm. The rattles make a noise like crickets. Hunnerds of crickets. Sound an heat an steam fill the tent. Move into me, through me, on an on. Till the edges of me start to blur. Till I lose all sense of time.

The light is around you, says Auriel. Let go, it's safe to let go.

I slide into the heat an the plant an the sounds. I leave my body, so heavy, so earthbound. An oh . . . the pain's too much. The hurt an the loss, the wrongness, the fear, the sadness. Too . . . too much to bear. Not jest me. All of us. Livin an dead an yet to be born. The darkest depths beckon me down. Somebody whimpers. It's me.

Her voice in my ears, in my head. Auriel whispers, In pain lies wisdom. Feel it. Let it take you. I promise it won't destroy you.

It closes over me. Fills my lungs. The black water of pain. Inside me. Outside. Beside me, beyond an around me. I cry pain out. I breathe it in. Over an over an over. My mother, my father, my sister, my brother. Helen an Tommo an Ike. People I know. People I don't.

I weep fer the livin. I weep fer the dead. I weep fer the yet to be born. An Epona. I weep fer Epona. Fer life so brief. Over so soon.

Yer friend, says Auriel. Her death was quick an proud. Yer hands on yer bow were merciful. Now she asks that you set her free. That you set yerself free. Let the dead go. Let all of the dead go.

My legs start to tremble. My arms jerk an dance. I'm

feverish hot. Freezin cold. Thin sourness leaps to my throat.

Auriel shoves the basin unner my mouth. I'm sick. Violently, suddenly sick.

She gives me water to drink.

From this moment, the Angel of Death is dead, she says.

She lays me down, the stars roll back an I'm in a still, gray place. A wide, flat plain at the edge of the world. It's the landscape of my dream.

† † †

There's a darkenin sky. The wind blows hard. The old man stands by the twisted tree.

Auriel's voice. In my head. Ask the pain what it wants of you, she says.

He holds a bow in his hands. It's white, like the twisted tree. Pale, silvery white.

To hold my bow in my hands agin, says I.

He holds it out. He offers it to me.

Will you take it? says Auriel.

I take it.

The bow was his, she says. My grandfather, Namid, the Star Dancer. The warrior who became a shaman. Now it belongs to you.

I feel its smoothness. Heft its weight. It's sweet. It's true. I swing the bow up. Fit a arrow to the string. It cleaves to me. Like it's part of me. My hands stay steady an sure. No shakes. No trembles.

It's one piece of wood, she says. The heartwood of the ancient whiteoak. It won't ever break.

Then the shaman's gone. I stand alone at the edge of the world. An I hold the white bow in my hands. I aim at the tree, now covered with leaf, green an fresh. The silver bark of its trunk an branches, rough with life.

I shoot.

The tree splits straight down the middle. There's a flash of lightnin. A rush of wind. Then the rumble, the thunder of hoofs.

The tree's gone. A body's there. Lyin there on the ground. On its back. Not movin. My arrow stuck in its heart.

I'm beside it. Kneelin down. My hand reachin out. To the dark red, blood red shawl that covers the face. I draw it aside.

It's Lugh. He's dead. My arrow stuck in his heart.

I draw the shawl aside. It's Jack. Dead. My arrow stuck in his heart.

Then it's me.

Then DeMalo.

He opens his eyes.

He smiles.

†   †   †

He sees me, I says. He knows me.

All right, she says, it's okay, I couldn't quite—I need you to think about him agin. Picture him. Don't block it.

Tall. Black robes. Metal body armor, breastplate an armbands. Long dark hair tied back. A watchful face. Strong, with broad cheekbones. Eyes so dark they're almost black.

Ah, she breathes. Tell me his name.

DeMalo, I says.

What does he see? she says. What does he know?

The shadows, says I. Inside me.

We need to look into them, she says. See what's there. Are you ready?

Yes, I says.

Don't be afeared, she says. I'm with you, Saba.

I'm crossin a lake in the mountains. In a bark canoe. I'm paddlin. Nero's huddled, a ragged shadow perched on the prow of the boat. He stares straight ahead.

My pilot. My watchman. My crow.

It's blackest night. It's bitterest cold. Above me, the hard stars stab. Like chips of ice.

The water parts as my boat glides through. My paddle dips an drags. It dips. An drags.

I don't look over the side. I don't even dare to glance. If I did look, if I dared to, night or no, I'd see 'em. I'd look down down down to the bottom. To the ancient bed of the lake. Where the dark things crouch. Where the old things wait. Where they crouch an wait . . . fer me.

Look down, says Auriel.

Saba! Saba! It's Lugh's voice.

Stay there, Saba. Stay with it, we're nearly there. Auriel's voice is calm.

Saba! Hey, Saba! Come quick!

Lugh. Callin. Lugh. Needs me.

Saba! he calls.

Lugh, I says.

Don't move, Auriel whispers.

A rustle. The shush of her rattles. Cool air slides in. It cuts through the heat. I shiver. She's gone outside.

I begin to rise from the dark deepness. Start to come up from the deep darkness. My self gathers itself.

I feel the ground, hard unnerneath me. The air's thick in the tent. Stuffy. Hot. I'm laid on my side, knees hugged to my chest. I'm shakin. My teeth chatter. I'm freezin one moment, burnin the next. My head's tight. It throbs.

The plant. The cactus tea. I let it in. It took me over. I set it loose inside me.

Voices outside the tent. Too loud. Hurtin my head. Lugh. Emmi. Tommo. I cain't make out what they're sayin. They're talkin on top of each other. Jumbled, tumbled words. Auriel's voice too, low an urgent.

I don't care, she needs to come now! Lugh's voice. So close, so loud, like a shock of cold water. An his hand on my arm, shakin me. Saba, c'mon, wake up!

Then I'm tryin to drag my eyes open an he's pullin me up to sit an Auriel's sayin, Lugh, stop it! You don't know what yer doin. If she comes outta the vision too quick, she might—

I know what's best fer my sister, he says. You bin here all night, that's time enough. Saba! Hey, Saba, there's somebody comin.

My eyes is open now. I see Lugh's tense face. His bright eyes. He's wound tight with excitement.

They're ridin into camp right now, he says.

My heart quickens. Jack, I says. It's Jack. He's here.

C'mon, he says. C'mon! He helps me to stand. I stagger. He grabs me. I'm dizzy, my legs shake, my stummick tilts.

Don't, says Auriel, please, Lugh, don't! Saba, we gotta—

But he's already leadin me outside, holdin me around the waist. The hard white light of day stabs my eyes. I shade 'em with my hand.

Look! he says. Look!

There's a horse an rider, comin towards us down the row of tents an shelters. The rider's low an slumped. The horse is slow. Heavy footed. Like they bin travelin too hard an too fast fer too long.

Nero an Tracker lead the way. Emmi an Tommo walk on eether side. People gather. Some follow, curious.

Auriel comes outta the tent behind us. Saba, she says,

please come back. We gotta finish proper. It's dangerous to—

Not now! Lugh says.

The rider's covered head to foot with the white dust of the Waste. Long hair in a wild tangle. It's a girl. I cain't see her eyes from here. But I know they're green. Deep an rich an alive. Like forest moss.

My breath catches. Then I'm stumblin towards her. Runnin towards her. Sayin her name.

Maev, I says. Maev!

† † †

I thought we seen the last of her.

It was the day we fought the Tonton at Pine Top Hill. We was outnumbered. Me, Lugh, Emmi an Tommo, Jack an Ash an Ike. Seven of us aginst Vicar Pinch an sixty some odd Tonton. Outnumbered, outwitted an about to be food fer the vultures. Till Maev showed up, that is. Thanks to her an her Free Hawks an that wild boy Creed with his Western Road Raiders, we beat 'em good. Well, that's what we thought at the time.

It's bin near enough two full moons since then.

I cain't credit that Maev's here. That I ain't still in my vision or seein ghosts. She don't look like nuthin livin, dusted white with the earth as she is. Emmi's beamin ear to ear. Tommo too. Nero shrieks an calls with excitement.

Lugh takes her horse's bridle an brings him to a halt.

Slowly she lifts her head. Almost like she's afeared. Then she turns her eyes on me. An in them, I read her ruin.

Maev, I says. What happened?

Her mouth moves. No sound comes out. She tries agin.

Saba. My name cracks from her parched lips.

Lugh, I says, help her down.

I found you. She sways in the saddle, her gaze fixed on me. Then she slumps an slides to the ground.

†   †   †

Lugh an Tommo catch her. Somebody comes runnin with a stool an they help her onto it.

Water! Auriel calls out. Somebody bring water!

Maev waves everybody away, weakly. I gotta talk to Saba, she mutters.

A woman rushes up with a full pan. Lugh holds it to Maev's lips. The moment she feels the wetness, she takes it in her own hands. At first, jest sips. Then gasps an gulps.

Down her desperate, grateful throat. Water trickles an spills. It snakes through the dust that coats her. Her face, her neck, her clothes. She drinks the pan dry.

As she gits her breath back, she looks at me. The Tonton came to Darktrees, she says. They cleared us out.

The cold starts in my stummick. Cleared out the Free Hawks, I says.

The Raiders too, she says. Right after Pine Top Hill, we started to hear rumors the Tonton was rallyin. Regroupin after the death of Pinch. We decided we'd all stick together. Safety in numbers. We kept pickin up little bits of news here an there, but nuthin to hang yer hat on. Ash an Creed was all fer leavin right away, but you don't abandon a place like Darktrees on a rumor. Good water an huntin ain't easy to come by. I dug my heels in. We stayed.

What happened? says Lugh.

They came in the middle of the night, she says. We had three on watch but it was so dark . . . There warn't no moon. An there was too many of 'em.

But the Hawks got away, says Emmi. Ash an Ruby an Taz an . . . everybody got away, right, Maev?

Her voice wobbles. She knows. We all do.

They come on us too fast, says Maev. Between heartbeats, it seemed. One moment quiet, the next there they was, on top of us. Most people was asleep. Some never even woke up. The lucky ones.

Silent tears spill down Emmi's cheeks.

No chance to fight, says Auriel. No chance to run. But here you are.

I was awake, she says. Me an Ash an Creed, we sat up talkin about the Tonton. Arguin, them two aginst me. What we oughta do, where we could go. They'd jest managed to talk me around. Finally convinced me it 'ud be the safest thing if we all left. We was gonna break camp in the mornin.

I says, How'd you git away?

I had help, she says.

Who from? says Tommo.

A Tonton, she says.

A Tonton helped you git away, says Lugh. Why would he do that?

She looks at me. As her hand goes to her neck. As she pulls a leather string over her head. As she holds out her hand. As she opens her fingers an shows me what's there.

It's a stone. A rose pink stone. The shape of a bird's egg. The length of my thumb.

Saba, says Tommo, ain't that yer heartstone?

It cain't be, says Emmi, she gave it to Jack.

I reach out. I take it. My skin knows it, so smooth an cool. My hand welcomes it like a friend. The coldness inside me starts.

It was him, says Maev. He's one of 'em. Jack's with the Tonton, Saba.

I stare at the heartstone.

I don't move. Don't breathe. The blood roars in my ears. It pounds in my head. Jack's with the Tonton. Jack. With the Tonton.

Saba! Saba!

It's Emmi. Callin my name, shakin my arm, draggin me back to the world. She stands in front of me. Auriel's nearby, with hunched shoulders, arms huggin herself. Watchin. Listenin. I half see Lugh an Tommo, as they half carry, half walk Maev to the tent.

Saba! D'you hear me? Em shakes me agin, her eyes fierce. It ain't true. It cain't be. I don't believe it an you shouldn't neether. Jack 'ud never be a Tonton. Never in a million years. You know him, you know he wouldn't. He helped Maev git away, that proves it!

I gotta think, I says.

No, you don't, she says. C'mon, we gotta find out what happened. C'mon!

She runs towards Auriel's tent, draggin me along behind her. Auriel hurries beside us. Tracker too. Em dives inside. Auriel blocks my way. Her face so young an so old. Her wolf-dog eyes that see everythin.

You ain't ready fer this, she says. We didn't finish. Yer too open, Saba. It's dangerous.

Open. I do feel different somehow. I feel bigger. I feel more than myself. Like I'm part of the air around me. Like I go on ferever an ever. Nero swoops down to land on my arm. I gather him in, hold him close.

I'm fine, I says. Stand aside.

† † †

They're jest layin Maev down on Auriel's cot.

Tell me everythin, I says. All of it. From the beginnin.

Hey, steady on, says Lugh. She's had it, she needs to rest. You can talk to her later.

I'll talk to her now, thanks. I shoulder him outta the way. Tommo's lightin the lamps an Em's fussin her with blankets an such. We prop her up. I crouch beside her.

So, everybody was asleep, I says. Jest you an Ash an Creed still awake. Then what?

Maev touches Nero's head with a gentle finger. Strokes him a couple of times. Then she says, You know what it's like there, Saba. At night. In the hills. In the trees. The silence there, it's . . . so deep. So vast. We're talkin around the fire . . . keepin our voices low, almost whisperin an then . . . outta nowhere . . . it's like the night rips open. The Tonton's on top of us. So many of 'em an . . . it's all so confusin, the . . . the horses an the screamin an they're tramplin down the tents with people still inside, still asleep an . . . pullin people out an . . . shootin 'em in the head.

What about you? I says. Ash an Creed?

We're on our feet right away, she says, but this one Tonton's already ridin me down. He corners me, then he jumps down an grabs me. An I'm fightin him off, no weapon, jest—Maev holds up her hands—but then I look at his face. He's dressed like the rest of 'em, in the black robes an the armor an all of 'em's got their faces covered, but I can see his eyes. They're Jack's eyes. It's him.

I hold out the heartstone.

He pressed it in my hand, she says. He whispers, Find Saba, give it to her, tell her—but he couldn't finish what he meant to say becuz all of a sudden, there was another Tonton right next to us, he was—

She stops fer a moment, collects herself.

Anyways, he could of heard, there was Tonton all over the place, so Jack lifts his knife, like he's about to kill me, an he says, loud so's anybody could hear, You've lost an yer the cause of it, so full of pride. You should of seen us comin by the moon, had more'n three on the watch.

But his eyes are movin, lookin this way an that, then he lets his arm go loose an I know that's my chance. He means fer me to run. So I duck an run an the horses, they've all fled into the trees away from the trouble, an I jump on the first one I

139

come to an I take off. I didn't look back. But I heard. Sound carries a long ways at night.

She ends on a whisper. We fall into silence. Led by her words to that mountain forest. On that quiet, moonless night. An I hear. I see. I smell. I feel. The chaos that came from the darkness. The panic. The terror. The pain.

The dreamers who won't ever wake. The dead who now walk with Maev.

My place was with them, she says. To stay an fight an die with them. I ran. Saved my own skin. All my fine ideas about myself. Every one of 'em a lie. This is who I turn out to be.

So he's joined the Tonton, says Lugh. I told you, Saba, Jack does what's best fer Jack.

That ain't true! says Emmi. He helped Maev git away, he saved her life!

I stare at the heartstone in my hand. No message, I says.

It was all so confusin, says Maev. Before I knew what was happenin, they're on us an I'm fightin this Tonton an I see it's Jack an then I'm runnin, I'm on a horse an . . . it's animal. The need to survive. I jest . . . went. The whole thing couldn't of took more'n three minutes.

Yer lucky you got away, says Tommo.

Am I? says Maev.

Of course, says Lugh.

Emmi kneels down next to me. What Jack said to you, she

says. You've lost an yer the cause of it. That don't seem like somethin he'd say. He don't talk like that.

Maev shrugs. He was right, she says. I am prideful, always thinkin I know best, not listenin to what nobody else says. It was—is my fault that they're dead. I should of had more people on watch. Right from the off, Jack an me never liked each other. It must of pleased him to rub my nose in my own defeat.

But he let you go, says Em.

I couldn't kill somebody I knew. Tommo's eyes go to me as he says it. He's thinkin of Epona.

He wanted you to bring the heartstone to Saba, says Emmi, to tell her somethin.

Tell her what? says Maev. That he's a Tonton now. That he don't care fer her. There you go, there's the message. Consider it delivered.

An there's this aginst him too, says Lugh. Darktrees is well concealed. You gotta know where it is, to know where it is. That's what y'all told me, right?

Maev nods.

So? says Emmi.

So, how did the Tonton find it? he says. Hidden away, deep in the forest, on a dark night. Somebody must of told 'em where it was, how to find it. Somebody must of led 'em there. Someone who'd bin there before an knew the way. Jack.

A voice inside me whispers, *Jack knows where Darktrees*

is. *Remember how he tracked you there from Hopetown? How he slipped between the trees, deep into the forest an past the Free Hawk guards?* I close my ears to its sly malice.

He wouldn't do that, I says.

How did the Tonton find it? Lugh lays his words out gently. They drift in the air an I breathe 'em in. What d'you know about him? he says. Really, I mean. Nuthin. He plays whatever side suits him at the time. He's a hollow man. A trickster. He's betrayed all of yuz. Betrayed you an deceived you.

Emmi's eyes fill with tears. I don't care what you say, she says. I know Jack in my heart. Saba's heart knows him too. He ain't no deceiver.

So, he's always told you the truth, says Lugh.

Like you, you mean? Auriel's cool voice. Our heads turn. It's the first time she's spoke. She's bin stood by the door all this time, watchin.

Lugh gives her a hard look. I ain't the one ridin with the Tonton, he says. He turns back to me. I will give him one thing, he had the decency to send yer necklace back. You seem a lot better. More like yerself. We'll rest today, pack tonight an be gone by first light tomorrow. C'mon, everybody, cheer up. We got the Big Water waitin fer us. A fine new life in a fine new land an I, fer one, cain't wait to git there. Whaddya say?

Let's go, says Tommo.

That's the spirit. Yer welcome to come with us, Lugh says to Maev.

She says naught. Jest lays herself down an turns her face to the wall.

Lugh an Tommo go off. The set of Lugh's back can say more'n most people's mouths do. Right now, it's shoutin to the world that he's right an that's that. His shoulders so certain. His arms so sure.

There's only one thing I'm sure of. Lugh's wrong. I cain't say how or why or what. But he is. He must be.

† † †

I walk by the river. Back an forth, back an forth, till I wear a path along the bank.

Jack sent me the heartstone. But no time in all the confusion to say why. Why he'd give it to Maev, tell her to find me, to give it to me. I gotta work this out.

Say Maev an Lugh's right. That he wanted me to have the heartstone back so's I'd know he don't care fer me no more. Even if that was so, would he choose a bloody attack on the Free Hawks as the ideal moment? Still, maybe he thought it 'ud be his only chance. But why do it at all? If you don't care fer somebody an they ain't around, you don't need to go to the trouble of tellin 'em so. You jest disappear from their life. Never send word an trust yer paths don't cross agin.

My mind sniffs at the problem. Licks at it, nibbles it, tears it apart. Over an over till it's like there's somebody shoutin at the top of their voice inside my head. Then I dive in the river an dunk myself till it shuts up. An I start all over agin.

I jest cain't git to what it means. How he might of come to ride with the Tonton. To be part of such bad deeds at Darktrees.

I ain't never got on with posers. Lugh's the twisty thinker. The one who's good at riddle-me-this an puzzlers. But I cain't ask him. He'd only carve more slices offa Jack's character. Give that nasty little voice inside of me even more to feast on.

You don't know nuthin about him. Not really.

He's a thief. A chancer. A rover.

A flash back to Ike. Outside the One-Eyed Man. He calls, Hey Jack! What is it you always say? An Jack turns, smilin that crooked smile of his. Sayin, Move fast, travel light an never tell 'em yer real name.

He'll play whatever side suits him at the time.

You know he ain't always told you the truth.

Auriel comes to talk to me, goin on agin about how we need to go back into the vision lodge, that it's dangerous to leave things like we did. I tell her I'm back to my old self. She jest looks at me a long moment, then goes away.

At middle day, the welcome committee announces a social. Tonight, startin at sundown, we'll have music an dancin. They figger it'll do the whole camp good to let off some steam an

144

have a little fun fer a change. Lilith an Meg promise to give a song, if they can remember any that's fit fer decent company.

What a lamentable waste of time. Apart from one thing.

It means that nobody bothers me. What with gittin stuff together fer the trip west an, now, doin this an that fer tonight as well, they let me alone. Lugh an Tommo an—at last, finally, three cheers an amen—Emmi.

All mornin she vexed me. Like a flea you cain't shake. There I am, tryin to think, an there she is, doggin my heels. Yippin an yappin her lamebrain ideas an stupid comments. I think maybe Jack meant this, an, D'you s'pose maybe Jack meant that? an, Why're you goin in the water agin, Saba? I'm gonna be a shaman like Auriel. Yip, yap, on an on the livelong day till I yell at her to shut the hell up or I'll wring her scrawny neck.

I brace myself fer the usual Emmi palaver. The quivery lip, the wobbly chin, the tragic eyes. But she jest grins an says it's nice to have me back. Then she skips off, sayin Meg promised to learn her the polka, an I ain't seen her since.

So, huzza fer the gawdamn social.

I throw myself down on the bank. I take off the heart-stone. Dangle it in front of my eyes. It turns an gleams in the sunlight, milky an dull an cool.

It's a heartstone, Mercy says as she puts it around my neck. Your mother gave it to me, an now I'm givin it to you. You feel how cool it is? A normal stone 'ud warm up next to your body. Not this

145

one. It stays cold until you get close to your heart's desire. Then the stone becomes warm. The closer you get to your heart's desire, the hotter the stone burns. That's how you know.

The heartstone led me to Jack. Showed me who he is, time after time. An time after time, I ignored its voice. Here is yer heart's desire. He is yer heart's desire. At last I paid heed. Now I know to trust it.

I gave it to him. He sent me it back.

I care fer you no more. Is that what it means? Or maybe this. Come to me, find me, my heart's desire.

I think about Jack. How he wouldn't be shook off. How he followed me, saved me an fought by my side. How he faced down death to help me find Lugh. Reckless, courageous, infuriatin Jack. He never let me down. Not once.

But.

Jack at Darktrees. Showin the Tonton the way to the Hawks, knowin full well they'd be slaughtered. Betrayin our friends, them who fought by his side only a couple of months before.

It cain't be so. Emmi says I know Jack in my heart. I gotta hang on to that.

I can only conceive of one reason he'd be with the Tonton. They must of nabbed him. He's traveled the wide an wild ways all his life. He knows every who an where an what an why. Miz Pinch used to call me her prize acquisition, when the Angel of Death was top draw in Hopetown. That's what Jack must be fer the Tonton. Their prize acquisition.

So what do I know fer sure? When we parted ways, he was headed east. To tell Ike's woman that he was dead. Molly Pratt, of the frilly red bloomers, with lips like ripe berries an curves to make a man weep with joy. She runs a tavern, in some place called the storm belt.

Jack must of run into the Tonton somewheres along the way. Still. Even if he was captive, he'd sooner kill hisself than ride with such men an be part of their wickedness. I know he would. I would.

I think till I cain't think no more. Till my head throbs. That plant tea Auriel gave me must still be swimmin in my blood. If I rest, jest fer a bit, it'll clear.

Everythin . . . all of it . . . it'll all become clear.

† † †

I wake with a start. I'm lyin on the ground by the river. It's dark.

Music rackets up at the camp. It bucks an kicks an hollers to yer heartbeat. Somebody's yodellin. Feet stomp. Hands clap. The let-off-some-steam social's in full swing. Torches light the sky. Joy sounds jig around me. The noise of it all must of woke me.

I cain't remember fallin to sleep. I bin out fer hours. I drag myself up to sit. The water of the Snake gleams, a silver ribbon in the moonlight. I lean my head in my hands. With a caw caw, Nero sails outta the gloom. He lands beside me with a flutter of wings. Cocks his head an gives me a beady stare.

I care fer you no more.

Come to me, find me, my heart's desire.

I know Jack in my heart.

Suddenly I know what to do.

Somethin ain't right, I says out loud. I'll go back. I'm gonna turn around. I'll go to that place—Resurrection, that's what Lilith called it—I'll go there an find him an make contact with him somehow. How hard can it be? I scritch Nero on his head. I managed to find Lugh, didn't I? We'll go tonight. While they're all asleep. Whaddya say?

The heartstone's lyin on the ground. Nero suddenly darts at it, snatches it in his beak an takes off. He sails above the river. He drops it. It's headed fer the drink.

No! I dash along the bank. Make a flyin leap. I soar through the air, my hand stretched out. Jest as I'm about to grab it, Nero dives. He nabs it.

I splash down. Face down. When I surface, drippin wet, gaspin fer breath, he's circlin above one of the cottonwoods on the bank. The biggest one, it's tall an tangled an wild. If he drops it in there, I won't never git it out.

Nero! No! Hand that over right now! While I yell, I'm wadin to river's edge, scramblin onto the bank an runnin towards him. C'mere, you bad crow!

He flies towards camp. He teases me, taunts me. To me, then away. To me, then away. Drops it, catches it, drop, catch. Almost lettin me git my hands on it, then snatchin it at the last moment. Almost makin my heart stop when he perches on the vent pipe of a privy shack an dangles the heartstone down it. The privy door's sealed. Chalked with a big white X. That means it's full.

Don't you dare! I shout.

I leap. Grab onto the pipe. Make a grab at him. The pipe bends. I tumble to the ground an he takes off agin. I go after him at a run. That stone's gonna lead me to Jack. I cain't leave without it.

The social's goin on in the big open space where we first saw Auriel. The junkband's up on the platform, playin like the Devil's whippin 'em on. Sawin at the stringboxes, wheezin the squeezebox, squealin the shrillie an whalin on the drums. Sweat flies offa their red faces.

Lilith sings. She belts it out in a big, brassy voice, swishin her skirts an flashin her eyes. Meg's perched barefoot on the platform edge, flirtin with some fella. Somebody oughta warn him to stand back a bit. She's packed her top-side fundamentals so tight into her low-cut dress that it's only a matter of time before she bursts her banks.

Everybody's dancin. They skip hand to hand, in circles. Twirl each other around by the waist. They shriek with laughter. Call to each other. Man, woman an child. Gone the world-worn faces of the day. The music's runnin in their blood. It shouts out life an livin. It shouts down death an kicks it in the pants.

Nero dives right into the middle. So do I. I duck unner flyin arms, slip between people, chasin him, yellin at him all the time.

Nero! C'mere right now!

Somebody grabs my hand. It's Tommo. Hey, Tommo, I says. Would you—

His arm's about my waist, he's swingin me around. Around an around, his dark eyes hot on me, holdin my gaze. I frown, rememberin what Auriel said.

The deaf boy. Take heed, Saba. He's in love with you.

Then I'm dancin with a stranger, a man. I break away. Nero! I call. I see Emmi. An Lugh. He's flushed. His eyes glitter. So wild an rattly as he dances that he almost looks feverish.

Suddenly, the music quickens. The circles break up. It's a free fer all. Somebody grabs my hand an sends me spinnin. I trip an stumble, bouncin from body to body, till I'm thrown right outta the heavin crowd.

Nero's flown onto the roof that shelters the platform. He caw caws his triumph at me. There ain't no way I can reach him there.

Dammit! I yell.

Bird trouble? It's Maev. Her an Auriel stand a few foot off, watchin the dancers. Maev looks pale an tired, but she's cleaned herself up. Her fresh-washed hair twists an glints its way down her back. It almost looks like a livin thing.

I'm still drippin wet from the river. Sorely vexed from chasin Nero. I glare at him, there on the roof, as I says to her, You said if I ever got tired of him, you'd take him offa my hands. Help yerself.

She pretends surprise. Did I? she says. I don't think so. I ain't really a bird kinda person anyways.

Lugh appears. He stands in front of Maev. The torchlight kisses his lips, smooths his skin, brushes his hair with gold. I'm so used to him, I sometimes fergit his beauty. Tonight it's a glittery, jittery, fevery beauty.

That look. I used to see it in Hopetown all the time.

You bin takin chaal, I says.

What? Don't be stupid. He laughs, gives a little shake of his head as he says, You cain't stand to see me havin even a bit of fun, can you? He holds out his hand to Maev. Dump these two misery guts, he says. Let's you an me dance. He takes her hand. C'mon, Maev, he says with a smile. Dance with me.

She breathes a soft sigh. I see it. I . . . I cain't, she says. Sorry.

His smile fades. His mouth hardens. He drops her hand, turns on his heel an walks off. His back's stiff with hurt.

Maev watches him go. I ain't got no right to dance, she says.

I ain't never seen him like that, I says. I'd swear he's on chaal, but—I turn to Auriel. I thought you said the camp's clean.

I did, she says, it is, I mean, I thought it was, but I guess I better—

There you are! It's Emmi. Shiny-eyed, jiggin from foot to foot, her cheeks pink with excitement. You slept the day away. Lugh wouldn't let none of us wake you. Hey Saba, ain't this fun?

No, it damn well ain't, I says. Jest then, Nero screams at me. An that damn bird's a thief. He took my heartstone an won't give it back.

Emmi points at him, laughin. Oh, look at him, way up there! He's a bad boy, all right. As she goes skippin back to join the dance, she calls over her shoulder, I told you he's a lost cause!

Her last words echo in my head. He's a lost cause. A lost cause.

Maev says somethin to me. I say somethin back, I dunno what.

You've lost an yer the cause of it. So full of pride. You should of seen us comin by the moon, had more'n three on watch. There warn't no moon the night the Tonton came to Darktrees, Maev said. *They came in the middle of the night. We had three on watch but it was so dark . . . there warn't no moon.*

Emmi was right. *That don't sound like somethin Jack 'ud say. He don't talk like that.*

The world goes silent. Shuts down. The music, the laughter, the voices. All but one voice. His voice. Jack.

Meet me at the Lost Cause, Saba. Be there at the next full moon. It's the rule of three.

He did send me a message. Surrounded by Tonton, with only seconds to spare, he sent me a message that wouldn't git Maev in trouble. Or him.

Jack's rule of three. He told me about it in Hopetown, while the place burned around us.

Him an me runnin. Swervin an leapin as bits of burnin buildin crash to the ground.

Ever heard of the rule of three? he shouts.

No! I says.

If you save somebody's life three times, their life belongs to you. You saved my life today, that makes once. Save it twice more an I'm all yers.

I'll jest hafta make sure that don't happen, I says.

He stops. Grabs my hands. It'll happen if it's meant to happen, he says. It's all written in the stars. It's all fate.

He pretends the rule of three's a game. A joke. But it ain't. Not to him anyways. It's how he binds hisself to people he cares about. How he binds them to him.

The Hopetown fire, when I sprung Jack from his lock-up in the Cooler . . . that was the first time I saved his life. The second time, it was the hellwurm. Once more 'ud make it three. Then his life belongs to me.

An while I'm workin all this out, while my brain's chewin it over, my eyes go on watchin what's happenin.

The band plays. The dancers dance. Meg still sits on the platform edge. Lugh's at her feet. He stares up at her. His hands circle her ankles, smooth her bare legs with restless intent. She jumps down. She takes him by the hand. She leads him off into the night.

Maev's seen it too. Her back's stiff, her arms hugged tight to her body. A hot tide creeps up her neck. She stands there a moment. Then, holdin her head high, she turns an leaves.

The rule of three. Save his life once more an it's mine. Save his—

Jack's life. He's in danger. The next full moon.

The next full moon. That's three nights from now.

The sounds of the world slam back. Hit me like a wall. Music, laughter, voices. The red hot kicks me in the gut an roars into life. My fingertips tingle. My belly burns. An I'm wound up so tight I could bust.

It's the way I used to feel before a fight in the Cage. Alive. Truly, fiercely alive. An thinkin clear.

I weave my way through the dancers an vault onto the platform, right in the middle of the band. Lilith's bellowin out a bawdy song. I put my hand on her arm an she stops, startled. The Lost Cause, I says. You ever heard of it? D'you know about it?

Sure, she says. Molly's place. Me an Meg worked there.

Where is it?

New Eden, she says. The Storm Belt, right in the middle.

Got it, I says. I start to go an she grabs my arm.

You cain't go there, she says, you got a price on yer head.

Don't tell nobody, I says. Swear.

But I—

Swear, Lilith!

She stares at me tight-lipped. She can see I'm fixed on it. Okay, she says, but you—

I'm already jumpin down, makin my way towards Auriel's tent. But I can hear her voice, even over the racket of the music. Callin after me.

Saba! Be careful!

† † †

Nobody follows.

Tracker's sprawled in front of Auriel's tent. He gits to his feet the moment he sees me. I hush him with a finger to my lips. I check that nobody's watchin, then we duck inside.

Lugh an Tommo's left our gear to one side. It's all packed up neat, ready fer a early start west in the mornin. I grab my barkskin sack an do a quick check of what's in it. Full water-skin, flint, knife, blanket, jerky. The bare bones of survival.

As I pull a tunic over my head, I consider weapons. I'll need somethin. My eyes go to Lugh's bow an quiver. No, it wouldn't be right. I take his slingshot instead. Stuff it down the back of my britches. I block out that I'm leavin him an Emmi an Tommo behind. Thoughts of how crazy worried they'll be when they find me gone. I swallow down the sudden, tight fright of bein on my own. Jack's in trouble. He needs me.

Move fast. Don't think.

I grab Hermes' gear. I shoulder my sack. Tracker's sat there. Watchin. Waitin. C'mon, I says.

I check it's all clear, then him an me slip outside agin. We hurry towards the bottom end of camp to find Hermes. Durin the day, the beasts got gathered up—horses, camels, mules an all—an penned in with a rope an peg fence in case they got spooked by the night's noise. Along the way, I whistle fer Nero.

When the pen's in sight, I stop. C'mere, Tracker, I says. He presses into my side. You cain't come, I says, it's too far. You gotta stay here with Auriel. She'll keep you safe. While I'm talkin, I take a loop of rope from my belt— tough, made from silverberry twine—an tie it around his neck. I lead him to a big cottonwood that stands behind the last few shelters an tether him to the trunk. His pale eyes follow my every move. Don't look at me like that, I says, it's fer yer own good.

He shoves his head into me. My nose prickles but I clamp

156

down firm. I ain't got time to cry. I rub his ears an kiss his rough fur. Thanks, I whisper. Now, you stay here. Hush.

Then I leave him. Fine creature that he is, he don't make a sound. Jest like I told him.

Nero drops outta the darkness. He lands on my shoulder, the heartstone danglin from his beak. Gimme that, you villain. I take it from him, put it around my neck. It 'ud serve you right if I tied you up an left you here, I says.

We reach the animal pen. Auriel's there. She stands at Hermes' head, strokin his nose. Star bright stargirl, wrapped in her dark red shawl. The glass beads in her hair glitter in the moonlight. Nero flies to perch on the rope fence beside her.

I walk up an throw my sack on the ground. I says naught. I don't look at her. Not even a quick glance as I saddle up Hermes with horse blanket an soft reed mat, as I lift his bridle over his head.

She helps me adjust it. Our eyes meet. I look away quick.

I'm goin after Jack, I says. To New Eden. He did send a message. He's in trouble.

I'll say this one last time, she says. Yer dangerously open, Saba. We didn't finish proper, we stopped at the wrong moment. Please, will you stay an let me finish.

I cain't wait, I says. I already wasted too much time.

Okay, she says, I done all I can. I brought you this.

She goes to the fence. Picks up a bow that's leaned aginst

it, a pale, silvery white bow. I stop what I'm doin. Cold shivers chase over my skin. Then I'm duckin unner Hermes' neck an I'm standin in front of Auriel. She holds out the bow.

Yer grandfather's bow, I says. Namid.

Yes, she says. Before he was a shaman, he was a great warrior. Now it belongs to you.

Heartwood of the whiteoak, I says. It cain't ever break.

You remember, she says.

I remember, I says.

I reach out. I take it. My skin tingles where it touches the wood. I feel its smoothness. Heft its weight. It's sweet. True. Perfect.

Auriel hands me a arrow. I swing the bow up an fit a arrow to the string. It cleaves to me. Like it's part of me. My hands stay steady an sure. No shakes. No trembles.

It'll do, I says. I sling it on my back. She hands me a full quiver. I better make tracks, I says.

Auriel holds Hermes' head as I mount. Music drifts, dips on the warm night breeze. The scratchy sweet whisper of a waltz.

There is a quicker route, she says. It's fast, but it ain't safe.

Tell me, I says.

Due north of here, you'll run into the old Wrecker road that skirts over top of the Waste, she says. If you ride fast, if you don't stop, you could be at the Yann Gap by sunup. The road ends there. Once you cross the Gap, yer on Tonton soil. The far north-west corner of New Eden. There ain't nobody there, you can slip in, unseen.

I ain't never heard of no north road, I says.

That's becuz them that take it, rarely make it. They call it the Wraithway, she says. There's all kinds of stories about it. The Wrecker spirits that ride its length, seekin vengeance fer their lost lives. Strange beasts. Skull collectors.

I'll take my chances, I says.

What'll I tell Lugh? she says. He's gonna come after you, y'know.

That's why I need a head start, I says. Stall him. Lie to him, whatever you gotta do. Jest buy me some time.

I start to move Hermes, but she grabs hold of his bridle.

Have a care fer yer brother, she says. He's— There's some wounds that run too deep to be seen. They're the most dangerous. An remember what I said about Tommo, he—

I ain't got time fer this, Auriel. Leave go of me.

This is important, you really—

I said, let go!

DeMalo, she says.

My stummick clenches. What about him? I says.

He's the Pathfinder, she says. You'll meet him agin. You ain't ready.

My palms go clammy. I'll try to steer clear of him, I says.

Saba, she says, yer only jest beginnin to know who you are, what you can do, who you can be. Remember, in the tent, in yer vision . . . yer right, DeMalo does know the shadows. His own, yers, the rest of us. We all have 'em. They're a powerful part of you, but you must learn to—

She stops on a breath. I can see her listenin to her voices agin, her guides. She nods. The time's outta joint, she says. The world moves on too fast. You'll hafta do this on yer own. Be very careful.

I gotta go, I says.

Nero takes off from the fence. He circles above, silent scout of the night.

She lets go the bridle. She steps back, huggin her shawl tight around her.

Don't stop on the Wraithway, she says. No matter what.

G'bye, Auriel, I says.

An don't lose sight of what you believe in, she says. If you do, we're all lost.

I nod a farewell as I leave. I set a course due north. An I don't look back.

Half a league outta camp, Nero circles back. He swoops past me, callin, callin, callin.

I turn to see what's his fuss.

Tracker comes runnin outta the darkness. He catches up with Hermes.

Tracker. Last seen tied to a cottonwood tree. There ain't no sign of his tether.

He don't say nuthin. Not a bark, not a glance of reproach. He jest settles into a steady lope alongside Hermes.

My heart gladdens. Lightens. It swells to fill my chest. What was it Auriel said?

He runs with you now. The wolfdog an the crow. Fit companions fer a warrior.

My crow. An now—it seems—my wolfdog.

He won't be left behind. I was wrong to do it. I won't do it agin. I should of known he wouldn't be tied.

THE WRAITHWAY

We ride through a land of stony plains. Of rock-bound lakes an spruce-choked forests, where the air stands heavy an chill. A place of the thick dark. The deep old.

The night's black. No stars. The moon shines white an hard. My every nerve's hummin. Hermes ain't easy. If I gave him his head, he'd fly. But, bad as I'd like that, I hold him steady. Steady, always steady. We got a long ways yet to go.

His hoofs drum the ground. The sound falls dull. Muffled. Somewhere in the distance, far, far away, I think I hear the beat of drums. Or do I? Hard to tell. Then nuthin. Gone. Stoneheart country like this conjures up bogeys in a person's mind. The Wraithway. Wrecker ghosts. Travelers who set off but never arrive.

I know all about ghosts now. Unquiet spirits. They don't hold no fears fer me. I reach fer the heartstone around my neck an I think . . . I think about Jack. Of how it'll be when I see him agin. When he's holdin me tight an I'm holdin him tighter an the heartstone's burnin my skin.

I think of what we might say. Him to me. Me to him. I ain't no soft girl. I don't know no soft words.

Be with me, Jack. That's what I'll say. Burn with me. Shine with me.

Nero flies ahead. Tracker runs behind. I check to my left

an my right. I'm alert, full of purpose, free. An fer the first time in a long time, I can breathe.

Here. Now. Alone. With none but my own heart fer witness, I'll say it. Without Lugh, I'm able to breathe.

He smothers me. Chokes me. Pens me in. Tethers me to him with his worry an sorrow an anger an fear.

Once I find Jack, once we're all together, I'll find a way to help him. I must. I swear I will. Jack an me, we'll find some way to help Lugh.

I see no wraiths on the Wraithway. But there's somethin ain't right. There's a deadness to the air. A flatness. It's a place that ain't one thing or th'other. Not quite alive, not quite dead. It waits. Like the moment between livin an dyin.

We pass a long line of rusted-out, crumblin cars. One after another, on an on fer a league an more. Nose to tail, all facin west. Like they was headed to the same place at the same time, but stopped fer some reason when they got this far.

Pa used to tell of when he was a boy an the winds unburied a car with four Wreckers inside. They still had their skins, shriveled onto their bones like dry seed pods. I'm thankful there ain't no dead inside these cars. The Wraithway's spooked enough.

When the night's half-spent its darkness, the country begins to change. I start to see wide, deep gashes in the rock. Scars as big as canyons. The earth's skin's bin scraped away. Its body blasted open. Over an over fer league upon league. Nature took no hand in this. The hands of people did. People long since dead. The Wreckers.

I slow Hermes to a walk. By the pale, cold of the moon, I look on their violent work. Their earth hate. The hulks of their great machines. The skellentons of their buildins. The toppled chimleys. The tangled heaps of iron an metal. All rusted. Silent.

No tree grows here. No moss. Not like most Wrecker places, where all of this 'ud be covered up. Hidden by the years, the countless years, of dirt an grass an scrub an trees as the earth gathers in what's dead an gone. But nuthin lives here. Only fire. Thin rivers, small lakes of fire. Wherever there's water, it burns. Low an ugly. Slow an thick. It oozes an roils, black an red. Like poisoned blood seeps from a fatal wound.

From the gashed ground, plumes of steam sigh.

If restless spirits ride the Wraithway, they ain't Wreckers. They're nature spirits. The spirits of earth an water. Of air an plants an creatures. With every right to ride vengeance on men.

No, Wrecker souls don't roam the road. This place, this hell, is their home. They're caught in their rivers of fire, always an forever drownin. Never, ever to be free. Their voices gutter in the flames. Take pity, fergive me, have mercy on me. Prisoners of their own destruction. Trapped till the end of time.

I hear them call. I make no answer. I turn my face from the murdered land.

† † †

We ride into kinder country. The rocky trail softens to earth in places. There's the open straggle of pine forests an small hills. There ain't bin no sign of traffic this whole time—no wheelruts, beast tracks, bootprints, nuthin. Looks like Auriel was right. Nobody travels the Wraithway.

When the sky's still dark, but you can sense the promise of day, we come upon a tipped-over wagon. It's blockin the trail. I slow Hermes to a walk while we go around.

It's bin smashed with a vengeance. There's a few scraps of pathetic stuff scattered about. Well-used eatin tins, a man's worn boot. Tracker noses an sniffs all around. Nero swoops down on somethin. He picks it up in his beak an shows me what it is. A child's rag doll.

Leave it, I says.

Whatever went down here, it warn't friendly. An not more'n a couple days ago, I'd say. The wheelruts still read clear. There's the hoofprints of a panicked pony. An some other tracks . . . beast, not human, but no creature I ever seen before. Each track's bigger'n my two hands spread out,

168

side by side. A two-toed beast. The inside toe's long, much longer'n the outside one. With a nail on it. It looks kinda like a hoof. But it ain't.

It's called the Wraithway. Them that take it, rarely make it.

I peer into the trees. The forest broods thickly on both sides of the trail, presses in, dark an unfriendly. Was that a movement, jest there? Tracker stares that way an growls. Maybe it ain't such kind country after all.

Tracker, c'mon! I says.

It cain't be far to the Yann Gap now. We hurry on. But Tracker keeps glancin to the right, into the trees on the south side of the trail. We go on another league or so. Tracker seems to relax an I can hear the rush of water up ahead.

Sure enough, a narrow stream cuts across the trail. It hurries outta the trees, gabblin to itself in a nervous rush. Hermes starts to slow as we approach. He tosses his head in complaint when I urge him on. He slows, then comes to a stubborn halt.

Don't stop on the Wraithway, no matter what.

No matter what. Well, I only got one horse an he needs a drink. Tracker too, he's bin runnin all night. We won't be long. A few seconds, that's all. I slide down from Hermes. The water's runnin fast an shallow over rocks.

Hang on, I says. I'll check it out, make sure it's—

Hermes pushes past me with a huffle as Tracker rushes into the stream an begins to drink. Nero lands on a rock an dips his beak in.

Guess it's okay, I says.

We drink long an deep. The water ripples an swirls, black in this light. It's icy cold an tastes flat, like stone. I look up at the sky as I sluice my face an arms. Dark clouds hide the moon. The last dregs of night tangle with forest shadows so's you cain't tell one from th'other. I squint. Looks like somebody's cut a path into the trees on the north side of the Wraithway.

Nero takes off with a squawk. I go fer a last scoop of water. Ow! I whip my hands out, an suck at my left wrist. The iron taste of blood. I must of nicked it on a stone. I plunge it back in the water, swish it about to wash off the blood.

We better git goin, I says.

In a flash, Tracker's outta the stream. He stares at it, stiff-legged, growlin.

I frown. What's the matter with you? I says.

Somethin slips around my skin. Somethin long an sleek. I snatch my hand out an peer into the stream. I cain't see proper, the light's so bad, the water's so dark.

The clouds clear the moon.

The stream's alive with snakes. Long, black, thick-bodied serpents, wrigglin an squirmin, more an more all the time. Suddenly, I realize my blood's still drippin. The water starts to boil with snakes.

Ahh! I scramble back. Tracker's goin crazy, barkin. Hermes

screams an rears. There's a snake writhin up his front leg. I lunge an fling it off. I grab a rock an wham it down on top of the thing. As I smash it dead, Hermes bolts fer safety. With a squeal of panic, he crashes off into the trees, down the path I noticed before.

No! I drop the rock an take off after him, Tracker at my heels.

† † †

Tracker an me run after Hermes. He's already well outta sight. We're on a good, bushwhacked trail that somebody's takin care to keep clear. Maybe hunters, maybe somebody else. It's the first real sign of life since we started this night-time ride, but I don't welcome it. The quicker I find Hermes an git outta here, the better.

Our feet fall silent on the forest floor, soft an deep with fallen needle. I slide my bow off, pluck a arrow an string it as I run. I keep turnin, checkin my back, my sides, ready fer any-thin. I can hear Nero above the trees, cawin to let me know he's with us.

The night's startin to wane in earnest, the day gainin ground fast. It's much easier to see now, even here among the trees. Not far ahead, I can see that they open up. Looks like it might be a clearin. To be on the safe side, I move offa the trail an slip along between the trees. Tracker keeps close to my side. A strange smell starts to tickle my nose, prickle the hairs on the back of my neck. It's sickly, thickly sweet. Then, sure enough, we're at the edge of a clearin.

An lookin at a huge Wrecker temple. A mighty ruin that's bein kept from fallin down completely by props, tarps an sheets of metal. Back when, it must of bin a sight to take yer breath away. Its stone walls still stand tall an proud, with arched window holes, fancy carvin work all around where the great door used to be. There's a iron cross, tall as the trees around it.

There ain't nobody in sight. Jest Hermes. He's standin in the doorway, takin a look.

Hermes, I hiss.

With a swish of his tail, he steps inside.

I curse to myself. Bow at the ready, I start to inch my way outta the trees, checkin, checkin, checkin in every direction. That funny, sweet smell's makin my scalp twitch.

Nero lands on the makeshift roof, peers in through a wide gap, then drops down an disappears. Great. First my horse an now my crow gone inside. But there ain't no sounds of alarm—beast or otherwise—so that's somethin at least.

I tread on silent feet across the clearin. Step around a pile of beast scat I don't recognize. Tracker takes one sniff an backs away, whinin.

I spot a feather, caught on a tree branch at shoulder height. White an fluffy. But not from no bird I know.

With my back to the temple wall, I sidle myself towards the black hole of the doorway. I peer in. The faint light of gray sky slants in through holes an gaps. Nuthin moves. It's all clear. I step inside.

I freeze. My skin goosebumps. Every hair on my head stands on end.

It's full of skellentons. Big an small an every size in between. They sit close packed, side by side, on long wooden benches. They gleam whitely, dully, in the dim light. They're all faced towards a raised stone platform at the far end. The wall behind it is covered, floor to roof, in skulls.

I take in the temple. It's one great room, much longer than it is wide. A long aisle splits it in half down its length, makin a straight path from where I'm standin, jest inside the door, to that high wall of skulls. The rows of benches sit both sides of the aisle. Along the side walls stand wire cages full of bones. In the middle of the stone platform, there's a shallow pit with a fire burnin. A heavy metal drum sits on a grill on top of the flames. Steam rises from the drum. That's where the hair-frazzlin reek's comin from.

It's also where Hermes is. He stands at the foot of the platform, helpin hisself to a pile of dried timbergrass heaped there.

I start up the aisle towards him, on tiptoes. My head turns from side to side, takin in the skellentons on the benches.

There's hunnerds of 'em. Wires run through each of 'em, tetherin bone to bone. They sit neatly on their bony backsides. Patiently. Fer all the world like they're waitin fer somethin. Well, they ain't none of 'em in a hurry no more, that's fer certain.

Some rest their hands on their knees. Some of the big ones hold hands with little ones. I keep espectin 'em to turn an stare at me with their hollow eyes. Nero hops from skull to skull, stoppin every now an then to stick his beak somewhere unspeakable. Tracker's close, lookin up at me with anxious eyes, whinin till I hush him with a finger to my lips.

Whatever's in the drum, it's bubblin like fury. The stink of it's jest about curdlin my liver. I step onto the platform to check it out.

The top of the drum comes to my chest. I cain't see in. On the ground nearby, there's a long pole with a tin bucket lashed to one end. A dipper. I pick it up. I lower it into the drum an fish around. Suddenly, it gits heavier. I got somethin. I lift the dipper out. I hand-over-hand the pole, bringin the bucket towards me. The smell's makin me gag now.

I stare into the bucket. Foamy water. With globby white bits in it. Somethin large bobs to the surface. It turns over. Lazy. Casual. A face looks at me. A human face.

Aaaah! I yell. I drop the dipper an stagger back. The head surfs out an plops at my feet. I leap aside, stumblin, aimin my bow at it without thinkin. At this . . . this nightmare that used to be a man. My hands shake as I stare down at it.

No nose. No eyes. No lips. One ear, with a silver hoop ring. A thick patch of long dark hairs. Some flesh boiled away to the bone. The skin that's left looks like a bloated, dead fish, drippin offa the skull in watery shreds.

Tracker's barkin like mad.

Somethin black swoops at me. I cry out an duck. It's Nero. Gawdammit, Nero! I says.

He caw caws as he flies to the wall of skulls in front of me. He perches on one. They grin down at me. Stare madly from their empty eye holes.

A temple full of skellentons. Cages of bones. A head bein boiled clean. A wall of skull trophies. The old stories that Auriel spoke of. Spirits an strange beasts. An skull collectors. Headhunters.

The fire. It's burnin hot an brisk. Somebody's tendin it. Somebody who ain't gone far an could come back any second. They could be watchin me right now.

I grab Hermes' reins an hurry back up the aisle towards the door. My head turns, my eyes scan everywhere.

Suddenly, a door opens in the wall of skulls. Somebody comes through it.

I read him in a flash. Barefoot. Bald. Painted white all over, but fer black slashes at his eyes an mouth. Dressed in a thick flutter of rag strips. Shriveled scalps hang around his waist. A blowgun around his neck. My bow's up. I aim. I shoot.

The second I spot him, he spots me. He grabs his blowgun an blows.

He's fast. But I'm faster. I duck. The dart zings over my head. I feel its wind in my hair. My arrow hits. It's a heartstrike. Perfect. He flies backwards. Crashes into the wall of skulls an thumps to the floor. Skulls rain down on top of him, around him, smashin on the stone floor with a fearsome racket.

Then. As the sound dies away, I hear 'em.

Drums.

Drumbeats. From the north. Comin this way. They mean one thing an one thing only. Fear an pain an a place in the skull wall.

No bogey. All too real.

Nero! I yell.

I turn an run. I belt outta that temple an onto the trail as fast as I can. Runnin faster'n I ever run before. I'm flyin, my feet hardly touchin the ground. I can hear Hermes an Tracker crashin along, well ahead of me. Nero screeches above the treetops. I burst outta the trees an hit the Wraithway at top speed. Damn. Hermes an Tracker's headed back the way we jest come. I holler at 'em as I pound the trail east.

This way! I yell. This way, gawdammit!

I can hear 'em, feel 'em, as they turn an come thunderin after me. I shift my bow to my back. Hermes slows down as he pulls up alongside. Still runnin, I grab his mane an swing myself onto his back.

Go, go, go! I yell. I stab my heels an he goes like the clappers. I grip hard with my knees, lean low along his neck. My heart hammers. My belly's tight. The red hot's runnin high an fast.

Wrecker wraiths. Travelers that set out, never to be seen agin. Headhunters, that's the truth behind the tales. When they find their firekeeper dead, they'll give chase. An we'll be easy to track.

As we pound along the road, my head pounds too.

I killed him. I had to. No choice. Still. It's one more life on my scorecard. It don't matter who, friend or foe, each life's a scar on my soul.

But oh . . . my bow in my hands. My whiteoak bow, the gift of the shaman.

Straight to his heart. No fear. No hesitation.

The beauty of it.

The power.

The beautiful, perfect, terrible power.

The dark thrill in my deepest self.

Tracker races at our heels. Nero speeds ahead. Hermes flies over the ground, tremblin with excitement. He's a wild wind. A streak of lightnin. His hoofs beat us into the hard yellow dawn, as we ride, flat out, fer the Yann Gap.

†   †   †

We reach it jest after daybreak. The Yann Gap. The end of the road. The border between here an New Eden. Across the Gap lies Tonton territory. An Jack.

The forest starts to thin out, then suddenly we're outta the trees an two fifty, three hunnerd paces on we're at the Gap.

There's two stone cairns, set well back from the edge, to red flag the danger that lies ahead. I stop at 'em, jump down an run to take a look.

Without the cairns to warn you, you'd be in real danger of ridin straight on an tumblin to a messy death in the canyon. Becuz that's what the Gap is. A dry canyon. A great deep gash in the earth, like somebody's took a giant axe to it. It's thirty foot across an deep, deep, deep. Too gawdamn deep fer comfert. Jagged rocks snarl at the bottom, like sharp teeth in a hungry mouth.

There ain't but one way to reach th'other side. By a rope an wood bridge that's jest wide enough to take a small cart. It's anchored to stumpy iron pillars. Two on this side of the Gap an two on the far side. They must be the remains of some old Wrecker crossin.

The wind witters an moans in the canyon. The bridge swings gently. I'm lucky there's any bridge here at all. Still, I cain't help but wish it was a lot more sturdy an a lot less swingy. I ain't never crossed a rope bridge. My bowels ain't keen on the idea, but my head's keen to stay attached to my body, so cross I will. Hermes too. I ain't leavin him behind.

I clutch tight to the rope railin an inch my way to the middle, testin it'll take his weight. I clutch even tighter as I jump—one, two, three times—makin sure I land hard. The slats feel strong. There's a couple that look new. Somebody's bin seein to repairs.

I rush back to Hermes. Rummage in my pack fer somethin to wrap around his head. I pull out a dark red shawl. Auriel's shawl. How the hell did it git in with my gear? Last time I seen it, it was around her shoulders back at the Snake.

My dream. The faceless body in the ground. The head wrapped in a blood red shawl.

I shove the thought away. I wrap it around Hermes' eyes an start to lead him across. Come, Tracker, I says. C'mon, boy.

He stays where he is. He runs to an fro, whinin an barkin. Damn. I'll hafta come back fer him.

With Hermes' weight on it, the bridge stays still. I soothe him, my voice low an calm. We go slow. One step, then another. I don't take my eyes offa his feet an where he's puttin 'em, not fer a second. Without even tryin to, I ferget my own nerves. Before I know it, we're steppin onto solid ground agin. We made it.

I unhood him, loop his reins around a nearby tree an head back fer Tracker. Poor devil, he's completely spooked. I tie nettlecord twine around his neck. Yer too big fer me to carry, I says. C'mon, now.

I haul on the twine an manage to git him onto the bridge. I pull an coax an he starts to crawl on his belly, whimperin all the while. Sweat trickles down my back, damps my armpits. Nero hops along the rope handrail, croakin encouragement.

C'mon, Tracker, I says. Good boy! That's it! Almost there.

Jest then, I hear a sound. So faint, I cain't be sure. No. Yes. Hoofbeats in the distance. Headed this way, movin fast from the direction we jest come. I cain't see nuthin fer the vast sprawl of forest. Must be the headhunters. They found the body. They're comin after me.

Sonofabitch, I says. I crane my neck around. The rope's bin coiled an wound around the pillars. It's pretty thick. Not too thick, I hope.

I hold out the cord to Nero an he takes it in his beak. Here, I says, help Tracker across.

He starts to hop along the handrail, leadin Tracker over the bridge.

I run to the far side. I grab my knife from my boot an start sawin at one of bridge ropes, near to where it joins the pillar. The rope's made from orange honeysuckle vine, woody an tough. An it's bin sealed with tree pitch aginst the weather, so it's hard goin. But I hack an saw an sweat over that rope like my life depends on it. Which it does. The rope starts to fray.

The riders is gittin closer.

C'mon, Tracker! I yell. C'mon, Nero, hurry up!

I throw a look their way. They're three quarters of the

way across. Tracker's still on his belly, froze to the spot. Nero's sittin on his head, holdin the cord in his beak.

I don't stop. I cain't. The rope's jest about cut now.

If I was you, I'd git a wriggle on! I call. Any time now 'ud be good!

Nearly through. Almost—

Tracker! I bellow. Shift yer gawdamn ass!

There's a great crackin noise. Suddenly, the bridge sags.

Nero takes off. Tracker leaps. He flies through the air towards me. He jest makes it.

The second his back feet hit solid ground, the rope snaps. The bridge tips. A few slats tumble into the canyon.

On this side of the Gap, the bridge is hangin by one rope only.

I run an start workin on that one.

There's a big cloud of dust headed this way. Must be a helluva lot of 'em. The red hot's runnin wild in my blood. I saw away like a demon.

Aaaaaah! I yell, the sound comin from deep in my belly as I hack at this last rope. Aaaaaah! Sweat stings my eyes.

Yellin from th'other side. Hoofbeats. Shouts. Screams.

Saba! Saba!

Voices callin my name. My name? But—

I'm through. The rope snaps. I turn, pantin.

To see the bridge swing down an dangle from the pillars on the far side. Useless.

To see four riders pull up on that same side of the Gap.
Lugh. Maev. Tommo. Emmi.

Eyes wide. Horrified.

To see another cloud of dust risin above the forest behind
'em. Rollin this way. The faint sound of drumbeats.

Dust. Drumbeats. The headhunters. They're comin.

†   †   †

We gawp at each other across the canyon. Then,

What the hell you done? Lugh yells. Are you crazy?

How should I know you was right behind me? I says. My
heart's poundin fit to bust my ribs.

Somebody's chasin us! says Emmi.

Headhunters! I says. It's me they're after!

You?! Lugh glares at me over the Gap, red-faced with fury.
Who's stuck on the wrong side of the gawdamn canyon! You
know what? That's yer problem right there! It's always about
you! Well, I'm sick of it!

No time to chat! Maev's already jumped down, run to
the nearest pillar an started reefin out the handrope from
the fallen bridge. You got some thin cord there? she calls
to me.

Nettlecord! I says.

Tie it to a arrow an shoot it over! she yells. We're gonna make a rope slide!

I rush to Tracker. Slip the nettlecord from around his neck, fumble to tie it to one of my arrows.

I see what her plan is. The handrope's still tied firm to the pillar on their side. She'll tie the end of the handrope to the nettlecord an shoot my arrow back to me. I'll tie the handrope to one of the pillars on my side. They can slide across to join me.

Maev's shoutin, Lugh! Tommo! Emmi! Yer gonna hafta hold 'em off while we do this! Take cover! Move!

The three of 'em's bin sat there in shock. But now they shift. Fast. They leap from their horses an rush to duck behind the rocks that edge the canyon.

The cord's ready. I nock the arrow. I shoot. It flies over an sticks into the ground, right at Maev's feet. She grabs it. Starts tyin the end of the handrope to the end of the cord. On my side, Tracker's barkin his head off. Nero's flyin back an forth, squawkin an callin.

Hurry up! cries Emmi.

By now, Lugh's figgered out Maev's plan too. It ain't gonna work, he says. The rope's too heavy. It won't make it to Saba.

Maev keeps workin as she says, Thanks fer that, Lugh, very helpful. You got a better idea? I thought not. Right, I'm ready here. You ready, Saba?

Ready! I call.

She loads the arrow onto her bow. The cord tied to the arrow. The handrope tied to the cord. Then she shoots. She aims high in the air. It arcs into the clear blue sky.

It so nearly makes it.

But Lugh's right. The rope's too heavy. We all watch as the arrow—a whistle shy of makin land on my side—falls outta the sky. I fling myself onto my stummick an lean over the edge. It's snagged on a bush that's growin outta the canyon wall, ten foot below me.

I look at them. They look at me. Maev goes to tug at the handrope.

No, wait! I says. Wait! Nero! I whistle fer him, pointin down at the bush. He sweeps down an lands on it. Looks at the arrow, then up at me with his clever black eyes. That's right, git the cord! I says. Bring me the cord, Nero.

He starts workin the arrow free with his beak.

The ground rumbles. Riders approach. The drumbeats grow ever louder.

They're here! yells Tommo.

Weapons! yells Maev.

They all load their bows. I scramble to my feet an do the same.

Look out fer the blowdarts! I yell.

Saba! I'm afeared! cries Emmi.

If you are, you ain't no sister of mine! I shout. Come at me agin!

I ain't afeared of nuthin! she yells.

That's more like it!

The headhunters ride into view. A dozen men. But not on horseback.

On bird back.

They're ridin birds.

Not flyin birds. Runnin birds. Huge. Eight foot tall. With black feathers an short white tails. Long, powerful legs. Big two-clawed feet. Small heads on top of long, stretched necks.

Like their temple firekeeper, these hunters is painted white over their entire body. Black slashes over their eyes an mouths. The rag strips that cover 'em whip in the wind of their ride. On their heads they wear helmets made from human skulls. A long black horsetail hangs down their backs. Some of 'em clutch spears, others ready their blowguns. Hatchets hang from their waists.

The drummer's at the back, two skinboxes slung eether side of his bird. He urges the hunters on, beatin fast with his heels. When they spot us, they start to make this fearsome noise. A high-pitched, endless yip. Uhluhluhluhla! Uhluhluhluhla!

Aim fer the birds! cries Maev. Go fer the necks!

The hunters race towards us.

Hold! yells Maev.

They're closer. That crazy war shriekin stands my hair on end.

Hold! she cries.

Closer.

Hold!

Then,

Fire! yells Maev.

One, two, three, four. I zing off the shots. Fast. Strong. My bow sings wild an sweet. I'm thirty foot back this side of the Gap, but my bow puts me right there. I bring down a bird. Two riders. They cry out as they tumble to death. A squawk, a flutter, an Nero lands at my feet. He drops the arrow with the nettlecord attached. I haul the string up an grab the rope the second it comes into view.

I got it, Maev! I yell.

I run to the nearest bridge pillar. I loop the rope around, make a slipknot an haul on it till it starts to pull taut. Till it stretches tight over the canyon gap. There's a little downslope on it. I tie the rope off.

We got us a rope slide.

Ready! I shout.

While I bin fixin the slide, Maev's bin gettin Em ready. Wrappin her belt around both her wrists, loopin it over the rope slide an bucklin it tight. Now she takes her by the waist, they yell, one, two, three!, an they're runnin to the canyon's edge an Maev gives her a shove.

Over the canyon flies Em, screamin all the way. I catch her at this side an set her free.

Keep shootin, Em, I says. We both fire away while Maev

sets Tommo on the slide with his belt. He comes hurtlin over the canyon so fast, he almost bowls me over.

Then there's the three of us—me, Emmi an Tommo—shootin from this side, with Maev an Lugh on th'other. Between us, we brought down half of the headhunters an a couple of the birds.

Lugh! shouts Maev. C'mon!

He hesitates. He'll hafta cross open ground to git to her.

Keep low! Move, gawdammit! she yells.

He makes a dash fer it, skippin an dodgin as spears an darts fly at him.

Stay down, yer too high! I yell.

There's one headhunter who's bin shoutin at everybody, tellin 'em what to do. Now he aims his blowgun at Lugh.

I see. I shoot him. A heartstrike. He tumbles dead from his bird. But he blew his dart. It hits Lugh in the arm. He keeps runnin. Probly didn't even feel it. He slides across the canyon. Tommo helps him offa the rope.

You bin hit! Pull it out! I says to him.

He sees the dart fer the first time. Yanks it out.

Then it's jest Maev left on th'other side. As we keep firin on the hunters, we're all yellin at her, C'mon! What're you waitin fer?

She's yellin somethin back.

What's she sayin? says Emmi.

She ain't got no belt, I says.

Cain't git across, says Tommo. She's trapped!

Maev, I yell, look out!

A headhunter runs at her, hatchet held high. Uhluhluhluhla! Maev whirls around an bends over. He tumbles over her back into thin air. He plunges to the bottom of the canyon, screamin all the way.

He's dropped his hatchet. Maev seizes it, takes hold of the rope with one hand an chops it free of the pillar. She runs at the edge. Swings herself across the Gap.

The hunters beat a retreat. They scoop up their dead, grab our horses an take off on their birds, back the way they come.

Then they're gone. That's it. Over.

Maev's bashed into this side of the canyon. She's hangin on the rope, startin to climb. Me an Tommo rush to help pull her up. She scrambles to her feet. Shakes her head at me. You don't make things easy, do you? she says.

They got Lugh in the arm, I says. Blowdart.

He's standin there, half outta his shirt, lookin at where it went in. There's a raised red welt on his upper right arm. Don't fuss me, he says.

Emmi, I says, where's the medicine bag?

She keeps it around her waist. She's already emptied it on the ground, sortin through little brown bottles an bags of herbs. I know what to use, she says. But we gotta git the poison out first.

I'll do it, says Maev. You got sage water, Em?

While they clean Maev's knife, me an Tommo sit Lugh down. We each take one of his hands. Grip hard, I tell him. He does.

Maev kneels beside him, knife at the ready. I'm sorry, she says. This is gonna hurt.

Jest do it, he tells her. As she cuts his flesh, as she slices a cross into his skin, he don't make a sound. But he almost crushes my hand.

Maev puts her mouth to the wound. She sucks out the poison an spits it on the ground. Agin an agin, till she's got it all out.

Done, she says an stands up. I'll see if Emmi needs some help.

Maev, says Lugh.

Yeah?

Thank you, he says. Yer . . . yer amazin. Jest now an . . . before too. I ain't never seen nuthin like it. You saved our lives. Their eyes meet. Briefly. But it's enough to kick a pink flush into her cheeks. A little smile onto her lips. Her an Tommo go over to Em.

Then it's jest me an Lugh. I'm still kneelin beside him, still holdin his hand. He looks straight ahead. His lips press together, his fingers twitch, his whole body quivers. He's in shock. From the ride, from the fight, from his injury.

I'm sorry I left like that, I says. Without sayin nuthin, I mean. But I had to. You would of stopped me an Jack needs

189

me. He sent fer me, Lugh, he's in trouble. He did send a message, I worked it out. I gotta meet him at the Lost Cause by the next full moon.

He turns his head an looks at me. I flinch. Not shock. Rage, sharp an white, hardens him. He yanks up our joined hands. Holds 'em in front of our faces.

We used to breathe together, you an me. We used to think the same thoughts. Feel the same feelins. Walk in each other's footsteps. The only reason we survived was becuz we had each other.

His voice lashes around me, tight an quick an low. With every word, his hand tightens on mine. Bit by bit, till the pain flashes red inside my head.

It warn't all that long ago, he says. Remember?

Yes, I gasp.

You knew I'd follow you, becuz you'd of done the same, he says. If it warn't fer Maev, we'd be dead by now. I'd be dead. An all becuz of Jack. All fer Jack. A man you hardly know. The man who helped kill yer friends.

I cry out with pain fer my hand. Stare into his eyes.

Tell me, Saba, he says. Does it hurt?

Yes, I whisper.

Yes, he says.

He lets go my hand. I cradle it to my chest. It throbs as the blood starts to flow. It's gonna be bruised. Lugh goes over to have Emmi doctor his wound.

They all bin watchin us. Nobody meets my eyes.

Fine.

Let him hate me.

Let 'em all hate me. The most important thing is, I'm where I wanna be. Where I need to be. An that's here. In Tonton territory. In New Eden. Headed fer the Lost Cause. Headed fer Jack.

✝   ✝   ✝

There's only one trail leadin away from the Gap. It goes into the trees.

I stick my knife in my boot, shoulder my bow an quiver an hang my waterskin on my belt. Then I whistle fer Nero an, with Tracker at my heels, I make fer the trail. When I git to th'others, I stop an says,

I gotta make tracks. I gotta be at the Lost Cause by the full moon.

That's two nights from now, says Maev. You got no idea how far it is or where it is. It ain't possible.

I smile to myself. What would Jack say now? It ain't impossible, I says. Nuthin's impossible.

You fergot Hermes, says Emmi.

It's my fault yer here, I says. That you lost yer gear an

yer horses. I'm sorry about that. More sorry'n I can say. I'll leave him an the rest of my stuff with you. You four can find another route outta here, back to the Snake. Head out west. Jack an me'll find you.

You cain't go on foot, says Maev.

I'll steal a horse along the way, I says. See yuz.

We squeeze along the path, me an Tracker. I duck unner low-hangin branches. Growth crowds in from both sides. It don't look like nobody passes this way much. Nero flits from branch to branch.

Wait up! Maev comes crashin after me. Mind if I tag along? she says.

You ain't got no love fer Jack, I says.

He's a gawdamn know-it-all, she says.

So'm I, I says. So're you, fer that matter.

Ezzackly, she says, he reminds too much of myself.

What he said to you, Maev, that was the message, I says. You've lost an yer the cause of it. So full of pride. You should of seen us comin by the moon, had more'n three on watch. It means, meet me at the Lost Cause at the next full moon. The rule of three.

Huh, she says. Smart. Well, yer set on goin an here we are. I ain't gonna let you go by yerself. There may well be more to this Jack thing than meets the eye. Anyways, she says—her tone oh-so-casual—I got me some vengeance to wreak with the Tonton.

An there it is, the real reason she wants to come with me.

I wish you'd speak to Lugh about Jack, I says. When I do, he don't hear what I say.

You don't git it, do you? she says. The way he sees it, while he was weak an helpless, Jack stole what belonged to him. You.

I stop. Turn to stare at her. Nobody stole me, I says. Lugh don't own me.

Try tellin him that, she says. An while yer at it, tell yerself.

I'll tell you to shut the hell up, I says. I go on, shovin my way along the overgrown path.

We better find some horses quick, she says. Two days ain't long to git to a place when you don't know where it is.

Saba! Emmi comes runnin after us. Lugh says you gotta come back, she cries. He says we gotta talk things over, make a plan.

He's got a tongue in his head, he can tell me hisself, I says.

Oh, he ain't speakin to you. She joins in behind Maev. Where're we goin?

The path comes outta the trees. We're standin on a little ridge. The land sprawls in front of us. What used to be a wooded plain with lakes, an mountains in the far distance. But the trees got some kinda blight—they're jest dried red sticks, trunks, branches, needles an all. Sad memories of trees, that's all they are now. The remains of Wrecker light towers here an there. We can see the trail cuttin pretty much straight across.

One road only. Headed one way. East.

I dunno where yer goin, I says. But I'm goin that way.

Hey! Lugh shouts from the trees behind us. Hey! He barrels up to me, his face a black cloud. Tommo's like a worried dog at his heels, leadin Hermes along.

I thought you warn't speakin to me, I says.

I ain't, he says. An you ain't takin another step till we got a plan.

I start to move down the ridge. Tracker an Maev follow. I got a plan, I says. I'm goin to the Lost Cause.

You got no idea where it is, says Lugh. It could be anywhere.

It's in the storm belt, I says. Lilith told me. Anyways, I didn't know where you was, but I managed to find you okay.

That's true, says Emmi.

Lugh stands at the top of the ridge, hands on his hips. He glares down at me an Maev. We keep on goin. You ain't got no horses, he calls.

We'll git us some! We'll steal us some! I call back to him. Go back to the Snake, Lugh. Take Hermes an Emmi an Tommo. Go back. I got a price on my head, I ain't safe company.

I knew there was a reason I liked you, says Maev.

We slip-slide through some scree the last few foot to the bottom of the ridge. We start runnin the moment we hit flat ground. Lugh's angry shout follows us. Saba! Come back here right now! Saba!

We set off across the plain, at a run.

† † †

Tracker feels it first. The rumble of hoofs behind us. We ain't bin runnin more'n a few minutes. He stops, looks back the way we jest come. He barks. Me an Maev stop too. Dammit anyways, I says.

Don't pretend yer surprised, she says.

Nero lands on my shoulder. We wait.

I don't want 'em to come. Truly I don't. It 'ud be best fer everybody if they jest did what I told 'em to.

Hermes gallops into view. He's got Emmi an Tommo on his back.

Saba! yells Emmi. Maev!

Hermes trots up an pushes his nose at my head.

Where is he? I says.

He's comin, says Tommo. He says he ain't bloody runnin.

They stare at me. I stare at them. They don't look happy. I don't s'pose I do.

We're comin with you, says Emmi.

You don't say, I says.

NEW EDEN

WE WALK EAST IN SILENCE.

Lugh's decided to stick with bein mad at me. It's like travelin with a storm cloud. One of them ones that hangs low an heavy. The kind that builds an broods an keeps on buildin an broodin till everybody's got a sick headache. I ignore him. Me an Maev keep the pace fast. Emmi rides on Hermes. Tommo keeps in with Lugh.

We gotta git some transport soon. But we don't meet nobody. No sight of no homesteads or settlements. Jest this endless forest of dead red trees.

Emmi tries to make cheery conversation with one or other of us. But she only gits a grunt or silence in reply, an it ain't long before she gives up. By mid-mornin, we bin walkin at least five hours. Lugh's the first to break.

We'll git us some horses! He says it in that sarcastical voice of his that I hate. We'll steal some! Gee, Saba, what horses should we take? There's so many to choose from!

Shut up, I says.

You shut up, he says. You an yer stupid ideas.

If it's so stupid, then why're you here? I says. Why'd you come, Lugh?

Becuz yer gonna find out that I'm right about Jack, he says. An when you do, yer gonna need me to pick you up offa the ground.

Go to hell, I says.

Don't need to, he says. I'm already there.

✝   ✝   ✝

Midday. A fierce orange sun fries the land. We come to a crossroads with a couple of crabby old sourfruit trees. They're about the only livin things we've seen since startin on this road. We argue the toss over which way to go. While they're still at it, I strike out east. Always east.

Somebody's yellin. Lugh. I break stride. Stop an turn around. He's still at the crossroads, wavin his arms over his head an shoutin at me. We glare at each other long distance. At last, with a curse, I trot back to see what's what.

Everybody's sat or flopped down in the shade of the trees.

What're you doin? I says. C'mon, git up!

I'm callin a rest, says Lugh. We're tired an hungry an thirsty. You are too, if you'd only admit it. But yer so damn stubborn, you'd sooner walk yerself to death.

We ain't got time, I says.

Too bad, he says.

All right, I says, but five minutes. No more.

I'll say when, he says.

I'll say when! says Maev. Fergawdsake.

I throw Lugh a look. I don't sit. I give my hot face an sweaty neck a swipe with my kercheef. Tommo shares out the eatables from my saddlebags. Dried deer strips, a few twists of berry jerky an a handful of hazelnuts. He portions out half an puts the rest aside fer later. It makes a poor meal, hardly worth the effort of chewin, but we do. I give Tracker my deer strip, but the other two beasts gotta settle fer what there is. Hermes tears at the sad-lookin grass. Nero nibbles the wormy sourfruit.

A gritty hotwind blows from the south. The sky's white an sharp an melts into heavy walls. Nobody speaks. We pull our sheemas low. Rub fat into our dry lips.

I pace back an forth. A naggin little voice starts up inside me. Pretty soon, it's shoutin so loud I'm surprised nobody else can hear it.

Go! it yells. Go! Go! Go! Jack's in trouble. He needs you. Take off on Hermes. Now! They cain't stop you. Go on, do it!

It's shameful. I know it. It's my fault they're here. It's me that's put 'em all in danger, nobody else. Still.

Go on! Take off! What're they gonna do, shoot you?

Don't even think about it, says Lugh.

Huh? I says.

What yer thinkin about doin, he says. You think I dunno what yer thinkin, but yer thinkin it so loud, I can hear you thinkin it. Don't even think about it.

I ain't thinkin about nuthin, I says.

Oh, yes, you are, he says.

Am not.

Are too.

Hey! I glare at him. I know very well what's goin on in my own head. Too bad some other people I know cain't say the same.

What's that s'posed to mean? he says.

Would you shut up? says Maev. Jest shut up! Yer drivin us all crazy!

What's the matter with Tommo? says Emmi.

He's dropped into a crouch on the trail. Laid his hands flat on the ground. He looks up. Wheels, he says. From the north. A wagon, headed this way. An a horse or maybe—

I grab his arm. How many horses, Tommo? How many?

One, he says. I think one. An a wagon.

Is it the Tonton? says Emmi.

They don't usually travel alone, says Maev.

The north road bends outta sight through the red tree forest. That's the way they're gonna come from. We look around fer cover. The two sourfruit trees. Scattered boulders. A light tower. There's one big slab of rock that stands between the crossroads an the bend in the north road. Whoever's comin, they're gonna hafta pass right by it.

I'm lookin at Maev. She's lookin at me.

Let's do it, she says.

Do what? says Lugh.

I'm game, I says to Maev.

Game fer what? says Lugh. What're you talkin about?

We need transport, says Maev, we're gonna git us some transport. On my signal, Saba an Lugh grab the horse. Tommo an Emmi cover the rear. I'll take care of the driver. If I don't like the look of it, we don't go. Okay, everybody outta sight. Weapons ready. Move on my word.

While she's bin talkin, she's swung herself onto Hermes an yanked her sheema down to her eyes. Now she pulls her kercheef up to cover her mouth an nose.

Hang on, says Lugh. There could be one horse, there could be ten.

Not ten, says Tommo.

Five then! We got no idea how many. We dunno who it is. You cain't jest go rushin at things without thinkin it through. We need to talk about this! He grabs Hermes' bridle.

Maev yanks down her kercheef. No, you need to listen, she says. This ain't Silverlake, an you ain't the daddy. Out here in the real world, the person who knows what they're doin is the daddy an right now, that's me. So. Do like daddy says an shift that tasty butt of yers. Unless, of course, you want it shot off.

She heels Hermes an they gallop into position behind the rock slab. I yank Lugh behind a boulder. He's red-faced. Tight lipped. His eyes spit blue fire.

Who does she think she is? he says. Hell, I don't even

know what she's talkin about—I ain't the daddy. I tell you, I am sick to death of bossy women an that includes you.

You ever hijacked before? I says. Stole a horse?

You know I never! But that ain't the point, the—

The point is to git to The Lost Cause by the full moon, I says. The point is that Maev knows what she's doin. Highway robbery, hijackin an horse stealin, that's her business.

An my business is keepin us alive, he says. You an me an Emmi. Th'other two can go hang fer all I care. I don't believe you, Saba. We was on our way to a good life. We had it in our sights. Now look at us.

C'mon, I says, you gotta admit this is excitin.

Not in my book, it ain't, he says.

Not like takin chaal, huh? I says. Not like what you got up to with that Meg?

I win with that shot. He looks away. Busies hisself coverin his face with his sheema an kercheef.

I do the same. We wait. Whoever it is, they ain't travelin fast.

But the slow rumble of wheels gits louder. Louder still. I keep watch from behind our boulder. My belly's tight with anticipation. A yellow cart lumbers into view. It's bein pulled by—

It's a gawdamn camel! hisses Lugh.

A fleabit wreck of a camel, shamblin along in front of the rickety cart.

The driver's singin. As he gits closer, we can hear the words.

She was queen of my heart all that summer
But when green leafs was turnin to gold
She slipped from my arms as a new day dawned
An left my heart broken an cold.

They're nearly on us.

Heeya! yells Maev. She heels Hermes. They dash onto the trail, in front of the cart. Hermes rears, squealin. Maev grips with her knees, a bolt shooter in each hand.

The driver hauls mightily on the reins. Whoa! he yells. Whoa there, Moses!

The camel bellows. He tramples an shies as he tries to avoid Hermes. Me an Lugh grab at his reins. Dust flies everywhere. The cart rocks, tips, then starts to settle. The driver reaches towards his feet.

Hands up or I'll shoot! shouts Maev.

He freezes. He sits up slowly, raisin his hands over his head.

Meantime, me an Lugh's bin draggin on the camel's bridle with all our weight. He resists, hollerin an spittin an rollin his eyes. Suddenly, without warnin, he sits down. We go flyin. But we're right back up, on our feet, grabbin our bows. We aim at the driver.

The cart's a high-sided wooden box, painted bright yellow, with suns an moons an stars all over. It's a ramshackle effort, lashed up with ropes an chains. It leans to one side. Two lanterns hang at the front. There's a little door at the back.

Tommo throws it open an checks inside. All clear, he calls to Maev.

She smiles at the driver. Stand an deliver, she says.

† † †

The driver stares at us. We stare at him.

He's a one-eyed, big-bellied, bald-headed old coot. With a filthy eyepatch, bushy sidewhiskers an a neck like a bullfrog. He's wearin a pink lady dress.

This is a hijack, sir, says Maev. We'll be takin yer cart an yer camel.

An if I say no? His voice creaks, like a rusted hinge.

Then I kill you, she says. We still take yer cart an yer camel but you won't be wavin us off. Climb on down. My associate here'll be happy to help you. We got you covered, so don't try nuthin.

She motions with her shooter to Lugh. He blasts her with a tight-lipped glare. But he shoulders his bow an gives his hand to the driver.

The old fella's bulky. He wheezes an grimaces as he squeezes hisself out from the driver's bench. As he climbs down, he leans on Lugh so heavy that they nearly collapse in a heap. I find the driver's firestick an toss it to Tommo.

206

Maev's jumped offa Hermes. Search him, she tells Lugh.

Do it yerself, he says.

The driver grins. Mutiny in the ranks, eh?

Shut up, I says. I pat him down. He's clean, I says.

You ever handled a camel before? he says.

His name's Moses, right? says Maev. We'll take good care of him, sir, don't worry.

Oh, I ain't worried, he says.

See what he's got in the rig, she tells me.

Beggin yer pardon, sister, he says, but the Cosmic Compendalorium ain't no ordinary rig. If you'll allow me—?

Make it snappy, she says.

The cart opens on both sides. He unties the right-side rope. Scuttles back as it swings down with a crash. It's a big cupboard, with shelves an drawers, crammed full of bottles an tins an jars of all descriptions an sizes.

A quack van, I says.

The driver counts off his stock briskly. Curatives, restoratives, prevellatives an laxatives, he says. Embarkations, emoluments an emetics. Oils an ointments, teas an tonics, powders an potions an pills. He takes a deep breath an goes on. I'll leech you, purge you, shave yer corns, test yer stools an worm yer guts. I cut hair, set bones, pull teeth an lance boils. I provide a complete eyecare service with a wide selection of spectaculars, an marriage guidance on a confidentiality basis. Doctor Salmo Slim, TPS. That's Travellatin Physician an Surgeon.

Like I said, a quack. I lift the side an tie it back into place.

Excuse me! He draws hisself up. You imprune my honor, sister. I come from a long line of medical perfessionals, startin with the legendary Sasaparilla Slim, way back in Babalingian times.

Save the spiel fer the mugs, says Maev. You young 'uns, hop in back.

Emmi scrinches her face. Do we hafta? she says.

Don't squawk, git in, says Maev. I'll drive.

No, I'm drivin. Lugh pushes past her an climbs in the front. You can ride shotgun.

You ever drove a camel before? she snaps. He shoots her a death look, but slides into the shotgun seat.

We ain't no savages, sir, Maev says to the driver, we'll leave you water an a weapon up the trail a ways.

Much obliged, he says.

She says, Fer a man about to lose his livelihood, yer calm does you credit.

He shrugs. Occupational hazard. No point gittin my knickers in a twist. Not that I wear none.

No hard feelins?

Not on my part. Say la vee, sister.

That's it, she says, slick as a whistle. We're outta here.

Emmi an Tommo clamber inside the Cosmic Compendalorium. I swing myself onto Hermes. Maev jumps in the driver's seat next to Lugh. She picks up the reins, an slaps 'em down on the camel sayin, Gee up there, Moses! Gee up!

He turns his head. Gives her a long, hard stare. Then he turns back an starts chewin calmly on his cud.

Lugh looks at Maev. Slick as a whistle, he says.

They climb down. They haul on the bridle. Pull the reins. Then they put their backs into it. They lean aginst his rear end an shove.

An all the time, Lugh's goin, Yer the boss, Maev. Yer the daddy. Maev knows what she's doin, Lugh. Hijackin an horse stealin's her business. Newsflash, girls. This ain't no horse. It's a gawdamn camel!

Shut up an push! she yells.

Fergawdsake, I says, how hard can it be? Emmi! Tommo! Come help!

They pile outta the back. Tracker barks. Nero dives an shrieks. But Moses don't budge. He bawls his head off, spittin an snappin with his vicious yellow teeth.

Ow! Lugh yells. He reels away, his hand clamped on his upper arm. Damn thing bit me! He curses an stamps his foot in pain.

The driver's jest standin there, watchin. Let me know if you need any help, he calls.

Gawdamn sonofabitch, I mutter. I leap offa Hermes an go fer the driver. I walk fast, loadin my bow, aimin it straight at his face. He throws his hands up. I stop three paces away.

Yer wastin my time, big man, I says. Git this beast on his

feet. Yer gonna take us where we wanna go.

Okay, okay, he says, keep yer shirt on, sister.

Move! I keep my bow trained on him as he waddles over to the camel.

Moses! he says, flappin his hands. Stand up, sir! Arise an walk, ye son of Egypt!

Right away, the stupid thing starts to git to its feet.

Yer drivin, I says.

He clambers onto the driver's bench. I squeeze in beside him.

Maev's pink-cheeked. Humiliated. The hard-girl hijacker, suckered by a camel. Without a word, she tosses me her bolt shooter an climbs into the back with Tommo an Tracker.

I don't believe this, says Lugh. He swings hisself onto Hermes. Lifts Emmi to ride in front of him.

I look at the driver. What're you waitin fer? I says. Move.

If I'm gonna take you where you wanna go, he says, you'll hafta tell me where that is. His one good eye blinks at me, pale an watery.

Oh no, you don't catch me that easy.

Where was you headed jest now? I says. My sheema starts to slip back from my face. My tattoo. Don't let him see. I yank it into place, scowl at him. Well? I says.

East, he says. We got a delivery to make in the storm belt. A tavern called The Lost Cause.

My stummick flips. That'll do to start with, says I. How far?

Three, maybe four days, says he.

Make it two, an I'll let you keep that eye of yers.

Two it is, he says.

†   †   †

The Cosmic Compendalorium rattles along. After we cover a couple of miles, the driver clears his throat.

You got me at a disadvantage, he says, moniker-wise, that is. You know my name. Doctor Salmo Slim TPS at yer service. Feel free to call me Slim. Might I have the pleasure of knowin who's hijacked me?

I says naught. I got one boot braced aginst the buckboard. Nero sits in my lap. He's bin givin the driver the beady eye since we set off.

That's a handsome bird, says Slim. Tame crow's, uh . . . unusual. Don't s'pose he has a name.

Nero, I says.

Nero stretches over. Flicks the pink dress with his beak an croaks.

Ha! says Slim. You wanna know about the dress, do you? I admit, it ain't every day you see a fella in a frock. It's a cautionary tale, friend Nero. A story of laundry an hard likker. Must be a week ago now. I warshed my clothes, britches an shirt, once a year like I always do. Rigged up a couple of branches, y'know . . . to hang it on, right next to the fire so's it 'ud be dry in the mornin. Well, you know how it is. I must of necked a little too much pop an passed out. Next thing you know, the gawdamn sun's up an my laundry's burnt to buggery. The whole shebang fell on the fire. Lucky I had the dress—it was my late mother's, bin keepin it fer sensamental reasons—otherwise I'd be sittin here in my birthday suit. Mind you, if I was, you might of thought twice about hijackin me, eh? Ha ha! Wouldn't that of bin a sight! Hooee!

Slim hoots an wheezes an cackles. Nero copies him, bobbin up an down, crow-laughin.

Well, don't lay a egg, I says.

Thing is, he says, in my line of work, you spend a lot of time sittin. A dress lets the breeze up . . . cool yer dingles down. There's a lot to be said fer a skirt.

I give him a look. We go on fer a bit, then he says, So, yer all headed to the Lost Cause.

Yer headed there, I says. We're jest hitchin a ride that far.

You know these parts pretty well? he says.

I says naught.

New Eden ain't no place fer travelers, he says. Let's hope we don't run into the Tonton.

Oh? I says.

New Eden's their land, they control it top to bottom, includin the roads. There's guardposts an pretty regular patrols. They stop everybody, check you got the right marks. Quartered circle brands fer Stewards of the Earth, slaves wear iron collars, an the rest of us git one of these. He shoves up his right sleeve, shows me a line of five small circles on the outside of his arm. Naw, he says, we don't wanna be stopped by them boys.

I aim my bolt shooter at his temple. Then you'll jest make sure we don't, I says.

We'll take the back roads, he says.

We go on fer a bit more. Then he says, They cleared out all the old folk, the sick, an the weak. Some people packed up an left—I know a fair few that headed out west. There's always one or two prepared to stand their ground, try to keep their land, but they're all worms' meat now, so much good it did 'em.

How come they let you stay? I says.

I'm useful to 'em, he says. I got special skills, knowledge handed down the ages. On the medicine side there's me, Doctor Wong an a sawbones called Hollis. We divide the territory between us. By the way, if you ever git gangrene, don't let Hollis nowhere near you. Cut off yer own leg, you'll be better off. Let's see, who else . . . ? A bunch of junkjimmies, of course—it never ceases to amaze me what them boys can make outta Wrecker junk. Uh . . . that's about it. Yuh, strong workers an healthy breeders is what they want most.

Breeders? I says.

Of course, he says. The Pathfinder's makin a new world. An only the right kinda people's allowed to live in it. If you don't wanna find yerself workin the land an breedin fer New Eden, you better watch yerself, you an yer friends. Yer jest what he's after.

The Pathfinder, I says, pretendin like I never heard of him.

That's the top man, he says. He's a great thinker, he has, uh . . . whaddya call 'em? . . . visions.

You ever met him? I says.

Me? Not likely, says Slim. Although I heard he rides with his men sometimes, slips in among 'em without their knowin, so maybe I seen him somewhere. Maybe he stopped me at some guardpost. Maybe—

Maybe you could stop talkin fer a bit, I says. You make my ears hurt.

He cain't stay silent fer long. Five of you, he says, only one horse. Makes me think you might of run into trouble somewhere. You didn't by any chance come over the Yann Gap?

We might of, I says.

You mean, you made it past them crazy skull collectors? he says.

Uh huh, I says.

Ha! He slaps his knee. Well, I'll be damned! Yer quite the thing, sister. I tell you, them weirdos has bin causin trouble there ferever an day. They caught my cousin Lister, oh, must be ten year back now. He was okay, Lister, fer a relation, essept he never knew when to shut up. Despitin that, I wouldn't of minded so much if he hadn't of bin wearin my best hat at the time. He borrowed it without tellin me. No, somebody oughta do somethin about that Yann Gap bridge.

I did, I says. It's gone.

He looks at me. Shakes his head an grins. Ha ha! Well, whaddya know! I give you my personal thanks, on behalf of cousin Lister an my best hat. You wanna be at the Lost Cause in two days? I'll git you there, by gum, I will.

Not at this pace, you won't, I says. Don't this mangy beast of yers go no faster?

You ever heard the old sayin, never judge a book by its cover?

No, I says.

Well, hang onto yer girdle, he says. Then he yells, Yeeha! an slaps the reins down.

Moses goes off like a shot. A startled squawk an Nero takes to the air. I only jest stop myself tumblin out by grabbin Slim.

He flashes me a yellow-toothed grin. Grand Champeen of the Pillawalla Camel Race! he shouts. Five years runnin! His bloodline goes back to the Great Pyramid of Egypt!

As the Cosmic Compendalorium rackets along in a cloud of dust, Slim starts to holler out a song. His voice rasps through the day like a rusty saw.

Oh, chase me, Suzie, run around town
Catch me, tickle me, tie me down
If you shiver my shanks, I'll buy you a gown . . .
But I'll be gone in the mornin a-rovin!

† † †

We leave the red blight forests behind. We ford wide brown rivers, shallow an sluggish. Skirt around the southern end of a giant, dyin lake. The sharp pong scours our noses. Makes our eyes water an our hair stand on end. The sticky white shore's alive with tiny flies that rise in black clouds as we pass. The iron skellentons of Wrecker buildins litter the shoreline.

We don't run into no Tonton, on patrol or otherwise. There's a small garrison at the top of the lake, Slim tells me, some fifteen leagues north. Why they're here is anybody's guess. They might of found a Wrecker mine site that's still got work in it. All he knows is, they don't patrol this far down. He says we shouldn't hafta worry about patrols an guardposts till tomorrow. But I'll keep us outta their way, he says. I know all the byways an I know the ways of the men in black.

I'd sooner be back in the Waste than here. It ain't till daylight starts to wane that we see the end of it. An then, the sight, the smell of livin trees—juniper, jack pine an fir—the sound of clean, runnin water, come as sweet, merciful relief. Like a cool hand on a brow hot with fever. Slim slows the Cosmic down an turns it off the trail into a little clearin.

What're you doin? I says. Drive on.

We gotta take a break, says Slim. Moses needs a rest. Yer horse does too, I'll warrant. We'll be safe here.

I press the shooter to his temple. I said, drive on, I says.

Slim raises his hands. Hey, hey! Calm down, sister. I said I'd git you to the Lost Cause in good time an I will. I aim to keep this eye of mine.

The man's right, says Lugh. You know he is. We gotta rest.

I'm numb with tiredness. We gotta keep goin, I says.

Don't be crazy, he says. When was the last time you slept?

As he says it, I try to think. Must of bin . . . no, I cain't think when. Weariness circles me, rubs itself aginst me, warm an friendly. I mustn't give in to it.

You cain't even remember, says Lugh.

He's dismounted an plucked Emmi from Hermes' back. Maev an Tommo's clambered outta the back of the Cosmic. I look at everybody's drawn faces.

Okay, three hours, I says.

Four, says Lugh.

At least, says Slim. You gotta be sharp here. Alert. Ready fer anythin. An it's plain foolish not to rest yer beasts proper.

All right, four, I says. But not a moment longer.

I'm talkin to myself. Everybody's bustlin around, helpin Slim set up camp an light a fire. I climb down from the Cosmic, stiff an sore all over. As I ease my back an rub my achin behind, I think, gimme a horse over a cart any day. I felt every bump of that damn road.

I stand apart. Exhausted but jangly. Like I don't know what to do with myself, how to be, once I stop movin.

Maev comes over. She glances at Slim, jibber jabberin to Emmi. He talks a lot, she says, but he don't say much. Makes you wonder.

I know, I says. Don't worry, I got my eye on him.

She crosses her arms on her chest. Stubs her boot into the ground.

Somethin on yer mind? I says.

I cocked things up today, she says. Talk about Jack bein a know-all, I take the cake. Any fool could of seen that stupid camel wouldn't move fer nobody but Slim. What the hell's wrong with me?

Well, you punished yerself, I says. You rode inside the cart all day.

It's the least I deserve, she says. I've lost my edge.

C'mon, Maev, I says. What about today? Back at the Gap? Gittin everybody across like that, fightin them headhunters . . . that was quite somethin.

She brightens. It was kinda fun, she says. She glances over at Lugh. He crouches, layin the fire. He must feel us watchin him becuz he looks up. Jest fer a moment, then he goes back to what he's doin. I was showin off, says Maev. Pathetic. Like some kid, wantin him to notice me.

Oh, he notices you, I says, never fear. You saved their lives, Maev. They was in danger—you all was—becuz of me. If anybody's lost their edge, it's me. You done good.

Well, at least I got their three lives to my credit, she says. But it don't make up fer what happened at Darktrees. Fer the Hawks an the Raiders. Nuthin ever will. If only I hadn't of bin so arrogant. If only I'd of listened to Ash an Creed. They kept sayin we should leave, but I wouldn't. Forty lives, Saba. My friends. Dead becuz of me. That's hard to live with.

It don't serve nobody to keep count, I says.

Oh, but it does, she says. I must. Every single one eats at me. Every time I close my eyes, I see their faces. They walk in my dreams.

I know, I says.

Ruby, she says. Taz. Ash. Creed. Jest thinkin their names feels like knives in my heart. So that's what I do. I think their names, over an over an over agin. I need to keep the pain sharp. Till I can make amends fer what I did. Maybe then I'll be able to sleep.

Maybe, I says.

We're quiet, then I says, D'you ever feel old, Maev?

I was born old, she says.

Her an me look at each other a long moment. Then she

nods an heads over to the fire. She passes Tommo on the way.

He stands in front of me. Gimme yer hand, he says. I hesitate. Then I hold out my right hand. The one that Lugh crushed in his anger an hurt. It's tender. Bruised.

Slim gimme this, says Tommo, as he unscrews the lid of a little pot an scoops out some goatweed unction. He takes my hand an starts to spread it over the bruise. He only uses one finger. He's so gentle, I feel a lump rise in my throat.

He looks at me. He shouldn't of hurt you, he says.

I hurt him, I says.

He gives a funny little smile. Is that how it works? he says. One hurt fer another? He drops his eyes. Concentrates on what he's doin.

Tommo's eyes was the first thing I ever noticed about him. Such a deep brown, they're almost black, with long dark lashes. Eyes like a deer.

When I first met him, back at Ike's, he was a boy. A pale bony jumble of elbows, knees an feet. He ain't that no more. Somehow, over the past months, he's growed to his man's body. He's tanned an lean. Thick, dark hair tied back from his face. Strong cheekbones. He's good-lookin an no mistake.

The deaf boy. Take heed, Saba. He's in love with you.

He stops what he's doin. He knows I'm starin at him, he can feel it. A flush creeps along his cheekbones. He don't lift his eyes as he raises my hand to his lips. He touches 'em to the bruise. I feel his breath on my skin.

I would never hurt you, he says.

Now he looks at me. He holds my eyes with his. Intent.
Serious.

No. No no no no no.

Tommo, I says.

He takes in a breath.

Jest as Slim calls out, How many eggs? One or two?

✝   ✝   ✝

One of Slim's patients gave him a cured leg of bristleboar
in trade fer yankin out his ingrowed toenail. He carves thick
slices an fries 'em up with pigeon eggs. Everybody waits,
eatin tins at the ready, mouths waterin, while he tends his big
frypan. Tracker crowds so close that he sits on Slim's foot.
He don't move his eyes as Slim turns the meat, spoons fat
over the eggs. His nose twitches. Drool hangs down in long
strings.

Hungry, eh, my friend? says Slim. Don't worry, there's
plenty fer everybody, man an beast. Never heard of a tame
wolfie before. Never heard of one with blue eyes neether. You
had him from a pup?

No, says Emmi. He belongs to our friend Mercy, but we
think she must be dead.

Well, we all gotta die, he says. You jest gotta hope you die good. Some folks wanna go in a blaze of magnificent splendor, like the sun itself. Others pray to go in their sleep. You think about these things when you git to my age. You know when I wisht I'd died?

When? says Emmi.

In my twenny first year, on a soft summer night, by the side of a sweet-runnin stream. I lay with a beautiful girl in my arms. An she told me that she loved me. A moment of pure joy.

That does sound nice, says Em.

Best moment of my life an I didn't even know it, he says. Sometimes that's the way it goes. Okay, grub's up. One line, no shovin.

There's a rush of feet, muttered thanks, then nuthin but the scrape of spoons on metal as we shovel in Slim's tasty food. I try to remember the last time I et. I cain't. My belly groans with relief. When we're done, we swipe our tins clean with our fingers. Emmi lifts hers an starts to lick it with little snufflin noises.

Emmi, fer shame! says Lugh. Yer a girl, not a beast, so don't eat like one. Good grief.

Slim was jest about to lick his too. He froze when Lugh barked at Em. He winks at her an they share a guilty grin. We all put our tins on the ground. Tracker goes around, polishin 'em with his long pink tongue.

Nero caught hisself a mouse earlier. A swoop, a squeak an a swallow. He's already fast to sleep in the branches above, his head tucked unner his wing.

Thanks fer the meal, I says. It's decent of you, considerin.

Even hijackers git hungry, says Slim. He stretches out his legs, settles more comfortable in his low slingchair an starts pickin his teeth with a twig.

You git hijacked much, Slim? says Emmi.

This is my first time, he says. It ain't half bad, neether. I'm glad of the company, Moses don't give much conversation. Nope, despitin our rocky start, this foolish old man is perfectly content.

Is that what you are? I says. A foolish old man?

His one eye gazes at me. Watery. Mild. Not too foolish to know that you don't want this young fella comin to the notice of the Tonton, he says. He nods at Tommo. A boy who cain't hear ain't safe. If they got hold of him, they'd kill him.

Tommo's flushed. His jaw set.

Nobody's gittin hold of Tommo, says Emmi. I'd kill 'em if they even laid a finger on him! She collects the eatin tins to clean.

That's the spirit, he says. You got a fierce champeen here, son.

I ain't yer son, he says. An I can take care of myself.

I'm sure you can. Now . . . I can tell that you three's kin. Slim points his finger at me, Emmi an Lugh. An Red here, well . . .

it 'ud be plain to a blind man how the land lies between you two. You cain't stop lookin at each other. He glances between Lugh an Maev. Oh, don't sit there blushin, he says, git on with it. Life's too short. Take her off in the bushes, my friend, an make her yer own. If you don't, somebody else will. Hell, I might jest make a play fer her myself. That 'ud put a rocket in yer pocket. Ha ha! How's about it, Red? You an me.

Shut yer mouth! Lugh glares murder at Slim. Hot color scorches his cheeks.

Slim jest cackles an slaps his knees. Oh, I hit the mark there! Naw, you ain't my type, Red. I like a hefty hen, a gal with a bit of meat on her. Slim turns to Tommo. As fer you . . . I gotta tell you, you innerest me very much indeed. You ain't no kin to these, you ain't got the look of 'em. Still, yer a helluva handsome boy. Gonna be a real heartbreaker. The moment I laid eyes on you, you put me strongly in mind of somebody. Who spawned you?

Emmi calls over from where she's scourin the eatin tins with pine needles. His pa's dead, she says. His ma too. It was a long time ago, but he don't like to talk about it.

Slim leans in, peers at Tommo by the firelight. I never fergit a face, he says. Cain't afford to in my line of work. Gotta remember who I deal straight with an who I deal crooked. Ha! I see a person once an I remember. The shape of the face, the set of the jaw, noses, eyes. Yuh, I'm sure I seen somebody. Not one of my customers but somewhere on my travels—

Tommo leaps to his feet. My pa's dead! He flings hisself on the ground at the foot of a tree. He curls up, his back to us, his jacket bunched unner his head. Emmi goes over. She lays down facin him. The quiet murmur of her voice starts to drift our way.

Slim shakes his head. Didn't mean to upset the lad. Still—nope, it's gone. Never mind, it'll come to me. He heaves hisself to his feet. Well, think I'll have a little zizz. He waddles over to the Cosmic an squeezes into the back. Then it's jest me an Lugh an Maev. Light from the full orange moon spills down into the clearin.

Maev sits in a copper pool of moonlight, gazin at the fire. She glows. She gleams. Her skin, her eyes, her hair. She looks like she slid down to earth on a moonbeam. She don't look real. I glance at Lugh. He's watchin her. An . . . oh my. . .

His face.

The look on his face makes my breath catch in my throat.

The hopeless longin.

The helpless yearnin.

He might as well lay at her feet an bare his throat.

Maev turns her head. Their eyes meet. Their eyes hold. The air goes still.

I know it ain't right that I should watch 'em. But I do. I ain't never seen Lugh like this before. Heart open. Nuthin hidden.

He's the first to look away. He catches me watchin him an his face closes down. There's a sharp pain inside me. I feel it in my gut. In my chest, I feel it. In my head. The pain you feel from a knife.

We're bein cut asunder, Lugh an me.

Bit.

By bit.

An it makes me think.

It makes me wonder.

Is this how he feels when he sees me with Jack? Do I look at Jack the way Lugh looks at Maev?

Helpless.

Throat bared.

Hopeless.

† † †

I'm runnin. Down a long, dark corridor. Torches light the way. Their jagged shadows dart an hiss an somebody whispers my name.

Saba.

Saba.

It brushes my skin. On a gust of cold air. The voice so dark an deep. The heartstone's warm in my hand. That means Jack ain't far away.

Then I'm climbin the staircase. Up the stone steps.

Saba, Saba, Saba.

The voice agin, strokin my spine. I know it. So well. It settles inside me. Deep inside.

I clutch the heartstone. Wait fer me, Jack. As the stones whisper, Saba, I run up the stairs. Then I'm at the top. At the wood door, old an scarred.

With the heartstone hot in my hand.

I turn the handle. I open the door. I step inside the room. It's near empty. Near dark.

Jack, I says.

Rushlights. A candle. A high-backed chair. Turned to the fire in the hearth. He gits up from the chair. He turns to face me.

Turns to—

Turns to—

Then it's gone. All gone.

It's jest darkness. An I'm fallin.

Down, down, down to the deep, vast dark.

I wake with a gasp.

It's a star-filled night. A mellow moon night. A breeze blows sweet in the trees. By the sweet, mellow light of the late summer moon, I see Lugh an Maev by the fire. They're kneelin. Facin each other. She touches his hair. His face. His lips. With gentle, tender care.

She moves towards him. She goes to kiss him.

He turns his head away.

She waits a long, long moment. At last she gits to her feet.

She goes an lays herself down. On the ground beside Tommo an Em.

Lugh sits on watch.

I pretend to sleep. But I'm thinkin about what I jest seen. He's drawn to her. He feels fer her. I read it in his face. I know. So why did he turn away?

† † †

I sleep shallow, driftin in an out on half-thoughts an almost-dreams. I crave the oblivion of deep sleep, but my brain's too busy.

A rustle an a whisper weave their way into my head. Unner heavy eyelids, I half-see Slim relieve Lugh on the watch, settle his bulk into his slingchair. Then I'm pulled down into a fevered muddle, of snakes an skulls an yellow medicine wagons.

An one dream, more real than the rest. Where Slim's openin the rear door of the Cosmic an takin out a bulky sack. He hushes Tracker, who's doggin his heels with keen inner-est. With a glance around the sleepin camp, Slim slips off into the woods. Tracker follows. Then it's rope bridges an lightnin storms an meet-me-at-the-Lost-Cause-by-the-full-moon.

When I come to agin, it's becuz Slim's touched my shoulder

to wake me. Then everybody's stirrin. As we break camp in silence, my head starts to clear. So strange, the visions that take hold of you in the night. Essept there's fresh mud on Slim's boots. An I could swear it warn't there when we went to sleep.

✝   ✝   ✝

We're back on the road agin while it's still dark. We head east. Always east. We'll be drivin into the dawn. Same as yesterday, I ride up front with Slim. Lugh an Emmi ride Hermes. Maev an Tommo's inside the Cosmic. Tracker sprawls over my feet. Nero flies above, swoopin down every now an then to see what's what.

Slim natters away, tellin me how there's a curfew between sundown an sunup. The Tonton don't permit no travel durin the hours of darkness. But we're on a mission, says Slim. The Lost Cause or bust. He's stickin to the main trail as long as we can to make better time. We'll jest hafta dodge off-road before we git to Maryville Drift. That should be some time around sunup. They got a guardpost there, so we'll take one of his little detours onto a side road.

Time an distance rattle away unner the wheels of the Cosmic. The landscape changes. We start to see the shadows of soft, folded hills. Stands of birch make thin silver ghosts in the darkness. Not long now till dawn.

Slim sits taller. His hands tighten on the reins. He ain't so cool about travelin these roads as he makes out. It ain't far to Maryville, he says. We need to start lookin out fer—

Fer what? I says.

He curses unner his breath. It warn't like this last time I passed, he says.

Jest ahead of us, to the left of the trail, there's signs of new settlement. A raw, razed parcel of birch forest. The felled trees, cut an stacked neat around the edges. The site's bin almost cleared of stumps. The thick chain an horse yoke lie ready to be used. An there's the horses. Two sturdy, shaggy mustangs. They're tied to a stake next to a tent.

A tent. Somebody's here.

I hold my bolt shooter on Slim. Take us outta here, I says. Fast.

Slim slaps the reins. Moses picks up the pace. Slim slaps agin an the camel really starts to fly. As we race by the clearin, we turn our heads to look. Somebody's comin outta the tent. They bin roused by the rumble of our wheels. It's a young guy. Short hair. Tall with broad shoulders. He's pullin on his shirt.

He calls, Long life to the— Hey! Hey, come back here! It's still curfew! Stop! Lemme see yer marks!

I press the shooter to Slim's temple. Don't even think about it, I says.

No fear of that, he says. Heeya, Moses! Heeya!

I grab the side of the Cosmic an look back. The fella's runnin fer the horses, shoutin. A girl, maybe my age, comes dashin outta the tent with two firesticks. She throws him one.

They're comin after us, I says. There's a girl too.

Damn, he says.

Hermes gallops up alongside us, Lugh an Emmi lookin over.

What now? says Lugh.

Take the child outta harm's way! Slim shouts. There's a hill comin up! Once yer past it, peel off to the right. Wait fer us at the long stone wall. You cain't miss it. Go!

Lugh's eyes meet mine. Don't do nuthin stupid, he says.

I won't, I says.

Hold tight, Em! He heels Hermes an they race off.

I stand up on the seat. Hang onto the edge of the roof as I peer back over it. The guy's on horseback. He's movin fast. The girl ain't far behind.

I slide back down on to the seat. They're gainin on us, I says. What'll we do?

You'll hafta kill 'em, says Slim. If you don't, they'll report that I broke curfew, that I didn't stop. Everybody knows the Cosmic. The Tonton'll be on the lookout fer us. His voice sounds matter-of-fact. Like he's talkin about the weather.

I blow out a quick breath. Hold her steady, I says.

I stand on the seat agin. I shove my bolt shooter into the

back of my belt. Pull myself onto the roof of the Cosmic. I lay flat on my stummick. The rig bumps an jolts. We hit a hole. I fly up. Land hard. If I don't crack a rib or git thrown off, it'll be a small miracle. I got a feelin Lugh might consider this stupid. But it's lucky fer me the Cosmic's such a wreck. Slim's wrapped ropes an chains around to keep her from fallin apart. I jam my feet unner one of the ropes. Make sure I'm well an truly braced. I pull out the shooter an lean on my elbows.

The homesteader's comin up fast behind us. The girl too. She draws level with him. Now she pulls ahead. I gotta wait till they're in range.

Nero swoops overhead, screamin. Git away, I shout.

They gallop closer. Closer still. Now I got a clear view of their faces.

Her smooth cheeks. Her round chin. Her hair flyin behind her, long an fair. She ain't seen more'n fourteen summers. An him. Despite his man's body, he ain't much older'n Tommo. A couple of youngsters.

I'll take her out first. I aim at the quartered circle brand in the middle of her forehead. Cold sweat beads my forehead. My upper lip. Wets my palms.

She grips hard with her knees. She's raisin her firestick.

Now. Now! Shoot her now!

Epona. On the roof. She smiles at me. She nods.

She starts to run towards me.

I cain't do it. I cain't shoot her.

Suddenly, the girl flies backwards. Arrow to her heart. She lands in a heap on the road. The boy opens his mouth. No chance to yell. A arrow zings into his throat. He tumbles offa his horse. They lie in the dirt. Neether of 'em moves. Their horses turn an race off together.

I peer over the edge of the Cosmic. At the far end, Maev swings into view. She hangs onto the doorframe with one hand, her bow held in th'other. She throws me a look. A what's-the-matter-with-you? look. She gives a little shake of her head. Then she swings back outta sight. No, Maev sure ain't lost her edge.

I free myself from the ropes. I slide offa the roof an back onto the seat beside Slim.

You do it? he says.

Yeah, I says.

We cain't leave the bodies there, he says. We gotta go back.

I shake my head. Drive on, I says.

But you don't—

I said, drive on! I yell it at him.

Tracker lays his head on my lap, whinin. I stroke his ears. A couple of kids, I says. I don't think he'd even started shavin.

I look at Slim, but he don't look at me. He keeps his face forwards. I cain't tell what he's thinkin.

I couldn't shoot the girl. My hands didn't shake, but still . . . I couldn't kill her. I lost my nerve. Without Maev, I might be dead right now. She saved my skin once more.

† † †

We find Lugh an Emmi at the long stone wall. They don't ask no questions. They don't hafta. They can see on our faces how it played out.

Slim's bloody detour. It takes us through such rough terrain, everybody's gotta pile out an walk while he leads Moses. Nero hitches a ride on Moses' hump. Tracker sticks with me.

Pushin an pullin, shovin an heavin, we coax Moses an the Cosmic along. Over hummocky prairie. Up an down an around hills thick with shad-bush an honeysuckle. We're caught out by a sudden patch of suck-mud. Somehow Slim manages to keep Moses goin, but the Cosmic's another thing. She sinks down a good foot an it takes us ferever to haul her free. In all of the shabibble, Emmi parts company with both her boots.

Where's this damn road? I says.

Not far, says Slim. Mind you, this ain't my usual detour. Guess you'd call it the detour of the detour. If I'm readin the runes right, we oughta run into another trail in a bit. That'll take us back to the road, then it's straight over the causeway into the storm belt an hey presto, welcome to the Lost Cause.

Less chat, more pace, I says. C'mon! Let's move it!

I urge us on. The sun beats down on our heads. I keep

lookin up, checkin its path. By middle day, I'm wound up tighter'n a spinnin top. I march back to Slim. He's wet through with sweat. Red in the face. I grab a handful of pink dress an yank him to me.

What kind of a gawdamn detour is this? I says. Where's the gawdamn road? If we ain't at the Lost Cause by nightfall, I swear, yer gonna be one dead fat man in a frock.

His one good eye stares at me. I never seen nobody so anxious to git to a hooch joint, he says. There must be a party I don't know about.

My bolt shooter's up. Pressed to his forehead. Don't be smart with me, I says.

It ain't a party, says Emmi, we're meetin—

Nobody, I says.

We need to push on, says Maev, that's all. Once we git there, we still got a long ways to travel.

Let the man go, Lugh tells me. We're all doin our best.

I let Slim go. You better not be leadin us wrong, I says.

Slim wafts his dress to cool down. My word's my bond, sister, he says. We'll be at the Lost Cause by dark.

C'mon, then, I says.

We keep on keepin on. An Lugh keeps on glancin at Maev. He makes sure he's beside her when we're haulin the Cosmic. At one point, she loses her footin an he dives to stop her from fallin. But the next moment, when she goes to thank him, he drops her arm like he's bin scalded an then completely ignores her. I see her frownin to herself. Givin him puzzled looks. An no wonder.

The Cosmic bumps an jolts. Her lanterns swing wildly. Slim winces at the rattle of glass from inside. If she don't fall apart before we git there, it'll be a miracle, he says.

Hey, Slim, says Emmi, what's the Lost Cause like?

It's what you'd call a lively establishment, he says. Hard hooch, rough grub an wicked wimmin.

You mean whores, says Emmi.

No, he don't, says Tommo.

Yes, he does, she says. Anyways, I know plenty of 'em.

Fer shame! says Lugh.

Ain't she the one! cackles Slim. Yes indeed, I'm talkin saucy mamzelles that know how to stir a man's stewpot. A word to the wise, gents, don't try nuthin with Molly. You'll be tempted to— by gum, she's a rare beauty—but you mess with her at yer peril. There was this one lairy cove—ha ha!—he snuck a look at Molly through the keyhole, in her bath all pink an rosy—oh boys, I pray fer that to be my last sight on earth, a curvy gal in a tub—anyways, there he is, this rapscallion, peekin at Molly's paticklers, an before you know it, he's tied backwards to his horse, trousers on his head, next stop Tillibunk Junction! Ha ha!

Tommo's frownin, positively glarin at Slim. Serves him right, he says. He shouldn't of looked.

Oh, he couldn't help hisself, says Slim. You'll see, when you meet Molly.

Don't talk about her like that! says Tommo.

You put me to shame, young man, yer absolutely right, says Slim. Molly's a respectable, clean-livin woman. Luckily, her girls ain't! Ha ha!

As we push an pull the Cosmic an Moses up another bumpy slope, I ponder on things. Slim knowin Molly. Lilith an Meg bein at the Snake River camp. I wonder if Slim's ever met Jack. When I stand back an look at the strangeness of everythin—how one thing's led to another an brought me here, almost like night followin day—it's as if this whole thing was meant to be. An that brings to mind what Auriel said. How we all got our parts to play. How all my roads, every decision leads me to the same place in the end.

Destiny. I hardly dare think the word in case Lugh hears me think it. I dunno, how could that be possible? Anyways, what does it matter? As long as I find my way to Jack, that's all I care about. That's where the road ends fer me. It's why I'm here, why I'm doin this. Fer Jack. To be with Jack.

Emmi barges into my thoughts by sayin, Y'know, Slim, yer too old to be carousin with whores. Yer time of life, you oughta be settled down with a good woman.

Hell, says Slim, no decent gal 'ud take up with a old fossil like me.

I don't see why not, says Em. They do say there's somebody fer everybody.

Believe it or not, missy, back in my salad days, I was what we

called a gay blade, he says. Had a fine manly figger. I had dash
an charm an . . . oh, I was devilish handsome, no word of a lie.
Females flocked to me, helpless moths to my deadly flame.

There you go, says Em. You jest need to scrub up some.

Where's the gawdamn road? I says.

I figger any moment now, we should—ah! Here we are!
says Slim. What'd I tell you?

As he says the words, we're suddenly bumpin onto a wide
dirt road that cuts across our path, east-west. Look! says Slim.
There it is! The storm belt! He points east.

Some ten leagues distant, straight on, the sky hangs low
an brown across the horizon. There's a little huddle of mountains. A thick plug of filthy-lookin brown cloud hangs above
'em, like a sullen lid. Forks of jagged lightnin flash down.

Where's The Lost Cause? says Em.

You cain't see it from here, says Slim. Over the causeway,
through a gap in them mountains an there she is, right in the
middle. It's all flat, open an empty, but fer the Lost Cause. He
leans in close to Em, makes his voice go spooky. There she
stands, he says, alone at the crossroads, with wind witches
shriekin an wailin around her all night long. Tappin on the
windows, scratchin at the doors with their long witchy claws,
let me in, let me in. Are you skeered of witches, little miss?

Em's bug-eyed. I dunno, she whispers. I never met one.

The brown cloud's sulphate, he says in a normal voice.
Rains down on the Lost Cause every single day.

Let's hurry, I says. It ain't far an it's a good road.

Slim's frownin, lookin up an down the trail. Too damn good fer my likin, he says. Somebody's bin workin on this. It's bin cleared. Made wider since the last time I was here.

The Tonton? says Lugh.

Roads is slave work, says Slim, not Tonton. Anyways, what it tells me is there's more traffic here. More people movin around. Everybody better ride inside till we git to Molly's. Anybody we do meet, I can explain the horse, but not all of you with no marks on you.

No way, I says. What's to stop you drivin somewheres an handin us over?

Look, he says, the Cosmic used to be the beast wagon in a travelin show. She's got air grilles in her walls so you can watch what's goin on. Shoot me if you don't like what you see.

We look at each other. Me an Lugh an Maev an Tommo an Emmi. Maev gives a little shake of her head. Don't trust him.

I ride with you, I says. The rest go in the back.

Did you not hear me? says Slim. I jest said, it's too dangerous.

An I jest said, I ride with you, I says. Me an the wolfdog.

As I tie Hermes to the back end, the rest of 'em climb inside, into the warm, dim stuffiness of the Cosmic. They settle theirselfs on the straw. Light slants down from the grilles, one high up in each wall, jest like Slim said.

Lugh's last in. I hope there ain't no fleas, he says.

Whatever happens, says Slim, whatever you hear, don't make a sound, don't make a move an don't come out till I tell you.

All of a sudden, he don't seem like the same person. His voice, his gaze, even his big body, they've gone sharp an tight. He looks tough. No mean feat fer a man wearin a pink dress.

Okay? I says.

They all nod. We shut the door on 'em. Me an Tracker jump in the front. Nero lands on my lap. The Cosmic pitches an creaks as Slim squeezes his bulk into the driver's seat. He gives Moses a brisk slap with the reins an, with a jolt, we're off.

† † †

Every turn of the wheels carries me closer to the storm belt. To The Lost Cause. To Jack. My hand goes to the heartstone around my neck. My fingers curl around its cool smoothness. Soon I'll be seein Jack. After all this time, after all that's happened, I cain't hardly believe it. My belly's tight. Jittery. Hot an cold. I crave his moonlight eyes. His heart-turnin smile. His lips, his touch, the warm sage smell of his skin.

Smell. Ohmigawd.

I'm sweaty. I'm all dickered with mud an I'm hot an—I must

stink like a polecat. I try to remember the last time I had a wash. I cain't. I got no idea. I turn to Slim. Do I smell? I says.

He throws me a startled look. Uh—

Ohmigawd, I do. I smell bad. How bad? Go on, you can tell me.

Well, he says, you don't smell as bad as some. But you don't smell as good as some neether.

I knew it, I says. What'm I gonna do?

Yer askin me fer advice? He shakes his head as he says, I'd remind you that I'm wearin a lady dress with no unders.

I stare at him, not seein him, in a panic. What a nightmare. I don't see Jack fer months an the first thing he does is pass out becuz I smell so rank. I'll hafta scrub up somehow. Wash an change my clothes an—

Wait a minute, I says. That fella, peekin through the keyhole at Molly. She's got a tub. I'll ask if I can take a bath. That's what I'll do. The moment we git there, I'll hop in an have a scrub.

I smile at him. Relieved.

Well, he says, would you look at that. The sun jest come out. I gotta tell you, sister, when you smile you are one fine-lookin female. He winks. If I know The Lost Cause—an I do—yer gonna hafta stop up that keyhole.

Late afternoon. The storm belt ain't more'n three or four leagues distant.

Not much further now, says Slim. I figger another— Whoa, Moses! Whoa, boy!

He hauls on the reins. The Cosmic groans to a halt.

Beside the road, there's a man lashed to a tree trunk. A fat iron spike's bin nailed through his throat.

He ain't bin here more'n a few days. He died hard. Hard an long. He's gaunt. Starved lookin. He had maybe forty year on him. Pa's age.

From his seat on my lap, Nero caws. I hold him tight. Crows like to have a go at a corpse. Somethin's already bin workin at this one, crows or some other dead eaters.

D'you know him? I says.

From a boy, says Slim. His name's Billy Six. Slim's mouth works. His big, jowly face has gone all red.

He starts to clamber outta the wagon an I grab his arm. Hey, hey! What're you doin?

I'm gonna bury him decent, he says. I cain't leave him like this.

An if somebody sees us? I says. Then what?

His lips thin. He breathes, loud an tight, through his nose as he stares at Billy Six.

Lugh's voice comes from the grille above my head. Why're we stopped? he whispers.

Somebody Slim knows, I says. We stare at Billy Six. We're all silent fer a moment.

No man oughta die like that, says Lugh.

He took to the woods when the Tonton came to take his land, says Slim. The Stewards moved in an Billy swore he'd make as much trouble as he could fer as long as he could.

I hope he made their lives hell, I says.

Slim turns to look at me. His face is bleak. We're gonna pass right by his old place. If we're lucky, we won't see nobody. But you should ride in back with the rest of 'em.

No, I says.

He shakes his head. We're on high alert now, he says. Walk on, Moses.

† † †

We go on fer a little bit, maybe half a league. Nero flies ahead. Billy's place comin up, says Slim. On the right.

A little house stands in the middle of fields. The grass roof, the walls of stone an wood an mud an tires make it look like it's dragged itself outta the ground. There's two planted fields, one field ploughed to earth an one—the furthest away—half-ploughed. In that one, there's a man hard at work draggin a shoulder plough.

Looks like good land, I says.

It should be, he says. Billy worked it these past twenny year.

The door of the house stands open. A young woman hurries along the path towards the road. She waves at us.

I'm gonna stop, says Slim.

Drive on, I says.

I said I'm stoppin, says Slim.

An I said, drive on! I shove my bolt shooter into his side.

He gives me a steady look. It won't take long, he says. Don't say nuthin. Keep yer face hid.

Fer some reason—I cain't say why—his calm look, his calm voice, makes me feel clumsy. Foolish. Dull-witted. Like I'm somehow . . . missin the point. But what point, I dunno.

Whoa, there, Moses. The Cosmic stops once agin. It creaks an lists as Slim climbs down. Me an Tracker jump out too. I adjust my kercheef an sheema so's nuthin shows but my eyes.

Me an Slim move around the Cosmic untyin the right-side flap, then the left.

Saba! Lugh speaks in a low voice, but I can hear him through the wall. What's goin on?

The people on Billy's old place hailed us, I says.

Keep quiet inside, says Slim. Don't move a finger. I'll git rid of her as soon as I can.

The woman runs up. Not a woman. Another girl. Pink-cheeked, bright-eyed, trim an neat. Sixteen or so. The black quartered circle brand of the Stewards of the Earth in the middle of her forehead. A bolt shooter in her waist holster.

She brings her clenched right fist to her heart. Long

life to the Pathfinder! she says. Her voice trails off as she notices Tracker. He stands beside me, my hand on his head.

Oh, don't mind him, says Slim, he's gentle as a lamb.

He makes the same sign as she—fist to the heart. I copy him.

Long life to the Pathfinder, says Slim. What can I do fer you?

I gotta have a baby. She speaks fast, her voice low. It's bin too long. If I don't git with child soon, he'll ask fer another woman an they'll slave me. She hesitates, jest fer a moment, then pulls a silver chain from her pocket an hands it to Slim. Will you take this in trade? she says.

Slim's one eye looks it over keenly. Nice, he says. Family heirloom?

The girl pulls herself tall an proud, firms her chin. My only family is the Earth, she says. The Pathfinder has chosen me to heal her.

Of course he has, says Slim. I got jest the thing. Now, where did I put that tincture? He starts checkin through his bottles.

The girl casts a quick look over her shoulder. The man pullin the shoulder plough's stopped work. He's makin his way over the fields, headin towards us.

Hurry, please, she says.

Slim says, I seen that fella nailed to the tree back there.

Oh, the vermin, she says. Eli caught it settin fire to the new bridge. Eli an the night patrol. About a week back.

Night patrol, eh? says Slim. Folks around here bin breakin curfew?

The girl's keepin nervous watch on Eli. But she rattles on, like she's glad of the chance to speak to somebody. She don't take no notice of me.

We bin havin trouble after dark, she says. Not jest us, other homesteads too. Ever since we got here. Wells gone bad, beasts missin, broke ploughs, fires, all sorts. Our horse disappeared last month. That's how come Eli's handploughin. So, he got everybody together an organized night patrols fer our sector. You sure you got that cure?

Slim starts lookin in the drawers. It's here somewheres, he says. So you figger this fella to be the cause of yer troubles?

Well, we ain't had none since Eli spiked it, she says. He says it must of bin livin rough in the woods.

Did Eli deal with the, uh . . . vermin hisself? says Slim.

I helped some. She gives a nervous giggle. It did make the most awful fuss.

Did it indeed, says Slim. Ah! Here we go. You take two drops in water twice a day. An not jest you, ma'am, yer, uh . . . Eli too. Not to be personal an you'll pardon my sayin so, but it takes two to make one.

He hands her a tiny brown glass bottle. She shoves it in her pocket. Two drops twice a day, she says.

Fer the next ten days, says Slim. It won't work otherwise.

RiverLee! Eli shouts her name as he charges up the path. Hair like straw. Built like a bull. Thick lips. Red-faced. He's holdin a firestick. There's a bolt shooter stuck in his belt.

RiverLee! he yells. Whaddya mean, hailin this scum?

I was jest askin fer news, Eli, she calls. Thought they might of heard somethin from along the road.

You! Eli grabs Slim. Quack man. Lemme see yer mark. What the hell's this yer wearin? He shoves up the right sleeve of Slim's pink frock, grunts when he sees the brand on the outside of his arm. He gives him a hard shove. Go on, clear off! I don't want yer kind on my good land. If I see yuz agin, I'll deal with you, d'you hear?

Slim an me's rushin about, foldin the Cosmic's flaps, tyin her up.

Loud an clear, mister! Slim calls out in a quavery voice. Long life to the Pathfinder!

I'll give you long life! Eli shoots the firestick at Slim's feet. Slim dances back as the shot slams into the ground. Eli laughs. Narrows his eyes as he notices Hermes tied to the back of the Cosmic.

That horse there's way too fine fer the likes of you, he says. I believe you stole him. Jest like some vermin stole mine. I lay claim to that beast, in the name of the Pathfinder. Untie him, RiverLee.

She hurries to do his biddin. My chest's gone tight. They cain't take Hermes. I won't let 'em.

Please, mister, don't take my horse! Slim whines.

Shut up! Eli jerks his head fer Slim to move beside me.

He keeps the firestick aimed at us. Tracker growls. He stops when I press my hand on his head.

I shoot mean dogs, says Eli. How come yer woman's all covered up? She too ugly to look at?

She's got the weepin pox, mister, says Slim.

Maybe I oughta shoot her, he says.

Nero's flyin tight circles a little ways overhead.

Here he is, Eli, says RiverLee. But he's awful nervy.

She's leadin Hermes. She holds his rope too high, too tight. He tosses his head, pulls an dances.

Yer holdin him all wrong, says Eli. Dammit, RiverLee, yer too stupid to live. Loosen up his rope a little.

He's still got us covered with the firestick. But he's distracted. He flicks a glance their way—jest fer a moment—but it's enough fer me to show Hermes my hand. I waggle it. He goes crazy, squealin an stompin. With one mighty tug, he yanks hisself free. RiverLee falls to the ground. She shrieks an covers her head as Hermes rears above her, flailin at the air with his front legs. Eli looks. I move.

I grab his firestick. Both hands. He hangs on. Both hands. Nero falls outta the sky at him, screechin. Tracker snaps an snarls at his legs. His hands loosen. Jest a bit. I smash the firestick into his face.

He reels back. The stick goes flyin.

Go go go! I yell at Slim.

As he hurries to jump in the front, I run to git Hermes.

He's skittered outta harm's way. But RiverLee's on her feet. Bolt shooter out. Aimed at me. She shoots. She misses.

I've pulled my own shooter by now. I raise it. A huge arm grabs me from behind. Hooks around my throat. Eli. He presses on my windpipe, chokin me. I struggle an scrabble, but he's too strong. He chops my shooter from my hand. Digs his into my temple.

Tracker's throwin hisself at Eli. Snarlin an snappin. Eli kicks at him.

Slim comes runnin, firestick at the ready.

I'll kill her! yells Eli. Put yer weapon on the ground, yer hands up! Cover him, RiverLee!

Got it, Eli, says RiverLee.

Slim throws down his firestick an raises his hands.

Call off yer dog! yells Eli. The crow too! I'll kill all of 'em!

Slim calls off Tracker. Nero's bin attackin Eli, divin at his head an shriekin.

Eli eases up on my windpipe. Jest enough fer me to croak, No, Nero! Go!

Nero retreats. He circles overhead, callin out his alarm.

You ain't no quack's woman, says Eli.

He yanks my sheema back. His eyes widen as he sees my tattoo. He smiles.

I'm facin the side of the Cosmic. There's a movement at the air grille.

Hey, RiverLee, says Eli, who d'you s'pose—

249

The thud of a bolt shooter.

Eli's head jerks back. His arms fly out. He hits the ground.

Eli! RiverLee starts screamin.

I'm on my knees, gaspin fer air. Lugh leaps from the back of the Cosmic, bolt shooter in hand.

RiverLee fires wildly at him.

He shoots her dead.

An it's silent.

Jest like that.

The shock of silence.

After noise an chaos an fear.

Lugh rushes over an helps me to my feet. Are y'okay? he says.

I nod. Yeah, I says.

Maev, Emmi an Tommo climb outta the Cosmic. They take in the sight of Eli an RiverLee lyin dead. Em starts to cry.

Don't weep fer them, little sister, says Slim.

What now? says Maev.

I'd like to burn the whole place an these two with it, says Slim.

Too much smoke, says Tommo. People might notice.

We'll hafta to bury 'em, says Slim. You lot do it. I cain't.

That's what we do. We dig a pit in the woods where Billy Six hid out. We don't make Emmi help. She cries quietly, with her back turned, an shrugs Tommo off when he goes to give her a hug. The rest of us work in silence. Our faces drawn with our own thoughts. Lugh's pale. He ain't so used as the rest of us to the shock of sudden violence. Of quick, brutal death. It warn't so long ago that I believed Hopetown had made me hard to it. But I ain't. An from the look on everybody's faces, they all feel the same. Apart from Slim.

As we start to cover Eli with dirt an leaves, Slim holds off Lugh's shovel. With his other hand, he reaches fer his shooter, but I grab it. Stop him.

You cain't kill a man twice, I says.

Slim looks at me a long moment. Then he spits in Eli's face, sayin, That's fer Billy, you sonofabitch.

We've jest about covered RiverLee with a thin layer of dirt when he says, Hang on.

He slides down into the grave. Feels in her pockets an pulls somethin from it. He pops it into the skinbag he wears around his waist, then holds up his hands fer Tommo, Lugh an Maev to help him out agin. I caught a quick glimpse as it went in his bag. It was the tiny brown bottle of tincture. Two drops twice a day so RiverLee could have a child.

That's what he told her, anyways.

†   †   †

As everybody climbs in back of the Cosmic, dusk is gatherin aginst the day.

Jest over a couple leagues to go, says Slim. Didn't I tell you I'd git you there by nightfall?

The huddle of mountains that looked so small when we first seen 'em now tower high an broodily dark. The storm belt, with the Lost Cause, lonely in the middle of the plain.

Meet me at the Lost Cause. Be there by the next full moon.

I'm comin, Jack.

I go to climb up front with Slim. Oh no, he says. Trouble loves you like flies love a dungheap. You wanna git to The Lost Cause in one piece? Ride in back with the rest of 'em.

I hesitate. I cain't think, cain't remember where he was when Eli seen my tattoo. It was all such confusion. But if Slim seen it too, then he—

He's pointin at the mountains. Look, there it is! he says. I brought you all this way. I could of handed you over long before now, gun or no gun to my head. C'mon, time's wastin.

Okay, I says. All right.

We're gonna go like the clappers, he says. Hang on.

Tracker stays with Slim. Nero's airborne. Hermes is gonna follow behind, untethered this time. I climb into the back of the Cosmic an squeeze myself between Maev an Emmi.

Slim yells, Gee up! an Moses takes off like a shot.

The Cosmic Compendalorium flies along. We brace ourselves aginst her walls. The road might be decent, but it's still rough. Too rough fer a rickety, rackety cart held together with rope an a hope. As she bounces an rattles an shakes an bumps, gaps start to appear. Between the walls. Between the walls an the roof, the walls an the floor. We look at each other, eyes wide.

Is she gonna fall apart? says Em.

Of course not, I says.

The gaps suddenly widen. The Cosmic groans.

Hit the deck! yells Lugh.

We all dive face down in the straw. The Cosmic hits a hole. She flies up. Slams down. The floor cracks. Breaks. Emmi screams. We fall through.

Here it comes—the ground, the wheels, the pain, make-it-quick-oh-mercy-it's-the-end-the-end-this-is-how-it-ends—

We don't land in the road.

We ain't on the ground. We ain't trampled an mangled. Our limbs ain't broke. Nobody's dead. We're still in the Cosmic, rattlin along. An we jest discovered her secret. She's got a false bottom. A fake floor with a hidey-hole unnerneath. That's what we've fell into.

As fer what we've fell onto.

Well.

✝   ✝   ✝

I'm starin down the barrel of a firestick.

It's wrapped in cloth. The top bit's slipped back.

Cloth-wrapped bundles, all different sizes and shapes, fill the hidden nest. Its walls an floor is heavy padded to pertect the Cosmic's secret cargo.

Everybody's lyin on top of me in a jumble of legs an arms an straw an shattered floorboards. We untangle ourselfs an stare. Lugh picks up a small bundle an pulls off the cloth. It's a bolt shooter. Emmi unwraps a blowgun. Maev, a sword. Tommo, a bundle of arrows. An there's some weapons I ain't never seen before. All clean an tidy an oiled an gleamin. Wicked. Ready fer action. My pulse starts to race when I see 'em.

But he's a doctor, says Em.

Doctor an arms dealer, says Maev.

Nobody says naught fer a moment. Then. The penny drops.

Ohmigawd, I says. There's a resistance.

What? says Lugh.

His friend back there, I says. Billy Six. Livin rough in the woods, sabotagin homesteads. Last night. We stopped there cuz he had a delivery to make. He went off when he was s'posed to be on watch, he came back with mud on his boots. I thought I was dreamin, but—he ain't no friend of the Tonton. There's a gawdamn resistance an he's the weapons man.

Maybe that's what he's deliverin to the Lost Cause, says Maev. Maybe it's a weapons drop.

Maybe Molly's with the resistance, says Emmi.

Probly meant some fer Billy Six too, I says, essept he didn't need none seein how he's nailed to a tree.

Hang on, says Lugh, where's the evidence? Jest becuz the guy runs weapons don't mean he's some kinda freedom fighter. Look at all of this, it's a bloody arsenal. Jest as likely, it's fer the Tonton. In fact, more'n likely. That's who's gonna be waitin fer us at the Lost Cause. Not jest unfaithful Jack but his nasty new friends in black too, I'll warrant.

Lugh looks straight at me now. You got a price on yer head, he says, an Jack's a man with his eye on the main chance. How fine would that be? Make his mark with the Pathfinder by handin over the Angel of Death. Slim knows Molly, Molly knows Jack . . . work it out. It's a set up. Slim's a Tonton spy. He knew who you was right from the start. He's bin playin us all this time. That's the story here. Not freedom. Death. Our deaths. All of us.

We stare at each other.

No, I says. No, yer wrong.

Am I? says Lugh. Think about it.

My breath's comin fast an tight. That moment when we first met Slim.

Where was you goin jest now? I said. My sheema starts to slip back from my face. My tattoo. Don't let him see. I yank it back, scowl at him. Well?

Uh . . . we was headed east, he said. We got a delivery to make. In the storm belt. A tavern called the Lost Cause.

Everybody okay back there? yells Slim.

Suddenly, I grab one of the firesticks. I smash it, butt first, through the front wall of the cart. Next to where Slim oughta be. I pull it out an smash it through agin. I shove myself through, biggin it with my elbows an shoulders. Tumble onto the driver's bench next to Slim. Tracker scrambles outta the way.

Slim throws me a startled look.

I aim my bolt shooter at him. Who am I, you sonofabitch?

Helluva time fer a identity crisis, he says.

We found yer load, I says.

Ah, he says. Okay, here's the thing— His eye flicks back to the road. Widens. Ohmigawd, he says.

I look where he's lookin.

Straight ahead a pillar of thick black smoke rises into the sky. It smacks aginst the sulphate cloud, like steam hittin a pot lid, an billows in every direction.

Somethin's on fire, I says.

It's the Lost Cause, says Slim. There ain't nuthin else there. Molly's in trouble.

My heart seizes. Starts hammerin in my chest. Jack's there. Waitin fer me. We gotta go in, I says.

You bet, he says. Straight over the causeway.

Up ahead a wide river in full flow cuts across the road. The road keeps on goin right over top of it. It's shored up eether side by banks made from rocks an boulders an concrete blocks. At the far end, it disappears through a gap in the mountains.

Black smoke billows through the gap. Tumbles along the causeway towards us.

I turn an yell into the cab, Fire up ahead! It's the Lost Cause!

Nero dives an swoops, callin out alarms. Slim starts to cough. Pulls his kercheef over his mouth an nose.

Lugh sticks his head through the hole. Sees the smoke. What're you, crazy? Stop! Turn around!

We're goin in, I says. Tell everybody.

He's about to argue. But there must be somethin in my face. With a curse, he disappears, an I hear him shoutin orders to the rest.

I yank my sheema up over my nose. Tracker's whinin. Anxious. I press him down to lie at my feet. Pull off my tunic an cover his head with it. Stay there, I tell him, good boy.

The Cosmic races over the causeway. The smoke billows an rolls in thick black waves. It tumbles. Crashes. Breaks. Six horsemen appear from inside the cloud. Riders in black.

Black robes.

Black riders.

The Tonton.

† † †

They gallop towards us. Six of 'em. In a tight group. Two by two by two.

My belly clenches. It's my first sight of 'em since the battle at Pine Top Hill.

I might of known, says Slim. Them Tonton bastards like to play with fire.

I shout back into the wagon, Tonton comin! Keep outta sight!

The causeway's narrow. Not more'n eight foot across. No room to pass.

They're headed right at us, I says to Slim.

How's yer nerve? Steady?

I guess, I says.

Ever played chicken before? he says.

No.

Watch an learn, he says. You better duck down. Seein there's a price on yer head.

My heart skips a beat. Our eyes meet. You knew all the time, I says.

Yer lucky it was me you hijacked, he says.

Who are you? I says.

A friend, he says. Git down, Angel.

I slide into the footwell, next to Tracker.

Heeya! Shouts Slim. Straight on fer Egypt, Moses! Heeya! We thunder along at speed. The Cosmic rattles an groans. Let's hope she holds together, he says.

I peer out. My shooter's ready in my hand.

Don't fire unless you hafta, he says.

Yer gonna hafta stop, I says.

I ain't stoppin. I'm gonna give these firebugs a little show. He pulls a big white hanky from his britches pocket. They'll jest see that old fool Salmo Slim, he says. Him an his fleabit camel outta control agin.

He heaves hisself to his feet an starts wavin the hanky over his head. Help! Help! Runaway camel! he bellows. With th'other hand, he keeps a death grip on the reins an holds Moses firm.

We barrel towards the Tonton. They come at us. Slim waves an hollers, Help! Help!

They come on. Holdin the line. Closer. Ever closer.

We're gonna crash! I yell.

You first-timers always panic, he shouts. Playin chicken's all about who holds their nerve the longest, who blinks first. It ain't gonna be me.

They hold.

Hold.

Hold.

I don't breathe. Don't move.

Thirty foot.

Twenny five.

C'mon, says Slim. Blink, you bastards.

Twenny.

Fifteen.

Blink, you gawdamn sonsabitches! roars Slim.

On the word, they split. Like they heard him. Three to the left. Three to the right.

I duck low. They thunder past, jest below us on the bank. A blur of hoofs an dust an robes an boots. A blast of smoke an sweat slaps me in the face. Fer one second—one heartbeat—I wonder if one of 'em's Jack.

A firestick cracks. Slim cries out. He falls back, sprawled on the bench. He's bin shot. His right shoulder's blasted open.

Slim! I yell.

Take the reins! he says.

I scramble onto the seat an grab 'em. I glance behind us. The Tonton disappear in a cloud of dust.

Hermes races along behind us, tucked in behind the Cosmic.

Slim presses his hanky to the wound. Grits his teeth aginst the pain. He hollers through the smashed wall into the Cosmic, blow up the causeway!

What? shouts Lugh.

Little balls with pins! yells Slim. Pull out the pins an throw a few!

I hold Moses firm. The road drives straight through the gap in the mountains. Disappears into the smoke.

Nuthin happens. Nuthin. Nuthin.

Suddenly,

BOOM! A great wallop of thunder cracks the air. Rocks the ground.

I dare a quick look over my shoulder.

Behind us, a colossal blast of rock an water an dirt slams into the sky. The causeway's bin blowed to bits. No sign of the riders or their horses.

Did we git 'em? says Slim.

I cain't tell, I says. Maybe not. They was movin quick. They might of got across before the blast.

If they did, they'll be lookin fer us, says Slim. So much fer sneakin you in without notice.

I glance over at him. Sweat beads his face. He's gray around the gills. What the hell, Slim, I says. You ain't no Tonton spy. Who are you?

His mouth twists. I think he's tryin to smile.

Jest git us to The Lost Cause, he says.

THE LOST CAUSE

MOSES BARRELS INTO THE WALL OF THICK BLACK SMOKE. I cain't see nuthin. My eyes stream. I cain't breathe. We're gonna crash. But quick as we're in it, we're out agin. The Lost Cause is straight ahead. Wild flames lick at it. Gobble it. They hiss an crackle an roar. Fire lights up the lonely plain. The low-hangin cloud glows bright. Orange an white an yellow an brown. The black smoke billows an curls. Waves of heat beat at the air.

The Lost Cause is lost.

We race towards it, there at the crossroads. I go as close as I dare, then haul on the reins. Moses slows, stops. He backs up, bellowin.

Slim slumps aginst me. Find Molly, he says.

Maev! Emmi! I yell. Slim's bin shot!

They come runnin an climb in the front, medicine bag in hand. Maev takes over an me an Tracker leap out.

Tracker, stay! I head fer the burnin buildin at a run. I'm coughin. The smoke stings my eyes.

Saba! Lugh's voice. Feet—his an Tommo's—pound behind me. Come back!

Jack could be in there! I yell. I slam into the heat. It's solid. Like a wall. It throws me back. Lugh grabs one arm. Tommo th' other. They pull at me, tryin to drag me away. I dig in my heels.

No! I yell. Lemme go!

Anybody in there's already dead, says Lugh.

No! I squirm an struggle.

It's one story. Made of flimsy Wrecker junk. The walls twist an buckle. Crack an shriek. The middle of the roof crashes into the flames.

Where's the still? says Tommo.

What? says Lugh.

Where they brew the hooch! he yells.

Omigawd, says Lugh, one spark an it'll blow! Run!

We turn. Start to run.

BOOM!

The blast flings us into the air. Sends us flyin. I land with a thump, face down. I scramble to my feet. Start to run back.

Jack! I yell.

No, Saba! Lugh tackles me. He throws hisself on top of me. He shields me with his body as The Lost Cause rains down all around us.

† † †

I'm still. Numb.

Git off, I says.

Lugh don't move.

Git offa me, I says.

He gits to his feet an holds out his hand. I ignore it. I make my way through the wreckage, go towards the burnin corpse of the Lost Cause. The fire feasts on the remains. It licks an crackles an snaps. The tavern sign lies on the ground. It's scorched, the paint flaked an faded. A little boat on a stormy sea, about to be swamped by a huge wave. I skirt around the edges, as close as I dare. My eyes search the flames. Lookin fer . . . I dunno what. Somethin. Anythin to stop this cold, heavy flatness of not knowin.

Tommo comes up. Yer shakin, he says. He puts his arm around my shoulders. I don't think he was in there, he says.

I look up at the sky. The sulphate cloud's startin to churn in sluggish clumps. The full moon shines faint in the darkenin sky. My hand's closed around the heartstone. It's cold.

He said he'd meet me here at the full moon, I says.

Tommo falls into step beside me. It's only jest dark, he says. Maybe he's still on his way.

Maybe, I says.

Suddenly, Nero caw caw caws. He's on the ground a little ways away, flappin his wings an bobbin his head.

What's he got? says Tommo. As he's sayin the words, I'm movin. We run to where he is.

Nero's perched on top of a hat. A brown, battered hat with a brim. There's a gray pigeon feather stuck in the band.

I stare dumbly. He stole it at Hopetown. Snatched it right

offa the owner's head. Emmi stuck the pigeon feather in the band, one night on our way to Freedom Fields.

It's Jack's hat.

Tommo crouches. He shoos Nero off an picks it up. He stands. Holds it out to me. As he does, it starts to rain. One moment nuthin, then a downpour. Brown, sticky rain from the sulphate cloud above.

I'm soaked through. Tommo's hair's plastered to his head. Filthy rain drips from his nose an chin. I take a couple of steps back. Then I swerve around him. Go past him, walkin fast, goin nowhere. Don't think, don't feel, it won't be true, it cain't be true.

My breath's tight. Throat's tight. Cain't breathe. I start to run. My feet slip an slide on the wet ground. I can hear Tommo behind me. The burnin ruins of the Lost Cause hiss an smoke as the rain starts to damp down the flames.

Jest then, twenny paces in front of me, somebody steps outta the smoke. The rain. The gloom. It's a woman. She's leadin a horse, a reddish longcoat.

She's got a gun.

An it's aimed straight at me.

† † †

I skid to a stop. Tommo too.

That's my hat, she says. I kill looters.

She's grubby an soaked wet. Her long tangle of blonde curly hair's pulled back in a tail. She's got full pink lips. Womanly curves in a long-skirted dress. Eyes smudged dark with sorrow. There's a scarf tied over her hair, pulled low on her forehead. Her drawn face tells the tale. She ain't known the mercy of sleep fer a long time. She's heart-stoppin beautiful.

Yer Molly, says Tommo. Ike's Molly.

Ike's dead, she says.

Where's Jack? I says.

Jack? she says. She frowns.

I snatch the hat from Tommo. This is his, I says. Where is he? Gawdammit, I yell, where's Jack?

I dunno, she says, I ain't seen him since—hey, who are you?

This is his hat! I says. Where is he?

He left it behind, she says.

He—he ain't here, I says.

Nobody here but me, she says.

The rain begins to stop. Bit by bit.

He ain't here, I whisper. He left it behind. Tears start to leak outta my eyes. I swipe 'em away.

I did tell him it was a crummy hat, she says, but . . . it ain't worth cryin over. As she's speakin, she's starin at me. Lowerin her gun. Leavin her horse an walkin towards me. She stops when she's a foot away. She's lookin at the heartstone.

Ohmigawd. She whispers it, like she cain't believe what she's seein. She lifts her eyes to mine. Jack's heartstone, she says. She reaches out. Pushes my sheema back from my face. Her fingers brush my birthmoon tattoo. They're tremblin. I can smell the drink on her.

Yer Saba, she says. What're you doin here? Where's Jack?

Whaddya mean? I says. He sent fer me. He's in trouble. I got a message to meet him here at the full moon.

But . . . how? I don't unnerstand. I thought he was with you, she says. I mean. . .

Saba! It's Lugh.

Emmi! calls Tommo. It's Molly!

Molly an me stare at each other as Lugh an Emmi an Tracker come runnin up.

Molly! Emmi shrieks. She dives at Molly, an flings her arms around her waist.

Molly holds her hands high. Hey, hey, who the hell're you? Slim?

Slim's makin his way towards us, bandaged up an leanin on Maev. His face is pasty an sweaty.

Ohmigawd, Slim, what happened? Molly puts Emmi aside an rushes over to him.

Tonton shot me on the causeway, he says. Guess they didn't like the dress.

She looks us over. How'd you run into these? she says.

He puts his one good arm around her shoulders an hugs her. I got hijacked, he says. A long story. You okay?

Yeah, she says. I bin espectin it. The Lost Cause is the last bastion of immorality an low livin. I'm sure they would of got to me sooner, but they know damn well I ain't got no customers. They chased or killed off all the rats an the Stewards don't drink or whore. I'm hardly worth the trouble, wouldn't you say? She gives him a funny little smile.

Well, that's the delivery off, then, he says.

Molly's eyes flick over us. Her face closes.

Oh, you can speak free, he says. They found the weapons.

We'll go to the fallback plan, she says. You deliver to Bram and Cassie.

I knew it! Maev jabs her finger at Lugh. There is a resistance! He runs weapons an the Lost Cause is a drop. Am I right or am I right?

You ain't wrong, says Slim.

I grab Molly's arm. Molly, I says, please, why'd you say you thought Jack was with me?

He said he was goin after you, she says. When he came to tell me about Ike. He was gonna go meet you. You was headed west, right?

When did you see him? I says. How long ago?

I . . . I dunno, she says. A couple months, I guess, I—

Molly! C'mon! I give her a shake. This is important!

As I shake her, her headscarf starts to slip back from her

forehead. I can see the pink, raised ridges of a wound startin to heal. I slide it off.

She's bin branded. Right in the middle of her forehead.

W.

I know it from Hopetown. The painted ladies an boys of Paradise Lane who'd lie down with a stranger fer chaal or hooch or a handful of beads. That's how the Tonton marked 'em.

W.

Whore.

✝   ✝   ✝

We sit on upturned boxes an such beside the Cosmic. A tin barrel of Molly's wormwood whisky survived bein blown in the sky. We all take a drink, even Emmi. It's killer hooch, worser'n Ike's pine sap vodka, an that was enough to blind you. It slices down my gullet like white pain.

How many of 'em? I says to Molly.

Two, she says.

Tonton, says Maev.

Molly nods. There warn't nobody in the tavern but me an Jack. After he told me about Ike, I—Jack's th'only person I know who'd travel so far to deliver bad news. I don't think I could of stood it if it was anybody else but him.

We're silent. I only jest met Molly. I don't know her, but we're bound together, her an me, through Jack an Ike. My heart cleaves to hers. It hurts on her account.

I told him not to, she says, but he stuck around to make sure I was okay. Then these two showed up. Tonton. Jack bein Jack, he . . . tried to talk us outta trouble but . . . two of them, one of him . . . they beat him pretty bad.

They beat him, I says. My skin runs hot an cold as I picture it.

Yeah, she says. Then, uh . . . one of 'em stayed with him while . . . uh . . . while the other one, uh—

Tears suddenly fill her eyes, spill down her cheeks. Sorry, she says, scrubbin at 'em. Afterwards, they branded me.

Emmi jumps up. Goes over an hugs her. Don't cry, Molly, she says. It's okay. We're here now.

Emmi don't unnerstand. She's too little. Molly's pain, so heavy, so thick, fills the air till I cain't hardly breathe. I glance at Maev, tears in my eyes. She's starin at Molly, her jaw set.

Slim's sat next to Molly, holdin her hand, squeezin it from time to time. Nuthin could ever ruin yer beauty, he says. He kisses her forehead, right on the dreadful brand.

She gasps a tearful little laugh. Yer such a liar, she says. Such a kind, dear liar. She wraps the scarf around her head agin an starts to tie it. After they left, she says, I . . . I jest wanted to be alone. She looks at me. I told Jack to go after you, she says. To follow his heart. I made him swear.

What did he say? I whisper.

He promised he would, she says.

I ain't seen him, I says.

Seems I was the last to see him, says Maev.

You? says Molly.

He gave her the heartstone to give to Saba, says Emmi.

An he jest happened to be ridin with the Tonton at the time, says Lugh.

What? says Molly. No. Jack would never ride with the Tonton. Never. I know him.

Maybe you don't know him very well, says Lugh.

I know that I don't like yer tone, she says. Jack is my friend. A very old, dear friend. I won't hold with you sayin things about him that ain't true.

Lugh looks away.

He was with 'em, Molly, says Maev. I seen him with my own eyes. Dressed like 'em an all.

They must of captured him, she says.

That's what I say, I says.

He was free, says Maev, not fettered.

Molly frowns. Takes a long drink from her tin an pours herself another. She catches Tommo starin at her. He ain't took his eyes offa her all this time.

What's yer problem? she says.

You shouldn't drink so much, he says.

What's it to you what I do?

Ike wouldn't like it, he says.

Whadda you know, anyways?

I'm Tommo, he says. Ike took me in. He talked about you. Told me about you. He said him an you an me . . . we'd be a family.

There ain't no gawdamn family, she says. Ike's dead.

He called me son, says Tommo.

Is that so? she says. Well, don't look to me to call you son.

Hard words. Hurtful words. Tears start to Tommo's eyes. They spill down his cheeks. He dashes 'em away an sets his jaw not to cry.

That was mean, I says.

Go to hell, says Molly. She's drained her tin. She pours another.

You got no call talkin to Tommo like that, says Em.

Hush, Emmi, says Lugh.

I won't hush, says Em. You ain't th'only one who loved Ike. You ain't th'only one who misses him. An it ain't Tommo's fault Ike got killed. He tried to save Ike. He loved him jest the same as you.

Molly's starin into her mug. Not the same as me, she says. Not the gawdamn same as me! Her voice rises to a yell. She flings her mug wildly. We only jest duck in time.

Molly stops herself. She's breathin high an fast. Fightin herself. Tryin not to fall apart. She gives us a tight little smile. I'm sorry, she says to Tommo. I had no right to speak to you like that.

He nods, not meetin her eyes.

Now what? says Maev.

Molly looks at Slim, nursin his shoulder, his face drawn with pain. We'll go to Bram an Cassie's, she says. Hide the weapons. We'll git Slim fixed up proper an work out what to do next.

I ain't goin nowhere, I says. Jack told me to meet him here an that's what I'm gonna do.

That's only what you think, says Lugh. You don't know fer sure. What're you gonna do, sit here all night? Wait fer him to turn up with the Tonton so he can hand you over?

Jack wouldn't do that, says Molly.

Whether he would or not ain't to the purpose, says Slim. Not at this precise moment, anyways. The point is, it ain't safe to be here. Not fer Molly, not fer Saba, not fer none of us. We got four dead Stewards on our tab, not to mention one blowed-up causeway. If any of them Tonton lived to tell the tale, they'll be lookin fer the Cosmic. Bram an Cassie run a safe house. That's where we all need to be.

The Tonton only know about you, I says. You an the Cosmic. Not us.

Hey, says Maev, we wouldn't be here without Slim. He took a hit fer us. Don't that mean nuthin to you?

Okay, then, the rest of yuz go, I says. I'll wait here fer Jack.

Yer faith in yer friend does you credit, says Slim. But I'll tell you this. If he's got hisself mixed up with the Tonton, he ain't master of his own fate. You'll serve him better by makin sure the same don't happen to you.

You ain't listenin, I says. He's in trouble, he needs my help, that's why he sent fer me. As I say it, I shoot a hard look at Lugh, darin him to bad-mouth Jack agin.

Even more reason to go to Bram's, says Slim. He'll know what's best to do. He knows these parts. He knows the Tonton.

They all look at me, wait fer my answer. My gut tells me to dig in my heels. If it was only me I had to think of, I'd dig in, no question. But my heart an head tell me I got Maev an Tommo an Emmi an Lugh to consider. They're in danger jest by bein here. Because of me. I look at Slim, wounded on my account. At Molly. Ike's Molly.

How far to this . . . Bram's place? I says.

Not far, says Molly. Three hours due north.

All right, I says, but I gotta leave him a message. Tell him where to find me.

I know jest the thing, says Molly. C'mon.

With her in charge, we gather up bits of the Lost Cause. Startin with the tavern sign at one end, we arrange it all alongside the northbound road in a line. But not so's you'd notice. Unless you was lookin, that is.

We need somethin to finish it off, she says. She looks at me. I don't s'pose—?

Jest as she says it, Nero comes flappin over. He moves slow

an low. Jack's hat dangles from his beak, held by the hatband. He lands. Drops it in ezzackly the right spot. He squawks with delight at his own cleverness.

If that don't beat all, says Molly.

I crouch. I anchor the hat with a couple of rocks. I touch it lightly.

See you soon, Jack, I says.

† † †

Before we leave, Molly goes to fetch her horse, Prue. Also a packed sack of necessaries she's kept hid aginst the day the Tonton would come to run her off. Then she does somethin else.

She goes to a certain spot, a little ways from the tavern an stables. Like any other lonely spot on this blasted plain, but fer a pile of rocks. A small cairn. She kneels beside it a long moment, her head bowed.

We look to Slim fer a reason why. He shakes his head an shrugs. When she rides up to join us, you can tell from her eyes that she's had a bit of a boo. We make like we don't notice.

So, as we git ready to move out, there's me an Molly on horseback. Lugh's drivin the Cosmic, with Tommo beside him. After their bad start, Moses took aginst Maev an won't budge one inch if she's anywhere in sight. Her an Em an Tracker's gonna travel in back with Slim. They'll do their best to keep him easy, but ridin on top of guns ain't a good ride fer nobody, let alone a wounded man. But he slams back a half-campbell of some thin green liquid—it'll blunt the pain, he says—an climbs in without complaint. We take one last look at the tavern at the crossroads. The fire's settled down to a low, steady burn of what's left.

Well, that's that, says Molly. No more Lost Cause. Me, my father, my grampa, his pa. I'm the last in a long line of deluded fools that stuck with this place. Misplaced optimism, that's what runs in my family. Always lookin fer a break in the clouds. Even in the storm belt.

As we turn our faces north an ride out, we pass Jack's hat. All my hopes set on one battered old hat. Misplaced optimism. I guess it runs in my family too.

SECTOR NINE

WE HEAR SIGNS OF LIFE LONG BEFORE WE SEE 'EM.

The faint strains of a junkband racket through the night. Down the road an over the trees. Foot-stompin music. The sound of voices whoopin. People havin fun.

Sounds like a party, says Molly. That's strange. The Tonton don't allow fun an it's after curfew. I wonder what's goin on.

Her an me move up next to Lugh an Tommo. Go slow, she tells Lugh. Hang back, stay outta sight till we find out what's what. Slim! She bangs on the side of the Cosmic. Somethin's goin on at Bram an Cassie's.

It ain't long before the farm comes into view.

Whoa, Moses, Lugh says softly.

We stop. We're at a bend in the road. Cedar woods on both sides. Tracker leaps outta the back an Em an Maev follow. They give Slim a careful hand down, but still he grimaces with pain. He's pale an drawn. The journey's bin hard on him.

Jest ahead lies the farm. Sprawlin fields in every direction with a big, square, hard dirt farmyard standin next to the road. A decent-sized house of tire an mud with a Wrecker junk roof stands one side. A lantern shines in the glass window. The party's goin on in the barn at the top end of the yard. The big doors stand open. Light an music an noise spill out into the night. A couple dozen carts with their horses parked up in a friendly muddle any which way.

We could take one of them an be gone in no time, says Lugh.

Ferget it, I says.

The mournful call of a pigeon comes from the woods to our right. Slim holds up a hand to hush us. The pigeon haroos agin. Slim makes answer.

Without a sound, a man slips outta the trees. A mountain of a man. Emmi gasps an ducks behind Maev.

A mask hides the top half of his face. It's a rough, savage thing of corn husks an bark. Not what you wanna see creepin out from the woods at night. Tracker growls.

The man holds his clenched fist to his chest. Long life to the Pathfinder, he says.

May he rot in hell, says Slim. Evenin, Bram. What's with the mask? Sounds like a party at yer place. Didn't think that kinda thing was allowed.

Special occasion, says Bram. First corn harvest in Sector Nine. Land's fruitful around here, thanks to the hard-workin folk the Tonton took it from. He takes off his mask an starts walkin towards us. Like the dress, Slim. Who you got with you? Is that Molly?

Hey, Bram, she says.

Bram's got a thatch of dark hair, a thick neck an eyes like a sleepy raccoon. He might have twenny two year on him.

He's got the black quartered-circle brand in the center of his forehead.

What're you doin here? he says. What the hell happened to you two? He frowns as he sees Slim's bandaged shoulder, as he takes in the soot smudges on Molly's face, the scorches on her clothes. Ohmigawd, they burned you out at last, he says. He helps her down from her horse, gives her a hug. You okay?

Yeah, she says. The Tonton shot Slim. We need Cassie to look at his shoulder.

Ran into 'em on the causeway, says Slim. Then we blew it up.

Bram whistles. His glance flicks over the rest of us. Who're all of these?

Friends, says Molly.

Friends we don't want the Tonton knowin about, says Slim. He motions to me. As I slide down from Hermes, Nero flaps off to perch on a branch. I go over to 'em. I hesitate.

Yer okay, says Slim. Go on, sister.

I pull my sheema back from my hair an face, so's Bram can see my birthmoon tattoo. His sleepy eyes snap open.

Bram, says Slim, meet Saba.

I don't believe it! Bram holds out a meaty mitt an we shake. You do know there's a price on yer head, he says.

Not now, says Slim. We gotta git the Cosmic outta sight. There was six Tonton on the causeway when we blew it up. If any of 'em got away, they'll be lookin fer me.

You got the weapons? says Bram.

You got somewhere to stash 'em? says Slim.

You bet, says Bram. Here, on the left. I'll guide you in.

Workin fast, we move Moses an the Cosmic off the road an into the woods. We cover our tracks as we go, like Bram tells us to. The way he takes us, there's enough room fer the Cosmic to git through without scrapin bark or breakin off branches. Mind you, at one point, it's such a tight squeeze that we only jest make it.

Lucky, says Slim.

No luck, says Bram with a smile. Good measurements.

He stops when we reach a small clearin, deep in the woods. Here we are, he says.

There ain't nuthin to see. Bram falls to his knees, starts clearin away the thick layers of damp pine needle with his hands. He feels around. He levers up a wooden hatch, lays it to one side, an swings hisself into the hole. He moves nippy, his head disappearin bit by bit. Must be a ladder. We crowd around.

It's a good sized unnerground room, down ten foot or so, there among the gnarled an twisted tree roots. Enough headroom fer Bram to stand upright. A stripped log serves fer a ladder, set at a sharp angle with crude steps hacked into it on one side. Lugh goes to climb down an Bram says, Mind the steps.

How come? says Lugh.

Number six ain't there, says Bram with a grin. But I only tell my friends. Okay, let's move. Quiet as you can.

We hurry to unload the Cosmic. Back an forth between the cart an Bram's unnerground store, where him an Lugh stack everythin into neat piles.

Where'd you git all this? I ask Slim.

He pulls me aside. Tunnels, he whispers. A Wrecker military place—Nass Camp—loads of stuff, buried unnerground. When we first, uh . . . met, I'd jest bin there to stock up.

Where? I says.

You know where you hijacked me? he says. Due north up that road, five leagues, give or take. He taps the side of his nose with a finger, points it at me. Our secret.

Emmi's gathered up a armload of Slim's lethal little balls with pins. She sets off with careful steps.

No, Emmi, let me take 'em, says Tommo.

I can do it! She glares at him. She trips. One of the balls goes flyin into the air.

Catch it! yells Slim.

Maev dives. We hold our breath. She snags it one-handed. Jest before it hits the ground.

Hoo! Slim wipes his brow. Sometimes them pins can be a little loose.

Shame-faced, Em gives up her armload to Tommo.

Once the Cosmic's empty of arms, we close the dump an move her deeper into the woods. Down a little ravine an behind a couple of giant deadfall cedars. She's a sorry sight after her trials on the road.

Poor old Cosmic, says Slim, shakin his head.

We'll mend her tomorrow, says Bram.

What now? says Molly. Our timin stinks, huh?

You could say, says Bram. Most everybody in Sector Nine's at our place tonight, every one devoted to the Pathfinder. But that wound of Slim's needs seein to an Cassie's the one to do it. I'm gonna sneak you into the house, all of yuz. I got a idea. But you gotta do ezzackly as I say, an Moses'll hafta stay here. We ain't got no camels in this sector.

He's gotta come with, says Slim. He'll bellow somethin fearful. Don't you got a stable to put him in?

Sure, says Bram, but—

He's pals with this here horse, says Slim. Hermes. He'll keep quiet if they're in there together.

Good grief, says Bram. A camel in the stable. All right, it won't be fer long, but you tell Cassie. She won't kill a wounded man.

Leadin Moses an Hermes, we follow him back through the woods, towards the road. Suddenly, the soft coo of a pigeon. We freeze. It comes agin. Bram answers.

Who's that? I says.

You ain't my only new friends, he says. It's bin quite busy around here.

Quick movement from both sides as two people slip outta

the trees. They stand in front of us. Masked, like Bram was. Bodies tense. Firesticks at the ready. They lift their masks.

He's wiry. Wild-haired. Barefoot. Tattooed. She's built to fight. Her waist-long hair hangs in dozens of plaits. Hard face. Wary eyes.

Creed. Ash.

Last seen at Darktrees. Presumed dead.

Here in front of us. Very much alive.

†   †   †

My breath catches in my throat.

Ash! cries Emmi.

She runs. She leaps. She clings to Ash like a burr an covers her face in rapturous kisses. Tough Ash softens, like she always does with Em.

She says, Still daft as a brush, I see.

She gives her backside a swat an dumps her on the ground. Creed ruffs Em's hair an winks as he shines his white-toothed smile on her.

Then I'm the one who rushes at 'em. As tears prick my eyes, I grab Ash in a tight hug.

Hello, my lovely, she says.

We thought you was dead, I whisper.

I'm way too stubborn to die, she says. What the hell're you doin here?

Jack sent fer me, I says.

Jack! Her face darkens. If I ever see that sonofabitch agin, I'll kill him, she says. He's turned, Saba. Gone over to the Tonton.

I says, No, Ash, it ain't like that.

We cain't say no more. Tommo's pilin in with the hugs an handshakes an Lugh as well.

Creed seizes my hand an holds it to his heart. I knew you couldn't keep away from me, he says. Suddenly, he catches sight of Molly. He goes still. Drops my hand like a hot coal. Good gawd, he says, who're you?

Bram says, Ash, Creed, this is Molly I bin tellin you about.

Creed walks right up to her, right in close, a look of wonder on his face. I'm gonna marry you, he says.

Molly curls her lip in scorn. As if I'd marry a grubby dirt-boy like you, she says.

He wipes a fire smudge from her cheek with his thumb. Tenderly.

You will, he says. Molly swats his hand off, like she would a fly. He jest smiles, an saunters away. She frowns after him, flushed with annoyance.

Creed, says Ash. She nods at Maev.

Maev ain't moved since Ash an Creed appeared, the dead risen to life. She stands stiff with shock. Her face gleams sickly white in the dimness of the woods. She looks worse'n Slim. Maev, who rode away from Darktrees as the Hawks an Raiders were being slaughtered by the Tonton, who left Ash an Creed to their fate.

Without a word, they go towards her. They pass her on eether side an head deeper into the woods. She stands there a moment. Then she turns an follows 'em.

They got plenty to talk about, I says. Bram, I need yer help. A friend of mine's in trouble.

Come to the house an meet Cassie, he says. We'll talk there.

†   †   †

Cassie turns out to be my age. A sturdy, pink-cheeked girl with a ready smile an careful eyes. She don't even blink when we all slip into her farmhouse as Bram keeps watch by the door. Jest a quick glance at my tattoo an Lugh's.

She sets out soap, clean rags an basins of hot water fer us to have a wash—Lugh an Tommo in one room an us girls and Nero in her an Bram's bedroom.

The little girl's gonna hafta stay outta sight, she says, an you, you cain't wear them clothes. You'll stick out. Yer taller'n me, but help yerself to what you can find in the chest.

She leaves us to it an goes to tend to Slim's wound. Me,

Molly an Em waste no time in strippin to our skivvies. Em's eyes jest about pop outta her head at the sight of Molly's womanly curves packed tight into her fancy red petticoat. Nero flaps his wings an shrieks.

Nero, quit it! Sorry, I says. He don't know he's a crow.

Molly laughs.

Em's still gogglin. Don't stare, I says, as I seize her rag an attack the back of her neck.

Ow! she says.

That friend of yers, says Molly, Creed. He's crazy, right?

No more'n any of us, I says. You better look out.

He better look out, she mutters.

Hold still! I scrub Em's face an ears. I says, Nobody believes me about Jack. Not Lugh, not Tommo. Maev says she does, but . . . I don't think so. Ash wants to kill him, probly Creed does too. It's jest you an me an Em.

I love Jack, says Em.

Do you now? says Molly.

Uh huh, an so does Saba, essept she's too—

I dunk Em's head in the basin. She splutters an squawks as I soap her hair.

I know how it is between you an Jack, says Molly. The moment I seen him, I knew he'd met somebody. I could see you in his eyes. Then he showed me the heartstone.

I feel myself flush. I set Em free an git to work on myself. Tonight's the full moon. An I don't care what Slim says, when

Jack finds the message at the Lost Cause, he'll come straight here. I'm gonna see Jack agin. My stummick does a nervous flip at the thought. I scrub an rub an rinse till my skin's tinglin.

I tidy my wet hair with my fingers. It's grown good since they shaved my head fer the cage fights in Hopetown. One day, it'll hang down my back the way it used to. Then Lugh an me'll have hair the same, an nobody'll ever cut it off agin.

Molly holds up her bone comb. Let me, she says. She combs rose oil through my hair. Here, she says, rub it in yer skin, it'll make it soft.

I gotta talk to Bram, I says, about Jack.

Leave it to me, she says. Before I can say nay, she's gone in a swish of skirts.

I oil myself an git dressed in a pair of plain britches an shirt that I find in Cassie's chest. They come a bit short on me, but not too disgraceful. Then me an Em join everybody else.

Slim's bin doctored an put to bed in a secret hidey hole in the wall. I look in on him, but he's already fast to sleep. Tracker lies at his feet, on guard duty. There ain't no sign of Creed an Ash. But Maev sits by the fire, silent, starin into the flames.

Molly's in a corner, talkin to Bram. Their heads lean together, her hand on his arm, her voice low an urgent. He nods his head from time to time.

The door from th'other room opens. Lugh an Tommo come out. I gasp. Their hair's bin cut short. Lugh's long, golden plait.

It's gone. He's had it since we was little. My heart clutches.

Why'd you do that? I says.

No long hair in New Eden, says Cassie, not fer men.

Lugh holds up his plait. It gleams, thick an golden, in the firelight. His eyes meet mine, a bit defiant. I was sick of it anyways, he says. Glad to see it go.

Bram turns back into the room, to the rest of us. Molly's eyes meet mine. A tiny shake of her head. I frown. Later, she mouths.

What now? says Tommo.

Nuthin, says Bram, this ain't the time. We cain't talk, cain't even be seen all together, it's too dicey. We gotta wait till everybody leaves. There's a lot to discuss—what to do about Slim, an you lot too. Fer now, Cassie an me better git out there before we're missed.

The two of 'em hand out masks to everybody but Emmi.

What's all this? I says.

Sometimes, the best way to stay outta sight is to be in plain view, says Bram. Tonight, it's the lone light in the woods that'll draw attention. Nobody'll notice a few more dancers in a crowded barn.

Why cain't we stay in here? I says.

It ain't safe, says Cassie. People's bin in an outta here all day. I don't s'pose any of yuz fancy crammin in the priesthole with Slim.

Don't take yer masks off fer nuthin, says Bram. Remember, you ain't branded. An everybody's on the lookout fer Saba an her tattoo. It'll be a great honor to hand her over to the Pathfinder.

If anybody asks, says Cassie, Saba an Tommo, you bin paired a month. You farm in Sector Seventeen. Lugh an Maev, the same. There ain't no Sector Seventeen, but none of these know that. They won't wanna look stupid, so they'll pretend they heard of it.

Sorry, Tommo, but it ain't safe fer you to speak, says Bram. Best to make like yer painful shy.

Dark color flags Tommo's cheeks. He nods.

How should we act? says Lugh.

Like them two at Billy Six's place, I says. Like you own the world an everybody in it.

We'll climb Emmi up to the corn loft, says Bram. Everybody's had enough of the damn stuff after today, so it's the last place they'll go.

Cain't I watch the dancin? she says.

You can look through the boards at what's goin on, he tells her, but you gotta keep schtum, okay? Not a footstep, not a squeak, nuthin, you unnerstand?

Emmi nods. Cassie an Bram put on their half-masks. We do the same. In one moment, who we are is hidden. We're unknown. Strangers, even to each other.

What about me? says Molly. What's my story?

Oh, I'm sure we'll think of somethin, says Bram. C'mon.

† † †

Molly's story turns out to be Creed.

He slips from the stables next to the house.

I thought he might turn up, says Bram.

Ohmigawd, I says, he's gone respectable.

So he has. Clean clothes, tattoos covered by long sleeves an a collared shirt, hair cut short an neat. He's even wearin boots. He looks completely different.

Yer positively handsome, Creed, says Emmi. I could never tell before.

He puts on his mask an falls into step beside Molly. He smiles at her. You look beautiful, he says. She says naught. You smell beautiful too, he says.

She don't even look at him as she says, Lemme set you straight, Sunny Jim. I ain't available. Even if I was, I wouldn't be available to you.

Ouch, he says.

You don't wear boots, Creed, I says.

Special occasion, he says. They ain't mine, they're Ash's. She's on lookout duty.

Bram takes Em to run her up the outside ladder to the corn-loft above the barn. Cassie leads the rest of us to the open doors. Inside, by the light of a dozen lanterns, everybody's dancin. Stewards of the Earth. Young. Strong. Workers. Breeders.

Everybody starts to go in.

Molly! I grab her hand an pull her to one side. What did Bram say?

I'm sorry, Saba, she says. If Jack shows up, you gotta stay outta sight. You cain't make contact with him.

My stummick drops. What? I says. Why not?

Bram's well set up here, she says. It's took him a long time to make connections—with Slim an me, one or two people around an about. Nobody would ever suspect he's anythin but a loyal Steward of the Earth. He cain't jeopardize that. You got a price on yer head, it's dangerous fer him to be har-borin you like this. He'll help you git outta New Eden, but that's it.

But . . . you told him Jack's a friend of yers, right? I says. It ain't jest me, you know he's in trouble, Molly. You know Jack.

I sure do. She sighs. Listen, Saba, Jack's bin tanglin with trouble his whole life, she says. He gits hisself into it an some-how he always gits hisself out agin. I know what Bram says don't seem fair, but you gotta look at the bigger picture. We gotta respect his wishes. This is his place. We cain't go puttin him an Cassie, all of us, in danger. Promise me you'll do as he says.

Jack sent fer me, I says. I ain't come all this way fer nuthin.

Once you leave, she says, you can do what you like. Take chances on yer own account. Promise me you won't do nuthin while yer here.

On my own. Once more, it's down to me, on my own, to do what I gotta do. That's fine. It's what I wanted all along. Bram's right, I cain't put everybody at risk. I don't want to. If Jack shows up here, I will stay outta sight. But I'll go after him, even if he's with other Tonton. I'll follow 'em till we're away from here. Wait fer the moment to make contact with him.

Promise me, Saba, says Molly.

I promise, I says.

We better go in, she says. C'mon.

My stummick's flutterin, like a butterfly caught in a spider's web. Right now, there's too much that's outta my control. Not jest tonight, but ever since we crossed the Yann Gap into New Eden. My hand's bin forced over an over. I ain't bin makin my own decisions.

Long before you was born, Saba, a train of events was set in motion.

You mean fate. I don't believe in it.

Not fate. Destiny. Fer you, all roads lead to the same place.

I jest need to see Jack, talk to him, have him explain everythin. Then we'll figger out what to do, how best to git away. The longer I'm in DeMalo's country, the more I feel things slip away from me.

Saba? says Molly.

Okay, I says. Here we go.

† † †

The band plays on a raised platform in the middle of the barn. All around it, bodies twirl. There must be fifty dancers in here. Their damp heat thickens the air. Smells crash together. Sweat. Soap. Earth on boots. The corn in the loft where Emmi hides. Roasted pig on the spit in the yard. Arms fly. Feet stomp. There in the beat, there in the bodies, somethin throbs an growls. Urgent. Rough. Dark. There's chaos in it. Wildness.

It's the masks. They're excited by 'em. They've unleashed somethin inside these young Stewards. Three girls, well on with child, sit on stools aginst the wall. Them an the band's th'only ones not wearin masks. One tune finishes an the players start another. It's a slow one, heavy on drums an bone shrillie. The dancers pair up. From the shrieks an laughter, not with their rightful mate.

Bram's back. He gives the tiniest of nods. That means Emmi's up above us, safely outta sight in the corn. We join in the dance. Molly an Creed. Me an Tommo. Lugh an Maev. Bram an Cassie.

It's easy enough to catch on. It's a tease of a dance. Slow. Shoulder to shoulder, hand to hand, back to back, oh-so-close but never quite touchin. Two steps forwards, two steps back, move in close an circle each other. Eye to eye through the masks.

Lugh an Maev talk, all intent, their heads close together. Creed talks to Molly. Molly pretends he ain't there. I keep lookin towards the open doors an the night outside. Not wantin to be here. Feelin trapped. It's too hot. I cain't breathe.

I need air, I says to Tommo.

We make our way outside. There's a few people standin around the pigroast pit. We hurry into the shadows. Outta sight, outta earshot. We rip off our masks. I close my eyes. Feel the cool air brush my hot face. Take in a deep breath.

With a rush, outta nowhere, Tommo's holdin me, kissin me, pressin tight up aginst me. Clumsy, urgent, unsure. Soft lips. A boy's lips.

I grab his hands. I move him away from me. Gently. Firmly. We stare at each other.

He says, I'm true an constant. Not like Jack. I love you, Saba. I love you.

He means it. He feels it. It's in his face. His voice. His eyes. What'm I gonna say? Whatever I say, it's gonna hurt him. I cain't bear to do that. He's bin hurt too much in his life already.

Tommo, I says, you . . . you an me—

Saba! Ash's voice. Hissin at me from the field nearby. I go towards her an Tommo follows me. She's crouched in the corn stubble.

Tonton comin! she says. Six riders. One cart. They'll be here any minute.

As she disappears, me an Tommo's pullin on our masks. We run back inside to find Bram an Cassie. Cassie's tappin her toes an watchin. Bram's takin a breather.

Tonton comin, I says to him.

Probly jest droppin by to check the party's all above board. Oh, he says, lookin at the pregnant girls, an it might be their time to be collected.

We look out over the dancers as we speak, pretend we're havin a casual conversation. Tommo's gone to stand with Cassie. Collected? I says.

They go to the baby house to give birth, he says. They leave the child to be wet-nursed an raised to be a Steward of the Earth, jest like them. Weak or surplus babies git left out in the open overnight. By the mornin, it'll be dead from cold or some animal will of took it.

Harsh, I says.

Only the strongest an best fer New Eden, he says. Molly spoke to you.

I nod. I unnerstand, I says. I won't make no trouble fer you.

Go dance, he says. Stick with yer friends. There's a door in the corner if you gotta make a quick exit. Head fer the fields.

He casts a quick glance at the ceilin. The cornloft's over-head. Emmi'll be watchin through the gaps. Yer sister, he says, will she have the wit to hide if they decide to search up there? You never know.

Of course, I says.

As he goes off, I take Tommo's hand an we slide back in among the Stewards.

We gotta talk, he says.

Not now, Tommo, I says.

As we move past Molly an Creed, she whispers, Where you bin?

Tonton comin, I mutter. Keep dancin.

Me an Tommo dance our way across the barn, with Molly an Creed right behind us. As we do, I see Lugh an Maev. Slippin through the little door. Hand in hand. Unseen by anybody but me. Where the hell're they goin?

Jest as I clock 'em, a ripple goes through the room. All heads turn to the main doors. A Tonton patrol. Six men, like Ash said. My heart seizes. Is Jack with 'em? Did he find my message at the Lost Cause?

The music falters, feet start to slow. But the patrol commander signals to the players an they keep on playin. The dancers keep dancin. There ain't hardly bin a pause. The Tonton move towards the three pregnant girls, clenched fists over their hearts, the sign of the Pathfinder. The girls salute quickly, as they stand up an start fussin with their clothes.

They're giddy with excitement.

I can barely see the back of the Tonton's heads. They all got short-cropped hair, clean, fine-lookin robes an gear. Nuthin like the grubby Tonton scum I know from Hopetown an Freedom Fields. I cain't tell if Jack's one of 'em.

I drop Tommo's hand. My bootlace, I says, it's broke. I drop down an pretend to tie it. I lose myself in the swirl of dancers, duckin, keepin low, movin bit by bit towards the door in the corner.

Lucky girls, says a girl nearby. They're off to the baby house.

I cain't hardly wait till it's my turn, says another.

My belly's tight, my heart's racin. I'm at the door now, pressin myself into the shadows. The Tonton patrol's movin towards the main doors, two by two, with the pregnant girls between 'em. The dancers nearby clap an cheer.

I gotta find out. I gotta know if Jack's with 'em. If he is, I'll follow.

Nobody's lookin. I lift the latch. I slip through the door.

† † †

I'm outside the barn. A big open shed stands opposite. I can make out tools, planks, bits of wagon, a plough. Stubbled fields to my right. The farmyard an house to my left.

I can hear a voice. Loud. Sure of hisself. The patrol commander. You two men, he says, split up, take a quick check around the barn, then we'll be on our way.

I dive into the shed. Hide behind a stack of planks. Suddenly, I feel it. The heartstone around my neck. I touch it. It's warm. The heartstone knows.

Jack's here.

He's here.

Right away, I'm tremblin. My breath comes fast an tight. Somebody rounds the front corner of the barn, holdin up a torch to light his way.

It's Jack. In his black Tonton robes an armor. Short hair. Clean shaved. He makes his way slowly along the side of the barn. Movin his torch high, then low, checkin that all's clear.

As he moves towards me, I watch him from the shadows. Time shudders. It stops. It waits. I take in the sight of him. His face, his lips, his crooked nose. His silver gray eyes like moonlight.

The heartstone burns, fierce an true. I bin wantin him so long. I bin missin him so deep. It hurts my heart to see him agin. I open my mouth to call his name. I stop myself. His head snaps in my direction. Like he knows I'm here. Did I make a noise? He lifts the torch. At the same time, there's a rustle overhead. I look up. Jack does too.

The side wall of the barn is directly opposite the shed. Set into it, at the top of a long ladder, there's a hatch door to the cornloft. It's open. Somebody's scuttlin down the ladder. It's Emmi.

Jack snatches up the whistle that hangs at his neck. He blows it. He's raisin the alarm.

My feet start to move. Two great arms grab me from behind. One hand clamps over my mouth, th'other one hauls me tight to him. It's Bram. Not a sound, he whispers in my ear. We watch.

Em's jumpin the last few feet to the ground, jest as more Tonton come runnin. One from the back of the barn, four from the front, includin the commander.

Gotcha! Jack yells. He lunges at Em an plucks her from the ladder. He swings her about, then backhands her across the face. Her head snaps back. She goes limp. He dumps her on the ground.

It's happened in a blink. Bram drags me further into the shed. We crouch there, listenin.

She must of bin hidin in the cornloft, Jack's sayin.

She looks a strong, healthy one, says one of the Tonton. If you ain't broke her neck, that is. He picks her up an heaves her over his shoulder.

Naw, says Jack, she's okay.

Let's hope she makes a good breeder some day, says another Tonton.

Nice work, brother, says the commander.

Jack salutes, clenched fist to his heart. I serve the Pathfinder an New Eden, he says.

They disappear around the front of the barn.

✝   ✝   ✝

Bram hangs on to me. Keeps his hand over my mouth. My breath shudders. My body twitches. It's lucky he stopped me. Lucky fer me, fer all of us, that he's as strong as he is. When Jack blew that whistle, when I realized Em was in trouble, the red hot kicked in an I jest went. An then he hit her. Knocked her out cold. If I'd of bin free, I would of gone fer him. With my bare hands, I would of tried to kill him.

Bram keeps his voice low an calm. We're gonna keep cool, he says. I know where they'll take her. We'll make a plan to git her back. Is she a smart girl?

I nod.

Then she'll be fine. Now, we ain't gonna make a fuss. We ain't gonna draw attention. That'll jest git us all in trouble, includin yer sister. We're gonna walk around the corner an wave 'em off, like the good Stewards they think we are. Nuthin's happened here, nuthin outta the ordinary fer New Eden. D'you unnerstand? Nod if you do.

I nod.

Okay, he says. C'mon.

As I follow him outta the darkness of the shed, Cassie slips outta the little door from the barn. The music rackets out behind her.

They found Emmi, says Bram. They're takin her.

Are we in trouble? says Cassie.

Nope, he says. We're grateful they found her. We knew somebody was hidin around here, we bin havin trouble.

Cassie takes one arm, Bram takes th'other an they walk me around the corner to the yard. We're jest in time to see 'em leave. The cart with the girls fer the baby house rattles outta the yard. Em's on horseback. Small an limp, she rides with the man who picked her up, his arms circled around her. The commander's last to ride out.

Bram raises a hand in thanks. We knew there was a mischief maker hidin around here, he says. Grateful fer yer help. Long life to the Pathfinder! Him an Cassie salute. The commander does the same. Then he heels his horse to catch up with his patrol.

Jack. He was smilin at the man next to him. Laughed at somethin he said.

The night swallows 'em. Folds around the sound of their hoofbeats. Then they're gone.

Emmi's gone.

The heartstone's still hot on my skin. The music an laughter an light spill outta the barn. Molly, Creed an Tommo hurry over to us. Where'd you go, Saba? says Molly. What's happened?

They took Emmi, Cassie tells 'em.

I feel dazed, like I'm in a dream. Jack was with 'em, I says. He hit her. Knocked her out.

What? says Molly.

He'll know she ain't here by herself, says Creed. He knows yer here, Saba, that Maev found you.

He took her, I says.

He didn't hafta, says Bram. He was by hisself. He whistled fer help.

He's turned, Saba, says Tommo. Lugh was right.

I back away. Strangers. Everywhere. All around me. My throat's tight. Where is he? I whisper. I want Lugh, where's my brother, I want my brother, where is he?

My body's shakin. I don't know none of these people, they ain't my people an all I want is Lugh an he ain't here, he's off somewhere with Maev when I need him an I ain't got nobody.

Hush. Cassie touches my arm. Come with me, she says. We cain't do nuthin fer now.

She starts leadin me towards the house. I can hear Bram sayin somethin to the men by the pigroast pit, hear them laughin.

We're passin by the stables. There's a couple of horses

standin outside. I shove Cassie hard. As she staggers back, I leap onto the nearest horse an we take off. He's facin the fields, so that's the way we go.

We fly over the stubbled cornfields.

I jest go.

Nowhere. Somewhere. Anywhere that's away from here.

† † †

Nobody follows.

I ride. An ride. An I cry. I sob my rage to the night. Nero flies above. Silent companion. My head's thick. It pounds. I'm trapped in my thoughts.

All this fer Jack. All fer Jack. I believed him. Defended him. An this is what he does. This is what he is. He's deceived me. Betrayed me. Lugh's bin right all along.

What d'you know about him? Nuthin. He plays whatever side suits him at the time. He's a hollow man. A trickster. He's betrayed you. Betrayed you an deceived you. You got a price on yer head, an Jack's a man with his eye on the main chance. How fine would that be? Make his mark with the Pathfinder by handin over the Angel of Death.

If Bram hadn't of grabbed me, if he hadn't of stopped me, I'd be in Tonton hands right now.

Trickster.

Betrayer.

Deceiver.

Jack lied about everythin. Who he is. What he is. How he felt about me. A means to a end, that's all I ever was.

I cain't stand to think about it. How stupid I am. What a blind fool.

Who cares what Molly says about him? What does she know, anyways? Look at her, stayin in that gawdfersaken storm belt years on end, waitin fer Ike Twelvetrees to come back to her.

The heartstone. It's a liar too. I wish Mercy'd never gave it me.

Without it, I'd never of looked at Jack twice. Never saved him from the Hopetown fire. I would of found Lugh on my own an we'd be out west by now. Him an me an Emmi. Everythin's wrecked. Ruined.

I wish I'd never met Jack.

I hate him.

Hate him.

Deceiver. Betrayer. Liar.

After a while, I cain't keep up the wild pace. I let the horse do what he wants. As he slows to a walk, I lie aginst his neck, worn out an cried out. We wander through the night. I don't pay no heed to where I am, to time passin.

The roar of fallin water rouses me. I lift my head an look

about me. We're in woods now, followin a rough track. The horse slows, stops. I slide off. I stumble through the trees. Suddenly, I'm in the open, on the edge of a high, rocky cliff. The cool spray wakes me. Water shoots out from the cliff face below. It thunders into a wide pool, a dizzy fifty foot drop straight down.

Nero shrieks as he circles above. Clouds clear the moon. I rip the heartstone from my neck. I throw it. It arcs. It falls.

Nero swoops to grab it. A black shape drops outta nowhere.

It's a hawk.

He knocks Nero.

Nero! I scream.

They tumble as they fall from the sky. Fightin. Shriekin.

They're gonna land in the water.

Nero's gonna die.

I leap.

I leap from the cliff.

WEEPING WATER

DOWN, DOWN, DOWN I FALL. I LAND SMACK ON MY BACK.
Knock the breath from my body. Sharp pain at my temple.

I plunge to the dark below.

Down to the bottom. Where the dark things crouch. Where the old things wait. Where they crouch an wait fer me.

The darkest depths beckon me down. Black water of pain, it closes over me.

Let go, it's safe to let go.

Betrayed.

Deceived.

Let go.

I open my mouth.

I let the darkness in. It begins to fill me.

Somethin grabs my wrist. A hand. Strong. No, let me be. I pull away.

Too strong.

Up.

Up.

Up from the dark.

Then.

Cool air hits my face.

I gasp.

Gasp.

Cough.

Breathe.

No! I says. I start to struggle. Let me be!

Don't fight me! Hand unner my chin, towin me. I'm hauled from the water. Laid on my side on rocky ground.

Nero, I says.

There's a rush of air. A splash.

I turn on my back an open my eyes. I'm lookin up at the night sky. Lyin on the edge of the rock pool. The roar of the waterfall from the cliff above.

Nero. The hawk got him. I drag myself to my knees. Nero! I cry.

A dark shape swims towards me, one-handed. It's a man. He holds Nero in his other hand, keepin him above the water. As he gits closer, I can see who it is.

My heart seizes.

It's DeMalo.

† † †

DeMalo. The Pathfinder. Master of New Eden. I'm dreamin. This cain't be true. He climbs outta the pool, gaspin fer breath, his chest heavin. He drags a wave of water with him an it splashes me. It's cold. Real. No dream.

He's alive, says DeMalo. Wounded but alive.

Give him here! I take Nero with careful hands, my breath caught in my throat. Nero! I says. His eyes glitter up at me. He gives a feeble croak. He's bleedin, I says, he's hurt, we gotta fix him.

I'm camped just over there, says DeMalo. Can you walk?

Yes, I says. I'm already gittin to my feet, my eyes checkin Nero over. There's blood on his breast an head.

When I saw it was you, I couldn't believe it, says DeMalo.

I hardly look at him, barely glance at him. Please, I says, we gotta hurry.

This way, he says. As he leads me away from the falls an the pool, he checks the sky. He gives a piercin whistle. It was my hawk, he says. Culan. I was night flying him. Not expecting visitors. I'm sorry.

I'm right behind him. My heart's racin. I'm coughin. My clothes an hair hang heavy with water, my boots squelch with every step. He's barefoot, bright in the night in his white shirt an britches. Water drips offa him too. He used to wear his thick black hair long an tied back. Now it's cut to his collar.

The path's rough. I stumble an Nero squeaks protest. How far? I says.

We're here, says DeMalo.

A simple tent among the trees. Nobody around.

Where's yer men? I says.

I'm alone, he says. This is my retreat. You're perfectly safe.

I hesitate. He holds open the tent flap. The crow's wounded, he says.

I follow him inside.

† † †

I hear him movin around. I can jest make him out, a shape darker than the dark. Then the sound of flint an a soft white glow lights the tent.

He sets the lantern on a table. Bring him here, he says.

Simple outside, simple inside too. Big enough to stand up in. A narrow bed, a stove, a chair, the table, a wooden chest. A few other bits. Some books. Good fer one, close quarters fer two.

DeMalo's fillin a bowl with clean water. He brings it to the table, then goes to the chest an takes out a blanket an a little tin box. He moves silent an smooth. He don't look to be in no hurry, but somehow everythin happens fast.

Sit, he says. He drapes the blanket around my shoulders as I sit on the chair, huggin Nero close, soothin him. Now, he says as he opens the box an starts takin bits out, we'll clean him up and take a look. He pours tincture in the water an dips a clean cloth. Move him close to the light, he says.

His voice is low. Deep. Warm. The few times, the few

words I heard him speak before—back at Hopetown, in the cells—unsettled me. Chilled me. Not now. Somehow, he don't seem like the same person. Or maybe it's me.

I can fix him myself, I says.

You're in no fit state, he says. He cleans Nero's head first. Gently.

I don't dare breathe till I see how bad it is. Jest a scratch, I says.

He dabs cranesbill salve on it. It's this other I'm worried about, he says. Okay, Nero, brave fellow. He starts to clean his breast. As the water in the bowl turns red, we can see the damage. A tear in the flesh, luckily not near to his heart.

It's not deep, says DeMalo. Looks like Culan just caught him with a talon. I don't see any damage to his wings or muscles. He's okay.

Oh! I gasp out, a sob, or laugh a shaky breath. I kiss Nero's head. D'you hear that? Yer okay.

It needs a couple of stitches, he says. Can he take it?

He can, I says. I dunno about me, though. I cain't abide a needle goin into flesh. I bin known to faint.

DeMalo flashes me a smile. A real, proper smile. I ain't never seen him smile before. His eyes light an crinkle, his teeth gleam, white an straight. He shakes his head as he cleans a thin bone needle. That's funny, he says.

Funny? I says.

He starts to thread fine gut through the tiny eye. I've seen you in action, he says. You're hardly short on courage.

Yeah, well, I says. We all got our weaknesses.

A quick flick of his eyes my way. Weaknesses, he says, or desires? D'you think it's important we learn to conquer them?

Jack. Betrayer. Deceiver.

Yes, I says. Nero croaks. Is he really gonna be all right? I says.

I promise, he says. Hold him still. DeMalo moves his hands slowly towards Nero. He slashes out at him, fightin, defendin hisself. I soothe him, hold his beak closed. DeMalo begins to stitch the wound. Nero struggles. He cries piteously.

Tears spring to my eyes. You're hurtin him! I says.

I'm sorry, it can't be helped, he says. Try to keep him still.

Jest hurry!

You're a mighty warrior, Nero, he says. A crow with the spirit of an eagle. DeMalo's hands work careful an sure. That's one, he says. One more to go.

Good boy, I whisper to Nero. Brave boy.

He cries in little peeps now. The same as when I found him lyin on the ground, fell outta the nest an his ma nowhere in sight. I'm cryin a bit too. I cain't stand that he's in pain. I feel it worse'n if it was me.

There we go. DeMalo's finished. Keep it clean, he says. Don't let him worry the stitches.

I take Nero on to my lap an dab the salve on his poor flesh.

How's that, my friend? DeMalo crouches in front of me.

Puts out a finger to stroke him. Nero gives him a sharp nip. I guess I deserve that, he says.

DeMalo looks so different with short hair. It's wet still. Messy. He smells of somethin green. Fresh. He takes the salve pot from me, dips his finger in it an, before I know, he's smoothin it gently on the cut on my temple.

An I let him. Fer some reason, I let him. I stare straight ahead, not movin, hardly darin to breathe.

DeMalo. I thought of him so many times. An them dreams I had about him, in the vision lodge an other times too. Always so strange an . . . disturbed me. But here we are. Like we know each other. We don't. I can count on two hands the number of times I seen him. An we never spoke, not really. You don't speak with yer enemy.

It's a long drop down Weeping Water, he says.

I give a little laugh. Weepin Water, I says. That fits.

Were you trying to kill yourself? he says.

I says naught.

When I pulled you out, you said no, he says. Let me be, you said.

I don't remember, I says. I—I jest jumped. Becuz of . . . Nero.

Now I do look at DeMalo. An he looks at me. Properly, fer the first time ever, we look straight at each other. The lamplight brushes his broad cheekbones, his lips, the smooth gleam of his skin. His face is strong. Watchful. Beautiful. With heavy-lidded eyes, so dark they're almost black.

I feel this pull towards him, between us. I felt it when I first seen him. Like there's a thin, tight, invisible thread that runs from him to me. An there's somethin about him—a kinda stillness inside of him—that makes me wanna tell him the truth. That believes he won't judge me.

Maybe I did mean to kill myself, I says. I didn't think it outright but . . . maybe the truth is, I didn't—I don't—much care one way or th'other.

To walk alone isn't easy, he says. What about your friends? Your brother and sister? Where are they?

I left, I says.

You're not the same as them, he says. You're nothing like them.

I don't unnerstand, I says. Why're you bein nice to me? I killed Pinch. You put a price on my head.

Silence. Then, the sudden patter of rain on the tent roof. A moment later, it's poundin down. It thunders onto the ground outside, splashes in through the flap.

As if we're not wet enough already, he says. He gits up an pulls the flap to an we're closed in. Alone. The air's suddenly heavier.

I stand up. Nero's cradled in my arms, already fast to sleep. I gotta go, I says. I'm shiverin. Shakin. My clothes hang chill an wet an heavy. My feet's numb with cold.

DeMalo's lightin another lantern. He don't look at me as he says, Somebody waiting for you?

Emmi. Lugh an Maev. Tommo an Slim. Ash an Creed an the rest.

No, I says.

He says, It's night, it's raining, Nero's been injured, you nearly drowned and you're suffering from delayed shock. Have I forgotten anything?

Yes. I bin betrayed by Jack. Deceived.

No, I says.

Well, then, he says. He takes Nero an settles him in a little crate next to the stove. I clutch the blanket around me, my teeth chatterin. DeMalo takes a pile of clothes from the wooden chest an puts 'em on the bed. Dry clothes, he says. He moves back to the stove an starts to feed it more wood. He crouches, his back turned towards me.

I scuttle to the bed an skin off my sodden gear. Use the blanket to rub the clammy wet from my body. I'm cold to the bone. I ain't never bin so cold. My teeth chatter in my head. I fumble into a soft shirt that hangs past my knees, thick socks. They're clean. They carry a faint smell of him. Now I know what it is. Juniper.

Come, sit by the heat, he says.

I dash to the chair by the stove. Pull my knees to my chest an the shirt down over 'em. I hug myself, shiverin. He goes an strips off his wet clothes. I can hear him. If I turned my head, jest a little, I'd see him. DeMalo. Takin his clothes off, not more'n a few foot away. This has gotta be the strangest thing I could ever imagine to happen.

I ain't fled. I ain't run or fought him or tried to kill him. I'd of espected the red hot to kick me in the gut the moment I seen who it was pulled me from the water. But no. Not a sign of it.

This ain't like me. But I ain't like myself. I'm . . . a me I never bin before. I feel unfettered. Light. Free. Free of Lugh an Jack an everybody else who especks somethin from me. Who especks me to be what they want. I don't owe them nuthin.

Right now, there ain't no world outside of this tent. It's as if everybody an everythin has faded away. Disappeared. Apart from DeMalo an me. An suddenly I know that this is where I'm meant to be. Right here. Right now.

All roads lead to the same place.

That's better, says DeMalo. I glance over. He's jest pullin a dry shirt over his head. I catch sight of a tattoo on the smooth skin of his chest. A red risin sun over his heart. My own heart quickens at the sight of his body.

He scoops up my wet clothes that I left in a heap an hangs 'em, along with his, to dry near the stove. Water's drippin through one corner of the tent. He sets a tin unnerneath. He pulls the plug from a green bottle an pours dark red liquid into two glass jars. He drags a stool over, sits on it an hands me one of the jars.

To chance meetings, he says.

To chance, I says.

We drink. It slips over my tongue, warm an rich an soft an

deep. Like a sad song. I ain't never tasted nuthin like it. What is it? I says.

Wine, he says. He holds his jar up to the light. Very old, he says, very rare. A whisper from a lost world.

The rain rains. The air's thick with the storm, heavy.

We drink some more. It's delicious. I'm startin to feel a bit warmer. A bit bolder. D'you have a name? I says. Besides DeMalo, I mean.

Seth, he says. But nobody's called me that for a very long time.

Seth, I says, tryin it out. I tip my glass to him. Thank you fer savin Nero.

What about you? he says. No thanks for saving you?

I says naught. I hug myself an drink the wine.

Three, he says.

I look at him.

That's how many times I've saved your life, he says. Once at Freedom Fields, once from Vicar Pinch and just now.

The rule of three. If you save somebody's life three times, their life belongs to you. No. That ain't nuthin but Jack's stupid nonsense. *Don't even think that name. Betrayed. Deceived. I hate him.*

The rain thunders onto the tent. Water drip drip drips into the tin. Wood crackles an spits inside the iron stove. I stare into my wine. Why did you? I says. Save me all them times? You shouldn't of. We warn't on the same side. We still ain't.

Whose side are you on these days? he says.

Nobody's, I says.

Not even your own, it seems, he says.

None of this makes sense, I says. You bein kind to me, fixin up Nero. Why didn't you let me drown? Ain't you the one who put a price on my head?

Yes, he says.

So, why all this? I says. What now? What d'you want from me?

We look at each other. I can smell the warmth of him. His skin. His hair. Somethin old starts to thrum in my blood.

The rain's slowin to a patter. It stops. He gits up, throws back the tent flap an checks the sky.

It's nearly dawn, he says. I'd like to show you something. Will you come?

What is it? I says.

He's pickin up a lit lantern. Something wonderful, he says. He sees my hesitation. Do you have to be somewhere?

They'll all be waitin. Angry with me about Jack, blamin me that he took Emmi, waitin fer me to make things right. I cain't face 'em. I cain't take no more of my own wrongness. Always wrong about everythin. Hate fer Jack burns in my gut.

Saba, says DeMalo. Are you expected somewhere?

No, I says. I drain my wine, put the jar on the table an stand up. Let's go see this wonderful somethin. Oh! I pluck at the shirt. Better put my clothes back on.

They're wet, he says. Look in the trunk. I'll wait outside.

There's only three things in the trunk—a green dress, womanly skivvies an a good pair of pigskin boots. More suited to Molly than me. I ain't never wore a dress in my life. What's he doin with gear like this?

I check my own stuff. He's right, it's all soppin wet. Nero sleeps in his little box by the fire. I mutter curses as I step into the dress an fumble with the buttons that close it up the front. I block out nigglin thoughts of Emmi as I pull on the boots. I duck outside into the cool air.

I find a pale, pink world. Dawn ain't far off. DeMalo's waitin. The hawk—Culan—sits in a nearby tree. He turns his fierce yellow eyes on me an ruffles his feathers. DeMalo looks at me in the dress. It fits well, he says.

He says it like he knew it would.

Nero's sleepin, I says, I—

We won't be long, says DeMalo. He'll be fine. Come, we need to hurry.

† † †

I follow him outta the trees, over a clear-runnin stream an through a lush, grassy meadow damp with rain. DeMalo keeps a check on the sky as he hurries us on.

This is good land, I says. I never seen finer.

This is New Eden, he says.

We come to a little hill covered with blackberry brambles. The air's heavy with the sweet promise of ripe fruit. There's a rusted metal door set into the hill, where it ain't quite so thick with bramble. It stands open.

Here we are, says DeMalo. The brothers will show you in.

What—? I whirl around. Outta nowhere, there's two Tonton suddenly with us. You said you was alone! What is this?

The two men bow their heads, clenched fists held to their hearts. One of 'em holds a lit lantern.

Everyone's here, master, he says.

What's goin on? I says.

You'll come to no harm, I promise, says DeMalo. They're an escort, that's all. I'll see you in a moment. He holds out his hands to the men. They grasp 'em, eagerly. She's an honored guest, he says. Thank you, brothers. Then, with a smile an a nod, he disappears around the hill, outta sight.

Me an the two Tonton stare at each other. Me. Two Tonton. I'm sniffin fer danger, on sharp edges, jest in case. The one with the lantern smiles an bows his head. Follow me, he says.

He goes through the door. I hesitate. Please, says the second one. We cain't be late.

I go through the door. He closes it behind us. In front, the first Tonton lights our way through pitch blackness. We go down some steps, into the ground. It smells dry. Musty. Thick, earthy silence closes around us. I hate bein unnerground, closed in. Sweat damps my forehead. He leads us through a long narrow room with wide shelfs set in the walls, like bunks. We go through a doorway into another room, then another, but there ain't nuthin in 'em.

What is all this? I says.

A bunker, says the man behind me. From Wrecker times. There was ten of 'em in here when the Pathfinder first come. Ten skellentons, that is. He says it was their hidin place.

What was they hidin from? I says.

Who knows? he says. War, pestilence, some kinda calamity.

We must be close to the center of the hill by now. At the end of a narrow passage, the lantern man opens a closed door an we go through.

Twelve heads turn towards us. Twelve quartered circle brands. Stewards of the Earth. Six boys an six girls. Young an strong, dressed simple. Their right hands fly, clenched, to their hearts.

Long life to the Pathfinder! they says. The two Tonton reply likewise.

I'm paused in the doorway, one foot in, one out. Not only my guide, but a few of the Stewards hold lanterns too, so the room's well lit. It ain't long an narrow, like th'other rooms we jest come through. This one's big, maybe twenny paces across each way. It's got white, smooth walls, built pretty much square but round in the corners. A white ceilin an floor.

I realize that all eyes is on me. Wary eyes. Starin at my birthmoon tattoo.

The one that the Pathfinder seeks has come, says the lantern man. She's his honored guest. Please, he tells me, come in.

As I do, noddin at the Stewards, they shift away. Nobody wants to stand too close to the Angel of Death.

If only they knew.

She's dead.

Auriel said so.

The second Tonton closes the door behind us. It disappears, becomes part of the smoothness of the wall.

It's time, he says.

Stand around the edges, says the first one. Backs to the walls. That's it. Now, blow out yer lanterns.

The puff of quick breaths an the light huffs out. We're all in the dark. The blacker than black.

It's silent. A deeper silence than any I ever knew before. All I can hear is the beat of my own heart. To my left, where the door is, a sudden waft of cold air. The faint tang of juniper. DeMalo's jest come in. Silence agin.

Then. The tiniest pinprick of light in the ceilin. Directly in the center of the room. A bird begins to sing. I jump. In the darkness of the room unner the hill, there's a bird singin. How did it git in here? I dunno what kind it is neether. I never heard this song before. Another bird joins in. A different song. Then another bird, with another song.

The pinprick grows to a weak beam. I start to see DeMalo, standin in the center of the room, right unnerneath it. He lifts a chunk of clear, glassy rock. The light beam latches onto it. The rock starts to glow with a faint pink light. An it ain't jest the rock that's glowin pink. It's the whole room. In front of us, beside us, behind us. Gittin brighter an stronger every moment.

The Stewards murmur an shift. Now the light's growin, changin to dark blue an red an gold. All around us. I can see now that it's the walls. They're changin.

The birds still sing. An somethin's joined in that ain't a bird. Sounds like a stringbox. It's singin along with the birds. I cain't tell where it's comin from. It's jest . . . here. In the room. Slow an sweet. It's the most lovely thing I ever heard.

The light brightens. Brighter an brighter. Golden, yellow.

It's the dawn. Dawn grows on the walls, all around the room. The birdsong fades an more stringboxes join in the song. Other musicmakers too. It's so beautiful, it sends chills up an down my spine.

The music gits louder an louder, quicker an quicker.

Suddenly, green leaps out at us. Fer a moment or two, I cain't figger out what it is. Then I see. It's grasslands. But I'm seein 'em like Nero must do. From above. All around me, on the walls, a bird's eye view of grasslands an blue sky an clouds. I'm movin fast, like the fastest bird that ever flew. The sound of wind weaves in with the music.

I'm a bird! I whisper. I'm a bird! Oh! I turn this way, that way, so's I can watch everythin, everywhere, all around me. Everybody else is doin the same, exclaimin. I catch DeMalo's eye. He smiles. I laugh.

Great herds of buffalo thunder over the plains. There's mountains up ahead. Vast mountains with snow on the top. We fly over 'em, into 'em, past eagles in the sky. We soar on the wind, on the music. There's animals I ain't never seen before. Shaggy big-horned creatures leap from crag to crag. I try to touch 'em. My hands go right through to the cold of the wall.

We look down on mighty rivers, swoop low to sparklin clear lakes where fish jump. Great forests of green trees. Then it's blue. Blindin blue an sunlight dancin on it. Water. Water. Endless water. Not a river. Not a lake. Somethin else.

Is that the Big Water? I says. I'm with DeMalo now, in the middle of the room.

Yes, he says. The ocean.

The roar of waves. Giant fish, smooth black with white bellies, leap high an splash down. Smaller ones, gray an sleek, burst to the surface an leap—six of 'em at once—fer the joy of swimmin free. Then we're unner the water. Hunnerds of fish swim together. Fast. Movin this way, that way. Other kinds of swimmin creatures. All sizes an shapes an colors.

Some of the Stewards sit on the ground, quiet. Others move around the room. I turn an turn. I gasp. Cry out at one wondrous sight after another. I cain't take it all in. My heart's beatin fast, like I'm runnin.

What is this? I says to DeMalo. Where is it? I wanna go there!

It's our world, he says. The way it used to be.

We're back on land, flyin over vast plains. Herds of beasts gallop below. Many kinds of springers an horses. Long-neck spotted ones, black an white striped ones. The rumble an dust of their hoofs. Huge, slow gray beasts bellow their long noses. Big cats roar an chase. Jackals chatter an tear at the dead. Birds of all colors shriek an squawk an take to the sky in dancin, rapturous flocks. Funny-faced creatures hang from trees by their long tails, their young clutchin tight. Great waterfalls tumble an roar. Trees. Flowers. Snow. Ice. Insects. Lizards. Butterflies. Strange, marvelous creatures, big an small.

We go to cities. By the sea. On the land. The lost cities of the ancient world. Their tall skyscrapers. Mysterious machines. So many people. Walking an eatin an laughin an playin an dancin. Travelin in cars, on two-wheelers like Em's from the landfill. They soar in their flyin machines that I seen when I crossed Sandsea.

Pa was right, I whisper. They did go up in the air.

Higher an higher we fly. Higher than any bird could ever go till we leave the wide wonder of the earth an sky behind.

Stars come out, all around us. On the ceilin, on the walls an unner our feet. Then on one wall, a little blue ball floats in a ocean of stars. On the blue ball, there's bits of green an white.

The music's slow now. Quiet. Tears track down my face. I ain't cryin. But I cain't seem to stop the tears.

Then the stars go out, one by one. The little blue ball gits fainter. The music fades. Till we're in darkness once more. Silence once more.

† † †

I feel DeMalo slip from the room. As the Tonton an Stewards light their lanterns, nobody speaks a word. It wouldn't be right.

We make our way back through the unnerground rooms, up the steps an outside. I blink as we step into the clear light of the mornin. One of the Tonton chains an locks the rusted door an pulls the brambles back to hide it.

DeMalo's waitin fer us in the sweetgrass meadow. The Stewards sit on the ground at his feet. I stand a little ways apart. The mornin breeze plays fresh an gentle. I let it dry my tears. We're quiet fer a bit. There's a solid, heavy ache inside of me.

At last DeMalo says, That was our Mother Earth. Our home. Before the Wreckers ravaged her. Desecrated her. Before they crawled over every inch of her body, stripping her, skinning her, gutting her. Poisoning her ground, her water and her air. Could you ever have imagined such beauty? It doesn't seem possible, does it, that such wonders were the everyday, right here, all around us. I couldn't imagine it. Until one morning, one glorious, unforgettable dawn, I heard music on the wind. It whispered to me, led me to that door in the hill, down the stairs, into that room. And there, as the new day dawned, I had the vision. It radiated through my body, just as you've seen today. Mother Earth revealed to me, through me, the unimaginable glories of our world as it used to be.

As DeMalo's speakin, he looks from one person to the next, holdin their eyes with his. Like he's talkin only to them. The Stewards lean towards him, each face shinin tight with hope, with belief. I suddenly realize I'm doin the same.

He goes on.

And she revealed to me my destiny. You are the Pathfinder, she told me. I have chosen you to heal me, starting right here in New Eden. You will choose only the healthiest, brightest, hardest workers to help you in this mighty task. Our Mother Earth chose me at that dawn, and she has led me to choose you. It's our life's work to heal her. Mine, yours, our children, our children's children. It's the work of many lives and it will take many lifetimes. It's the greatest work that anyone has ever undertaken. We'll do right by her this time. We won't fly too close to the sun, the air is for the birds. The bounty of the earth and the clean waters are enough for us, and those we share in harmony with the creatures, who have as much right to be here as we do. Remember this day—when your body's tired and your spirit's weak—remember my words but, more than anything, hold fast in your heart that wondrous vision of the world as it was. The vision that I have shown you. We are the chosen ones, my friends, you and I. This is the dawn of a new day on earth.

The Stewards come up to him, boy with girl, two by two, an kneel at his feet. He touches each one on the forehead, four times, on the point of each quarter of their circle brand, sayin, earth, water, air and fire, we serve the Earth, our sacred Mother. He kisses the brand. Then he joins their hands together an they go off through the meadow.

DeMalo nods at the two Tonton an they follow the Stewards. Then it's jest him an me, standin in the grass with the blue sky above. The day wraps around us, the cool freshness of the air beginnin to warm.

Did you take them from their families? I says.

We brought them to New Eden to show them this, he says. To teach them, to share with them the good news. That something amazing will be accomplished and they're going to be a part of it.

Where're they goin now? I says.

To start their new lives, he says. To work for the common good of the earth and the earth's people.

Auriel's camp. The exhausted an unwanted, huddled on the banks of the Snake River. I think of stolen land an Billy Six, spiked through the throat.

Not all people, I says.

Who are the best stewards of the earth? he says. The old and weak? The sick? Or the young and the strong? Whose children will best serve the earth? Those born to the scum of Hopetown? Weak children born to the weak? Or the children of these people?

I dunno, I says. I ain't never thought about it before.

Resources are precious, he says, rare. There isn't enough clean water or good land to go around. You know that.

We sink down into the meadow grass. It tickles my bare legs. He leans back on his elbows. His hair shines like a crow's wing.

I wish I'd never seen that, I says. All them wondrous things. I wish I didn't know that's the way it used to be.

I felt the same when I first saw it, he says. But I couldn't leave. I kept returning here, dawn after dawn, and the vision would come, over and over, until I was possessed by it.

I cain't ever ferget it, I says. But it's long gone. Lost. An there ain't nuthin I can do.

But there is! He kneels in front of me, takin my hands. You've already started, don't you see? You didn't just survive Hopetown, you conquered it. You destroyed it and you did the same at Freedom Fields and Pine Top Hill. You killed

Pinch. You began to clean the infected wound. That's what I'm doing here.

I did all that fer my brother, I says.

You and I are willing to make the difficult decisions that have to be made, he says. To act on those decisions.

I think of Epona. Yes, I says.

We have the courage to act in the service of something greater than ourselves, he says. Don't think I don't have a conscience, that I don't constantly question and challenge myself. I do. The consequences of my decisions, my actions . . . I'm well aware of them. I'm awake in the dead of night, thinking about it all. But we—people I mean—we can't go on as we are. There's no meaningful future for us or this earth. You do see that?

Yes, I says.

The first time I saw you, he says, I looked into your eyes, just for a moment.

I remember, I says.

And I knew you, he says. For who you really are. Who you can be. You're extraordinary. Think of what you've already done. Now, imagine what you could do. You've only just begun to discover what you're capable of. Tell me. How does it feel? To master your fears and weaknesses. To win in the Cage, time after time, against all the odds. To stand in your own power at the top of the hill.

I cain't look away from him. The beauty of his face. The

beauty of his voice. The way I heat wherever he touches me. The thread between us tightens an tightens.

It feels right, I says. I feel . . . right.

That's the power that changes the world, he says. If you can do that for your brother, imagine what you could do for the earth. To bring back—even just a little of that wonder you saw in there.

I feel such . . . sorrow, I says. Like somebody I love jest died. I know what I said before, but I'm glad I seen it.

Feeling sorrow is fine, he says. It's right. But you need to use those feelings, channel them into action. Just as you did with your brother. You have such strength, such courage, such power within you.

I would never have let you drown, he says. I've been waiting for you.

Waitin fer me, I says.

My whole life, he says.

He leans towards me. Slow. Real slow, so's I can move away if I want. I don't. He kisses me, sweet an soft.

I feel a drop of water on my face. Then it's pourin. It's sunny but pourin with rain. I shake my head, blinkin in surprise.

We laugh. Then he grabs my hand an we run.

✝   ✝   ✝

We dash inside his tent, shakin ourselfs like dogs, gaspin an laughin a bit. He grabs a cloth an gives his hair a quick rub. He tosses it to me as he pours wine into the jars. He holds one up an I go to take it from him. My heart lurches. He's so close to me. So warm. The smell of him, damp an green, makes my skin jump all over. There's three books laid out on a small table.

You got books, I says. I seen one of them before.

Books are very rare, he says. They're so delicate, not many have survived. Would you like me to read you something? He takes one with gentle hands.

I dunno, I says. I dunno what that means.

He opens it, turns over a couple of paper leafs an starts to speak.

There was a time when meadow, grove and stream,

The earth, and every common sight,

To me did seem

Apparel'd in celestial light,

The glory and the freshness of a dream.

It is not now as it hath been of yore;

Turn wheresoe'er I may,

By night or day,

The things which I have seen, I now can see no more.

He stops. He spoke slowly, restin each word on the air like it was precious. My heart ain't big enough to hold the beauty.

It aches from tryin to. He closes the book. He lifts his eyes an looks at me.

You spoke how I feel, I whisper. About what I seen in there. If I had them words in me, that's jest what I'd say. How did you know?

Suddenly I move, in a rush, an I'm kissin him. His lips, his mouth, the words he spoke. Smooth an warm an rich. His arms bind me. Pull me tight to him. Kisses that burn. Kisses that sear. Feverish an ancient.

I fergit everythin an everybody. Jack. Betrayal. Myself. I lose myself. In the touch of him, the taste of him, the smell of him, till I feel the moment when the edges of me start to blur. I let go. An I melt into the dark, blank heat.

I don't remember movin, but he's sittin on the chair an I've climbed on to his lap an I'm runnin my hands through his hair, over his shoulders an arms, while we kiss. Feelin the strength of him, the life in him. He drags his lips along the inside of my arm, wrist to elbow. Trailin shivery fire on my tender skin till I'm quiverin head to foot. A rush in my belly, hot an ancient.

The tent's dim an gray. In the dark of his eyes, I see a tiny reflection. It's me.

A flush flags his cheekbones. I can see myself in your eyes, he says.

I touch a finger to his lips.

I'm drowning in you, he whispers.

I lead him to the bed. We lie down together.

An the rain, it rains an rains.

† † †

I wake with a start an blink in the bright mornin light. I'm in DeMalo's arms. In his bed. We're both bare as the day we was born.

My eyes meet his. I feel a hot tide crawl up my neck. The whispers. The cries in the closeness of the tent. Me. Him. Him an me together. I cain't believe that was me. What was I thinkin of? I couldn't of bin thinkin. No, no, that ain't true, I knew full well what I was doin. I wanted to do it.

Then another thought crashes in. Emmi. I gotta git back to Bram's, we gotta find Emmi. Lugh'll be frantic, worryin about both of us, probly searchin fer me.

Seth, I—

You amaze me, he says. We're perfect together. He turns my head to the side. Touches his lips to the back of my neck. Your first-time mark, he whispers. You chose me to put it there. Above all others, you chose me.

Yes, but I—

You gave yourself to me, he says. And I gave myself to you. Freely. Not just our bodies, it's more than that. Much more.

You felt it too. I know you did. We're going to be so beautiful together, he whispers. So perfectly beautiful. In our perfectly beautiful, perfect new world.

His eyes is hot as melted rock. He kisses me an I kiss him an I'm lettin go an fallin once more an—

You could be carrying our child already, he says.

A baby, I says.

A cold sweat breaks on my skin. It never crossed my mind. No. No, it couldn't be. Yes, it could. Easily. It happens all the time.

Think of it, he says, a child, Saba. A son, a daughter. Yours and mine. What could be more wonderful?

I know about the baby house, I says. I ain't no breeder.

He laughs. Of course you're not, he says. We'll raise our child—our children—together. The simple fact is, people are born with different abilities. We were born to rule, you and I. It's not an easy life, but it's a meaningful, important one. You and I will change the world. So will our children.

With every word, the panic rises higher. My heart's beatin madly. Seth, I says, I, uh . . . I'm sorry, I gotta go.

No, he says. His arms tighten around me.

I cain't breathe. I push him offa me. Shimmy quick into the first things I git my hands on. The girly skivvies. I shouldn't be here, I says, I dunno what I was thinkin of. This ain't right, it's . . . all wrong.

Nero hops outta his box, starts squawkin as he hears the

ruckus. I'm snatchin the green dress from the floor an yankin it over my head. Haulin the boots on.

DeMalo's on his feet too, pullin on his britches. He grabs my arms. What d'you mean, wrong? How? he says. How is it wrong? Tell me.

My breath's comin fast. I cain't, I says, I dunno, I—I jest know it is.

You'll have to do better than that, he says. Have I lied to you? Have I forced you to do anything you didn't want to do?

No, but I—I'm sorry, I says. This is . . . this was a mistake.

His hands tighten on me. No mistake, he says. We're the same, you and me. We're meant for each other, made for each other. I knew you'd come to me and so did you, from that very first moment. The price on your head was just a safety net.

Lemme go, Seth, I says.

Where are you going? he says. Who's waiting for you?

Nowhere, I says, nobody. Lemme go.

You'll be back, he says. You won't get far. Of your own free will, you'll come to me again. And again and again. I'm a fever in your blood now, Saba. As you are in mine. He lets go of me. Stands back.

I snatch Nero from the table an dive outta the tent.

An I run.

† † †

I scramble around the pool, an start clamberin back up the rocks beside Weepin Water. I gotta let Nero fly. I cain't run nor climb if I'm holdin him. He breaks away with a joyous squawk an flies free. I'm trapped by my thoughts, poundin in my head over an over.

Above all others, you chose me. Our child, Saba. A baby. No, it won't happen, it cain't happen. Yes it can. It could. Ma had me an Lugh when she was my age. Ohmigawd, what was I thinkin of?

I warn't thinkin. I stopped thinkin. I was so blinded by rage an hurt an hate fer Jack an Lugh warn't there to stop me an—

You gave yourself to me. And I gave myself to you. Freely.

Freely . . . my gawd. What we did together in the closeness of his bed. The shameless way I was with him. Don't think about it, pretend it never happened. There cain't be a baby, there mustn't be. Back to the rest of 'em as quick as I can. Git Emmi an git the hell outta this place. Lugh's right. We never should of come.

You're extraordinary. You've only just begun to discover what you're capable of. Imagine what you could do for the earth. To bring back—even just a little of that wonder.

The sights, the sounds of that lost world. I won't never fergit. What if he's right? What if we could go back to that?

I'm hurryin so much that I slip. Fall a couple of times an scrape my knee. The dress, DeMalo's green dress gits torn an dirty.

It fits well. I knew you'd come to me. He must of got it with

345

me in mind. How long had he bin keepin it in that trunk? I yank at the tear, rip it even more.

I'm hot an sweaty by the time I reach the top. Nero's nowhere in sight. Damn bird. I whistle fer him as I head in the direction of Bram an Cassie's place.

A horse's head pops up in the middle of a wild wheat field. It's Bram's horse, grazin peaceably. He whinnies an comes gallopin up. I swing myself onto his back an heel him home-wards. As his hoofs tear up the ground, I try to block out DeMalo's voice in my head.

I'm a fever in your blood now, Saba.

A fever in my blood. That's almost what Jack said.

Yer in my blood, Saba.

Jack. He deceived me. Betrayed me. This is all his fault.

An Emmi. I ain't hardly spared a thought fer poor Em an what she might be goin through. I'm the worst sister in the world, the most selfish.

I keep on whistlin fer Nero. He don't show.

I cain't stop to look. I cain't go back. He could be anywhere. But I got this funny feelin. This kinda prickle that he's some-where jest outta sight. That if I jest turned my head quick enough, I'd see him.

I don't. I don't.

Dammit, Nero.

THE ROAD TO RESURRECTION

I reach Bram an Cassie's jest past middle day. If I act like all of this . . . DeMalo . . . if I make like it never happened, then it never happened. All I gotta think about now is gittin Em back.

There still ain't no sign of Nero. It's quiet at the homestead, nobody about. As I pass the stables, I do a quick check on Hermes. He ain't here. Where is everybody? As I come to the house, I hear raised voices. Cassie an Bram. I take a deep breath an open the door. At the click of the latch, their heads turn quick. They're tight faced, tight lipped. Alone.

Bram pulls me inside an slams the door shut. Where the hell you bin? he says.

Where is everybody? I says. Where's Lugh?

Cassie's keen eyes flick over my face. The dress. The boots. What's all this? she says. Where's the clothes I give you?

Nero got attacked by another bird, I says, an I had to climb up this cliff to git at him. Yer stuff got ripped to shreds. I stole this the first chance I got.

As I speak, I know how lame it sounds. What a obvious lie. Cassie glances at Bram. Even ruined, she can tell it's a finer dress than any settler would own.

You put everybody at risk goin off like that, says Bram. What if you got caught?

349

I wouldn't of squealed on yuz, I says. I'm sorry. I was upset. I had to git away an think.

Did it never occur to you that yer friends, yer brother, might be worried sick about you? says Cassie. That they might of spent most of the night lookin fer you?

I said I'm sorry, I says.

Well, while you bin off lickin yer wounded feelins, she says, Bram's bin workin out a plan to git yer sister back. Seein how you couldn't be bothered.

My cheeks flag hot with shame. I stand there, shoulders hunched, while her spiky tongue lashes me.

All right, that's enough, says Bram. Everybody's waitin at the ammo dump. I was jest on my way there.

I'll come with you, I says.

You sure as hell will, he says.

I hesitate. He nods at the door. Wait outside, he says. I do as he says, feelin low an shabby an stupid. I only jest met Cassie an Bram, but their good opinion matters to me. Specially Bram. Last night, he kept his head better'n anybody I know could of.

My head's whirlin. I dunno what to do. Everythin's gone so wrong. I pace back an forth. I can still smell DeMalo on me. My skin. The dress.

Bram comes outta the house behind me. We hurry along the road towards the woods. Cassie sure don't like you, he says. She don't trust you. She asked me not to go. Says we oughta leave you to sort out yer own mess.

But yer gonna help git Em back, I says. You made a plan . . . she said.

Slim says you'll go fer yer sister with or without my help, he says, an if it goes wrong an you git caught, they'll put it all together. Yer sister, you, an that'll lead 'em right here to us. That won't jest be our whole set up blown, but me an Cassie an Slim—maybe even Molly—killed. So I'm gonna make sure you do it right. That we're in an out quick an clean, we git yer sister, then all of yuz leave New Eden an never come back. I want you gone, d'you hear me?

Yes, I says. My humiliation burns my face. He's right. Every word.

Slim likes you, he says, gawd knows why, he must be goin soft in the head. He could be a wanted man after what you did on the way here. The Cosmic's easy to spot, even from a distance, an we got no idea if them Tonton got away before the causeway blew up. We'll hafta hide him in the woods till we know if he's safe or not. If he ain't, we'll hafta smuggle him out somehow. We only jest got started on this an thanks to you, I could lose my main man. He don't jest run weapons, he's my eyes an my ears. I'd sooner wring yer neck than help you, but . . . aw, hell, I'm sick of talkin about it.

He don't say no more. When we're deep into the trees, he gives the signal—the pigeon call. Answer comes back. We move forwards an we're at Bram's rootbound arms dump. An here they all are. Tommo an Maev. Ash an Creed an Slim an Molly.

Tracker comes runnin. He shoves me with his big head, almost knockin me over. As I rub his ears an fuss him, I take it all in. Everybody looks completely different. Tommo an Creed wear Tonton gear. Maev, Ash an Molly all ragged an filthy, like they bin livin rough. Nobody comes to speak to me. A quick glance when I first show, but that's it. They keep on loadin the Cosmic's secret compartment with ammo an weapons. She don't look nuthin like she used to. She's bin pretty much rebuilt. Changed to a open cart with new boards, all chalkwashed.

An there's Molly's mare Prue an my Hermes. He greets me with a toss of his head an a whuffle. I kiss his soft nose. Stroke his face. At least the beasts seem glad to see me. All but Moses, of course. The Grand Champeen of the Pillawalla Camel Race sits off to one side, chewin his cud an givin me the evil eye.

That's it, says Slim. Lugh! All done!

Lugh climbs outta the arms store, my bow in his hand. He's dressed like a Tonton too. He don't look nuthin like my brother, like my Lugh. His birthmoon tattoo's now covered up with some kinda face paint. His eyes take in my dress, the new boots. He comes right over, grabs my arm an takes me into the trees, away from everybody.

Where you bin, Saba? he says. What're you wearin?

It's Cassie's, I lie.

I was lookin fer you half the night, he says. First Emmi, then you. What was you thinkin, runnin off like that? Don't you ever use yer head? He pulls me to him. Hugs me tight.

Is this yer way of pickin me up offa the ground? I says.

Why couldn't you listen to me about Jack? he says. All I ever wanted to do was pertect you, stop you gittin hurt.

Where was you? I says. When they took Emmi? I needed you. I wanted you, Lugh.

I'm sorry. He puts me away from him. I was—I couldn't of done nuthin anyways, he says.

You was with Maev, I says.

So? He's a bit flushed on the cheeks, a bit shifty.

So . . . you love her, I says.

No, I don't.

I seen the way you look at her, I says. Did she take away the shadows fer a time? There in the cornfields, in the moonlight?

Fer a time, he says.

Maybe that's all there is, I says. The most we can hope fer.

I said about maybe comin west with us once we git Emmi back, he says, but . . . she said no. She's stayin here.

How did you ask her? I says. Did you say, come with me Maev, be with me, we're meant for each other, made fer each other, yer a fever in my blood.

I go still. His words, DeMalo's words, it's like they're runnin in my head all the time, over an over, behind the words I speak, the thoughts I think. He's right, he's right, he's a fever in my blood, in my head, in my bones—no, no, that's what Jack said.

Saba? says Lugh.

Yeah, I says. So . . . did you say that to her?

No, he says. Of course not. Here. He hands me my bow, an we go back to th' others.

† † †

Bram's changed into Tonton gear, too, like the rest of the boys. He's cleared a patch of forest floor an hunkers down, stick in hand. He scratches a map in the dirt as he speaks.

Okay, he says. Full attention. Everybody. No matter how well you think you know the plan. They'll of took Emmi to Resurrection, to question her. It's Tonton headquarters, the middle of the spider's web. I know the outside pretty good. I done a fair few scouts from the lake, but I ain't never bin inside.

What? I says.

You heard, he says. Let me tell you what I do know. Resurrection stands, like a great slab, in between the lake on this side an a big field of boulders an rubble on the approach side. The Field of the Fallen Mountain. There's only one gate, in an out. We go in through the gate, an out by the lake, droppin down by rope into boats. Okay so far?

We all nod our heads. He goes on, Resurrection's a strange buildin. Huge. Long an narrow, maybe half a mile long, half a mile high.

Half a mile? I says. What the hell was it?

Bram shrugs. I dunno, maybe somethin to do with the lake. Hard to tell. From the approach side, it looks jest like a big slab of concrete. We got five floors, runnin right along the top. Bottom floor—let's call it one—that's their kitchen an stores. At this end, there's a kinda landin stage that juts out over the lake. Floor two, we got sleepin quarters. We avoid that. Floor three, I dunno what goes on there. Floor four, I dunno, floor five, I dunno. I only know what I could see from the lake. Lights goin on an off, people comin to windows. Speakin of which— windows, that is—they run all along the buildin on both sides, every floor but kitchen level, that's only got a couple. We'll try to drop ropes from a window on the third floor.

Why don't we leave by the landin stage? I says.

Kitchen level's always busy, he says. All night, every night, there's people comin an goin.

Where will Emmi be? I says.

We dunno, says Lugh. She could be anywhere in there.

We all look at each other. This is hopeless, I says.

Don't you dare say that, says Lugh. It's yer fault she's in there.

That's enough, says Bram. By the way—Bram looks at me—Ash, Creed an Maev's asked to throw in with us, an I said yes. Glad to have 'em on board. This is their first official op.

Right, I says. I look at the three of 'em, but they keep their eyes on the map.

So, Bram says, this is how we git there. Tommo, me, Lugh, an Creed's the Tonton. We're bringin four women to be interrogated. That's Molly, Maev, Ash an Saba. The story is we caught you doin sabotage in Sector Ten—I bin makin a little trouble there lately, so that story should hold water. You women ride in the cart, me an Lugh drive, Tommo an Creed on horseback behind. We go through three guardposts on the road, here, here an here, where we'll hafta give the password.

What is it? I says.

Different every time, he says. They got a bunch, they use 'em in random rotation. You can tell which one from the color of the flag on the gate. I spent many a hour spyin on guardposts when I should of bin workin. Slim's bin a great help with that too, gittin round the place as he does.

Slim shrugs, but looks pleased.

When we git to here, says Bram, we split up. Molly, Tommo an Saba take Hermes an Prue an head to the far end of the lake—it's called Glasswater Tarn. They'll tell you what to do, Saba. In the meantime, Lugh an me an Creed, in the cart, drive into the gatehouse, perched on top. Right through the main gate with our suspects fer interrogation, Ash an Maev.

I only half-listen as Bram goes through the rest of the plan. I'm outta the main action. I won't be part of Emmi's rescue. They don't want me. They don't trust me. I ruined everythin fer everybody becuz of my blind belief in Jack. Deceitful betrayer. If I ever set eyes on him agin, I'll kill him.

I gotta be there! It bursts outta me.

They all look. No, says Bram. Yer a liability.

They could well be usin Emmi fer bait to draw you in, says Slim. You cain't go nowhere near the place.

But I—

What's the most important thing? he says. That we git the little gal back, right? You think on that, big sister, an leave yer pride here. Moses an me'll roast it fer supper. Ha ha!

We leave it at that. While they close the arms dump an say farewell to Slim, I hurry into the trees with a pile of raggedy clothes. Slim's right. Bram's right. Lugh's right. I ain't nuthin but wrong. About everythin an everybody. I ain't no judge of character. No judge of my own heart. I'm prideful, arrogant an stubborn.

I rip the buttons open on DeMalo's hateful dress. I'm about to take it off when suddenly Tommo's here, his dark eyes intent.I jump, my heart racin, cover myself up agin. Tommo! Don't sneak up on me like that, I says.

I gotta talk to you, he says.

Not now, I says, this ain't the time. Later, I promise.

He looks at me a moment. You cain't put me off ferever, he says. Then he nods. Later, he says.

When he's outta sight, I haul off the dress an scrabble at the roots of the tree. I stuff it deep into the earth. Bury it. Bury him.

Jest what I need, more trouble. Trouble. Ohmigawd, what if I do have a baby in me? No no, don't think about it. If I don't think about it, it cain't be so. Where's that Nero got to? As if I don't have enough to worry about.

Saba? It's Molly. Yer talkin to yerself, she says. Here. Let me give you a hand.

I jump to my feet. No, it's okay, I—

But she's already pullin a raggedy shift over my head. Her eyes flick over the girly skivvies I'm wearin, the boots.

Stand still, she says. She starts to cover up my birthmoon tattoo, dippin her baby finger in two little pots of paste, brown an white, mixin on the back of her hand till she gits the color right to match my skin. Where you bin? she says. Where'd you git the fancy gear?

It's Cassie's. I tell the lie agin. If I tell it often enough, I might even start to believe it.

Fine, she says, keep yer secrets. You smell nice. What is that, juniper?

I dunno, I says.

Okay, that's covered up. An you look truly wretched in them clothes. You'll pass. Now . . . She runs a keen eye over

358

me as she rummages in the little bag at her waist. This hair of yers . . . She's pulled out her comb an started combin an fussin an movin around me. Before I realize, before I can stop her—

Oh! She goes still. She's seen it. On the back of my neck. My first-time mark. His mouth. His lips.

Above all others, you chose me, Saba. His smell on my skin. His voice in my head. His mark on my body.

She smooths my hair to cover it. There we go, she says. There, now. You look fine.

Tears start at her kindness. I grab her hand, comb an all. Molly, I whisper.

Our eyes meet. Beautiful Molly. So tough, so kind, so sad.

This might not mean much to you right now, she says, but fer what it's worth, I'll tell you. Maybe I know it better'n most. Life ain't black an white. People ain't neether. Family, friends, lovers. It's all a lot more complicated. The longer I live, the more I see, the less I know fer sure. Especially when it comes to matters of the heart. So dry yer tears. Whoever he is, he won't be cryin over you. Men never do. That's the one thing I do know fer sure. Now, muck up them boots a bit.

She pats my cheek an heads back to th'others. She's comin! she says.

They're already headed fer the road by the time I pull myself together. Tommo an Creed lead the horses through the trees, while Bram an Lugh an Ash wrestle the cart along the narrow track. Molly an Maev hang back a bit, waitin fer me.

Ready? says Molly.

Tracker's tethered to a big tree, on a short rope. Bram decided it's better that we leave him here. He's whinin, lookin anxious. This is where we part ways, him an me. I cain't bear to look at him.

C'mere, sister, says Slim. Give a smelly old man a hug before you go. He hauls me into a awkward one-armed hug. Check my right pocket, he mutters.

I dig into it, outta sight of Maev an Molly. I pull out a tiny brown bottle. The silent enemy, he whispers. It's called eccinel. One drop in a full cup, a man'll sleep eight hours. Two drops, he'll do a whole day, maybe half of the next.

An three? I says.

The longest sleep of all, he says. Use it with a cool head.

I throw my arms around his neck an hug him tight. Thank you, I says. I'm sorry about everythin.

I shall rise agin, never you fear, he says. I seen you fight at Hopetown, heard word of what you did at them other places. You don't know it, but yer a bit of a legend.

No, I ain't, I says.

Anyways, he says, when I seen who it was hijackin me, I had this idea you might join us. We'd be able to kick things

360

up an march on to glorious victory. Well . . . I'm jest a foolish old man with romantical notions. I'm honored to of knowed you. Good luck, m'dear.

An you, Slim, I says.

I give Tracker a last kiss on his head. Molly takes my arm an Slim waves us off. Tracker starts howlin.

I keep lookin back over my shoulder. Till the trees hide 'em from view. Till all that's left is the sound of Tracker's distress, ringin among the trees.

† † †

I'm next to Ash in the back of the cart. Molly an Maev sit opposite. We're tied at the ankles an wrists, good enough to pass inspection, loose enough to slip free quick. Creed an Tommo bring up the rear on Prue an Hermes. Lugh an Bram sit tall on the driver's bench with Bram's work horse, Ted, in the traces.

We ain't long on the road, maybe half a league from Bram's place, when a dot appears on the road behind us. It gits bigger an bigger. Ash leans around me to squint. What is that? she says.

A smile starts to crawl over my face. It's Tracker, I says. It ain't long before he catches us up. He's runnin flat out.

Tommo an Creed give him room an he takes a flyin leap into the back of the cart.

What a boy! cries Ash.

He flops on top of our legs an rests his head on my lap. I shake mine as I stroke his ears. The dog that won't be left behind. When will I learn?

A little bit later, a familiar call has me lookin skywards. It's Nero, cruisin along above us.

I ain't seen him fer hours, I says.

He drops down. He's got the heartstone in his beak. Nero! Come here!

He ignores me an lands on Molly. The furthest he can git from me. He dumps it in her lap.

Well, Nero, hello, whatcha got here? she says. She holds up my heartstone. Did you lose this, Saba?

I give him a death glare. He jibbers at me. Smart-alec crow. That's what he flew off to find this mornin when he disappeared. It must of washed up down at the rockpool. So, I didn't imagine him jest outta sight. He's bin lurkin around all day with it, on purpose waitin till now when everybody's here.

No, I says. He stole it agin. He's a thief an a menace an I'm gonna trade him in fer a umberella.

He laughs at me, bobbin up an down. Molly notices the stitches on his breast. She shoots me a quick glance as he takes off agin. Mission accomplished, he settles into a steady pace ahead of us. Molly tosses me the heartstone. I shove it in my pocket.

Scuppered by my gawdamn bird. Not fer the first time. An, if I know him—which I most surely do—not fer the last time neether.

† † †

We roll through the warm afternoon. We aim to be in place by curfew. Nightfall. Ready to go. Ready to move. Sadly fer our rear ends, the Cosmic don't ride no smoother than she did before. Along the dirtpack road we rattle, in an outta the shade of cool, sweet-smellin woodland. Over clear-runnin streams. Past Stewards in their fields who stop what they're doin to watch us go past.

They're thinkin, I'm glad it ain't me in that cart, says Molly. Wonderin if their turn will come one day.

Wouldn't they like to know what we're sittin on, says Ash. I am dyin to have a go with them little pinballs of Slim's. I sure would like to of seen that causeway go up. Ka-boom! She winks at me. Ash, never more cheerful than when she's got trouble to look forward to.

Bram kicked Tracker out. He's keepin up with us, slippin through trees, runnin low through fields, disappearin from

363

time to time, then showin up agin a bit further down the road. He knows he's gotta stay away from other people.

Creed an Tommo ride close behind the cart. Creed cain't take his eyes offa Molly. He tries, but eventually he gives up an jest outright stares. She ignores him fer a bit. But you can see her windin up. Gittin more hotter an crosser an vexed by the minute. Finally, she snaps.

Stop starin at me, she says.

Stop bein so gorgeous an I'll stop starin, he says. Smile at me, Molly, please. One little smile an I'll die a happy man.

You tire me, Creed, she says.

That's my strategy, he says. I'm gonna wear you down, like water on rock.

I wouldn't paddle in a shallow stream like you, she says. She sinks into her corner an glares at the road ahead.

He winks at the rest of us. I'm makin progress, he says.

Tommo's makin every effort not to meet my eyes. What a relief. I couldn't take trouble from that quarter too. Not at the moment.

Creed an Ash an Maev seem to of reached some kinda unnerstandin of what happened at Darktrees. Some kinda peace between 'em that's led 'em to decide to stay here an work with Bram an Cassie to build the resistance. To do what has to be done, in the service of something greater than ourselfs. DeMalo agin. I cain't git away from him. Right here in front of me, it's what they're all doin.

Maev's quiet. She makes answer if somebody speaks to her, but I can tell she ain't really here. She's somewhere deep inside her own head, her own heart, tryin to work things out. Like me. I glance at the back of Lugh's head as he talks with Bram, as they sit there, shoulder to shoulder on the driver's bench. They seem to be gittin on pretty good.

Lugh an Maev probly won't git the chance to be alone before we hafta leave New Eden. After this is over, after we git Emmi back, we'll be straight on our way. An even if he did git a moment, knowin Lugh, he'd funk the chance. He'd never admit what he feels fer her. If Maev knew, maybe she'd change her mind an come with us. Maybe not. Maev ain't run of the mill. Love ain't all there is. An, like Molly said, you cain't know nuthin fer sure, least of all the ways of the human heart. Still. I think she needs to know.

I jig her with my foot an she looks up. I slide my glance to Lugh, then back to her. I look at her steady. She goes pink. He loves you, I mouth at her. She goes even pinker, looks flustered, her eyes goin to him. Then back to me, with a little frown. He told me, I mouth. Do you love him?

She hesitates. Then, her eyes soften. Her face. She smiles. I give a little laugh.

What's funny? says Ash.

Nuthin, I says. Nuthin.

The land we travel is rich an fruitful an kind. Lugh's head keeps turnin to look at this an that. He asks Bram about crop rotation, irrigation an all sorts an I remember what Auriel said about him. *Lugh dreams of a settled life. He longs to plant himself in one place, plant the land around him. His hands itch to work good earth, put food on the table that he's grown hisself, raise children. That ain't you.*

She's right. The thought of workin the land don't heat the blood in my veins. Too bad. I gotta fall in with what's best fer all of us.

We pass a little slave gang. Three women an two men with iron neck collars, chained together at the ankles. Watched by a Tonton, they're clearin stones an rocks from a field right beside the road. They all stand, easin their backs, as we rattle past. One woman raises her hand in greetin. Low, outta sight of the Tonton. I nod in reply. I wonder what they did to end up like this. Probly nuthin but be the wrong sort of person. Not fit into the new order.

With every roll of the wheels, every rattle of the cart, what DeMalo said repeats an repeats. The old an the sick. The sick an the weak. The old an the sick an the weak.

Precious resources. Water an land.

People like me. People like us.

The young an the strong.

Some of the people. All of the people.

I ponder his words. Who deserves a share of what little there is? Who decides?

Have I lied to you?

The lies that lurk in the shadows of truth.

† † †

It's comin up to dusk, nearly curfew. My belly starts to tighten with nerves. We passed through the first two guardposts no problem. Bram shouted the right password fer the color of flag tied to the barred road gate, an the Tonton guards lifted it an waved us on. We left the farms behind some time ago. Ahead of us, the road disappears. Swallowed up by a vast plain of giant boulders, great glints an rock slabs the height of ten men.

The Field of the Fallen Mountain, says Bram. We should see Resurrection any— there it is.

It comes into view.

Holy crap, says Creed.

I ain't never seen such a gigantic Wrecker buildin before. A massive, sheer wall of concrete rises up from the boulder-strewn plain below. It stands half a mile long an looks to be jest as high.

Remind me, says Maev, how high did you say it is?

I make it seven hunnerd foot, says Bram.

There's the four floors with windows he told us about. They run along the top of the vast wall. Otherwise, it's faceless. Solid.

There's the gatehouse, says Bram.

It's perched at the end nearest to us. It looks like a dot. It's jest like he told us, when he was takin us through the plan. He drew it, we seen it, I imagined it, but now, seein it fer real, the size of it—

Unbelievable, I says.

Now I know what a flea feels like, says Molly.

She looks grim. As do we all. But not Ash. A half-smile crooks her mouth.

Fleas plague you, she says. Swamp skitters can kill you, an a little thorn—so small you hardly notice—it can work its way unner the skin an after a bit, yer hand's infected. Maybe you lose a couple fingers, maybe the whole hand. Maybe yer blood goes bad an you die. Tiny things can cause plenty of trouble. Cheer up, people!

Okay, says Bram, we're comin to the last guardpost. This time of day, their mind's on other things. All they wanna do is lock the gate an git their supper on to cook.

Ahead of us, on the left, a stone-walled hut with a door onto the road. As we approach, we can see the barred road gate. It's up. No colored flag. The rumble of our wheels brings a Tonton from the hut. He's holdin a chunk of flatbread in his fist, chewin. When he sees who it is—four Tonton with a cartload of prisoner women—he waves to come on through an goes back inside.

What'd I tell you? says Bram. He clicks at the horse an we pick up the pace.

We ain't more'n thirty foot away. Another Tonton rounds the back corner of the hut, twitchin his robes into place. Call of nature. When he sees us, he shouts somethin an breaks into a run. Th'other guard comes dashin outta the hut to pull down the gate. Bram curses.

What is it? says Ash.

There shouldn't be a commander here, he says, He's too high up. Okay, they're stoppin us. No problem, we done this before. No eye contact an I do the talkin. He slows Ted to a walk. The Tonton in charge—the commander—steps into the road.

Long life to the Pathfinder! Bram calls, clenched fist to his heart.

We all make the sign too. The commander replies the same. Bram pulls Ted to a stop. Evenin, sir, he says.

The guard who closed the gates comes runnin up. Check the women, the commander tells him.

We go tense. Me, Maev, Ash an Molly.

We're from Sector Ten, sir, says Bram. We caught 'em doin sabotage. Takin 'em to headquarters fer interrogation. Nuthin unusual.

The commander ignores him. Check their faces, he tells the guard.

A chill shivers my skin. *You won't get far.*

What's goin on, sir? says Bram. Some kinda trouble?

The commander says, How's the roads in yer sector, brother?

Nero lands on the closed gate. We keep our eyes down as the guard starts movin around the cart, lookin at each of us in turn. Ash first. He leans in to look at her. He trades nods with Creed an Tommo. He moves on to me. I stare straight ahead.

Creed coughs an shifts in the saddle. You bin out here long? he says to the guard. His gun hand rests, casual, on his weapons belt, fingers touchin his bolt shooter.

He's pricked a grievance.

Too damn long by far, the guard mutters. A sour look towards at the commander, listenin to Bram rattle on about the state of the roads. His eyes scan me quickly an he moves on, happy to have Creed to complain to.

I bin here two days, says the guard. Me an my partner was set to be relieved at sundown an then he shows up, my partner gits to go back to barracks an I gotta stay.

He barely even looks at Maev.

How long? says Creed.

Only a brief glance at Molly. Another two days, says the guard. With this jackboots.

That ain't fair, brother, says Creed.

Well, you tell 'em that at Resurrection, he says. An like it ain't bad enough bein stuck here four days, you should—

You! calls the commander. I didn't see you check that one! He goes on talkin to Bram.

The guard throws him a filthy look. What one? he says. Sir?

Mind yer tone, he says. The one with the short hair.

He means me.

The guard comes to stand at the foot of the cart, right beside me. I stare across at Maev. Hold her eyes. Sweat starts to trickle down the back of my neck.

Turn yer head, says the guard. Lemme see you. Slowly, I turn towards him. I hold my breath. Keep my eyes dropped. Clammy hands. He stares at me. Then he leans a little closer, licks his thumb an drags it over my cheekbone. His eyes widen as he sees my tattoo.

Sir! he yells.

Then he's dead. Double dead. Two bolts through his head. Creed an Tommo.

Another shot. Two shots, three, four.

Saba! screams Lugh. Saba!

✝   ✝   ✝

We all hit the deck at the first shot. Me, Maev, Ash an Molly. Now we scrabble free of our ropes an tumble outta the cart as Tracker comes runnin. Creed an Tommo jump offa the horses.

Both Tonton lie dead on the ground. Bram hangs halfways outta the driver's seat, face down. He's bin shot in the back.

Lugh's standin in the footwell. Bolt shooter clutched tight in his hand. Face white. Eyes wide.

A rush to pull Bram free, lay him on the ground. Me an Maev run to Lugh.

Lugh! I cry. I clamber in beside him. Lugh, what happened? Are y'okay?

I killed him, he chokes out. The Tonton went to shoot Bram, so I shot at the Tonton an . . . Bram moved. He got in the way an I killed him instead. I killed Bram.

I take the shooter, put my arms around him an sit him down. His whole body's shakin.

Two shots. Creed looks up from Bram's body. One to the head, one in the back.

Eether would of killed him, says Tommo.

You don't know, I says to Lugh.

I think they was lookin fer Saba, says Ash. They know she's here. They must of got Emmi to talk.

I says naught. I hope she's wrong. I cain't think about the Tonton frightenin Emmi, maybe hurtin her to git her to spill all she knows. I hope it was DeMalo put out the order to look fer me.

There's silence. No hue an cry. Nobody to hear the shots an the screams. Jest the empty road behind us. The closed gate ahead. An, on the other side, the Field of the Fallen

Mountain with the road leadin up to Resurrection.

What about Cassie? says Tommo.

Cassie sure don't like you. She asked me not to go. Says we oughta leave you to sort out yer own mess.

I dunno, says Molly. Fer now, she'll have to leave the farm, I guess. We cain't let nobody find Bram here.

Bram. If it hadn't of bin fer his cool head last night—only last night—things could of gone real bad. Fer Emmi, fer me, fer all of us. Thanks to me an my blind faith in Jack, we blundered into Bram's set up an nearly wrecked it. An now he's dead. He should of listened to Cassie. All of this ruin becuz of me.

What a gawdamn mess, says Ash.

What're we gonna do? says Tommo.

We go on, says Maev. We do the job.

We look at her. She ain't said a word till now. But the old Maev's back. She stands tall. Head held high, green eyes dark with determination.

Ash stands up, a smile creepin over her face. The Free Hawks is back in business, she says.

We'll operate right unner their noses, says Maev. An I got a mind to let the boys join this time around. Creed?

I'm in, he says.

Me too, says Molly, if that's okay.

Whaddya have in mind, Maev? I says.

We'll go through the gate an escape by the lake, she says,

jest like Bram planned. But that's as far as it went, remember. He'd never bin inside, so we ain't really no worse off. We'll jest be one person down. Lugh? You okay to go on?

He's pale an shaky still, looks a bit sick, but he nods. Yeah, he says. We gotta git Emmi back. I'll drive.

I hug him. Good man, I whisper.

Hang on, hang on, says Creed. There's a password. A different one fer each gate, dependin on the flag color. Bram's th'only one who knew 'em. They won't let us into Resurrection without it.

We all look at each other.

I know what I gotta do.

I know the password, I says.

What're you talkin about? says Lugh.

The Angel of Death has a price on her head, I says. We're gonna hand her in. I'm the password.

†   †   †

Three dead. The two Tonton, an Bram. We leave their bodies concealed by rocks. Hid from view. Safe from dead eaters. Once Emmi's safe an we're on our way, the rest of 'em'll come back fer Bram. Take him home to Cassie an send him back to the sky with warrior ceremony.

The blood on the road gits shuffled to the dirt. The stone hut's closed. The gate left open. Fer all the world, it looks like post deserted. Maybe fed up guards who took a hike. Nuthin as it seems.

We empty the Cosmic's secret innards. It don't take long. She's only packed with enough to do the job. Lugh an Creed an Tommo stock their weapons belts, slingin as much hardware on 'em as won't attract undue notice. I make sure Tommo's got my bow an quiver on his back. Molly an Ash pack what they need onto Prue an Hermes. Thinkin she's on the sly, Ash slips two of Slim's bad-tempered pinballs in her saddlebag.

Hey! Ash! You warn't supposed to bring them, says Maev. We agreed, no explosives.

I ain't gonna use 'em, Maev, says Ash. I jest like the feel of 'em.

In case we meet anybody comin down from Resurrection, Creed an Tommo's gonna ride the horses till we part company with Molly an Ash. Till that time, they ride with me an Maev in the back of the cart. I'm trussed up with rope, way too much fer the purpose. Hopefully, it won't draw notice. Nor the fact that Tommo's got a rope coil hung on his belt.

Lugh jumps on the driver's bench. The wheels start to move. Through the Field of the Fallen Mountain we go. Bram's good horse, Ted, slips along the road, around the boulders. Nero flits from one to the next. Tracker paces behind.

If DeMalo's there . . . if he's there . . . please, please, don't let him be there. Why would he be? He was at his retreat camp this mornin. Mind you, so was I.

It ain't no part of our plan to hand me over. I'm jest to smooth us through the gate. Once we're inside, in the belly of the beast as Slim calls it, we make haste to find Emmi an git out quick. We dunno what to especk once we're inside. We'll hafta depend on sharp wits, fast thinkin an swift moves. But. But. If all goes wrong an fer some reason I end up facin DeMalo once more, I know somethin about him.

I seen his weakness. The flush on his cheekbones. The whispers. The cries in the closeness of the tent. Not jest mine. His.

Of your own free will, you'll come to me again. I'm in his blood. I'm a fever in his blood. It ain't jest him that's got power now.

An it ain't jest DeMalo that preys on my mind.

The heartstone hangs around my neck. It'll lead me to Jack. If he's there, I'll find him. An I'll kill him.

Betrayer. Deceiver.

Of Maev an the Hawks an the Raiders. Of the forty dead at Darktrees. Of how many more that I don't know about. Of Emmi. Of me.

The silent enemy—the tiny brown bottle—tucked aginst my breast.

A sharp knife deep in my boot sheath.

The anger starts to burn, deep in my gut.

We drop Ash an Molly where Bram planned we should. As the Field of the Fallen Mountain ends an the start of the treeline marks the final approach to Resurrection. They'll beat fast through the woods, skirtin along the edge of the lake to the far end. Glasswater Tarn's a league in length, near enough.

Bram hid three canoes aginst the day they'd be needed. He nursed high hopes of his newborn resistance. Up to now, he'd only used 'em fer his night-time scout expeditions to watch an learn what he could about Resurrection.

With a wave, Ash an Molly slink into the trees with Tracker an the horses an we jolt off. We won't see 'em agin till we have Emmi safe with us. Then we'll make the drop by rope down to where they'll be waitin fer us in the canoes.

Ted pulls strong up the last bit of the slope, then we're at the top. From where we are, the road runs a flat approach to the blank iron gate of the gatehouse.

Creed, Lugh an me, our priority's Emmi, says Maev. Quick as we can, we find where they're keepin her an we snatch her. Saba an Tommo, you git the ropes in place. Stick close to each other, okay? Everybody good?

We all make assent.

We know this ain't a great sitchation, says Maev. But we're smart, an fast. We go in, we find Emmi, we git her out. That's it. An if you gotta kill anybody, do it quiet. All right, Lugh. Drive on.

My fingertips tingle. My insides judder. My stummick's atwist with nerves an fear. My mind thinks clear. My eyes see sharp. It's jest like I felt before fights in the Cage. I'm ready fer anythin. The red hot smolders, ready to burn.

As we roll towards the gatehouse, Nero rides the cold mountain wind that whips around us.

There's a guard tower on each side, one guard in each nest. They point their firesticks at us. Password! calls one.

I got better'n a password, brother! Lugh calls back. Shine yer lights down! See what I got in the cart!

Tommo an Creed haul me to my feet so's I face the gate. Strong lanterns cut through the gloom. They settle on me where I stand. Creed shoves up my chin, so's they git a good look at my cheekbone tattoo.

It's the Angel of Death, says Lugh.

Someone shouts out a order. With a groan an a shudder an a creak of chain, the gate starts to slide to one side. They're lettin us in.

Here we go, says Maev.

RESURRECTION

WE DRIVE INTO A BIG OPEN COURTYARD WITH A SWEPT DIRT
ground. It's torchlit. Quite a few Tonton movin about. A
little group on one side stretch an lunge an turn, all together.
Graceful, one move flowin into the next one. None of 'em's
Jack.

We stop next to a gibbet, right in the middle. Two Tonton
hang from it, still in their black robes. Their flesh ain't decayin,
it's bein et. By birds, insects, rats. The stench is gruesome.
Jack ain't one of 'em. That's all I got time to take in.

Eight or so Tonton's already runnin at us. As two of 'em
grab Ted's head to stop him, the rest swarm around the back
of the cart an it's all a blur, a confusion, an inside of me the
red hot pops an snaps, as they unhitch the back flap an bundle
out Maev an me. Creed an Lugh an Tommo jump down.

The commander salutes. Long life to the Pathfinder!

Our boys do the same. Eyes on the commander. Playin
the part of loyal Tonton. The commander smiles. He's got
snaggly teeth. His thin blonde hair's in full retreat from his
forehead.

Nice work, brother, he says to Creed. I'll take her straight
to the Pathfinder.

I break into a cold sweat as one of the guards hands him
the end of my rope.

But, sir, we caught her, sir, says Creed. It's only right that we hand her over.

I shouldn't hafta remind you, brother, that we serve New Eden, not ourselves, says the commander. But under the circumstances, I'll pretend I didn't hear that. Who's this other female?

We caught her sabotagin, sir, says Lugh. Sector Ten.

You an yer patrol can hand her in fer interrogation, he says. That's all.

Four Tonton start herdin 'em towards a door in the guardhouse walls. The commander starts walkin me towards another one. There's two other Tonton with us.

We got inside Resurrection. But that's all. The plan's a bust already. I got no control. I'm tied so well, I got no chance to git away. But I can stumble.

I trip myself up. Twist to look to the darkenin sky. Nero! I yell.

The commander's kept a firm grip on me an, even as I cry out, he's yankin me upright an on we go. But Nero's heard. He comes swoopin down at the Tonton, the commander an the two others. They duck, flailin at him an yellin. Nero's a fearsome sight, screechin an flappin as he attacks.

Do somethin! yells the commander. Stop him!

Tommo's already runnin this way. Nobody else moved to heed their commander. Must be skeered of birds. Or maybe jest crows.

You, the commander says to Tommo, you brought her in, didn't you? Take the bird.

Nero's settled on my head. Fluffin up his feathers an makin mean. Tommo lifts him offa my head.

Follow me, says the commander. The Angel of Death an her crow. That'll please the Pathfinder.

We go through the door an it clangs shut behind us. We're in dank gloom, lit only by a few wall torches. Almost right away, we're goin down a open metal staircase. The commander goes first, pushin me ahead of him, behind us a Tonton guard, then Tommo holdin Nero, then the second guard bringin up the rear. We go down two floors.

We turn left. Then we're marchin down a long, wide corridor. Rushlight torches gutter an smoke as they throw jagged pools of filthy orange light offa the walls, ceilin an floor. All concrete. It's cool, a bit damp. We pass wooden doors on both sides. Each one the same, spaced regular. Each one bolted shut. My skin shivers. It's my dream.

I'm runnin. I gotta find Jack. I know he's here. Down a long, dark corridor. Torches throw ragged shadows across the stone walls.

I try to think how the buildin's put together. Bring up in my mind's eye Bram's drawin in the dirt, the plan of this place. What he told us about it. We must be movin along the fourth floor. Behind each of these doors there's a window. The lake should be on my left. The Field of the Fallen Mountain to the right. Okay, I know where I am. That's somethin, anyways.

383

Our feetsteps echo, the commander's heels a brisk strike on the stone floor. I cain't turn my head to look at Tommo behind me. As we approach other Tonton, they move aside an stand with their back pressed flat to the wall, until we pass.

Suddenly, the commander stops. I'll take her on from here myself, he tells the two guards. He nods at Tommo. Yer with me, he says.

The Tonton give the clenched fist salute, turn snappy an march off in step, back the way we come. Now it's jest me, Tommo, Nero an the commander.

He straightens his robes. Wants to impress the Pathfinder. Hand me in an take the credit.

You look good, I says.

Shut up! He yanks on my tied hands an hauls me behind him. The corridor goes on an on. We ain't passed nobody fer a bit. Gotta take a chance. I shoot a glance back at Tommo. He nods. Do it now. Now!

I slam myself sideways into the commander. Knock him off balance. Nero attacks. Beak slashin, wings flappin. His hands fly up to pertect his face. Tommo charges at him, runnin him into the wall. The back of his head smacks aginst the stone. He crumples to the ground.

We pause fer a second. No runnin feet. No outcry. Untie me, I says to Tommo.

As he does, I glance around. A little ways ahead, there's a shut door on the right. When I'm free, I run to it an shoot the bolt. It's empty. The bluish light of early night shades the window.

Tommo's already draggin the commander towards it, the rope dumped on top of him, Nero ridin on the rope. I take his feet. We lay him down. I feel his neck fer a pulse.

He's alive, I says to Tommo.

We gag him with his own kercheef. Bind him with his own belt, ankles to wrists. We start to gather the rope in tidy loops. We're both breathin hard. I check outta the window while we work. It's a long way down to the Field of the Fallen Mountain below. A sheer, sick drop.

Now what? says Tommo.

We stick to our part of the plan, I says. Git this rope in place. Third floor, any lakeside window.

What if they cain't find Emmi? he says.

We gotta trust each other, I says. We jest gotta do our bit of the plan. Right, let's git outta here.

He shoulders the rope. I scoop up Nero. We bolt the door shut on the commander.

Sweet dreams, I says.

Back in the corridor, I only go five steps along when I notice. The heartstone's warm aginst my skin. I touch it. Not a lot warm. But some. My flesh goosebumps. I stop. I turn my head to look behind me.

Nobody there. The room we jest left with its bolted door an the commander tied up. One gutterin wall candle. Then darkness beyond. I turn back. Tommo's waitin fer me. He waves me to hurry. With every step that I take towards him, the heartstone starts to git cooler. By the time I reach him, it's cold. I look back the way I jest come.

Jack. He's somewheres nearby. The red hot tightens within me.

What's the matter? whispers Tommo.

I look at him. You go on an git the rope fixed, I says. I'll come find you. I got somethin I gotta do.

He frowns. What? No, we gotta stay together.

I won't be long, I says.

I'll come with you, he says.

No, this is somethin I gotta do alone, I says.

He's about to say somethin else, so I kiss him. On the lips. Trust me, Tommo, I says. Here, take Nero with you.

I put him in his arms. Tommo hesitates, starin at me. Thoughts chasin over his face. Then, with a nod, not lookin happy, he goes off.

To kiss him like that. When I know how he feels, what he'll think it means. Fergive me, Tommo. But needs must.

He's got my bow with him. That's okay. I slide the knife from my boot. I softpad back down the corridor. The heartstone starts to warm. No sound but my breath, my heartbeat.

One wall torch, almost out. Then darkness beyond. Darkness an silence. I take the torch from the wall. I hold it up to light my way. I don't go far. The corridor ends after twenny paces. A stone staircase winds sharply upwards.

I'm at the bottom of a stone staircase. It's steep, winds sharply upwards.

Saba. Saba.

The voice runs along the walls an up my spine. It settles in the dark places, deep inside of me. Like it belongs there.

Prickles run over my skin. Cold an hot at the same time. No. No voice. That was jest a dream. I feel the heartstone. It's much warmer. I start to climb the stairs.

When I git to the top, there's a wooden door. Old, scarred. The heartstone's burnin hot. He's on th'other side. I open the door. I step in the room. Near empty. Near dark. Rushlights. A candle. A high-backed chair. Turned to the fire in the hearth.

He gits up from the chair. He turns to face me.

I reach the top. There's a wooden door. Old an scarred. That's all there is. The stairs don't lead nowhere but here. The torch goes out.

The heartstone's hot on my skin. Jack's inside. The red hot crackles an hisses.

Betrayer. Deceiver.

Of Maev an the Hawks an the Raiders. Of the forty dead at Darktrees. Of Emmi. Of me.

I clutch the knife tighter.

Slowly, slowly, I turn the handle. Slowly, slowly, I open the door.

I hold my breath. The door don't make a sound. Not a sigh. Not a whisper. I inch it open, my knife ready at my side. A dim room. Rushlights. Rugs on the floor. A large table off to the left, covered with a cloth. One end of it set fer a meal with a chair, plate, cup, an lit candles.

The crackle of a fire. A solid, dark wood, carved settle chair, turned towards the fire in the hearth. Nobody in sight. A door to the right, slightly ajar. It's another room. The light of a candle spills out. I can hear somebody movin around. Quiet sounds. One person.

Jack's in there.

I slide inside. Ease the door to. I start to move towards the open door, my feet silent on the soft rug, knife clutched tight in my hand. My cold hand. I can feel the sweat on my upper lip. The heartstone sears me.

Where's your escort?

DeMalo's voice.

My heart leaps to my throat. I whirl around, the knife low at my side, outta sight.

DeMalo's jest got up from the settle chair. There's a book in his hand.

My escort, I says.

Two Tonton come through the main door, holdin trays

with covered dishes. The smell of cooked food comes in with 'em.

Here they are, I says quickly. Right behind me.

Long life to the Pathfinder, they says, with a bow of their heads.

Put it on the table, brothers, he says. Set another place for my guest.

They rush to do his biddin.

My breath's comin short an sharp. The blood's roarin in my ears.

A woman comes outta the room with the open door. A servant woman who don't raise her eyes as she scurries past me. Not Jack. The Tonton's liftin the dish covers.

That's fine, says DeMalo. We'll serve ourselves. You can leave everything. He follows 'em to the door.

My mind's workin cold. I drop the knife. Tuck it unner the edge of the rug with my foot.

Thank you, brothers, he says. I don't wish to be disturbed. He closes the door behind 'em an locks it. He puts the key in his pocket. He looks at me.

The heartstone burns, fierce an steady. Like the heart of the fire in the hearth. Where's Jack? He must be here somewheres.

You came, says DeMalo. Just like I said. Of your own free will.

So. He don't know how I got here. Not yet anyways.

There's somebody still in that room, I says.

I don't think so, he says. He comes an pushes the door open. Shows me. It's a bedroom. Whitewashed walls, a plain bed with a plain white cover. A small chest. Candles on the walls. No, he says. No one but us.

No Jack. Nowhere fer him to be hidin. He ain't here. But still the heartstone burns.

We're alone, I says.

Yes, he says.

But there was somebody else here, I says. Before I come in.

Just me and the servant, he says. And then the two guards, but you came in with them. Are you all right? You're flushed.

I'm fine, I says, fine.

He touches my face. We have so much to talk about, he says. There's so much I want to tell you, so much I want to know about you. But we've got all night. Tomorrow. The rest of our lives. I have something for you.

He goes to the chest an takes out a red dress. He hands it to me.

Another dress, I says. I take it with reluctant hands. You got a sister or somethin?

Or something. He smiles. Get changed and we'll eat. He goes out an shuts the door.

There's a lookin glass on the wall. I'm starin straight into it. He's right, my color's high. The heartstone burns, but I ain't got time to think about what that means. Not now. I jest gotta git outta here as fast as I can. Without no trouble, without raisin no alarm. How long since I left Tommo? A few minutes, no more.

The red hot's runnin high in me. But I cain't use it to fight, not in the normal way. This ain't the Cage. DeMalo's stronger'n me in body an mind. That means I gotta turn it. Try to use the red hot in my head, not my gut. I know what he does to me, I know the danger. I cain't let him drown me like before. Disappear me.

I pull on the red dress an lace it up. I check myself in the glass, turnin this way an that. The dress dips low at the neck, nips tight at the waist, like somethin Molly might wear. I hardly recognize myself. I look womanly. That must be what he wants.

If you know yer enemy's weak point, go fer it hard. I gotta be outta here in five minutes. Time starts now. I tuck Slim's tiny brown bottle safely aginst my breast. My stummick's fluttery with nerves. I take a deep breath. I open the door.

He's pourin wine at the table. He looks up. You're beautiful, he says. He holds a cup of wine out to me. I go over an take it.

A toast, he says. To a new world.

To you an me, I says.

We drink. His eyes look heavy. Bruised. Exhausted. Somehow I gotta distract his attention so's I can doctor his wine.

The food's ready, he says. Shall we eat?

You look tired, I says. I take his cup from him an put it on the table with mine. Sit, I says. He does.

I slide onto his lap, facin him, an put my arms around his neck. Shut my body to the burn of the heartstone, the heat of his arms about my waist.

I'm sorry I ran away this mornin, I says. The truth is . . . nobody's ever made me feel like you do. It was all too much. I had to be by myself, to think. About what you said. About who I am an what I can be an . . . I realized yer right. The way things are now, it won't do. We need to find a new way. A meaninful future, that's what you said.

He smiles.

There ain't no point to this life, I says, to all that we go through, if we don't at least try to make things better. I wanna make the world a better place. With you.

I knew we were meant to be together, he says. That first time I saw you.

I whisper in his ear, I cain't stop thinkin about bein with you.

I slide offa his lap, take his hand an lead him to the bedroom. Jest like that, he comes with me. I cain't believe how easy it is. The power of a red dress.

We sit beside each other on the bed. I stroke his hair back from his face. Yer eyes look heavy, I says.

I . . . get these headaches sometimes, he says. I can't do anything about them.

I can, I says. Lie down, I'll be right back.

I slip outta the room, hurry to the table an fill the two cups with wine. One of 'em's got a little dent in one side. I reach into my dress an pull out the brown bottle. My hands is steady, ice cold as I unstop it. I can hear Slim's voice in my head.

One drop, a man'll sleep eight hours. Two drops, he'll do a whole day, maybe half of the next.

An three?

The longest sleep of all. Use it with a cool head.

I check over my shoulder. I can hear DeMalo movin in the bedroom. I hold my breath as I drip the liquid into the dented cup. One drop. Two. I hesitate.

His bruised, weary eyes.

I shove the stopper back in the bottle an tuck it into my dress. I swirl the tainted wine. Take both of the cups an head back to DeMalo.

He's lyin on the bed, rubbin his head with one hand. He's barefoot, no shirt, jest his britches. With the door key in his pocket. I sit beside him. Hand him the dented cup. We drink. I suddenly realize I ain't got no idea how long it takes to kick in. Slim didn't say an now I curse myself fer not askin.

Lie down with me, he says. Take off your boots.

I don't wanna. But I cain't think of a good enough reason not to, so I do. He pulls me down beside him an holds me in his arms. The candlelight plays shadows over his face. Gleams on the smooth skin of his chest. He smells like a mountain forest on a cold, dark night.

That's better, he says.

What does this mean? I says. I touch the tattoo over his heart, a red, risin sun.

Every Tonton gets one, he says. Once they've proved their dedication to the good of the earth. To New Eden. To me.

How? By killin? I says.

Cleaning the infected wound, he says. You've done the same. At Hopetown. Freedom Fields.

Then I'll hafta git one too, I says.

He touches my bare skin, jest above my heart. It shivers at his touch. No, he says. You're perfect as you are.

He tugs on the end of the string that laces the front of my dress. It starts to slip free. The bottle, he mustn't find it. I grab his wrist. Harder than I mean to. He frowns.

What're these? I says. I touch the thin silver band that he wears around his left wrist. I noticed it earlier in his tent. It's got strange marks etched into it.

Nothing, he says. He frees hisself, leanin closer to kiss me. I stiffen.

What's the matter? he says. His hand brushes aginst the heartstone. He pulls away quick. It's hot, he says, surprised.

It's a heartstone, I says. The closer you get to your heart's desire, the hotter it burns.

Am I your heart's desire? he says.

That's what the stone says. I start tracin his face with one finger. Lightly. Slowly. His forehead, his eyebrows. His cheekbones, his nose, his lips. I'm sorry, I says. I hafta git used to . . . bein with you like this.

I wanted to tell you, he says. I've found something amazing. If it's what I think it is, it's going to change everything. It's going to make it possible for us to—

Shhh, I says.

His eyelids start to droop. So heavy, he murmurs. Feels like I'm being . . . pulled under. Feels like . . . Ahhh, he breathes. The wine. You put something in it. Are you killing me, Saba?

By the candlelight, in the dark of his eyes, I see a tiny reflection. It's me.

I kiss his lips softly. G'bye, Seth, I says. His eyes close. His chest rises an falls. Rises an falls. His breathin deepens.

Seth, I says. Seth?

No answer. He's out.

† † †

I grab the knife from unner the rug, unlock the door to DeMalo's room an hurry down the stairs. Then I hitch up the red dress an, boots in hand, I run. Fast as I can, quiet in bare feet. A night-time hush thickens the air. Down the long, long corridor of the fourth floor. Past the bolted room where the weak-chinned commander dreams of crows.

As far as I can tell, I was only with DeMalo a few minutes. But his room, his tent, the Wrecker bunker, they're all places outta time. Where real life stops. An this place . . . Without the sky to tell me, I got no idea how much of the night's passed. It's like bein trapped unnerground.

Tommo must of put the rope in place long ago. He'll be in a panic, wonderin where I am. What if they all left without me? What if I'm trapped here? If I am, I got nobody to blame but myself. Set on revenge when all I should be thinkin about is Emmi. Lugh's right. I'm obsessed with Jack. If I do git outta here, I'll make it up to her.

Suddenly—not more'n fifteen foot ahead of me—a door opens. I press aginst the wall. Two Tonton come out. They stand in the corridor, talkin in low voices.

I don't breathe, don't even blink. I clutch the knife tight, ready to slash out. Inside my head, I'm screamin at 'em to move, to go. Somethin drips on my head. Hot. Painful. I raise my eyes. I'm right unner a wall candle. A drip lands on my forehead. I don't even wince.

At last, they start to move, still talkin. I let myself breathe agin, let my face screw in pain. I wait till their footsteps fade. Then I hurry after 'em.

Finally. There it is. The open metal staircase that runs up

the middle of this place like a spine. It's all clear. I make my way down one floor, silent, knife at the ready, boots in my hand.

Okay, third floor, any window, lakeside. Fix the ropes an down we go to the waitin canoes. As I step offa the last stair into the third floor corridor, I catch a flash of movement to my right. About thirty foot along, I'm jest in time to see a Tonton open a door. It's on the lakeside. He slips inside. My flesh goosebumps. I know the back of that head. I stared at it all the way to Freedom Fields. The heartstone's warm aginst my skin.

It's Jack.

The red hot slams to life. I pull on my boots with tremblin hands an poundin heart. I tiptoe along the corridor, clutchin the knife.

Hold fast. Hold fast to what he's done. If it warn't fer his deceit, none of us 'ud be here. An I wouldn't of lost myself to DeMalo. Lost myself in DeMalo.

I used to know who I am. I don't no more. An it's all down to Jack.

I stop outside the door. The heartstone's hot. I move slow, silent. I turn the handle.

I open the door. An I step inside.

✝   ✝   ✝

It happens fast. In a flash.

A tiny room. Like a cell. Dark. Moonlight floods through a small window, waist high.

Jack's leanin out of it. As I come in, he whips his head around, eyes wide. No! he hisses.

A rope stretches across the room an out the window. Tied at this end to the door handle. Our rope. He's holdin it. Clutchin it.

Sabotage.

Even as I take in all of this, I'm at him. On him. Knife held high. The room's so small, he ain't got time to dodge. He grabs my knife hand. My rush jest about topples him outta the window. He's off balance, tippin backwards. Keepin the knife high with one hand, hangin on to the rope with his other. He pushes back aginst me with his lower body. Scrabbles at the floor with his feet.

No! he gasps. Emmi!

I dig my boots into the floor. With all my strength, I push aginst him. I inch the knife towards his face.

Emmi! he chokes out. Rope!

Hands seize me from behind. Throw me offa Jack. I stagger into the wall. It's Maev. Her an Jack's both got hold of the rope. They're pullin aginst it, like there's a weight on it. A person.

Shut the door! hisses Maev.

What? I says.

398

Door!

I do as she says an the rope pulls taut. My head's poundin an crashin. The wild rush of redness that took me over. I'm pantin fer breath. Suddenly, I realize what Jack was tryin to tell me. Emmi's on the rope.

I dash to the window. Pull Maev away an lean out next to Jack. Emmi's clingin to the rope about ten foot down, swingin back an forth high above the waters of the lake. Five pale faces look up at me. Molly an Tommo in one boat. Ash an Lugh in another. Ash tows a third boat—empty—behind her. Creed's treadin water. He shakes his head an starts swimmin fer the empty boat.

Emmi! I whisper. Are you okay?

She looks up an sees me. Breaks into a great grin. Jack was helpin me, she says, an then the rope jerked an I nearly fell off an Creed fell in the water.

Jack? I says. Helpin you? He knocked you out cold.

I was play actin, she says. I saved yer life. We bin havin the best fun, me an Jack!

Fun? I says.

Okay, Em, Jack whispers from beside me. Down you go. Slow, like I told you. Don't be afeared.

I ain't, she says. See you later. An down she goes, inch by careful inch towards Molly an Tommo.

I look at him. At Jack. Play actin? I says.

I didn't have time to think, he says. I jest had to move.

She's a loose cannon, that girl. She got all excited when she seen me, that's why she came bustin outta the loft like that. I knew th'other guy was gonna come from the back of the barn any second an I couldn't take the chance she might blurt out somethin about you. The moment I seen her, I knew you must be nearby. I told her to pretend I hit her an she did the rest.

Why warn't you at the Lost Cause? I says. Did you find the message I left you?

No, he says. I couldn't git away. I got moved to a different patrol a few days ago. They switch us around to avoid factions. No loyalty to anybody but the Pathfinder. We warn't nowhere near. I'm sorry.

Maev's at the door, bolt shooter out, keepin watch. Saba, she says, yer next. Time to go.

My heart lurches. What? I says. No, I gotta—hang on, what's goin on here? Why does everybody essept me seem to know what's goin on? You go next.

I'm last out, says Maev. It's my operation. We already bin here too long.

Maev, please, says Jack.

Two minutes, she says. She slips outta the door.

Then it's jest me an Jack.

We're standin by the window, facin each other. The moon streams in through the open shutters.

I take a breath. Start to sp—

Jack's hooked my waist with one arm, clapped his other hand over my mouth an pulled me close.

We ain't got time fer you to yell at me or fer me to tell you everythin that's happened, so I'm jest gonna cover the main points real quick an then I'm gonna kiss you, he says. I went after the guys that raped Molly. One thing led to another an I seen a chance an ended up joinin the Tonton. I'm deep inside now. Nobody suspects me. I sent the message with Maev becuz I wanted you to work with me. I'd be on the inside, feedin you information, you'd be on the outside, actin on it. A team. You an me . . . we're good together. We'd work to stop this thing before it goes any further. But I thought you'd come by yerself, that you'd slip away. Th'only way this could work is if nobody knows about me, jest you. I cain't trust nobody else. This is my life we're talkin about. But here you are, with this huge crowd, an they all know I ain't real Tonton. If I was, I would of raised the alarm. Instead, I led 'em to Emmi's cell an opened the door.

I wave my hand to speak.

I ain't finished, he says. He takes a deep breath. I ain't comin with you, Saba.

Tears spring to my eyes.

I'm sorry, he says. You came all this way fer me. But it

didn't work out like I thought. It was a long shot. I never bin much good at playin them. Yer gonna go to the Big Water with yer family. I want you to have a good life. I'm gonna stay in these parts an do what I can to stop this. If I don't, one day they'll reach yer land of milk an honey an I don't want that.

I watch him while he speaks. His high cheekbones, his shadow of a beard, his gorgeous crooked nose. The little dip in his top lip. His silver, moonlight eyes.

Okay, that's the main points, he says. Now I'm gonna kiss you.

He takes his hand away. He kisses me.

I'd almost fergot how it feels to be kissed by Jack. To be touched by him. To be held by him. The fierceness of it. The tenderness. The tinglin all over my body, like lightnin's about to strike me. How we fit together, chest to chest, thigh to thigh. Like we was made fer each other.

He brings me alive. He lets me breathe. He's open skies an wide spaces.

Now that I'm here, with him, I cain't believe that I lay with DeMalo. That I freely gave myself to him. Jack never betrayed me. I betrayed him.

Nobody's like I thought they was. Nuthin's like I figgered it. Nuthin's like I thought it would be.

Tears spill down my cheeks. He brushes 'em away with his thumb. Kisses 'em away with his lips. That only makes it worse. I thump him on the chest. Hard. I rest my forehead aginst his. Gawdammit, Jack, I says.

A soft knock on the door. Maev comes in. Sorry, she says. Time to go.

Come away from here now, I says. Come with us. We'll help you git away. At least do that.

He shakes his head. I got somethin I gotta do, he says.

What? I swipe my eyes on my sleeve.

He smiles. I do like you in a dress, he says.

Please, Jack, I whisper.

Off you go, he says.

My heart breaks. I hear it break. I feel it.

I sit on the window sill. I grab the rope. We look at each other, one last time.

G'bye, Saba, he says.

You sonofabitch, I says.

I swing myself around, an I go.

✝   ✝   ✝

I go down a couple of handholds. Then I stop. Still so close. I could go back. Make him change my mind. Tell him—

I cling to the rope. Rest my head on my hands an screw my eyes shut. I won't cry, I will not cry. Somebody below gives the rope a jerk. I look down. Creed motions me to hurry.

No. He's made his choice an it ain't me. A surge of strength, of purpose, kicks through my body. I start to climb down towards the boat below. Now I'm movin fast. Too fast. My jerky movement sets the rope swingin. I swing out an then—I cain't believe it—straight towards the closed shutters of a window on the second floor. The sleepin quarters. I swing straight into the shutters an hit 'em with a loud thump. I freeze to the rope as it swings out over the lake agin.

The shutters fly open. Bang aginst the stone with a crack that splits the quiet night. A Tonton blinks at me, sleepy eyed. Jest woke up. Big, meaty fella.

I glance down. Too far to jump. No choice.

Knock knock, I says.

I swing towards him, feet first, my legs held stiff. Straight into his chest. He tumbles backwards into the room. A cell bedroom. I jump in after him. He starts to scramble to his feet, yellin fer help. I leap into a split kick an catch him unner the chin. He spins off, arms flyin, an bangs face first into the wall. He falls on his back, out cold.

I leap over him, open the door an head fer the stairs in the middle. Behind me, I can hear cell doors startin to slam open.

A girl! someone yells. In a red dress!

As I reach the stairs, Jack's already on his way down from the floor above, Maev at his heels. Down! he says. All the way!

The sound of doors slammin open. More yellin. Poundin feet. Shouts of, Intruder!

We cain't afford a fight, says Jack. Go left at the bottom.

The sound of shots behind us.

We race along the kitchen corridor. Duckin unner men with trays, knockin over boys with pots. Startled faces turn to look. Collared slaves, not Tonton. Stay where you are! Jack yells at 'em.

We burst through a door. We're outside. Straight ahead, a long platform juts out over the lake. It's the landin stage. There's wooden barrels piled on top of each other. We run to the edge of the platform an look down. We look at each other. It's gotta be a fifty foot drop to the water.

Lucky you can swim, says Jack.

Where's Maev? I says.

We whirl around. She's behind us. She stands in the doorway. Her right hand braced aginst the frame. Th'other hand pressed hard into her left side. Her blood's on the loose. Her life soaks away into her shirt, her britches. It drips on to the floor. My eyes meet hers an there I read her end.

Maev! I run to her.

She's unbucklin her weapons belt. Gimme yer dress, she says. That's all they know, a girl in a red dress. Help me. Move!

No, I says, but I'm already yankin my dress over my head, pullin it over hers.

Put my belt on top, she says. Pull it in tight. Tighter. As I do, she cries out in pain. Okay, she gasps, okay.

I'll draw 'em off, says Jack. Good luck, Maev. Then he's

gone. I can hear him yellin, This way! an blowin his whistle.

Help me, she says, over there. We stagger behind the barrels. She starts checkin her two bolt shooters. Now, git outta here. She unhooks one of Slim's pinballs from her belt. As far as you can, she says, as fast as you can.

No, I says, I ain't leavin you. I won't leave you, Maev.

It's okay, she says, really. I must be crazy, but I'm happy. Fer the first time in a long while, I'm doin what I know to be right.

She pulls herself up to stand tall. Jest like the first time I seen her back at Hopetown. Her copper tangle of hair hangin down her back. Head held high. Maev, the warrior queen.

Please, Maev, no. I got tears in my eyes as I hug her neck.

I got no idea what all this means, Saba, she says. Maybe you'll figger it out.

I kiss her lips. Don't let 'em take you, I whisper.

She smiles. I'm a Free Hawk, she says. Go.

I turn an run straight offa the end of the platform. I leap into the air. An as I soar through the darkness, high above the lake, Maev starts to shoot.

† † †

Creed pulls me outta the cold of Glasswater Tarn. I crouch in the front of the boat, shakin, wrapped in a blanket. He took a soakin too, but he warn't in so long as me an he's tough as rope.

He paddles a path to the top of the lake, keepin to the shadowy shoreline. We don't talk. The other two boats—with Ash an Lugh an Emmi, Molly an Tommo—glide along a little ways ahead. We got Emmi. No. Not we. They. Th'others got her back. I didn't have nuthin to do with it.

Eight of us when we left Bram's. Six of us now.

Nobody follows. The sound of gunfire goes on fer longer than I'd of thought it would. Or could. Then one big explosion. Slim's pinball.

The sky lights up fer a long moment, a sudden blaze of angry orange that spills onto the smooth black skin of the water around us. I look back. The landin stage is gone. Where it was there's a gapin hole in the buildin. Flames shoot into the night. DeMalo will hear that a girl in a red dress held off his men fer a time an then blew herself an them to pieces.

Nero flaps down. He lands on the prow in front of me.

I'm crossin a lake in the mountains. In a bark canoe. I'm paddlin. Nero's huddled, a ragged shadow, perched on the prow of the boat. He stares straight ahead. My pilot. My watchman. My crow.

It's blackest night. It's bitterest cold. Above me, the hard stars stab. Like chips of ice.

The water parts as my boat glides through. My paddle dips an drags. It dips. An drags.

I don't look over the side. I don't even dare to glance. If I did look, if I dared to, night or no, I'd see 'em. I'd look down down down to the bottom. To the ancient bed of the lake. Where the dark things crouch. Where the old things wait. Where they crouch an wait . . . fer me.

Not long after that first explosion, there's another one. Much, much bigger. It shudders the water of the lake. Cracks the night in two. The boats in front of us slow. We all turn to look.

The top left corner of Resurrection's bin blasted to the sky. Fire rampages. While we watch, that whole side of the buildin collapses an tumbles into the lake.

Creed's eyes meet mine. The ammo store was in that corner, he says. D'you think—?

I got somethin I gotta do. That's what Jack said.

Take me away from here, Creed, I says.

†　　†　　†

Ash an Molly land their boats well ahead of us. By the time me an Creed reach shore, they bin hauled into the trees an well hid with branches. We do the same, then follow a little path through the woods to the cave campsite that Bram told us about.

There's a bite to the air. A sting to the mountain breeze.

A sharp warnin of winter to come. Creed looks to the sky. Snow on the way, he says.

It's too early fer snow, I says.

Yeah, maybe, he says.

He stops. Lugh's standin in front of us in the path. He stands aside to let Creed go past.

She's dead, says Lugh.

I nod. I clutch the blanket tight around me, shiverin. She saved my life, I says.

You'd think I'd be thankful fer that, he says. I don't feel particularly thankful.

Tears start to my eyes. Please, I says. Maev was my friend.

Well, I got one up on you, he says. I loved her.

She knew, I says. I go to touch him, to put my hand on his arm, but he steps back.

I'll give Jack one thing, he says, without him, we'd of never got Emmi outta that place. But she shouldn't of bin there at all. As fer him sendin that message, draggin us into this, an you—he's as selfish as you are. I blame the two of yuz fer everythin. Them four settlers, Bram, Maev . . . I lay all their deaths at yer feet. An fer what? Where's the prize?

There ain't one, I says.

You've betrayed me, he says.

Lugh, I says.

I ain't got nuthin left to say to you, he says.

He's like a stranger with his short hair an Tonton clothes.

His most well beloved face is closed to me. I asked too much of him. Took too much from him. With no care fer him.

I'm sorry, Lugh, I says. I cain't tell you . . . how much. Please. I need you. I love you.

He holds up both hands, shakin his head, as he backs away from me. He turns an stumbles off towards the cave.

We're at some kinda end, Lugh an me. I feel it, a sharp, cruel pain, deep inside of me. In the safest, oldest, most joyful part of me. I wait till I git my tears unner control, then I follow him.

The cave's a good size. Big enough fer Hermes an Prue to shelter inside as well. There's a small fire goin. Ash an Tommo an Creed sit by it, warmin theirselfs. Lugh's joined 'em, but a little ways apart, starin into the flames, not seein.

Tracker greets me with a nudge of his head. Molly wraps another blanket around my shoulders, starts rubbin warmth into me. Her eyes search my face, full of questions. Emmi comes up. She puts her arms around my waist an hugs me tight. Jack ain't dead, she whispers.

Of course not, I says.

I didn't think so, she says. I'd feel it if he was.

Molly's eyes meet mine.

I brought some of my lethal whisky, she says. Put on some dry clothes, then come have a drink.

Me an Em stand there, her arms around me. She's strong an steady when nuthin else is. She says, Slim said some people hope they'll die in a . . . blaze of magnificent splendor, like the sun. I think that's what Maev hoped.

I kiss her on the head. I'm a bad sister, I says.

You ain't bin havin a easy time, she says.

No, I says.

The important thing is we stick together, she says. You an me an Lugh an Tommo. Will you be okay, Saba?

I dunno, I whisper. This time, I really don't know.

She holds a blanket up while I crouch behind it to strip an change. I send her back to the fire, then I ball up the skivvies DeMalo gave me an toss 'em into a dark corner. As fer the fine boots, they're my only ones. Much as I'd like to, I cain't git rid of 'em. Anyways, I've told the lie that they came from Cassie, so I'll stick to that. I wrap myself in Auriel's shawl, an go to join everybody. Set my boots to dry by the fire. I stare into the flames in silence, like the rest of 'em.

I'm hollowed out. I walk, my heart beats, I breathe, but I ain't here. It's like I bin losin parts of myself all along the way. Back in the Waste with the ghost of Epona. With Auriel. With DeMalo. I wonder if the fire got to his tower room. If it burned him as he lay sleepin. An the last of me here, in this place. With Maev. An Jack.

Jack. It wouldn't matter if I never saw him agin, as long as I know fer sure that he's alive. That he didn't git caught in the explosions or the fires. That would be enough. But some-how—like Emmi—I believe I'd feel it if he was dead.

Skins of Molly's wormwood whisky pass around. Lugh broods in the shadows. He don't look at me. He don't look at nobody, an don't say a word. Tommo sits beside him, the same.

Bring on sweet oblivion, says Creed. He takes a long drink.

There ain't no such thing, says Molly. I should know. I tried often enough an hard enough.

When it's my turn, I pass. I'm numb already. Nero sits in my lap an I stroke his feathers. When the skin gits to Lugh, it don't go no further. He steadily works at it, him an Tommo, passin it back an forth between 'em. The fire hisses an pops. Everybody stares into it. Thinkin what they're thinkin. Feelin what they're feelin. Not speakin. Till Ash says to me, Guess you'll be on yer way in the mornin.

To the land of milk an honey, says Creed.

I stand up, holdin Nero.

I'm goin fer a walk, I says.

With Nero in my arms, I make my way through the trees towards the lakeshore. The kindness of soft needles unner my bare feet. I reach the water's edge an stand there fer a moment. The moonpath gleams down the middle of the lake. Cold an sharp. It looks real enough to walk on. Clouds scud across the moon an it disappears. They clear, an there it is agin.

Footsteps behind me. Lugh! I turn an my breath catches when I see who—

Oh! I says, it's you, Tommo! I didn't recognize you in them robes.

He comes closer. With purpose. He's got my bow slung over one shoulder. I realize he's bin carryin it since we left Bram's.

Where did you go? he says. When you sent me off? You was gone a long time.

Fergit it, I says. It don't matter.

He stands in front of me. The night shadows his face. I'd hardly know him in this light. He looks different. Older. A shiver runs over my skin. I rub my arms. It's cold, I says.

What happened to yer clothes? he says. Where'd you git that red dress?

My heart jumps. How could he have seen? He was in the canoes with the rest by the time I showed up.

What dress? I says. I didn't have no dress on.

Don't lie, he says. I notice everythin about you. Things other people don't. When you looked down, from the landin stage, I seen you.

I, uh . . . ran into a little trouble, I says.

Trouble? he says. What?

I'd rather not say, I says. I . . . it was foolish, but . . . I'd rather jest fergit it. It don't matter.

He takes my arm. Don't treat me like a child, he says. I'm a man. I care about you.

I know, I says.

You said to trust you, he says. You kissed me.

Hot shame fer that false kiss tightens my heart. Tommo, I says.

He's pullin me to him, leanin in, meanin to kiss me agin. I pull back. Turn my head away. A heavy beat of silence.

I'm sorry, I says. I shouldn't of. It was wrong.

You deceived me, he says.

I'm sorry, I whisper.

Here. He shrugs off my bow an hands it to me. Carry it yerself. I ain't yer beast of burden.

He turns away. I stop him with a hand. He looks at me, his eyes so dark in the night that I cain't read 'em.

The dress, Tommo, I says. Nobody . . . I don't think anybody else noticed. Please. You won't say nuthin.

His mouth twists. You can trust me, Saba, he says.

A mockin echo of my words to him. My hollow words. A tiny bow of his head an he starts back up the path to camp. I watch till he disappears outta sight.

† † †

I set Nero to fly. Barefoot, my bow on my back, I start to scramble my way over the rocks. I gotta be alone. I gotta think.

It's carved from the mountains, this Glasswater Tarn. A rough, unfriendly shoreline. I nearly fall once, scrape the skin of my hand as I save myself. The sharp shallow pain feels good. I clamber to the top of the biggest rock yet. I'm lookin down on a wide stretch of stony beach.

What was a large Wrecker buildin sprawls along the top. Broken steps, wide an shallow, rise to it from the beach. Made of white stone, the place stands a ghost in the mountain night. It's collapsed, but fer one end. You can see it was two floors high. Lots of big windows to look out onto the lake, still shards of glass in a few of 'em.

Keeled over onto its side, halfways up the beach, a big boat dreams as its body flakes to rust. There's the memory of what looks to be a waterwheel at its stern. A boat with a water-wheel. I never thought of such a thing.

I climb down to the beach. My bare feet wake the sleepin stones. They shift an whisper to each other. I walk up the stairs an step inside the bit that's still standin.

It was one big room. The floor's crumblin, the ceilin too. In the middle of the floor, a ball lies smashed, some of it still covered with tiny glittery bits of lookin glass. I crouch an pick up a piece. I wonder what this place was. Parts of wooden chair scattered about. A long stone-topped table on iron legs, partly buried unner rubble. I go to it.

On the floor, unner the middle of the table there's two dusty old boxes. I drag 'em out an put 'em on it. I open the smaller one first. A stack of round plates inside. They're stiff black plastic, a little hole in the middle of each one. I lift the lid on the bigger box. Some kinda Wrecker tech. A round heavy metal plate, a spindle in the middle, a metal arm with a tiny needle. I study it fer a moment.

There's a crank stickin outta the right-hand side. I give it a go. It's stiff, but I manage to turn it a few times. The round plate starts to spin. I slip a black plate onto the spindle. I lift the little metal arm. Drop it on the plate. Sound blares out. I snatch the arm off an back away. I stare at it, my heart beatin fast.

I put the arm down agin. On the very edge of the black plate. This time I take gentle care. Music starts to play. Sweet, sad music. Stringboxes. A woman starts to sing. Words I ain't never heard, that I don't unnerstand. It slows down. It stops.

I stare at the machine. It only lasted a few seconds. It was like the music in DeMalo's bunker, but with a voice too. Wrecker music. Sounds from time past. From a gone world.

I turn the crank round an round till it won't turn no more. Then I set the music to play agin. It flows out. The singer, long dead, long fergot, starts to sing.

I go an sit at the top of the crumblin steps. I lay my bow beside me. I gaze down the silver gleam of the lake an I listen.

It's the song of a heart to the cold night sky. To moonlight on dark water. The song of a heart that yearns fer somethin it won't ever have. The music breathes in me. Aches in me.

I don't know nuthin no more. Why DeMalo reached me the way he did. Why the heartstone burned fer him. I don't hate him. I know I should, but I don't, an I don't want him to be dead. To of died in the fire. I dunno why Maev had to die. An Bram. Lugh's right. It was my fault. What happened to them is down to me. I dunno how to put things right. I don't think I can. It's all gone way beyond sayin I'm sorry.

I ain't got no peace, anywhere in me. I don't think I ever will.

Thick, soft flakes of white drop around me. It's snowin. Creed did say snow was on the way. I look up at the sky. Nero soars across the face of the moon, turns an starts flyin towards me.

Then. From across the lake. From the edge of the night. From the place where the darkness ends an the moonpath begins, a boat glides into view.

A man's paddlin. All the tiny hairs on the back of my neck prickle.

The heartstone starts to warm.

I stand. I take a step forwards. Then another an another till I'm halfways down the beach. There I stop. The long-dead singer sings her song as Nero guides the boatman into shore.

The paddler's head is bowed to his task. Then he lifts it. An I see who it is.

✝   ✝   ✝

He lands the boat. One last stroke of the paddle, then a watery swish, a pebbly crunch, an he's jumpin over the side an pullin it outta the lake.

Nero swoops down. He raises a hand in thanks. Nero rises agin with a cry of farewell.

He walks towards me, up the beach, his boots loud on the rocks. His head's down, like he's watchin his feet. My heart beats with his footsteps. The heartstone burns in the hollow of my neck. He stops close to me. Still lookin at the ground. Then, slowly, like he ain't sure of hisself, he raises his head.

I ain't never seen Jack at a loss fer what to say before. But he jest stands there. Lookin at me. The music stops.

I speak first.

I thought—that second explosion, I says. The ammo store. Creed thought it might be you set it off.

I did, he says. But I chose somethin with a long fuse.

I knew you couldn't be dead, I says. I would of felt it. I'd know.

Oh, he says.

What're you doin here? You said what you had to.

Not everythin, he says. We was kinda rushed.

Please, Jack, I says. Don't make things harder'n they already are.

He brushes the snow from his hair. From mine. His hand falters. Drops. It's snowin, he says. There's some cover over there. Can we talk?

I look away. I give a little shrug. He follows me up the beach, up the steps. We go into the room with the music box, now silent once agin.

He hugs hisself, lookin around. I hate these Wrecker places, he says. Full of ghosts.

My poor eyes. They're hungry fer the sight of him. His hands, his neck, his hair, his shoulders, everythin. I let 'em look their fill. I cain't possibly hurt no more'n I already do, so what's a bit more heartache?

He catches me at it. He looks his fill of me. I missed you, he says.

Don't, I says.

A lotta things have happened since we last seen each other, he says. Not jest to me but you too. Emmi told me some of what's gone on. What a time you've had, how hard it's bin. It was wrong of me to bring you all the way here. To drag you into this. I was only thinkin of myself an what I wanna do. I'm sorry.

Is that it? I says.

Not quite, he says. He comes closer. I know it's selfish of me to even think of sayin this. You deserve a guy who'll . . . pluck the stars from the sky an lay 'em at yer feet. I'm the kinda guy who'd step on 'em on my way out the door. I ain't got nuthin to offer you. He takes my hands in his. I jest want you to know that . . . how I feel about you hasn't changed. No. That ain't true. It has changed. It's grown stronger. He touches my face. You run deep in me, Saba.

Oh, no. I shake my head, break away from him. Don't do this, this ain't fair, Jack. Gawdammit, why didn't you send me a proper message? Tell me what was goin on?

You know I couldn't, he says. You see how this works. I couldn't put me or Maev at risk if anybody overheard, if they caught us.

Much good it did Maev in the end, I says. I'm gonna ask you somethin an you gotta answer me true. Did you lead the Tonton to Darktrees?

He looks at me straight. No, he says. They didn't need me to. The camp had bin scouted out some time before. I couldn't stop it. All I could do was give Maev an Ash an Creed a bit of cover so's they could git away.

If yer Tonton, you got a blood tattoo, I says. Who'd you kill to git it?

I told you I went after the guys that attacked Molly, he says. I followed 'em to their camp. They drank too much an passed out. When they come to, they was trussed up, slung over their horses an on their way to Resurrection. I handed 'em in to the Pathfinder. Told him what they'd done. He invited me to pull the trigger on 'em an I accepted. That's how I come by my blood tattoo.

Jack knows DeMalo. The thought of 'em in the same room together . . . I cain't begin to think about it.

You should never of left me, I says. If you'd jest come with us in the first place, none of this would of happened. Everythin's ruined. Why couldn't you come?

You know why, he says. I had to tell Molly about Ike.

Why couldn't you of sent a message with somebody else? I says. One of the Hawks?

He runs a hand through his hair. Okay, he says. Here's the thing. Me an Molly have history. We had a child together. I was very young, she was very kind an . . . it happened. These things do. Her name was Gracie. She lived five months an three days.

The cairn at the Lost Cause. Molly kneelin beside it. Their little girl. Molly an Jack's daughter.

You had a child, I says.

We never loved each other, he says, not in the way of lovers. Friends. The greatest of friends. I would of stuck with her, even after Gracie died, but Molly's a lot smarter'n me. She sent me packin an she was right. Some time after that, I innerduced her to Ike.

Did he know? I says.

Yeah, he says. It didn't make no difference to how he felt about her. Or her about him.

I cross my arms over my chest. Stare down at my bare feet, turnin blue with cold. Would you be like that? I says. If I'd . . . bin with another man?

Hey. C'mere. He comes to me. Wraps me in his arms an kisses the top of my head. This is me yer talkin to. I've racketed all over the place. I'm hardly in a position to judge anybody.

I love you. I whisper it into his sleeve so's he don't hear. I'm afeared, Jack, I says. Everythin I thought I knew, pretty much all of it turns out to be wrong. Some of the things I seen of late . . . that I felt, I . . . I ain't the same as I was. I dunno who I am no more.

We don't choose the times we're born in, he says. That's the business of the stars. The only choice we got is what we do while we're here. To make it mean somethin. I'm done with bein a dodger an a chancer, that's all.

Maev. Smilin at me. I got no idea what all this means, Saba. Maybe you'll figger it out.

What'm I gonna do? I says.

I cain't tell you that, he says. Nobody can. You gotta figger it out fer yerself.

Wait here, I says.

I go to the table. I crank the music box an set the music spinnin agin. I walk back to him. Dance with me, I says.

Look at you, he says. No boots an it's snowin. Stand on my feet.

I do. He gathers me into his arms. We stand there fer a moment. Not movin. Jest standin. Our bodies so close together. Thigh to thigh. Chest to chest. He starts to move us. Slowly we dance, among the ruins, with the snow fallin all around. Once more, the voice from long-ago times sings her song of the moon an what lies in the heart.

He rests his cheek aginst my forehead. His skin's warm, his stubble rough. I put my hand over his heart. I feel it beatin, strong an steady.

So, how're we doin with the rule of three? he says.

We're two all, I says.

Huh, he says.

We stop dancin.

I'm gonna hafta kiss you, Jack, I says.

I wish you would, he says.

I breathe him in. Breathe the light of him into the dark depths of me. I kiss him. Lightly. Like thistledown. A feather driftin over his smooth, warm lips. He takes my face in his hands an kisses me, over an over an over agin. My lips an my cheeks an my eyes an my lips, oh my lips. An I kiss him back. My whole body's shakin. On fire. He's shakin too.

I think of what we might say. Him to me. Me to him. I ain't no soft girl. I don't know no soft words.

Be with me, Jack, I says. Burn with me. Shine with me.

I'll stay till the moonpath fades, he says.

An he does.

He does.

†   †   †

He watches from the rocks. Unseen. Unheard.

He came to tell her again how angry she'd made him

How she'd hurt him. Betrayed him. Deceived him.

The drink he took earlier keeps him warm.

But then he arrived. Jack. In his boat.

He can't hear what they say, but he watches them.

They talk. They dance.

He watches until he can watch no more.

*Then he creeps away. Unseen. Unheard. Back to the
   cave where the others are sleeping.*

He lies there, awake, and stares into the dark.

Hurt.

Betrayed.

Deceived.

ACKNOWLEDGMENTS

To Sophie McKenzie, Melanie Edge, Gaby Halberstam and Julie Mackenzie, my ever grateful thanks.

Thanks to my agent, Gillie Russell, and my editors, Marion Lloyd and Karen Wojtyla, for their patience, support and wisdom.

And thanks to Paul Stansall. For everything. Always.